PRECIPICE

THE FIRST INSTALMENT IN THE CHAOS TRILOGY

K.T. MOON

First Edition: 2026

ISBN: 979-8-9947172-0-2

Website: www.ktmoonauthor.com

Formatted with Vellum

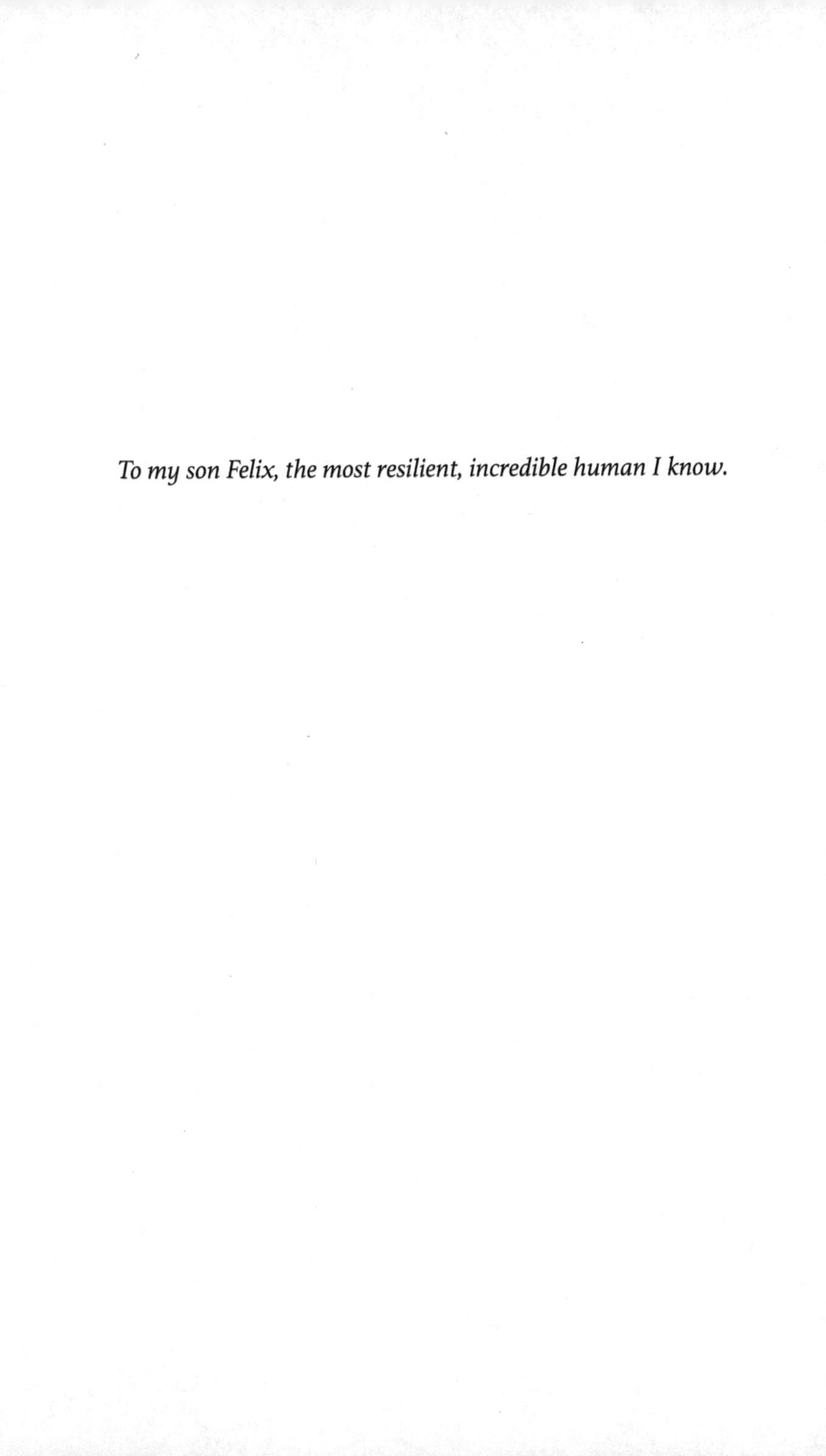

To my son Felix, the most resilient, incredible human I know.

1

PROLOGUE

An explosion of glass shards erupted in slow motion. Her lungs seized as black fumes poured into the Lada. Next to her, her husband (the most beautiful man, if one could use such a term) was dying from a shard of the windshield that pierced his breastbone. She grasped his hands, their eyes locked, tears streaming from both as his breath rattled. The old stories about fairies were true, she realized; their eyes changed color as they approached death.

"You are the one," he sputtered, his gaze piercing her soul. She suppressed her rising grief, leaning in for one final kiss, careful not to push the glass deeper. She watched his eyes frantically cycle through colors and emotions - fear, love, horror, and anguish - in a final instant before they went black.

Releasing his hand, she wiped her face, climbed out of the wreck, and stumbled toward the figure known as the Impaler. Slung over his shoulder, like a heavy sack, was a lifeless body. There were a million choices, an infinite number of paths, but in that moment, she knew she had only one.

The Impaler's mouth curled into a smirk. "So, it's done, yes?"

"Yes," Julia muttered, her gaze fixed on the body, no doubt some poor, frail woman, she thought.

"Her? She's a whore. But the resemblance is uncanny, wouldn't you say? Almost a spitting image of you!"

Julia merely nodded, unfazed. She wasn't afraid of Vlad; in fact, she could smell his fear.

"Good. The plans are in motion. GO. NOW!" he commanded.

Without a second's hesitation, Julia fled toward Havana under the blanket of darkness. A surge of adrenaline displaced all other feeling. Her sole objective: reach the garden and disappear from this life, unseen.

Entering the garden, she checked over her shoulder out of habit. She laughed at the precaution; only one other person knew of this place, and that person was fast asleep.

She looked into the fountain, took a deep breath, and prepared to take the plunge, to disappear from this earth forever. She failed to notice the toucan perched atop the mahogany tree at the garden's center. The bird muttered, "Here we fucking go," with a hint of cynical glee before taking flight.

2

Anna Drozdov, perpetually hungover, prepared a "mojito con vodka" for the mysterious man who ordered it. As she crushed mint and sugar with a pestle, taking out her life's frustrations on the drink, she avoided eye contact, staring instead at the water and thinking about the same recurring, despair-inducing dream she had every night.

In the dream, she was at the bottom of a marble staircase in a jungle, leading up to a blurred, enchanted dome. A bird, either a macaw, toucan, magpie, or crow, depending on her mood, perched on one shoulder, and a despised snake or iguana on the other. Draped in a gauzy dress whose color shifted with her mood, she always reached the eleventh, final step, but never the top. Waking up brought only frustration and a vodka- or rum-induced headache.

The man interrupted her thoughts, telling her, "You could smile, Rusa." Per the usual, he was an older man. Whilst he looked Afro-Cuban, his Spanish was perfect yet unaccented. He could be an American spy. She remained on guard. She was only 21, but felt she had lived countless lifetimes and hated the way customers patronized her.

"What is there to smile about?" she retorted.

"The fact that you're not just a shitty bartender, but so much more," he smirked, settling into his seat. Anna studied his smug, familiar-yet-unplaceable mannerisms. They were quick and smooth like a lizard. She felt certain this "asshole" would return, a common occurrence in Miramar, where she served plenty of arrogant officials from the Embassy.

She started cutting limes in anticipation of the upcoming lunch rush of Soviet officials and tourists who sought the kiosk for the sea breeze. Her kiosk, run with her brother, was a state-allowed marvel, the only one in Havana serving the "Mojidka", her personal nickname for the "perfect blend of two cultures" (mojito con vodka). Small talk unnerved her, but she enjoyed correcting the clientele with "Mojidka." Cubans, meanwhile, stuck to their traditional mojitos and canchancharas, enjoying the steady supply of mind-numbing refreshments.

The Mystery Man spoke again, knowing her name despite not being a regular or Party Member. "Anna, how comfortable are you with this life? So much is waiting for you out there," he piped up, his voice unnervingly ethereal.

"Do I know you, comrade?" she asked acerbically, cautious about displaying her anxiety. She noted his non-Cuban accented Spanish and linen clothes, wary of the CIA agents and American sympathizers rumored to be crawling around Havana. Her suspicion was validated by the disappearance of her school friend, Yuri.

"I know what you're thinking. No, I'm not American. I have no interest in politics of this realm. My concerns are for something much larger," he hissed as he stared piercingly. His guayabera and Panama hat annoyed her, but it was a deeper, unidentifiable quality about him that made her want to tell him to fuck off. Another man playing mind games.

She resumed chopping limes, waiting for her brother to return with the sugar ration. Following her deceased mother's tradition, she refused to pre-pluck the mint leaves, a small way to hold onto the memory of a woman who was a mother, a sister, and an adversary in an instant, and who once cryptically told her, "I knew you before you were born and will know you after we depart this earth."

The Mystery Man looked at her again, not with lust, but with a smug smile. As she locked eyes with him, she thought she saw a star colliding in his irises. *"I'll return. You will as well. You have done your penance. You need to return. You do not belong here,"* he communicated, his lips unmoving.

A shiver and a sudden flash in her brain made her wonder if he was using new CIA telepathy technology. As she breathed deeply to control her anxiety, she became even more convinced he was American.

He laughed. "Humans did their job to revive your lost humanity. Your bitchy façade doesn't hide your essence. Say what you want, but your actions speak louder."

Nope, she thought, *not telepathic,* or he'd know that bartending can destroy one's faith in entitled individuals. "Ok Comrade, whatever you say," she muttered.

"I'll be back," he said out loud before walking into traffic, narrowly missing cars and seemingly vanishing. Preoccupied with the idea of the CIA recruiting her, Anna poured herself a vodka to take the edge off.

———————

Mikhail Drozdov, or Misha as his nickname went, returned from his supply run, their precious sugar ration secured. Even after the ten-block walk under the relentless sun, a five-kilogram sack rested on a perfectly sculpted shoulder. He looked impossibly immaculate in the unseasonable January heat. Women, drawn by his effortless grace, charm, and chiseled body, regularly engaged in conversation with him no matter where he went. Men and women ogled at him. Yet, Misha remained aloof. The men, for their part, wanted to be his friend, drawn to his easy confidence and natural athleticism.

Anna, standing behind the cramped counter of their *kiosk*, was his antithesis. Where he was bronzed, brunette, and effortlessly fit, she was perfectly, resignedly average for a Russian. She often wondered how they could be related. Her complexion was pale and sometimes turned red under the summer heat. Anna never had issues with fucking the men of her choice, but she had issues with keeping them around longer than a one night stand. A few professed their love for her, but she wasn't interested.

"Careful, honey. Your brow looks like someone dug a ditch in it. Keep making that face and it'll stick," Misha chided as he dropped the heavy sack of sugar onto the worn countertop with a soft thud. He noticed the tightness around her eyes, the unusual furrow in her brow. Anna's face was more troubled than usual, betraying a deep-seated agitation that even she rarely allowed to surface. Empty glass clutched tightly in her hand, she turned slowly to face her brother.

"Have you ever served a guy in here that looked like he was a ghost from one of those American magazines from the early fifties? Like a Cuban matinee idol, but too perfect, almost staged?" she asked, ignoring his casual insult about her expression. "His whole look was too Cuban. There was something *odd* about him. Like he didn't belong anywhere."

Misha leaned against the counter, his smile softening

into a half-frown of sibling exasperation. "Are you sure it wasn't just your sparkling personality that drove him away? Or maybe your stellar customer service skills? You know, the kind that makes people regret asking for the item you're selling?" He paused, his gaze drifting pointedly to the empty glass in her hand. "Or did you drink too much of the product again? Which, by the way, we really should talk about at some point, Anna."

She felt the familiar, hot rush of shame. He *never* took her seriously, relegating all her concerns to either her moodiness or her drinking.

"Fuck off, Misha," she spat. She immediately turned her focus back to the array of glassware behind the counter, those mute inanimate objects that offered a silent comfort. She polished a tumbler finding a strange solace in the repetitive, mindless task.

Misha was the only person in her life capable of launching Anna into an emotional tailspin while also prompting her to question everything. Siblings.

Anna Drozdov, a Russian expat raised entirely in Cuba, was a woman who never quite fit in anywhere. Her displacement was a fundamental part of her being. She felt like a permanent outsider, never quite Russian enough and never truly Cuban enough. Only her parents had ever believed in her and even that was a hesitant at best. Since their untimely deaths, she felt resigned to live out the life of a Russian tragedy. Her brother, Misha (tall, perpetually charming, naturally athletic, and flirty) would inevitably marry some beautiful Cubana, securing his place on the island. And Anna would languish in the kiosk.

The intense love her parents had shared felt utterly foreign to Anna. She viewed it as an impossible myth. However, there was one person who had managed to draw her in unlike anyone else: Ivan. When she was sixteen, in a rare moment of genuine vulnerability, Anna had confided in her mama that her almost frightening attraction to Ivan felt ancient, like they had been lovers for an eternity, destined for each other from before Anna was born. "It's fleeting, Anna. That intensity is only meant to take you on a ride. The flame will be extinguished, it always is. And where will you be after that? Broken." It was a harsh truth. There was no time for infatuation. There was only the present, and the grim knowledge that everything was ultimately temporary.

———————

The next day, like countless others before it, unfolded with the familiarity of Anna's routine. Her hands ground the limes into a pulp with the stone pestle. She aimed for that perfect balance of sour and sweet, the foundation of every good mojito. Around the one-hundredth glass, the inevitable lunch rush began.

The vanguard of the Soviet embassy staff arrived, a parade of red, sweating faces, their linen shirts already clinging to their backs in the tropical heat. They came in search of their refreshing mid-day reprieve: a potent, icy mojito. It served as the momentary escape from the swelter and the bureaucratic drudgery of their work. Their coping mechanisms for the relentless stress of life in a tropical, politically volatile outpost were few and predictable: the discipline of morning exercise, the view of the crystal waters of the Gulf of Mexico, and a steady supply of vodka. At least they had this vibrant, if perpetually sticky, paradise, a stark contrast to the vast, frozen motherland, a connection to Mother Russia, minus the bone-chilling winters.

Anna had become an unintentional anthropologist of the new arrivals, hearing the same conversations, the same grievances, the same bewildered observations every single day from the perpetually rotating embassy staff.

"It is so hot here. A relentless heat. Why would anyone choose to live here for too long?" one would inevitably groan, mopping his brow with a handkerchief.

"But the fruit! The mangos and papaya, they are simply amazing. We cannot get anything like this in Moscow. Why would we ever leave?" another would counter, already thinking of his next bite of sweet, dripping fruit.

"Ach, but it is like living inside a banya, twenty-four hours a day," a third would complain, adjusting his tie unnecessarily.

Then would come the inevitable political paranoia, whispered conspiratorially: "Watch out for the Americans. You never know which *Cubanos* are actually working for them."

A beat of uneasy silence, then, "Do you think any of *us* are working for them?"

"No way, comrade. Not at all. We are loyal." The denial was always too quick, too loud.

A final, dramatic sigh: "If I have to have another meal of just black beans, rice, and fried plantains, I swear, I will jump into the sea."

"It is really difficult to pickle herring here, it spoils so quickly, but I know a guy..."

Anna's ears perked up at that last comment, a tantalizing glimpse into a world of smuggled comfort and defiant tradition, but she never managed to get the elusive guy's name.

And then, with predictable regularity, usually about once a week, a particularly judgmental staffer would eye Anna: her practical shorts, her worn flip-flops, her simple tank top, her thick, frizzy blonde hair piled messily on top of her head. He, and it was always a man, would deliver the cultural indictment. "How is my child supposed to get *cultured* here? Look at the poor kiosk kids. They are barely Russian. I bet they have never read anything by Tolstoy or seen a proper ballet." The disdain was palpable, a casual dismissal of Anna's life and her mother's choices.

At this cue, which she met with a weary but sharp anticipation, Anna would reply, her voice ringing out in perfect, unaccented Muscovite Russian, cutting through the general chatter. "My mother named me after Anna Karenina. I have read all the works of Tolstoy. Every single time the Soviet National Ballet company came to Havana, my mother took my brother and me." And every time she delivered this perfectly rehearsed defense, the comrades would collectively gasp, an audible intake of breath, as if only just realizing that a complex, cultured human being stood before them, not merely a servile bar maid. Anna was long accustomed to their shock. It was utterly, painfully predictable.

During the peak of the lunch rush, the humidity seemed to coil around them, a heavy, suffocating blanket. Although it was ostensibly January, the heat was inexplicably oppressive that day. Anna felt a sheen of sweat plastering her thick, blonde hair to the back of her neck. She squatted down behind the counter, reaching for a lower shelf in search of a rubber band to secure her unruly tresses.

As she straightened up, she bumped her head sharply on the underside of the counter. The jar of lime juice and sugar, already prepped for the next batch of drinks, teetered and then overturned, dumping its entire sticky, acidic contents directly down the front of her tank top..

"¡Hijo de puta!" Anna swore.

"Is it really so bad?" a cool, melodic voice chided from the other side of the counter.

Anna was about to snap back with something equally

biting but the words caught in her throat. She stared at the woman who had spoken. She recognized the woman immediately, not in the way one recognizes an acquaintance, but with a sense of familiarity, even though she knew that she had never seen her before. Anna found it difficult to catch her breath, the heat suddenly irrelevant. The woman was stunning: shoulder-length, tightly curled black hair, large, hazel eyes, and her skin was the color of caramel. Beyond her physical beauty, she possessed a quiet power that Anna could not pinpoint. Anna *knew* there was a connection to the Mystery Man. Anna's detachment evaporated, replaced by a consuming intrigue. Two complete strangers in one week, neither of whom seemed Cuban nor Russian.

As if summoned by the sight of an attractive woman, her brother, Misha, sauntered over, a charming smile already in place. "Anna, I'll help the lovely *señorita*. Go, rinse off." Anna felt a relief at the excuse to step away. This woman made her feel even more unsettled and apprehensive than the Mystery Man had. Besides, Misha never missed an opportunity to flirt his way into a side hustle, often by offering questionable salsa lessons to unsuspecting Russian staffers or naive tourists. He could easily pass for Cuban, but any true Havana local knew instantly he was an amateur instructor at best.

"Mojito con vodka, por supuesto," the woman requested, her voice a low, smooth purr.

"Coming right up," Misha replied, his focus entirely on her.

Misha plucked the mint leaves, launching into his tritest conversational gambit. "You aren't from around here, are you?" he asked.

"You could say that," she replied with a subtle, enigmatic smile.

"Well, welcome to Havana. The greatest city in... Cuba." They both shared a small laugh at the expense of the island's self-importance. Anna rolled her eyes, still wiping the sticky residue from her chest, and continued to prepare drinks for the steady stream of Cuban regulars who typically followed the Russian lunch crowd.

"So what are you doing here?" Misha pressed. Anna instinctively kicked his leg from behind the counter. Too many direct questions, she knew, often led to trouble in this surveillance state. But perhaps, since this woman was neither Cuban nor Russian, the rules were different. Still, Anna couldn't deny her own consuming curiosity and figured it was better for her suave, less-guarded brother to risk the interrogation.

"I am Ara. I'm visiting an old friend," the woman stated, but as she said it, her eyes locked onto Anna's, looking directly into her soul. Anna's breath hitched again. There was a sudden, fleeting flash, a fragmented memory. It was gone as quickly as it came. Anna was jerked back to the present by a regular customer yelling, "Anna, *oi!* Mojito con vodka!" She snapped out of her trance and focused on her work. A wave of new information had just hit her but she could not retain a single piece of it.

"Anna, you met my other half, Oragan, yesterday," the woman stated smoothly, the knowledge of Anna's name a final, unsettling confirmation of their intentional presence.

Fuck, Anna thought, a genuine spike of alarm hitting her. *How and why did all of these strangers know my name? Am I on some sort of list?* She mentally scanned her life for any possible transgressions. She had no intention of ever turning for any government, Russian or American. But maybe, just maybe, this Mystery Duo was something far more than simple spies. Desiring a little deviation from the suffocating norm of her life, she decided to engage. *Hell,* she thought, *this is shaping up to be one of the most exciting, least mundane days of my entire life.* As long as she towed the party line, she would be fine. Besides, in a country full of overeducated and underemployed citizens, gossip about mysterious, powerful strangers was one of the most potent, and certainly the most dangerous, currencies.

"I did," Anna replied cautiously, meeting the woman's gaze. "And he is your husband?"

"He is my other half," the woman corrected, her expression unwavering.

"Okaaaay." Anna and her brother exchanged a quick, skeptical smirk that spoke volumes about the woman's cryptic answer.

The woman settled onto a stool, staring out to sea with the exact same unnerving, distant expression that the Mystery Man had worn. Her perfectly shaped nose had a slight curve that reminded Anna of a bird's beak. Men waiting for their drinks or sipping their beverages winked and muttered various clumsy pick-up lines as she sat. She ignored them all with a chilling composure. The women in the line stared at her with a mix of awestruck admiration and unconcealed envy. Anna couldn't deny it: this woman was otherworldly by all of Havana's standards.

The line of customers finally died down, leaving a momentary lull.

"Anna," the woman began, her voice dropping, "as my other half said, we are beyond the politics of this realm. There are some big decisions to be made. Transportation. Revelations. Transmutations." She almost squawked the last two words, the sound briefly breaking the human smoothness of her tone.

This realm? Decisions? Choice? The very idea of choice

scared Anna more than any other aspect of the conversation. She had rarely made any significant choices in her 21 years. All major choices had been made for her. The USSR had chosen for her parents to live in Cuba. They chose to send her to a Cuban public school instead of the Russian school. Her mother chose for her to be a competitive swimmer, out of all the other sports she could have played. And instead of sending her back to Russia for a university education, which she had easily qualified for, her mother had insisted that it was best for her to maintain an ordinary life, working in the family business. Anna had not fought her mother. Now, she was intrigued, and highly skeptical of this strange interloper. Anna was terrified of making any decision, no matter how mundane. But a *realm*? What did that even mean?

"Ok, lady, whatever you say," Anna replied, attempting to project a cool, unbothered exterior.

Misha's face was etched with a concerned frown. The Mystery Woman looked directly at him, her eyes darkening. Her voice became authoritative. "I am not in the CIA. Nor do I work for any government." Misha's worried expression relaxed, just slightly. Then, as abruptly as she had appeared, the Mystery Woman rose from the stool and walked away, disappearing into the distance in a manner that mirrored the sudden vanishing of the Mystery Man the day before.

"Anna, what the hell was that? Not even a *who*, but a *what*?" Misha whispered, his voice trembling slightly. "Like a witch from Papa's old Georgian fairytales. And who is her 'other half'?" Well, well, well. For the first time, Misha was actually going to believe Anna. Her brother's perfect, carefree emotional façade finally cracked, just for a few precious moments.

"See? I told you! It wasn't me being the usual freak,"

Anna exclaimed in validated frustration escaping her. "I have no idea. Her fucking weirdo 'other half' showed up yesterday with the exact same shady vibe. Both reassured me that they aren't Americans and that they don't work for the CIA. I'm still not sure, as their Spanish accents are flat. But both of them knew my name, and I have never met either of them." She felt a strange combination of vindication and profound dread. Perhaps she was in danger, but better to be in danger and validated than slowly going crazy, Anna thought grimly.

"It is never, ever good when a stranger knows your name," Misha said, his brooding face looking out over the sea. Anna knew exactly where he was: he was thinking about the disappearance of his closest friend, Piotr. Piotr was physically stunning and charming, just like her brother, and a talented artist whose work teetered on the edge of political acceptability, but never quite crossed the line. One day, a strange, anonymous Russian came to the kiosk and ordered a simple drink. He asked Misha if he knew of Piotr Petrov. "No, comrade, that name is not familiar to me," Misha had replied, easy and breezy as ever, refusing to betray his friend. Misha had tried to warn Piotr later that day, but he never saw his friend again.

"It'll be fine," Anna said, forcing a calm she didn't feel. "Nothing *exciting* ever happens to us. This might just be... interesting, *zanuddny*." She maintained her typical unamused smirk, a necessary mask to keep her nineteen-year-old baby brother calm, but deep down, she was terrified of the unknown Mystery Duo and what their visit meant. Mama always told Anna that her intuition was the truest thing about her. "Trust your intuition, Anna. Your greatness lies in it," her mother had always said. That was all Anna had to rely on. No great beyond. No heaven. No hell.

No comfort in prayers to higher beings. "You are your own goddess," her mother had instructed. Only intuition and accepting people as they are, most of whom were neither purely good nor purely bad; they simply *were*.

The two of them spent the rest of the afternoon working in a strained silence. Anna didn't dare speak of the Mystery Duo again, afraid that naming them might conjure them back. As they were scrubbing the sticky lime residue from the glasses, Misha leaned over and whispered, a secret just between them, "Pedro has some new American music. The best thing I have ever heard. We can listen at home tonight."

The one thing about America that Anna genuinely loved was its music. She could not care less about their lifestyle, their messy politics, or their aggressive foreign policy. She was, if she were being honest, a little afraid of the American power structure itself. But their music—she could not get enough of it. Misha's taste in music was eccentrically refined, completely different from almost everyone else's, save for their best friend Manny. It was heavy on the synthesizer, an electric, futuristic sound. He once earnestly called it "New Wave." But sometimes, he surprised Anna with the latest, most infectious American pop music.

"Exactly what I need," Anna replied, a genuine smile finally breaking through her worry. "A distraction from an unknown potential danger with something that is certainly illegal. I'm in."

Finally, she had something concrete to look forward to.

3

Autopilot took the siblings home. Both were oblivious to the silence of the other, each lost in the bizarre events that had unfolded moments before at the kiosk.

The heat was suffocating. Dewy sweat perpetually remained on the surface of their skin. It was relentless. No matter how slowly they ambled along the cracked, sun-baked pavement, the sweat poured down their backs. People were calling this oppressive wave the *Infierno de Enero*, the Hell of January. Everyone was hot, miserable, and generally irritable, a stark contrast to the perfect, temperate weather that January in Cuba usually promised.

As they approached their apartment, Anna bent over the stoop to pet the familiar, well-fed neighborhood cats littering the doorsteps. They were pampered by the entire building's residents, evidenced by the uptick in mice. The wrought iron gate into their old, converted Spanish colonial building was, as always, never locked, a casual disregard for security that was typical of their community. Faded coral-colored paint peeled off the side of the building, showing decades of tropical sun and neglect.

They began the climb up four flights of stairs. The building's acoustics amplified the cacophony of their neighbors. They were unable to hear anything except the deafening, disparate streams of salsa music echoing up from the various open windows. It was a rhythmic, welcome muffle for their own impending musical misdeeds. Misha pushed open the door to their shared one-bedroom apartment and flicked on the light. The sudden illumination sent a small army of roaches scattering into immediate hiding. The sight of them always highlighted one of Anna's long-standing complaints about Cuba. Even though she was certain that the bitter cold of most of the Soviet Union was too harsh for cockroaches to survive, her Georgian papa's voice would echo in her mind. "Anna, cockroaches are in the Soviet Union. Cockroaches are everywhere. The self-serving and vile shit-eating creatures are everywhere in the universe."

Misha motioned her over to the corner of the room where their tape player rested. He reached for a hollowed-out book, a common, clandestine hiding spot, to reveal a cassette tape. The replica copy was starkly labeled with a single, evocative title: "Thriller." They possessed many such forbidden tapes, pirated copies of Western music and films hidden throughout the apartment, but this one felt different. While it was a replica, and Anna hadn't yet heard the music it contained, she knew instinctively that it was going to be something truly extraordinary. She snatched it from her brother's hand, only to recoil. It felt hot to the touch.

"That shit music downstairs only serves one purpose," Misha muttered, nodding toward the floor. "A great buffer for our misdeeds," he said with a wicked smile. He placed the tape into the deck. Anna rolled her eyes at him; he knew perfectly well that she loved salsa. However, Misha's cultural taste, despite their upbringing, was impeccable. She couldn't fault his beloved Depeche Mode, a tape he kept hidden securely in the back of his closet, suggesting the depth of his devotion to it.

As the music started, Misha looked at Anna. The left side of his mouth curled upward in a knowing, confident half-smile. He gave a single, emphatic nod of his head, as if to confirm, "God damn, this is magic." Anna's eyes widened. She started bobbing her head to the beat, her body instinctively translating the foreign rhythm into the familiar.

Neither of them could understand a single word of what Michael Jackson was singing. But they didn't need to. They knew, instantly, that he was a musical genius. He was possibly revered in America with the same level of intellectual respect that Igor Stravinsky commanded in their birth country. Listening closer, Anna perceived a dark undertone. Judging by the man's vocal cadence and eerie mood of the music, Anna knew that this Michael Jackson must be telling a horror story of some sort.

As the chilling chorus started, an intense wave of nausea hit Anna. She stumbled backward, a cold sweat breaking out over her skin, instantly replacing the humid heat. A sour bile and the faint, unexpected flavor of mint rose in her throat. She steadied herself on the counter, her thoughts spiraling. Perhaps the mid-day mojito con vodka had been a bad idea. Or worse, maybe their vodka was poisoned by the omnipresent Party, a genuine fear in their world. Life seemed to swirl around her, the music's powerful sound reverberated in her head. Almost everything she had eaten that day felt like it was making a determined journey up her throat.

Meanwhile, her brother, completely oblivious to her

sudden distress, continued to move. He shook his hips and moved his feet to the beat with a serious expression on his face as he began choreographing his own dance to the music.

"I'm going to the toilet," she managed to say. She walked unsteadily toward the small bathroom, barely able to stand upright. Her brother ignored her, as he tried to memorize the garbled English lyrics. "Eee cose toom idight..." The bathroom was a necessary retreat, regardless of the source of her sudden illness. Anna looked at her reflection in the spotted mirror, splashed cold water on her face, and desperately slurped water from the faucet. As she looked up to dry her face, she jumped with a gasp. Sitting on the windowsill behind her were two creatures: a Macaw, resplendent with the most distinguished, vibrant plumage, and a perfectly lined Iguana. Her mouth fell open in disbelief.

"Hello Anna," they said in perfect unison, their voices chillingly synchronized, not unlike the creepy twins from an American horror film she had recently watched with Misha on a stolen reel-to-reel in an abandoned building.

She blinked hard, attempting to clear her vision. Some Cubans believed in Santeria. Magical Realism. Talking animals. Russians, however, believed in Mother Russia, the power of pickled foods, and inevitable tragedy. Animals did not talk. Except, perhaps, for bears, and usually only after one had consumed copious, mind-altering amounts of vodka. She had only had a couple of mojitos that day. A small voice in her mind insisted: *The vodka must have been poisoned.*

"We understand that you may not recognize us, but we both visited you earlier today."

Oh great, these fuckers again, she thought, the realization hitting her hard. She instinctively knew that they were trouble, but she could not yet grasp the extent of it. Could the vodka cause her to hallucinate such an elaborate vision? She made a frantic mental note to visit the library tomorrow to research mental illness or poisoning.

"I would tell you to get the fuck out of my house, but there are talking animals in my bathroom, so I think *I'm* the one who's going to get locked away for this," she stammered, stumbling back a step. Her body shook with an uncontrollable, nervous giggle that was completely out of sync with her terror. Anna sank onto the toilet seat and looked at the pair. People who started to see and hear impossible things in Cuba were often never seen or heard from again.

"I really need to contact the embassy immediately and inform them that the vodka shipment is poisoned and they should dump it." She was about to scream Misha's name for help when the Macaw elegantly fluffed her plumage, a gesture of impatience.

"Anna, stop it. There's no time for your existential crisis," the macaw said, her voice perfectly unaccented and crystal-clear in Spanish. "This is far bigger than you. Kala needs you. Only you know how to bring order to the chaos."

"Mama, is that you?" Anna said, a sharp wave of sarcasm cutting through her fear. *No time for feelings* had been her mother's constant, weary refrain.

Anna started chewing the inside of her cheek, a habit from her childhood. She didn't know what else to do in this moment of profound regret and confusion. Stall? Think? Demand answers? "What in God's name are you talking about? Kala? Chaos and peace? Are you crazy? *Am I* crazy? I am a bar girl. A boring bar girl. A kiosk bitch. Whatever derogatory name you want to call it. I live in a cramped apartment with my brother. My parents died when I was 17. I grew up in Havana. It is my home. I do not know what the hell you are talking about. And why are you *talking*? You are animals!"

Anna's entire perception of reality was shattering. She had just spoken to a parrot as if it were a long-lost, annoyingly cryptic relative. The Iguana's tongue flickered out, a quick, silent snap as it caught a few stray mosquitos, and then it began talking after swallowing.

"Where do you go to escape from your life?" The iguana's voice was dry and raspy, sounding as irritated as an iguana would.

"To a bar," Anna shrugged, the simple truth.

"You fool, no. You're more of a mess than we could have imagined," the iguana chastised, carefully enunciating the last word. "Where do you go to find *peace*?"

"The walled garden, near la Plaza Catedral in Habana Vieja." As she spoke the name, a good idea formed in her mind: she should go there immediately after these creatures left to clear her head.

"Have you ever seen anyone else in that garden?" the Iguana stated matter-of-factly, his eyes unblinking.

Thinking back, her mama had first introduced her to the garden. It wasn't in a particularly hidden place; no place in bustling Havana was truly a secret. But some places, she now realized, were only visible to those who were truly looking for them. Anna and her mama would go to the garden when the weather became too hot to bear, when Anna had a bitter fight with her brother, when they suffered a serious lime crop blight... it was for any occasion that made things feel uneasy or unstable on this Earth. They went mostly to rejuvenate themselves. When she visited the garden, she felt an undeniable, calming presence in her own skin. It was the only place in the whole city where she felt like she genuinely belonged.

She had *never* seen anyone else there. It seemed so obviously located, too. Standing in front of the old plantation owners' decrepit hacienda, one merely had to veer to the left and walk down a short dirt path in an alley that led the seeker between two colonial buildings: one painted bright blue, the other bright green. Unlike the rest of Havana, they never seemed to decay. Anyone, or so she had always thought, could walk 25 meters down the alley to a low wrought iron gate. She had always been enamored with the gate because it had the distinct design of a macaw and an iguana woven into the ironwork.

"Oh..." Again, she felt suddenly breathless, this new realization settling in her stomach.

The macaw squawked with a dry, knowing glee and said, "And think about the garden. Have you ever seen a dead flower? Any mosquitos? A groundskeeper? Overgrowth?"

Anna thought again, the image of the garden impossibly clear in her mind. Not only had she not seen any of those things, but the hibiscus and plumeria were always, perpetually in bloom, their rich fragrance always filling her nostrils. At first, the visitors had brought her only fear and dread of the unknown, but as they continued to speak, her deep-seated curiosity was piqued. Their voices were so oddly, intensely familiar. Her brain frantically ran through all the scenarios under which she could have met them, hitting a blank wall of confusion every time.

"Stop speaking in riddles and questions and tell me what is going on," she demanded, swallowing hard to prevent herself from crying out of frustration and the crippling fear of being crazy.

"ANNA! COME OUT! ARE YOU OK? YOU HAVE TO HEAR THIS SONG!" Misha's muffled voice boomed from the other side of the bathroom door.

"Meet us in the garden on Saturday at noon. Be ready to leave this realm. Do not be late and make sure that you are not followed by any other being." Their ominous voices echoed in the small bathroom in perfect, unsettling unison.

"But I have the lunch rush!" she protested, her life suddenly colliding with the absurd. "What am I supposed to tell my brother? This is insane. This *is* a result of bad vodka. And what realm? I happen to be perfectly okay with this realm most of the time." Except, she thought bitterly, when strange creatures decided to show up and invade her life.

"ANNA! Who are you talking to? Come out!" Misha yelled, his impatience growing.

"HOLD ON!" she yelled back at the door, her voice strained.

She turned back to the windowsill, but there was nothing there. The Macaw and the Iguana were gone. The only evidence of their impossible visit was a single, impossibly bright red macaw feather resting on the sill. She quickly tucked the feather into her bra, a strange talisman, and exited the bathroom to the driving, angry rhythm of "Beat It" now playing on their tape deck.

4

Falling for an eternity. Anna, naked, plummeted into the abyss. Fear didn't exist, only smug power. Her body jolted to a halt inches above red clay earth. Serpents, thick as Anna's torso and shimmering with dark scales, slithered from the surrounding shadows to bind her body in cold, constricting coils. Torches flared to life, casting an eerie, flickering orange light across the circular, subterranean pit where she was suspended.

Anna, with a detached and almost clinical curiosity, examined her legs. They were fused, covered in rough, red-tinged scales that trailed off into a grotesque, fish-like tail—a terrifying parody of a mermaid, demonic and utterly grotesque. She had to concede a certain theatrical flair to Dalv. Their last encounter in his smoke-filled lair had been equally dramatic, featuring her suspended midair with her legs deliberately splayed open. Always one step ahead of the base motives of men, even deified ones, she had concealed a powerful, protective enchantment within her pussy. Predictably, Dalv attempted to greet her with a casual insertion of his left forefinger. The enchantment triggered instantly: a toucan beak, sharp and impossibly solid, had manifested and brutally ripped the digit clean off at the knuckle.

As she floated in this state of unwelcome suspension, waiting for Dalv's inevitable, tiresome theatrics to begin, a sense of weary anticipation settled over her. What was the spectacle this time? Another transparent power grab? A clumsy, ill-conceived attempt at rape, as trite and predictable as the plot of a badly written play? Such banal ambitions for a horrific being.

"Oh look, the great Dalv has finally taken his true, magnificent form," Anna spat the words out, heavy with sarcasm. He emerged chiseled and impossibly muscular, stark naked, his skin was a shocking, vibrant red. His black eyes blinked in unsettling unison as he took a deep.

"Did you freshly shine those impressive horns for my benefit? They look remarkably... polished. And your wings, Dalv," she continued, her voice dripping with feigned pity, "they're looking a bit tattered, worse for wear. Pity." The pure, unadulterated hatred she harbored for him was a constant.

In an instant, before she could utter another syllable of venom, a serpent coil snapped around her face, gagging her mouth with its sinuous body, the smell of dust and musk filling her nostrils.

"Do not for one second think this spectacle is for you, Anna. You are merely the necessary prop. They are coming for us. The Others. This humiliation is the only way I could force you to listen, to be still. They are coming for us. You know who I speak of..." His voice was a low, guttural rumble that vibrated through the air.

Anna woke abruptly, the final words of this stranger's warning dissolving. Who was Dalv? The sound of her neighbors, a man and woman fighting again resulting in a symphony of slamming doors and shouting, incoherent Spanish, yanked her back to the harsh hot reality of Havana.

The dream, the one with Dalv and the abyss, was the worst of all her recurring nightmares. Not because she was terrified, but because she *wasn't*. Objectively, it was a terrifying vision of hell, yet her primary emotion was a cold, pragmatic annoyance.

A repulsive, fuzzy film coated the inside of her mouth, a stale reminder of sleep. Water. She needed water first. And immediately after that, a toothbrush to scrape away the remnants of the previous night.

She and Misha operated on a strict, alternating schedule: one day off each week while the other worked the kiosk alone. After the head-spinning, logic-defying events of the previous Tuesday, she was profoundly grateful that her turn for rest had fallen on Wednesday. Her brother, a creature of relentless energy, had skipped out of their small, sun-drenched house precisely at 9:00 AM to prep the kiosk. She, meanwhile, remained collapsed on her woven floor mat, savouring the stillness.

She gently clutched the single, vibrant red feather, the bizarre token left by the Mystery Duo, as she attempted to process the cascade of absurdity from the day before. A Mystery Duo, a man and woman seemingly appearing from the humid air of nowhere, had cornered her, calmly informing Anna that she was essential in a cosmic plan to return control to their realm. As a final, unsettling detail, they possessed the ability to transfigure themselves into a macaw and an iguana, which happened to be the exact two animal figures intricately carved into her garden gate.

"What the actual fuck?" she finally said out loud, the question directed at no one, least of all the silent red feather.

Convinced that she was losing her grip on sanity, she decided a dose of routine was the only cure. It was time to find breakfast and then dive into the sea for a swim before the mid-day sun could singe her pale skin. Anna forced herself into motion, forced herself to trudge through the motions of preparing for a swim, and left her apartment.

The comforting smell of *café con leche*, with that distinct, slightly burnt tang to the steamed milk, permeated her neighborhood. She navigated the crowded sidewalk, stepping carefully past the long, ration line and the equally interminable bank line. It was only a five-block walk to her preferred cafe, a sanctuary run by Elena, the ancient, seemingly immortal *abuela* who had been a fixture of the neighbourhood since Anna was a child. Even after her mother's death, Anna had clung to their weekly breakfast ritual: strong *café con leche*, a hearty plate of leftover black bean stir-fry, and perfectly scrambled *huevos revueltos*. Elena had always treated Anna not just as a customer but as her own granddaughter, earning her a place on Anna's very short list of three trusted friends.

"*Buenos días* Elena," Anna said, the words a sigh of relief as she stepped into the familiar cool darkness of the cafe. Relief flooded through Anna as she saw Elena's soft smile wrinkles crinkle around her eyes. Her shiny black hair was tightly bound in an intricate braided bun atop her head.

"*Buenos días* Anna. How are you today?" Elena replied. But then, an unusual hesitation. She stopped short, her lips pursed, as if she desperately wanted to ask a torrent of questions but physically forced her mouth shut. This was profoundly unlike Elena, who was normally effusive, direct, and inquisitive.

"I am... ok. You seem concerned," Anna said, her own voice cautious. She had no clear gauge for what was real or whom she could truly trust after the surreal events of yesterday.

A deeply serious, almost pained look settled over Elena's

face, dispelling the last vestiges of the warm, cafe *abuela* facade. "I can tell that they came to you. Be extremely careful. You are uniquely special, *mija*. You have no idea how important your destiny is. They understand your destiny. But their motives are rarely pure, and their attention always comes at a price. They are the reason you are here, on this planet, in this life."

Well. At this point, the capacity for surprise seemed to leave Anna entirely.

Keeping her expression carefully measured, she asked with a flicker of genuine curiosity, "So, you know... the Mystery Duo?" It was the only name she had for them.

Elena deeply inhaled, held it for a deliberate beat, and then exhaled completely. Anna unconsciously started sucking on the inside of her cheek, a nervous habit that intensified as her thoughts became untethered by Elena's subtle but profound shift in demeanor. Elena usually exuded an aura of confidence, certainty, and was known for her quick, sharp retorts. Deep breaths and pauses were atypical for Elena. *Misha claimed Anna was paranoid or hypervigilant,* but Anna knew it was a product of her own precise, razor-sharp perception.

"Anna. Nothing in this world, this dimension, is truly as it seems. What I am about to tell you will not make logical sense. As a matter of fact, you'll think that my mind has finally gone to shit. Maybe it has," Elena said, a dark chuckle escaping her mouth.

"I don't find this particularly funny, Elena," Anna said, her brow furrowing in genuine distress as she continued to chew and suck on her cheek.

"To understand, you must go beyond the physical act of seeing and fully commit to the act of believing. Those two, the ones I know well, can be incredibly tricky. It is their job, their cosmic mandate, to see only the grand, big picture of everything, completely ignoring all the small consequences and the very humanity that they occasionally feign interest in. They consistently fail to understand that the tiniest contributions, the smallest acts from each being, great or small, make the universe what it is. They often punish deities and *mythans* - think of them as powerful magical creatures - unfairly in the tyrannical name of balance. And sometimes, Anna, they use these beings for entertainment, like chess pieces. They have existed for an eternity. It has been a very, very long time. And one day, their hubris will inevitably get them in trouble," Elena said, closing her eyes in a gesture of profound, internal thought. It appeared to Anna as if she were receiving a direct, instantaneous infusion of information.

"As a matter of fact, it will happen sooner than even *they* think," Elena warned, her eyes snapping open.

"I don't understand any of this." Anna tried desperately to slow her breath, to force her mind to make sense of this terrifying, new reality. Hearing ominous warnings from a strange man when no one else was around was easy to dismiss: the man was clearly crazy. Hearing the same thing corroborated by a woman, with her brother present, meant that either the woman was crazy, or Anna was in serious trouble. When the message was then amplified and expanded by two talking animals, Anna had reverted to the safe thought that it was *her* solitary problem. A delusion. But now that Elena, her most grounded anchor, was corroborating and expanding the story, there was no denying that at least some essential, terrifying part of it was true. In that moment of intense clarity, Anna's gaze fell upon Elena's pendant. It was a silver tree, exquisitely detailed, with various animals carved onto its branches, including, unmistakably, a macaw and an iguana.

"So you like this pendant, eh?" Elena winked, her usual sparkle returning for a brief moment. "I'm not just a cafe *abuela*, you know. But come back later, Anna, when you are fully ready to hear the truth. You'll be ready. Your kind always are. This day was meant to come." She gave Anna a soft, knowing smile. "And *unknit* that brow, *mija*. You'll look like a sun-fried Party wife." Anna responded by instinctively knitting her brow even tighter and continuing to aggressively suck on the inside of her cheek.

As Anna frustratedly and quickly ate her breakfast, washing it down with her strong, slightly burnt coffee, she studied Elena with new, suspicious eyes. Elena had striking, beautiful jet-black hair with three distinct, shocking white streaks that ran through it. She possessed the softer, comfortable mid-section of an *abuela*, which was lovingly accentuated by her brightly colored, fitted polyester shirts. She owned one in every imaginable color of the rainbow along with her breezy cotton skirts that covered her knees. Her calves, however, were the calves of someone who had stood on concrete for decades, muscled with prominent veins and tiny, burst blood vessels around her ankles. Her arms and hands were muscled, showering her physical strength.

"*Hola* Elena! *¿Qué tal*?" another regular customer walked in, nodding a greeting to Anna on his way.

"You can always ask me for help, Anna," Elena said, her voice dropping to a low, intimate promise, accompanied by a final wink and her most comforting smile. With that, she turned swiftly on her heel and walked towards the new regular, the *abuela* facade snapping back into place.

Anna was reeling, her mind a frantic, buzzing hive of

fear and disbelief. An open water swim was the only activity that could regulate her system and calm her frantically frayed nerves. A feeling, a physical sensation like a bonfire, radiated from her heart, spreading outward to her limbs. Since her parents had died, she had painstakingly tried to build a simple, predictable life for herself and her brother, only to have it all completely derailed. Motherly advice be damned. She would *not* wait the requisite ninety minutes after eating before swimming. What was the absolute worst that could possibly happen if she didn't wait?

———————

In a rare, almost desperate surge of optimism, she convinced herself that the swim would instantly clear her head, purge her body of any emotional and physical poison. Talking animals. Magical, omniscient *abuelas*. What the hell else was waiting to happen? Asking that question aloud felt like an invitation for exactly the answer she didn't want to hear.

She took the bus toward Santa Maria del Mar, the closest proper beach to Havana. It was a bumpy thirty-minute ride. She ensured she got a window seat in the back left of the bus to avoid the inevitable extra attention that came with her unnaturally pale skin turning beet-red in the tropical heat, and to get a view of the endless sea, which was the only thing that truly soothed her soul. When Anna arrived at the beach, she quickly removed her dress and flip-flops and tossed them onto her towel beneath the scant shade of the only available palm tree. The sand was brilliant white. The water was an impossibly clear, inviting blue. For a fleeting, perfect moment, she forgot about being spoken to in riddles.

Anna mentally braced herself for the onslaught of whistles, muttered comments, and brazen catcalls, not because she considered herself particularly striking, but simply because it was the pervasive, relentless norm in Cuba. Anna was numb to it now.

Right on cue, the catcalls began. She managed to filter out the noise, focusing only on the burning sand beneath her feet as she sprinted toward the sea. The moment she dove into the sea, the water doused her anxiety and fear. She was instantly able to think clearly. That bilateral, rhythmic swimming motion was a cure for her racing mind. She set out for the furthest crab trap, a small buoy about 300 meters away, and started the methodical process of piecing together the puzzle, as Elena had challenged her to. The repetitive wash of the waves combined with the rhythmic nature of swimming made this Anna's ideal, necessary way to solve the bullshit riddles, if they were even solvable at all, and not just the product of a grand, vodka-fueled hallucination. *Did her mama know about these others?* She must have. How else did she know to choose a garden with a macaw and an iguana on the gate? Could it have truly been a coincidence, a massive, cosmic joke? Why had her father or Misha never gone to the garden? *Was Elena some sort of sage? A Guardian?* Perhaps everyone in her life was secretly mixed up in the local Santería beliefs. Anna couldn't imagine her mother, Julia, practicing Santería, but you never knew with Elena or the Mystery Duo.

Anna flipped onto her back to float for a while, letting the sun warm her face. She started to giggle. *None of this made sense! How could any of it be real?* She was oblivious to a growing, far-off commotion near the shore, until she heard a single, piercing whistle. She stopped floating, began treading water, and looked towards the shore to see people frantically swimming inward and a group of others on the sand motioning wildly for her to come in.

"SHARK! SHARK!" people screamed, making the unmistakable motion of a fin slicing through the air near their heads.

Anna had only ever seen sharks from the safety of the shore. As she tread water, she quickly scanned the horizon and the water around her to pinpoint the location of the threat. Of course, it was circling the crab trap, only about 10 meters away. It looked enormous and distinctly like a bull shark.

"*Hijo de puta*," she muttered, a curse of profound irritation.

The shark, with the terrifying, deliberate speed of a predator, swam directly toward Anna.

Anna gulped a massive breath of air and dove under the water's surface, instinct overriding panic, knowing she shouldn't look like easy surface prey.

The shark, with its immense body, swam directly up to her and, impossibly, nodded. "I will not hurt you, Anna of Kala," it said in an even tone.

Anna choked on the salty sea water as she violently shook her head back and forth underwater. Her grip on reality, already frayed, was bending and fading in real-time. She didn't *feel* crazy. However, she knew that most deluded people probably didn't feel crazy either. A man-eating bull shark was speaking fluent Spanish to her. Anna did the only thing she could think of: she nodded back and decided to simply go along with the conversation with the bull shark.

After observing the shark for another moment, she quickly surfaced for a desperate breath of air and waved emphatically at the panicking crowd on the shore to indicate that she was okay. At that exact moment, she noticed a small rowboat had been launched and was heading for her. She dove back down.

"I understand the concept, in theory," she sputtered, the water distorting the sound, and filling the space between her words. What else do you say to a shark?

"But *how* do I understand you?" she asked, demanding an explanation from the bull shark.

"You are Anna of Kala. Of course you understand me. I have only heard tales of that realm," the shark said, its voice as wistful and distant as a shark's voice could possibly sound. "Kala is supposed to be a glorious planet." Then, staring at her with its huge, flat, black eyes, it added, "Maybe I'll make the transition in my next life."

"What did you just say?" Anna was shocked, a specific phrase leaping out at her. Her mother always used to say those exact words when talking about her dreams of globe-trotting or becoming a famous dancer.

The shark abruptly dove down and started efficiently picking off smaller fish near the sea floor, the conversation apparently concluded. Anna was about to pursue the talking shark, as utterly ludicrous as that sounded, when a pair of strong hands grabbed her under the armpits and yanked her violently into the rowboat.

"Anna! That shark was right there! What the hell were you thinking?" Manny, Elena's grandson, was leaning over her, his face a mix of relief and accusation. He smiled, and the faint, familiar smile wrinkles around his eyes were the exact copy of his abuela's. She almost answered honestly, about the talking shark and Kala, but thought better of it at the last second.

Sweat dripped profusely from his face while his curly black hair blew wildly in the breeze. Manny had always possessed a strange, uncanny knack for being in the right place at the right time for both Anna and her brother Misha. He and Misha acted like brothers, inseparable and fiercely loyal. Sometimes Anna wondered if their bond was even closer than that of true siblings.

"*Oi, puta*, why did you pull me out? It wasn't trying to kill me," Anna said, a tone of deep resignation entering her voice. The shark would have given her answers, she was certain, but she had been ripped away by the second of her three closest friends.

"You and my *abuela* are exactly the same. Always making light of the most serious situations," he winked. She had always suspected that Manny was somehow different from most of the boisterous, often crass Cuban men she knew, but now she was certain.

"Maybe she's part Russian," Anna muttered with a dry, tired sarcasm.

Manny chuckled, a genuine, deep sound.

While he began to row with methodical strokes, she couldn't stop the phrase from looping in her mind: *Maybe I'll make the transition in my next life.* With each row of the heavy oars, Manny inhaled and exhaled forcefully, his energy pouring into the effort.

Anna sat slumped over the narrow plank, trying desperately to shield her frying skin from the sun in any way possible, even though the rowboat had no sail or cover. Other *beings* might think she was "Anna from Kala," a supposed deity, but Anna in Havana was simply a pale-skinned girl acutely prone to brutal sunburns. She could feel her skin searing as they rowed toward the shore. Her pale complexion had been exposed to the unforgiving tropical sun for far too long. Her brother, Misha, never fried, but she always paid a painful price for spending even a few minutes too long at the beach.

"You know, your skin is absolutely frying," he stated, matter-of-factly, not looking at her.

"No shit," she grumbled back.

He just smiled, a flicker of genuine amusement, and increased the speed of his rowing.

She stared intensely toward the rapidly approaching shore line. It was drawing terrifyingly close. She couldn't bear another second of the sun searing her skin, but she was trapped in the middle of a damn rowboat.

"You should really go to my *abuela*, Anna. She can help you if you just ask. I can help you, too."

These fucking mysterious, vague ways that *everyone* had suddenly adopted lately. Anna threw her hands up, the gesture dripping with exasperation, and yelled, "Great! Great! I'll go to Elena for the second time today and have my goddamn mind blown *again*! Is that what the hell you people want?"

"Um... I... she just has aloe plants. The Canadian tour guides all go to her for the remedy. It is no big deal, Anna. We only want to help you." As Manny looked at her, Anna noticed unsettling depth to his eyes, filled with a knowledge far exceeding his years.

"Yep. Ok, sure. I will go to her." Her head began to pound, a deep, throbbing ache. Usually, the vigorous swim alleviated all her physical and mental ailments. She winced, rubbing her temples to try and relieve the pain.

Just then, the boat scraped against the sand. She vaulted over the bow and purposefully strode toward her towel, dress, and flip-flops, all while the noise around her became a deafening hum. She could hear the amplified *gringo* comments and the cautionary, high-pitched yells of people telling her that she was frying. Her skin sizzled. While she could not wait to get out of the sun, which she loved and hated in equal, intense measure, the more pressing issue was that everyone on the beach was talking about her. The buzz was a deafening wall of chatter. Years ago, she had painstakingly mastered the art of ignoring strangers as they talked about the pale-skinned freak. This was different. It was as if she was vibrating with the hum of strangers talking about her, almost like she was absorbing their energy.

"How does a person get that red? I have never seen a *puta* so red! And they are as red as you get! *Oi*—I've never fucked a red woman." She heard every single, intrusive comment.

"*Vete a mierda*!" Anna screamed, the steering pain between her eyes forcing the curse out.

The asshole who had just spoken laughed. "Her hair is beautiful though—I want my hair that color." "Why did that *maricon* Manny save her?" "Don't say such a thing!" "She is a *bruja*. No other explanation for surviving a shark attack." *That was the only possible explanation,* Anna thought to herself, a bubble of dark humor rising in her throat. She chuckled to herself at the thought of being a witch. As usual, people were talking as if she were deaf, but this was a slightly more entertaining topic than her pale skin.

On and on it went. She abandoned the beach as quickly as possible, pulling on her dress and running toward Elena's cafe, dodging carts, cars, bicycles, and the occasional street dogs and cats with desperate speed.

"Elena!" Anna said loudly and breathlessly as she burst through the cafe door, Manny right on her heels, his breathing ragged.

The cafe patrons all stopped their socializing and stared at the frantic, red-faced, blonde-haired girl. They collectively realized that it was just another weird white tourist, needing Elena's famous sun remedy, and went back to their conversations.

Elena strolled from the back of the kitchen with a

serene, almost unnervingly calm look on her face. Anna guessed that she was about to launch into one of her mystical riddles about a goddamn talking animal, another realm, and the overall bizarre new vibe of Havana.

"*Mija*, your poor skin is fried. Come here. I have a poultice of aloe, hibiscus, and plumeria ready for you."

That was a relief to hear. At least *something* in her day was rooted in mundane reality: a bad sunburn.

"Anything to prevent the burn from fully setting in." Anna knew that she wouldn't feel the true, crippling pain for a few hours, but once the burn settled, it would be almost impossible to feel or think about anything else.

"Manny!"

"Yes, *abuela*?"

"Please tend to the comrades. I need to help Anna right now."

"*Por supuesto*."

Elena's aged, strong hand took Anna's already hot, red one and led her to a small, back room off the kitchen. Elena pointed to a weathered wooden stool, wordlessly ordering Anna to sit. Once Anna sat, Elena stood behind her as she prepared the thick, green salve. Anna could tell that the *abuela* was barely stifling a grimace as she reached back to help Anna remove her sundress.

Elena sucked in her breath sharply.

"*Oi, hija, qué lástima*!"

"I know, I know. I had an unintentionally long day on the water. It was really fucking disturbing, actually." With that, Elena applied the first strip of cotton, thoroughly soaked in the poultice, directly to Anna's shoulder.

It took Anna's breath away. It felt like frozen metal against her burning skin. She sucked the air sharply through her teeth as the salve was quickly, expertly applied.

"Shit, that's cold," Anna winced.

Elena smiled, a slow, gentle curve of her lips. "Cue the talking animals everywhere." She let out a gentle, soft chuckle that Anna, in her pain, found genuinely offensive. Seeing Anna's expression of offense, Elena softened her tone.

"My dear, I understand that you have not been enlightened or come to realize the full truth about yourself. No one in your position ever does until it is the appointed time. Would you like me to tell you the truth, now that you have fully seen?"

Anna nodded. With each passing, bizarre moment, either her sanity or her deep-seated cynicism was fading, and she couldn't decide which.

"You are one of the very few humans, a tiny fraction compared to the billions on this planet, who serve as a powerful deity for those in another realm." She placed a comforting, knowing hand on Anna's shoulder and paused in deep thought. "Well, there are a few thousand of you here at any given moment, as far as I know. Some non-deity magical creatures as well. But contrary to the rumors, Anna, I truly don't know *everything*." Elena winked with that last statement.

Here we go, Anna thought.

"The other realm, the one that has been swirling around you and invading your life this past week, is a planet far, far from here. Believe me or not, it doesn't matter to the truth," Elena said, as if she had just flawlessly read Anna's mind. "It is the absolute truth."

"Sure," Anna nodded flatly, pursing her lips into a tight, thin line.

"It is Kala, one of the most exquisitely beautiful planets in the entire multiverse. I have only been once, myself.

Perfectly lush jungle forests, vibrant beyond your imagination. Temples and deities that, sometimes, answer the prayers of their worshipers. People living in harmony with all the animals. But there is an insidious dark side to this paradise, as there is with everything in the multiverse. Nothing is truly perfect by any standard. Most perfection is a facade, a carefully maintained illusion, as I am sure your mother taught you."

"Right." The cynicism, her lifelong shield, was starting to creep back in as Anna nodded slowly. Sanity was still technically there, but it was clinging on by a thread. How much, if any, of this cosmic nonsense should she believe?

"You must believe me!" Elena said, this time letting out a powerful, full-bodied chortle and throwing her head back with unexpected force. "But in all seriousness, my dear, you have no choice but to believe now. Dark forces have far more sinister things in mind for you."

"There is an unknown, powerful force that inevitably creeps in when controlling powers come into play, and power itself becomes the sole determining factor for all actions. Kala is under a deep siege right now, a slow rot, and its people are unsure how to stop it. It takes a deity or a powerful demigod," her eyes bored a deep hole directly into Anna's soul, "to break the decay and restore both chaos and peace. And sometimes, Anna, the attempts are fruitless." Elena shrugged, an unsettling gesture of fatalism, as she said that last line.

At that exact moment, Anna realized that her skin was no longer the color of a freshly bloomed hibiscus. The throbbing, searing heat was gone. Elena began to pull off the wraps. Anna realized, in a sudden, shocking flood of clarity, that the intense hibiscus-red color had drained completely from her skin. As Elena unwrapped the bindings, Anna saw that her skin was its usual pale, flawless color, and the agonizing stinging sensation was entirely gone. The healing had been instantaneous.

"Demi-god? Deity?" Anna said flatly, the words hollow. "Chaos doesn't sound peaceful in any world," she added, trying to cling to basic logic.

"Oh, it's far better than the absolute alternative, Anna. Better to get all this truth out now because the simple truth is that you can die a gruesome, meaningless death here on Earth, or you can embark on your destined path... where you *could* die, but you may also restore the balance to an entire planet. Your mother, Julia, was a powerful deity from Kala. You are a deity from Kala. Your brother, well..." Elena trailed off, the omission hanging heavy in the small room.

Anna could feel the blood draining from her face. Her mother and father had died in a simple, tragic car accident years ago.

"Wha..." she trailed off, her throat constricting. She could hardly think of what simple question to ask, and then sputtered out the first thought that broke through her shock:

"Wait, what are *you*? You have known me since I was a little girl, a customer, a child! But you wait until *now* to tell me all of this? What are you playing at?" Anna swallowed back a surge of pure, white-hot rage. Blood rushed back to her face, a flush of anger. Her mother was dead, a victim of a roadside accident, not a goddess.

Elena gave a wry smile and took a deep, steadying breath. "I am one of the thousands of Keepers of the knowledge and magic that flows between the various realms and Earth. We serve as information portals and keepers of the cosmic archives in the multiverse. Deity protection and meticulously keeping all knowledge are our number one objectives. And our number two objective is to look like ordinary, unremarkable people in the most plausible way possible."

Thousands? Anna wondered, the scale of this hidden world suddenly crushing.

Just then, Manny burst through the kitchen door, smelling of coffee and flour. "*Abuela*, Anna, it's getting incredibly busy out there. I can't work this rush on my own. Anna, tell your brother that he doesn't need to bring anything for music night." Anna nodded mindlessly at whatever Manny was saying, the information barely registering.

With that, Anna stood up, her body feeling healed. She mumbled a thank you to Elena for healing her unbelievable sunburn, thanked Manny for pulling her out of the water (even though she was in no real danger from the talking shark), and walked home in stunned, terrifying silence. There was no way Misha, the pragmatic one, would ever believe a single word of this.

Anna arrived at the quiet, empty house and had it all to herself, as long as she didn't count the roaches. Her brother had three more hours at the kiosk. She decided that she was going to listen to Thriller, despite everything that happened the last time she listened to it.

As she put the cassette into the tape deck and pressed play, she heard the foreboding nature of the music for the first time. She had listened to it last night, but she hadn't *heard* it. She gingerly handled the red macaw feather, turning the vibrant object over and over in her palm as she listened. As she began to hum along to the strange, foreign melody, she realized with a cold certainty that she understood the English lyrics to the song, perfectly, even though she didn't speak a word of the language.

She wanted to smash the cassette player against the concrete floor, but she couldn't. She drifted into self-reflection as Michael Jackson sang. The desire for a stable, uneventful life had manifested itself through a deep desire for control. She never wanted to do more than work in the kiosk, or so she had told herself. She never wanted to leave Cuba, or so she had told herself.

After her parents died, she had convinced herself that stability and consistency led directly to security. It was only now, under the terrifying weight of cosmic circustances, that Anna realized that she had no control over her fate. Maybe it would be worth disrupting her life.

Anna stopped the tape and put in her other favorite cassette. It had songs by David Bowie and Dolly Parton, two of her all-time favorite singers. Her odd taste in music would surprise no one. *Of course*, she thought, *David and Dolly probably aren't from earth.* As the music played, Anna pulled the *sala* from the fridge, spread it thickly on a slice of bread, poured three fingers of vodka, and plopped onto the worn couch, trying to rest in this moment of normalcy. A searing, blinding pain suddenly erupted between her eyebrows.

"*Puta madre*," she gasped to no one, wincing and sucking in her breath. The pain was so unbearable, so intense, that she dropped her glass. She clamped her hand over her forehead and fell backwards onto the couch, only she didn't stop at the couch. She continued to fall through an endless, silent void. She awoke lying on the perfectly manicured edge of a pristine lake. Ahead of her, a series of intricately carved stone steps led to a massive, circular marble platform floating unnaturally in the middle of the lake.

"Come, Anna." The low feminine voice was a disembodied command. She looked frantically around, seeing no one. Pain still radiated, pulsing from between her eyes as she forced them open wider. It felt as if an invisible, powerful rope had pulled her towards the floating platform.

She teetered as she stepped onto the first stone step. The water was transparent down to the sandy bottom, but there were no fish, no frogs, no algae - nothing. It was void of any visible life.

"What a terrifying fucking dream this is," Anna said to herself. Yet part of her knew that it was no dream at all.

As her foot stepped onto the cool surface of the floating marble platform, Anna's entire body started to hum. Logic was trying desperately to override the experience, her mind demanding to know the impossible science of how the platform was floating.

"Dream, this really is a dream, I'm still on the couch," she repeated, trying with desperation to convince herself.

The platform was immense, easily the size of her entire apartment building back in Cuba. Ornately carved marble columns anchored each of the four corners. Resplendent detailed carvings of tropical birds, lush flowers, and tall trees were synced perfectly. She swore that the carved birds were actually flapping their wings and flying within the stone.

A feeling of profound elation washed over her, something she had never felt before in her life.

"Maybe not a nightmare," she said to no one, a genuine smile finally breaking through her fear.

"Anna, this isn't a dream. This is only the beginning." An apparition of a naked woman shimmered into existence. She looked as if she had been carved out of a single, massive block of glowing amber. Her long, dark hair was wildly unkempt but Anna found her oddly beautiful feeling a strange, primal attraction to her perfect, naked body.

Shocking herself, she never found women attractive in Havana.

Anna narrowed her eyes, responding with sarcastic agreement. "You're absolutely right. This is definitely reality. My brother is going to have me committed to an institution."

The woman's voice grew agitated, losing its soothing quality. "I am Taris. My *ziblings* and I called you forth. Your *fortuna*, the very essence of your power, was stolen from you through nefarious, powerful means. Your foolish, childish antics on Earth were punished. As a result, all of Kala is being punished and decaying."

Fuck, here we go again with Kala. With each bizarre occurrence, Anna's doubt about her true, cosmic identity became increasingly difficult to uphold.

"Look, lady, I have no idea what a *fortuna* is or what you're talking about," Anna said, with disarming honesty, hoping that she might receive a more coherent explanation.

"Your ignorance is unappealing, Anna, and deeply disquieting. The *fortuna* is the source of your power here on Kala. Without it, your abilities to serve your people and restore balance are severely limited. You must find and restore your *fortuna* to me and my ziblings," Taris commanded.

"Listen, if I knew *anything* about a *fortuna* or whatever it is, I would find it and give it back to you immediately," Anna said, again sucking on the inside of her cheek. Taris genuinely frightened her. If Anna could procure what she needed, she absolutely would.

"You fool! You deities are utterly self-absorbed and willfully blind!" Taris's amber body shimmered violently, and then she disappeared in a silent puff of golden smoke.

Moments later, a crackly, male voice called her over to the ornately carved column on the far side of the platform.

"You have irritated my sister, and she has little patience left for you. Best not to test me as well. I am Zaris, the portal protector."

A naked man with equally unkempt hair, also looking as though he had been meticulously carved out of amber, levitated before her at the opposite end of the platform. Learning from her disastrous interaction with Taris, Anna approached him with curiosity.

"Dear Zaris, please tell me what I need to know about the portal," she motioned around the entire platform with her hands.

"I ensure that you have seamless, safe travel between the worlds. Only you, Anna of Kala, and a select few others, can travel through this specific portal, and only with my deliberate, conscious presence," he stated authoritatively, his amber eyes boring directly into hers.

"Seems dangerous, no? And how is it that anyone, even a deity, can travel through a portal at all?" Anna was genuinely ignorant of the science and magic of inter-dimensional travel and was asking the question in earnest.

"Now you are mocking me with your faux ignorance. I will not be tested as I cannot serve a deity who refuses to return and reclaim their destiny!" Zaris screamed, the sound echoing painfully across the empty lake. He then dove headfirst into the water, and a cloud of swirling smoke remained in his wake. Anna was confused. She had been earnest, for once.

"Wait! I was being honest!" she yelled, a desperate attempt, but she clearly didn't know the social rules in this realm.

"Anna of Kala, I am Qaris, the head of your power. Without you, there is no us. Without us, there is no you." A third amber-colored figure, with their hair pulled into a messy, elegant bun, floated into position at the center column. This figure had the clearly defined female top half of their body and a male bottom half. Their hair was just as wild and untamed as their ziblings'.

"I am everything and nothing of your power, understand?" Qaris said, their voice balanced between two octaves. "My ziblings have not forgiven you for your absence and your denial. But you must return to us and make it right." They held a magnificent trident. The far left prong of the trident was embossed with a blinding array of sapphires. The far right prong of the trident looked like a marble carving of an intricate skeleton key. The middle prong of the trident was a dull green color. A faint, sputtering hint of a flame was captured within.

"I'm really trying my best to understand," she said with pleading, earnest eyes.

"Bring your entire body, your full consciousness, through the sanctioned portal. Restore your *fortuna*. Restore the compassionate, true rulers of Kala. Only then can you begin to restore Kala itself. Trust very few." Qaris had a flat, unreadable look on their face, refusing to reveal any emotion.

"So, this restoration, does it mean that I must permanently reside here? Or..." Anna's mind was finally coming to grips with the new, terrifying reality. Between Oragan, Ara, Elena, the talking shark, and now the *ziblings*, the wall of doubt she had built her life upon was almost completely gone. Anna tasted her own blood from nervously chewing on her cheek. Fear had ruled her adult life, her Havana life. Fear of the oppressive government. Fear of the invasive Americans. Fear of losing friends, family, and lovers.

"You have two final choices, Anna: restore Kala and reside here as the Goddess you are, or face permanent exile in the Nothing Lands." Qaris was growing visibly irritated, the amber of their body flickering. Suddenly, Taris and Zaris reappeared, flanking Qaris in an intimidating, three-pronged front.

"Now LEAVE!" They roared in unison, a sound that shook the platform, and shooed Anna away with dismissive, angry gestures of their hands.

Anna woke up violently, lying splayed on her concrete floor. She lay there in silent, numb shock for the next few hours while she processed the entirety of the events of the past few chaotic days.

5

Manny counted down the minutes until Misha was scheduled to arrive at his apartment. He flitted about, attempting to clean anything with a surface even though nothing was dirty. Manny thought about the invisible current that coursed between them every time he looked into Misha's glacier blue eyes. Misha felt it as well. They would hold each other's gazes just a little longer than comfortable. A hand would firmly linger on a shoulder. They would exchange winks and smiles over the benign transactions of vodka mojitos or cafe con leche.

Manny wasn't sure what to do. He reflected up on his past lovers and how they were usually good friends, but they mutually fulfilled physical needs more than emotional ones. Deep love, beyond friendship, never manifested in those relationships. This felt different. A knock on the door startled him as he was lost in thought. Misha.

Manny opened the door to see Misha standing before him, grinning devilishly. His wavy, short brown hair was perfect. His chiseled jaw line framed his beautiful lips. And those piercing blue eyes. Manny could feel starbursts in his stomach. Humans got butterflies. Keepers got starbursts.

"Come in, Misha," he said with an equally provocative smile. Misha walked in and casually grazed his hand across Manny's shoulder as he made his way to the kitchen counter with a bottle of vodka. "I always come prepared," he said in a sing-song voice. Manny casually and cautiously regaled him about his sister's adventure to make small talk, walking a bit closer to Misha with each sentence. Manny handed him two glasses, purposefully resting his hand on Misha's during the transfer, lingering a bit too long. Misha did not pull away. Once he finished the story, there was an eternity of complete silence. Manny could feel that they both enjoyed the buildup of tension. Misha smelled like toasted marshmallows, fiery sweetness. Manny couldn't help but inhale deeply. Keepers had a heightened sense of smell.

Manny seized that moment. He moved to within an inch of Misha's face, almost nose to nose, and whispered in his ear "You. The way that you move. The way that you exist. The way you care. The electricity of you is irresistible to me." Misha froze in place. Manny wondered if he misjudged their hidden flirtations and nuances in his behavior. Misha's breathing grew heavier. No longer did he smell like a toasted marshmallow, but of a leather jacket and a campfire. The smell of pure desire. Misha stood at the counter while Manny wrapped his arms around him, something that Manny has wanted to do for awhile. Misha's body shuddered as he reciprocated the embrace, grabbing Manny's arms, shoulders and lower back as if to test every muscle. Misha's face conveyed an unreadable intensity. His eyes pierced Manny's. For a second, Manny wondered if he made a mistake. Misha gently ran his fingers through Manny's thick, curly hair, cupped his face and brought it towards him.

"May I kiss you?" Misha asked gently. Manny nodded as Misha leaned in for a passionate kiss. As their bodies pressed against each other, Manny could feel that he and Misha were both fully aroused. Manny hurriedly took Misha's shirt off and then his own. He grabbed Misha's hand and led him to the couch to sit. Manny straddled him, alternating between kissing his mouth and neck while grinding against him. Misha threw his head back and moaned. Misha now smelled like a heavenly mixture of cinnamon and musk. Manny never smelled pheromones like that before and it drove him wild.

"Do you want to go to my bedro-?" Before Manny could finish, Misha led the way. No need for clothes, Manny thought as they hurriedly undressed each other. Manny threw Misha on the bed and explored his naked body from head to toe. Using his mouth, he tasted every inch, taking pleasure in Misha's excitement, eventually engulfing his aroused cock in his entire mouth. Manny bobbed up and down, enjoying every delicious moment until Misha exploded. Misha then pulled Manny up to his face, kissing him passionately, fully tasting himself in Manny's mouth. He threw Manny back on the bed for his turn to explore Manny's toned body. Manny was about to explode from having his nipples sucked while Misha gingerly played with his balls. Eventually Misha swallowed his dick in his mouth. Manny felt fireworks. Visions of joy, birth, death and rebirth passed before his eyes in that climactic moment.

Misha crawled next to him and held him.

"You know, Misha, you -" Misha put a finger to his mouth before he could finish.

"You don't have to speak like a poet every time you talk to me. You can say something like 'I fucking love you'," he said with a sly glint in his eyes.

"Misha, I fucking love you," Manny said with a huge smile.

6

Anna woke up the next morning to the sound of her brother making coffee and whistling a jarring, upbeat Cuban tune. Her head felt thick and heavy, a painful fog from the night before, as she stumbled out of the small bedroom and into their tiny kitchen.

"Why are you so fucking chipper?" She asked, wincing as the sound of her own voice sent a fresh spike of pain behind her eyes.

Misha turned, a *cafe con leche* in his hand, his usual carefree smile slightly strained. "Anna, what the hell happened yesterday? The whole *barrio* is talking. I heard that you were almost eaten by a shark. Then I come home to see you got shit faced. Clearly that shark rattled you more than you let on." He moved towards her, his expression softening into an unfamiliar, urgent sincerity. He continued, "You are the only relative that I have on this earth. You cannot leave me."

A flicker of suspicion ignited in Anna's bleary mind, slicing through the haze of her hangover. "What do you mean by this earth?" she said suspiciously. She grabbed the edge of the mahogany table to steady herself. Anna was physically present but she felt as though she was observing from a distance, the recent events racing through her mind as she sought a rational narrative.

His brow furrowed. "Planet earth? Here? Cuba? Russia? Anywhere?" He gestured vaguely toward the window, where the sun shined on the Malecon.

"How could I leave? Where would I go? What would I do if I went there?" She interrogated him, her gaze sharp, searching for any tell-tale sign that he was concealing some piece of this bizarre puzzle. Was he in on this as well? Anna sat heavily on the wooden stool, bleary eyed and waiting for the much-needed caffeine infusion.

Misha sighed, pushing the cup of coffee across their old mahogany table. "I know that you had a near-death experience. I'll entertain the existential talk for a moment. So, did you really almost get eaten by a shark, or is this just another rumor for the gossip queens?" He said the last part almost as a challenge, his eyes holding hers. There was something *off* about Misha, but she couldn't quite pinpoint the difference. If she called him on it, he would immediately deflect, claiming paranoia brought on by her lack of sleep or excessive drinking. But this felt different. It felt like fear.

Her eyes narrowed as she took a swig from her coffee. Scenario calculations swirled at light speed in her brain, a rapid-fire assessment of her new reality. At this exact moment, Anna did not know if a.) any of the encounters over the past few days were real, b.) if they were real, if her brother was in on all of it, and c.) if he *was* involved, then she couldn't trust him. Anna made a calculated choice to be unbothered, at least on the outside.

"No, I didn't. Everyone overreacted, per the usual," she lied smoothly, taking a slow, fortifying sip of the brown elixir. "There was a shark, yes. But I wasn't in any real danger." Anna knew that she would most definitely sound certifiably insane if she told her brother the whole truth: that the enormous predator had somehow communicated with her, a brief, silent reassurance that she wasn't a part of its dinner plans.

Anna noticed the subtle lines around his mouth ease as his jaw unclenched and he offered a genuine smile. "Ok. Well, get your ass to the kiosk. It's my day off, and the early tourists will be thirsty soon."

"Hey," she said, raising a curious eyebrow, "you always give me shit for something, but I heard something interesting about *you*."

"What?" he said a little too aggressively, the tension returning as his jaw clenched again, making the muscle twitch near his ear. Anna knew instantly that her suspicion was correct. He was hiding something, but she decided to continue with a benign line of conversation, testing the water.

"Yesterday, Manny let slip that he was going to see you last night to listen to music."

Misha froze, his posture becoming rigid. His jaw remained steadfastly locked. "SO? We listened to music last night. Maybe today we'll watch a movie, an old Soviet classic." He tried to sound casual, but his voice was strained.

"Be careful, is all. I don't want you to get caught with anything contraband. I've heard they're cracking down hard on anything that they think is American propaganda, or any deviation from the Party line," she cautioned, her grip tightening unconsciously on her coffee mug.

"There is nothing to be careful of," her brother spat back, unusually flustered, his reaction a silent, damning confirmation of Anna's deepening suspicions that he was involved, somehow, with her shitty current circumstances.

"What the hell? If you're disappearing, getting caught for listening to music is the stupidest reason to rot in a prison cell," she balked, attempting to sound like the pragmatic, annoyed sister. "Not to mention I don't want to pay a fine or deal with the kiosk alone for a week while you're in jail." *Cagey and reckless*, she thought, noting the shift in his personality. Two traits totally unlike her brother.

A look of profound relief washed over Misha's face, as if she had just swerved away from a cliff edge. "Oh sister, no worries there. Our yankee music supply is secure." His energy shifted back to its normal, breezy state. Anna gave up the interrogation, deciding she had pushed him far enough, and resigned herself to follow his orders and get to work.

Uneasy banter with her brother. No talking animals in sight. A cold, small voice in her head reminded her that they were only thirty minutes into their Friday. The talking bird's directive, "Meet us in the garden on Saturday," played on a loop in her head.

After picking up the fresh mint from the day's beverages, Anna arrived at the kiosk on the edge of the Malecon. She unlocked the shutter and rolled it up with a grinding squeal of rusty metal. Her head on a swivel, she glanced behind each shoulder, half-expecting a fantastical stranger to approach her, but the usual runners getting their daily exercise front of the sea. A minuscule sliver of tension melted from her neck.

She entered through the side door and started to prepare the glasses and slice the limes for the day. Anna hummed the infectious baseline of "Thriller" as she slipped into her meditative drink-prep rhythm, the familiar, comforting motions a balm to her chaotic mind. Once she realized *what* she was doing, she stopped herself abruptly.

She was afraid that the song held some sort of summoning power.

"Oh now you have really lost your shit, Anna," she muttered out loud, trying to shake the ridiculous thought.

"Anna, what did you say?" a warm, familiar voice came from out of nowhere, causing her to jump.

Summoning indeed. If Anna could accidentally summon anyone at any time, it would be Ivan.

"Privyet, Ivan. Can I help you?" she said, turning to face Ivan. Ivan was her inexplicable, unrequited love. Anytime he showed up, an involuntary smile spread across her face, and her heart skipped a beat. She didn't know the specifics of his job other than "Cultural Attaché," but if he were an *actual* cultural attaché, then she was the actual Anna Karenina come to life. A tragic but beautiful thought. His mother was a Cuban senior communications official, and his father was a Russian senior trade official, giving him all of the access to information and the financial privilege afforded to the Party elite. Ivan occasionally "found" black market vodka for them in times of shipping crisis and blockades. He was the lifelong object of her intense, one-sided, unrequited affection for as long as she knew him, which felt like an eternity.

"A mojito *con vodka* of course. And tell me, was it true that you were in a shark attack yesterday?" He placed his hand on hers across the bar, his touch sending a sharp, pleasant tingle through her arm and down to her *chocha*. Was he flirting? Often when comrades flirted, their delivery was clunky at best and completely offensive at worst. Not Ivan. His delivery was always perfect, a subtle blend of concern and charm. Ivan's eyes, usually a light hazel, looked intensely soulful. Ivan knew how to make you feel like the only person in the world when he wanted something. Anna didn't care. She wanted to feel like the only person in the world to someone, even if it was for a fleeting moment.

"Shit, if I didn't know any better, I would think that we lived in a tiny village where news travels on the wind," she said, pulling her hand away to wipe it on her apron with feigned indignation. "Does it look like I was in a shark attack yesterday?" She turned around and motioned dramatically, as if modeling a new dress.

"Definitely not, you are perfection," he countered, leaning an elbow on the bar, "however, a Russian bartender in Havana very nearly gets eaten by a shark. I imagine you're hard to miss as you swim, practically glowing against the blue water," he said with a wink. "People are going to talk, Anna. You know how they love a good disaster." Even though his eyes were hazel, she swore that she saw a blue flicker in them, like a brief, hot flame. Anna was lucky that her face was permanently flushed from the oppressive heat, or else her skin would surely betray her private thoughts. His hand returned to hers, his touch deliberate. He *was* flirting.

He leaned in, his voice dropping to an intimate whisper that smelled faintly of sweet cigar smoke wafting off his curly black hair. "I also wanted to discuss something else that I heard. There are questions about you and your brother's residency here in Havana." *Definitely not flirting now*, she thought, the sudden professional shift a cold slap of reality. If she could pull him over the bar at that moment and fuck him senseless to stop the conversation, she would.

Even though she was raised in Cuba, her parents were Russian, and she had inherited the famous Russian ability to keep her face impassive. She kept her composure, her voice calm and measured in response, though her thoughts were a million at once, intertwined into a complex, anxious web of emotions.

"Of course, Comrade. What would you like to discuss?"

"Well, make this drink on the house, and I'll let you know the latest rumors," he said with the same charming smile. Anna knew that everything he did was transactional, especially with women, but his allure was intoxicatingly toxic. And yet, his fleeting attention made her feel special, chosen.

"Of course," she sighed, already reaching for the mint.

"I've heard that they are considering returning all Cuban-born Russians back to the USSR within the next year, to make them more loyal to the Motherland," he said gravely, watching her face for a reaction. "I am excluded, of course, being half-Cuban, but you and your brother are on the list for consideration."

Anna kept her face flat, her heart sinking into her gut. "When will this be decided?"

"In six months. I will try to keep you as informed as possible," he promised. His eyes had the look of pity, and his tone sounded genuinely concerned, but Anna couldn't help but wonder what else he wanted in return for this information.

"As a worker, who spreads Soviet culture to Canadian and European tourists through the fine art of the mojito con vodka, I feel my job is important for the image of the USSR," she parroted, a lie so flimsy neither of them believed it.

"Anna, cut the shit. I'm not the one you need to impress with your commitment to the Party. But I will do what I can to help both you and your brother," he said, lowering his voice again. "Who in the hell would want to live in the Soviet Union after living here?" He didn't finish the thought, merely shaking his head.

By not responding, he knew that she agreed completely. She poured him a shot of vodka, on the house. They took it together, the fiery liquid a brief anaesthetic against the day's grim news.

"Anna, I have a bad feeling about things," he murmured, his eyes searching hers. "Something bigger than us is happening, a change in the political wind. But I will always be honest with you. Whatever happens, we can get through it together." Their eyes were locked, and both of them started breathing heavier, the proximity and the intensity suddenly overwhelming. Both of his hands had clasped hers across the sticky bar top.

She turned a shade of crimson, her skin betraying her secret thoughts about Ivan, the simple, intense desire for him. She was speechless, but knew nothing had to be said—the moment was communicating enough.

Just then, her first real customer of the day, an overly chatty Canadian in a white sun hat, arrived at the kiosk, shattering the tension. Ivan gave her a quick, almost panicked look and walked away breezily blending into the crowd. Anna, almost collapsing from the intensity of the exchange, gripped the bar for a moment, then started her job for the day, plunging back into the mundane rhythm of mint and vodka.

An uneventful, exhausting day followed. Russian comrades. Cuban comrades. A loud Canadian tour group that kept her too busy to think.

She arrived home to find her brother prepping the black beans and rice in the kitchen. He was humming one his favorite songs from Depeche Mode, and had a small, contented smile on his face.

"Why are you so happy, even for you, dear brother?"

"I watched a movie today with Manny. Elena made us a

delicious meal after. Good food and entertainment. What more is there?" He practically sang as he spoke, his movements light and fluid.

Something is missing from this story, she thought, noting the careful gaps in his narrative. Anna decided not to press and not to ruin her brother's day off with the truly awful news from Ivan. She figured it could wait until tomorrow, when she had a plan.

The next morning, they walked to the kiosk in a humid, oppressive silence. The weather continued to be unseasonably and brutally hot, a dense, wet heat that felt unnatural. As human nature dictates, it was all that anyone could talk about.

"What do you think is causing this? It feels like the air is boiling," Anna said, pulling her hair back from her sweaty neck and knotting it haphazardly.

"I don't know, but I'm not sure how we'll keep up with the extra ice required if this continues," Misha muttered, looking worriedly at the sky.

They paused as the kiosk came into view, and Anna's blood ran cold. Two despots from the embassy staff, recognizable even from a distance, waited by the counter: Vlad and Boris. Misha froze mid-step, his jaw going slack. Anna's pulse quickened, hammering against her ribs.

Inhale, one two three, hold one two three, exhale one two three. Anna's body begged her to turn and run, to sprint down the Malecon and throw herself into the sea. Through sheer willpower, she remained rooted to the spot, standing shoulder-to-shoulder with Misha.

"Misha, I know why they're here," she whispered, her throat dry. "Rumor has it that they're sending Russians back to the motherland to 're-acquaint' us with our Soviet culture."

"Is that what *he* said?" Misha sputtered out, attempting a nervous, hollow laugh.

"Why are you so nervous? What the hell did you do, Misha? This isn't just about the music, is it?" Like any good sister, she knew her brother was full of shit about something vital and terrifying.

"No." He sighed, the sound heavy with resignation. "There is something you should know. But you cannot tell anyone else, ok? Especially not them." His eyes flitted frantically between her face and the ominous figures waiting at the kiosk.

Here we go again, she thought with a strange sense of déjà vu. She rolled her eyes internally. "Let me guess! You're a vampire. NO! A werewolf? A fairy? A mystical transfiguring shark in a human suit?" Anything felt possible now.

Misha cocked his head to the side, pursing his lips together tightly. Silence hung between them, charged with anticipation.

"Ok, ok, what is it? Tell me," Anna held her breath, gripping his arm. Nothing between them had ever been this serious, this world-shaking.

"Well, I am a fairy," he sputtered out, the admission a rush of air.

Anna's mind momentarily spiraled, the sheer absurdity of the statement colliding with the established reality of talking animals.

"With Manny," he added quickly, studying his feet with intense focus. The spiral stopped. *Manny didn't tell Anna that he was a fucking fairy?* God dammit, she thought, annoyed that she was out of the loop.

"I know, I figured that part out. You were just at his house," she said, being unintentionally obtuse, still processing the 'fairy' part.

"No, we really like each other. In a forbidden way," he winced, his eyes looking off to the sea, unable to meet her gaze.

"OH! OH. Oooooh...." Anna was speechless. Flirty, handsome, charismatic Misha, who had irresistible charm with women, was in love with a man. She could see that he was fighting back tears, looking both relieved that the secret was out and terrified of the potential consequences. She took his hand and squeezed it gently, a silent, powerful reassurance.

"Brother, I don't care about that," she said earnestly, looking directly into his tear-filled eyes. "We will figure this out together. Until then, be careful. You know the punishment here. I don't want us to be deported or worse."

They walked towards the kiosk, both of them wearing their perfectly practiced, Soviet trained, blank faces.

"Priviet, comrades," the siblings said in unison, a chorus of false politeness.

"Priviet, Anna and Misha. Hot today, no?" said the one who goes by Vlad, with the behind-the-back nickname of "The Impaler" because he was rumored to torture perceived dissenters. It was whispered that he had a collection of sophisticated interrogation weapons at his disposal in the embassy basement. Vlad was an imposing figure, a man carved from granite. He was taller than almost anyone Anna had ever met and looked as though he could effortlessly lift a car. His smiles were usually the result of his inner sadism asserting itself. While he had a handsome, angular face by traditional standards, Anna was certain that no self-respecting woman would consider a relationship with him.

"I know you aren't here to talk about the weather, Vlad," Anna said, her smile wide and artificial. "Have a seat while we prepare a drink for you two. On the house."

"Thank you. We're here on official business," said the

one named Boris. Just Boris, aka The Impaler's dumb sidekick. Anna noticed that Boris wasn't looking well, even for him. He was always doughy, but today he seemed extra pale and sweaty. Mosquitos swarmed around his head. *At least he functions as mosquito repellent for the rest of us*, Anna thought darkly.

Playing dumb, Misha kept the conversation going, leaning across the counter. "Oh, did the vodka shipment arrive? We were so worried. I was afraid that we'd have to switch to rum exclusively. Horrible, horrible situation. Nothing like the clean, pure taste of our national beverage, eh?" Misha winced internally as the propagandist words came out of his mouth.

"Yes Misha, the vodka has arrived, but that is not why we are here," Vlad cut in, his eyes fixed on Anna. "We are considering returning all Cuba-born Russians back to the motherland to reintegrate back into Soviet culture and society. While Cuba has much to offer for the cause, it is a little too close to America for our comfort. Too much access to American culture can rot your brain, no?" Vlad's lips turned up in a thin, chilling smile as he said it. Anna detested him, his mere presence causing her to fantasize about his violent, drawn-out death. The desire to annihilate him was now equally a part of her core as her desperate, unrequited love for Ivan. It troubled her deeply that both men caused such deep, yet violently opposing feelings, at a molecular level.

On top of all that, it's the music, she thought, a fresh wave of panic and fury. *The fucking Thriller album and everything else.*

"I do not believe that I have been contaminated by American culture, comrade." Anna started pounding out the limes with aggressive force, as if his evil face was at the bottom of the glass. "As a matter of fact, our parents instilled pride in Russian arts and culture from a young age," she said through a fake, tense smile that didn't reach her eyes.

"Yes, we are aware. May your parents rest in peace. Good people," Vlad spat the words out with a casual cruelty. Anna thought she saw a faint, alarming red flare in Vlad's eyes at that moment. He must have noticed her gaze, because he quickly looked off towards the Malecon as he continued. "However, it is a different time than when you were young. We've heard accounts of American pop music making its way into Cuba. We want to ensure that no one here is promoting its spread, or corrupted by it."

"Comrades, rest assured that we only enjoy the amazing music that we find here in Cuba and the beautiful classical music from our own country," Misha stated in his usual breezy way, leaning on his casual charm. "We don't even like Russian pop music, except for Trololo," he added, a twinkle in his eye. Anna had to suppress a cackle; they both hated that ridiculous song, but knew that it was a favorite of uptight, older people.

That seemed to put Vlad and Boris at an unnerving ease. Vlad's smile contorted slightly, a subtle sign of satisfaction. Boris merely swatted at the persistent mosquitos that swarmed around his sweaty, pale head.

Anna slammed their drinks on the bar. Luckily it was so hot outside, or else she would have no excuse, other than pure rage, to explain her bright red face.

"You know, we would hate to find out that you two, both exemplary workers of the people, are aiding and partaking in American culture," Vlad said, his voice dropping to a low, chilling register. "We would not want you to go the way of your parents." Boris laughed, a wet, unpleasantly high sound, as the words came from Vlad's mouth. Vlad took a long, slow gulp from his mojito, never breaking eye contact.

All of the blood drained from Anna's face. Her stomach churned violently. She crouched down, pretending to get clean glasses, but instead took deep breaths, fighting back a surge of tears and a boiling rage deep inside of her. She heard a faint buzzing coming in from the distance and gathered herself. Composed, she informed them that their parents' death was a tragic accident and could they please let her continue preparing for the day. The buzzing sound got closer, louder.

Her brother had his back turned to them, completely absorbed in chopping limes. His jaw clenched with every precise slice, and his eyes narrowed at each piece of fruit with exacting focus. He was getting a great deal of satisfaction chopping the limes. She knew exactly what he imagined the limes to be.

"Hey – there are a few.. hey..." Vlad and Boris paused, their conversation derailed, before they realized what was happening. "BEES!" A terrifying, dense swarm of angry bees suddenly enveloped Vlad and Boris, stinging them relentlessly and viciously.

"BEES! AAAAAAH!" Both men screamed like five-year-old children, shrieking in horror. "We'll return! Take care of the bee problem!" And they bolted, running clumsily toward the sea, swiping frantically at the insects. As they got further away, the bees dispersed, peeling off in mid-air and going on their way, vanishing as quickly as they had arrived. Vlad gave her a terrifying, venomous look over his shoulder as he ran, but she didn't care. Anna was laughing so hard, a wild, hysterical sound, that she was near hyperventilation. Her brother, however, was less amused.

"What the fuck was that, Anna?" her brother demanded, his voice ringing with incredulity, turning around to face her.

"What was what?" she said, wiping the tears of laughter from her face with the back of her hand.

"The bees. It felt like you controlled them, you *puta bruja*," he hissed. "Anna, that is impossible," he finished, his face a mask of disbelief.

"Don't be ridiculous, Misha." Although he wasn't wrong. In the frenzy of the bee attack, she had felt a strange sense of power, a powerful, reassuring connection with the insects, as if they were acting on her behalf.

"Now it's my turn to tell you a secret. But let's wait until after work, I need a drink and a plan," she intoned, the humor gone.

"I always knew that you were a lesbian!" He smiled, a genuine, relieved smile now.

"Ha ha, very funny. However, I'm sure you will think it's fucking crazy. But it may be our only hope," she shrugged her shoulders and shut her mouth firmly as a customer approached.

When they finally arrived at home that evening, exhausted and tense, Anna told Misha everything. Absolutely everything. She recounted how the exotic duo, relationship unknown, were also a talking macaw and iguana. She explained the non-shark attack and the surreal communication. She revealed the existence of Elena, the enigmatic Keeper of Gods-Know-What, and detailed the secrets of her and her mother's hidden garden spot. She told him that their mother was a deity in exile. That there are other realms, including a planet called Kala. Finally, as a grand, inexplicable flourish of her new reality, she also told him that she understood all the lyrics to "Thriller," a song sung in a language she could barely speak.

His face was blank, registering zero shock.

"You know all the English lyrics to Thriller?" he asked, completely deadpan. She punched him on the arm.

"I know it doesn't make sense," she rushed on. "But whatever it is, it must be real, right? I have to decide I should stay and face deportation or go with the talking lizard and macaw. What would you do in my situation? You have a fucking lover, so maybe don't answer," she said, cutting herself off. "Shit, it is all confusing. I wish our parents were here to help," she finished pensively, running a hand through her hair.

"I don't want to believe you, Anna. You sound fucking mental," he admitted honestly. "But I must believe you. It's the only thing we have now other than deportation to our frozen homeland." He stood up, pacing the small living room. "Anna, think back though. You seem to forget the strange reality of our lives. Our lives have *never* been 'normal'. Your life has never been that way! We had so many strange occurrences during our childhood that you simply took for granted." He stopped pacing, his eyes becoming distant, wistful. "Mama seemingly talked to animals, remember? I was jealous of the way that she would take you off without notice and you both would return completely rejuvenated. Father, well he was Georgian. He told the folklore from Georgia as if it were absolute, literal truth, not fairy tales."

"I haven't decided if I should meet them in the garden," Anna confessed. "Elena warned me that they could be trouble. I would do anything to stay here with you."

"Anna, this is bigger than our current reality, and you know it. You must go," Misha said with a newfound urgency. "And maybe you will finally learn the truth about Mama and Papa. I hated the way Vlad talked of their death today. I wish we were talking about *his* death."

"Do you think that fucker was involved? There was something about him, beyond his usual Rasputin vibe, that was insidious," Anna said. He shrugged, but their eyes met, confirming they were thinking the exact same, terrifying thought.

"Hey, check this out," Anna said, wanting to lighten the mood and prove the last, most absurd point of her story. "You know how terrible my English is. Put on Thriller and I'll show you something."

He fast-forwarded the cassette to the exact spot in the tape deck, about a minute in, and pressed play.

That familiar, dizzy feeling came over Anna, the world momentarily blurring at the edges. She grabbed her brother's hand and led him to the bathroom, guessing that the macaw and iguana would be in the window. *Voila, the dynamic duo,* she thought with a weary sigh.

"You called us? Oh! And your brother too!" squawked the macaw. She bounced up and down on the window sill, then settled, precariously perched on the ledge. "He is lovely, but I get the feeling he doesn't fancy macaws." She winked, a disconcerting gesture on a tropical bird. The iguana rolled his eyes with human-like exasperation.

Misha's mouth was agape, a perfect, stunned O. He instinctively sat on the toilet to steady himself.

"So now we can't listen to Thriller without being graced by your presence?" Anna said sardonically, crossing her arms.

"Thriller is a cautionary tale, Anna," the bird commanded, her voice dropping in pitch. "It's about Kala. He is singing of the current situation in your land, using it as a call for help. Listen closely."

She brought the tape deck into the bathroom and rewound to the beginning of the song. As she listened again, absorbing the bird's words, her body felt a visceral reaction, as if it was going to decay into the earth, a sudden, grotesque sense of vulnerability. Yet, the feeling was set to a catchy beat that she couldn't ignore. She tried not to be emotional, but the thought of widespread suffering and fear in another realm, one she was connected to, caused her to feel distraught.

"Can someone tell me what the hell the song is about?" a frustrated Misha pleaded. "I still can't understand the English words!"

"There is a dark force controlling the Kalan realm and turning their idyllic slice of the universe into a draconian hellhole," Anna recited, the understanding flowing from her effortlessly. "No one is safe. Balance is gone. Light is gone. Free thought is impossible." Her brother looked as surprised as she felt about the expert analysis coming out of her mouth.

"I still don't understand how *I* can help," Anna said, feeling the weight of the universe settle on her shoulders. "What can I do? I am nothing! I am a bartender."

The iguana flickered his tongue, then looked at the macaw as if he were asking her permission to continue speaking. The macaw nodded a curt assent.

"Jesus Christ, you're dense, Anna. You are a goddess," the iguana said, completely deadpan.

"Is this really the time to flirt with me? I mean, I probably would have slept with you as a human, Oragan, but absolutely not as an iguana," Anna retorted, giving him the side eye.

The iguana rolled his eyes. "In your dreams. You aren't my type. Many so-called humans are actually deities learning a lesson. Deities tend to behave badly and need a break from all that power, a nice long exile," he explained in a rush. "You're a goddess in Kala. After a bout of exile, worshippers often miss the gifts of the deities. There's an increase in festivals, altars, sacrifices, and prayers to bring them back. Some return and do more harm than good while others clearly learned their lessons. Since your exile, Anna worship has been on the decline, as we expected," he said nonchalantly.

"My *what*?" Anna retorted, stunned. He ignored her and continued talking.

"You're in exile. You were a total self-absorbed bitch before your exile, apparently. People haven't really forgotten. They aren't worshipping you yet, like they used to. Your numbers are off. You're not supposed to return for a while. But we're speeding things up. We greased a few universal wheels, probably breaking some major space-time-continuum laws in the process," he rushed on. "All with good intentions though. We want to bring order and normalcy back to Kala. And you are the only one who can do it," the iguana said breathlessly, even though he sat perfectly still.

"During time in exile, the Keepers, like Elena, keep you steady and safe from external factors. Think of the Keepers as deity protectors so you don't get in too much trouble in this Earthly realm," he concluded.

"Any questions?" Ara asked brightly.

Misha's mouth opened again, as if he were catching mosquitoes. Anna flicked the bottom of his chin. He closed it.

"Yeah, who wants a drink? Because I do," Anna said, feeling the desperate need for a dose of normalcy and vodka. Misha immediately raised his hand.

The menagerie and Misha followed her to the living area.

"All of this is unbelievable," Anna said, pulling a bottle of vodka from the freezer, the alcohol smelling clean and sharp. She poured a shot in each glass, squeezed a couple of limes, added a tablespoon of sugar, and handed the drink to Misha. "Which is leading me to believe it, as it is the only thing that I have going for the two of us right now."

"Deportation or whatever this is," she said, motioning towards the talking animals with her glass.

"What about him?" she said, pointing to her brother.

"He has some 'magical' qualities," the macaw stated matter-of-factly, sipping the air. "He's a demigod or maybe a wood-sprite. They manifest differently when deities have offspring on earth. His powers will come within time. You're like a parasite to him, Anna. Your powerful presence essentially sucks them out of him. His powers will only grow stronger when you're not around."

She was so matter-of-fact that Anna couldn't get mad. And yet, the word "parasite" felt like a knife to her heart. Anna would never drain her brother. Not intentionally, at least.

"Wait what? I have powers?" Misha muttered in disbelief, clutching his drink.

"That's the other thing. Your deportation," the macaw said, ignoring Misha's question entirely.

"Vlad is also from Kala and—"

"He's a bad guy?" Misha finally said with mock surprise.

"Well, he's not the most benevolent deity," the macaw conceded. "He's another deity, neither good nor bad in the human sense. He didn't learn his lesson on earth and needs more time here before he returns. Best to keep him at bay and act naturally around him with what little time you have left," the Macaw cautioned.

"Fuck it. I'll be at the garden tomorrow at noon," Anna

declared, slamming her glass on the table. "Misha, what will you do if Vlad and Boris stop by?" Out of the corner of her eye, Anna swore that both animals flinched visibly when she said Vlad's name.

"Don't worry about me. I will figure something out," he said, forcing a brave smile. He didn't quite believe the words coming out of his mouth, but he managed to regain his composure.

"As long as you're around Elena, you will be safe, Misha," the iguana interjected. This was the first time the lizard had said his name.

"Are you sure?" Misha muttered, his face pale. Fear. He was genuinely afraid.

"I can't leave him!" Anna exclaimed before the duo could respond.

"Anna, I'll be fine. You must leave for me to become powerful," he said in a feeble attempt at bravado, a sacrifice in his voice.

"We're required to tend to other matters," they said in unison, ignoring the last, painful exchange. And with that, they vanished, leaving behind another exotic red feather. Her brother grabbed it and began to examine it closely.

"Keep that close and I'll keep mine close," Anna said, retrieving the first one she had found. "I have one from a previous visit. I figured that this may be a gift from our visitors, no? If nothing else, a beautiful feather from a talking macaw will at least be decorative."

"Sure. Whatever you say," Misha said, his disbelief slowly giving way to a dawning, terrifying understanding.

Misha sat on the couch and stared at his feet, his eyes boring through the ground, lost in thought.

Maybe x-ray vision is his power? Anna joked to herself, trying to lighten the mood. She recognized that look. Either she had the definitive confirmation that she wasn't crazy or, at least, she was crazy in good company with her brother.

Anna ejected the cassette and hid it securely in their well-worn copy of *The Odyssey*.

Anna chewed on her cheek and stared into space as she began the long, slow process of accepting that she is, in fact, a goddess.

By her estimate, Misha was in a state of shock. Bargaining. Disbelief. He wasn't close to acceptance. Their lives had been prescribed from the time they were born, a comfortable certainty. They were supposed to have the same mundane lives in beautiful Cuba that their parents had. It was not always bad. It was not always good. But it was consistent, predictable. There was a certain peace of mind that came with that consistency. And now? Now chaos was the only certainty.

The next day, Anna opened the kiosk early and thought about the perfect excuse for her brother to give to Vlad and Boris. Her absence would definitely raise suspicion. There were two things that all men accepted, without question, as an excused absence from women: explosive diarrhea or talk of their periods. She figured that she would combine both for extra, undeniable emphasis.

As she stared at the tranquil blue sea, a feeling of smugness bubbled to the surface. Or was it pride? She had never been truly smug and only a bit proud ever in her life. Whereas before learning that she was a goddess, she took pride in the kiosk, now it looked like a sort of shitty outdoor bar with a nice view.

"Really what am I doing here? I am better than being a barmaid," she said aloud, waving her hand dismissively toward the counter. She stared off wistfully in the direction of the Malecon, a world beyond her reach.

"Oh for fuck sake, stop waving your hands around. You're not a witch, you're a defunct deity in exile," Misha growled, intensely preparing the limes. "Keep your center, ok? Take it down a notch."

Anna concluded that Misha had a bit of jealousy. He could be a demigod, or a fairy, or a regular Russian expat. Either way, Anna was a confirmed, bona fide goddess.

"You aren't being worshipped here and now, so get to work," Misha snapped, clearly still in the angry phase of learning about their lifetime of illusion.

Anna rolled her eyes and lined up the glasses. Hand crushing the ice block with her fists released a significant amount of frustration. Time passed excruciatingly slowly. She hoped that a large tour group would arrive to speed up time.

Five minutes later she heard "Hola Anna! I have a Canadian tour group that wants to your signature drinks." Her brother shot her a look as if to say, "did you have something to do with this?"

She shrugged, having a distinct, powerful inkling that she did, in fact, have something to do with the sudden, convenient appearance of a thirsty, time-consuming tour group. The Canadians stood in a polite single file line, asking earnest questions about this odd cultural mélange. How did they move here from the USSR? Who made up most of their customers?

Finally, agonizingly, it was 11:30 in the morning. Anna started to feign cramps, a theatrical performance of plausible pain. Whether it was a fake period or fake diarrhea, no man wanted to know about it. At that precise moment, Vlad and Boris the potato showed up.

"Priviet comrades. How is today? It seems that you took care of the bee problem," Vlad said with a cold smirk.

"Fine, comrade, but it seems that my sister has suddenly come down with gastritis that has been poorly timed with her woman problems," Misha said with an unforced grimace, playing his part perfectly. Diarrhea and periods made him as viscerally uncomfortable as any man. Yet he agreed to the disgusting charade.

"Anna, please. Come to the embassy. We can help with your stomach problems," Vlad suggested, his darkness tempering Anna's smugness with a wave of icy fear.

Anna could only think about the bees, mentally begging them to come back and sting this man into oblivion. They did not come. She started sweating out of sheer nerves and crouched over a bit, wrapping her arms tightly around her midsection. Vlad smiled, a predatory curve of his lips as his brows narrowed.

"You seem to have a fever. Please join us," he insisted. The Impaler had a sinister look about his face. His imposing physique and unnervingly steel-blue eyes did nothing to assuage anyone. Meanwhile, Boris was as soft and sweaty as ever, like a pathetic, pale dumpling.

Anna tried desperately to hide the panic in her eyes. She was afraid of missing the mysterious rendezvous, thus resigning herself to deportation and cold, gray mundanity at best, or something far more depraved at worst.

Suddenly, Boris, looking profoundly confused and agitated, said "Vlad, come on, we *fuckers* have that important report due today. The one with the new quotas."

The Impaler's face contorted with shock and fury. It looked as though he was fighting a severe internal battle. He finally gave up, looking equally confused and exclaimed "Of course! Thank you for the reminder, Boris! We *fuckers* have the report. Let's go."

And with that, they turned and left, rushing off as if the

report was a fire that needed extinguishing. Anna looked at her brother with an expression of total shock.

Misha, looking equally perplexed, said "I... um... that might have been me. Unsure how I did it, but I wished for it. All I could think was 'surely those fuckers have some annoying bureaucracy to tend to, like a report. And then they did," he finished, a wide, relieved smile spreading across his face, a sudden injection of confidence that he had something going for him after all.

Involuntarily, Anna threw her arms around her brother and whispered "Thank you, Misha. You have always been special, even before today."

She stepped back and looked into his eyes, a final, intense connection. "Misha, if I never see you again, know that I love you more than anything, no matter what." She feigned doubling over in pain for anyone that was watching from afar.

He smiled and mouthed the word "Go."

With that, she started walking briskly towards the ruins of the old colonizer's compound, her heart hammering. She sped up, and the pulsating sound of "Thriller" started up again in her head, as if it were playing on a massive loudspeaker, overwhelming all other sound. She looked around, panicked, and realized that no one else could hear it.

"Anna!"

Ivan. Why now? The worst possible timing.

She picked up her pace, pretending like she didn't hear him over the mental music.

"Anna! Please! Stop!" He yelled, his voice carrying clearly.

Anna turned around. She was only 100 meters from the alley that led to the garden. She turned and walked slowly back towards him, trying to force out a coherent sentence. He was her magnet. Irresistible, down to her very core.

"Ivan, hola. How are things? I'm a bit ill today. Gastritis and the monthly cycle," She scrunched her face and wrapped her arms around her midsection to feign cramping intestines. She wanted to die, right there in that spot, because she just divulged that grotesque information to the man she loved.

Unable to get the music out of her head, and trying to distract Ivan from her fake period and diarrhea, she asked "Do you hear that?"

"Hear what? No. I am sorry to hear about your issues," he said, looking genuinely concerned. "But you there is something that you need to know," He grabbed her hand, and an intense, electric jolt shot through her body, nearly making her knees buckle. It was almost enough to make her stay in Havana.

He flinched violently. Blue flames momentarily lit up his perfect hazel eyes. He felt the intense connection too, but instantly ignored it, shoving the feeling away.

"You need to know that Vlad and Boris are keen to get you and your brother back to the USSR. Something about being too powerful? That's what I gathered," he said, looking puzzled as the bizarre words came out of his mouth.

"Anyways, I will try in whatever way possible to ensure that you stay. *Whatever. Way. Possible.*" His perfect, hazel eyes bore into hers, the blue flames burning brighter with intent. He leaned in, as if he was going to kiss her, and she finished the rest, pulling his powerful body to hers, kissing him passionately, desperately.

For a moment, Anna lost track of her surroundings and her mission, the world shrinking to the press of his lips. She almost *came* from the kiss, the sheer intensity overwhelming. But the pulsating, insistent sound of "Thriller" swirled in her head, a chaotic, divine alarm clock that brought her crashing back to reality and the urgency of the task ahead of her. She stepped back from his embrace, forcing herself away.

"I have gastritis!" she yelled, a final, ridiculous cry, broke free of his hand, and ran towards the alley, leaving him standing alone and confused. That brief moment with him felt like an eternity of exquisite torture. She kept running, slightly hunched over, while a thousand panicked thoughts swirled through her head along with the stupid, loud "Thriller" song that was playing so loudly that she could hardly concentrate. *I just told an incredible specimen of a human that I had my period and diarrhea,* she thought, mortified. This magical realm better be fucking incredible to be worth this humiliation. Anna didn't dare look back to see Ivan's heartbroken face.

Anna approached the ornate iron gate that led to the garden, the one with the Iguana and Macaw pictograms. She never noticed how the animals were cleverly incorporated into the wrought iron, in a perfect yin-yang formation, until now. The gate was nondescript wrought iron from a distance, but upon very close examination, there were symbols carved into the iron: complex pictograms that seemed to tell a story. No time to study it now though. She pulled the single, soft red feather out of her bra and clutched it tightly in her hand as she grasped the latch. It was hot. Almost unbearably so, as if the iron were heated from within. She passed through the gate, and it slammed shut behind her with a heavy, final clang.

The garden was as pristine, as otherworldly, as ever. She inhaled the deep, sweet scent of plumeria, a tropical perfume that always reminded her of her Mama, and smiled. She continued around the central, ancient palm tree, looking for the Mystery Duo. She walked towards the beautiful stone fountain for respite from the heat, while still clutching the red feather, the sound of "Thriller" still pulsating in her head, a thunderous soundtrack to her destiny.

"Anna, can you hear me?" Her brother. His voice, or rather his *thought*, was as clear as if he stood next to her. "YES! Misha! I can hear you!" She started thinking instead of speaking, the strange communication surprisingly easy even with that damn song playing at a volume of 11. "I am in the garden waiting."

"Good. I will meet with Elena soon to tell her what I know and get more information from her," his thoughts appeared and vanished like disappearing ink she had seen in movies.

She sat on the cool, stone edge of the water fountain, looking at the beautiful, stylized peacock spigot as it poured out pristine, clear water. Anna reached her hand towards the spigot to cup the water when suddenly the water formed into strong, clear hands and grabbed her by the shoulders, starting to pull her violently towards the pool of the fountain.

Anna shoved the red feather back into her bra and began to struggle, fighting against the water attempting to drown her. She stopped struggling immediately when she saw the clear reflection of the macaw in *human form* at the bottom of the fountain, waving her in. And with that, she released her breath and allowed the watery hands to pull her towards the deep, waiting bottom of the fountain.

7

Her lungs were on fire. She couldn't breathe. The portal tore at her, pulling her at light speed through a black, burning void. Every part of her body was excruciatingly raw. Screams went nowhere. The brutal passage was lethal to humans. Only powerful deities, rare magical humanoids, and a few other universal mythans survived portal travel.

She was =close to losing consciousness when the immense force of the water shot her upwards, rocketing her into the open air. Time seemed to stretch and slow into an agonizing moment as she dropped towards the pristine lake below. With the instinct of someone accustomed to survival, Anna inhaled a deep breath just before she plummeted into the water.

In that single inhalation, her body absorbed the reality of the land: the scents of blooming hibiscus and plumeria around the lake's edge filled her nostrils. Simultaneously, metallic-sour smell of bird shit aggressively assaulted her senses. A deafening clamor of chattering toucans and raucous macaws filled her ears. Beneath it all, she registered two more primal scents: the heavy, musky odor of a large, predatory cat lurking somewhere near the perimeter, and a faint, unsettling whiff of decay. Her senses were beyond heightened. Seconds of a sensory onslaught lasted for an eternity.

She felt the sting on her skin as she belly-flopped into the lake. Dizzy and disoriented, she opened her eyes and instantly recognized the floating, marble platform as the same one from her recent dream. She propelled herself out of the water and onto marble surface. Unlike Earth, however, this ascent was utterly effortless, as though she could levitate.

Her clothes, a casualty of the portal's violence, did not survive the journey. As she looked down at herself, she saw her skin had taken on a new hue: an iridescent olive complexion. She pulled at her hair, realizing her once-blonde locks were now shiny silver, styled in perfect, frizz-free curls. Staring at her reflection in the glossy marble, Anna almost failed to recognize herself.

"My ziblings aren't here," a slightly despondent voice announced, startling her. It was Zaris. Anna jumped slightly and instinctively crossed her arms, a futile attempt to cover her sudden nudity.

"Goddess, you have been naked and then some before me." His tone carried a familiar hint of cheekiness, yet it was layered with a profound sadness.

"Well, I – " she sputtered. "Anyways, I wish that I had some dry clothes." Before the thought was complete, an outfit materialized: cut-off denim shorts and a simple black t-shirt, identical to her standard, comfortable clothing in Havana. A dry pair of sneakers, *Dvamyachi* - a USSR brand worn only by elite athletes - also appeared at the base of what she now realized was Zaris's marble column. Uncertain and bewildered by the instantaneous manifestation, she retrieved the clothes, pondering their apparition as she quickly pulled them on.

Zaris swooped closer to her, his form shimmering with anxiety. "She kidnapped them," he said, his sadness now a palpable, heavy weight in the air. "I am utterly alone, here to waste away."

Remembering his volatile nature from her dreams, Anna chose her words with cautious precision. "Do you know anything about their disappearance?"

"The entity who stole your *fortuna*," he stated, his voice tight. "It happened before I even knew what was happening. I couldn't stop her. She needed them to activate power. They are mutable, adaptable. I am fixed. I am helpless in their rescue." Anna could clearly see tears beginning to well up in his eyes.

"Sorry to hear that. What does that mean for me, being here... uh, now?" Anna ventured, already dreading the answer, certain this entire situation was spiraling into disaster.

"YOU? YOU? You always think this is about you!" And with that characteristic, volatile outburst, the temperamental Zaris vanished. Anna was left standing alone on the marble platform. The sun blazed hot in the sky. She squinted as she scanned the perimeter of the lake. She immediately understood she needed to help Zaris, regardless of his tantrum.

"I'm sorry, Zaris!" she yelled toward the empty air where he had been, in his general direction. No response came. Unsure of what her next move should be, she made her way across the platform toward the shore.

A lush, vibrant tropical jungle bordered the water as far as her eyes could see. She walked on a series of equidistantly placed marble slabs that led to a stretch of white, soft sandy shore. The water gently lapped at the banks. The shoreline was lined with trees adorned with the most resplendent flowers: hibiscus, plumeria, and birds of paradise. All the tropical blossoms she loved most on Earth were here. She scooped up a handful of the soft, white sand, letting it sift through her fingers. It was even finer and softer than the sand of Varadero, her favorite beach back in Cuba.

"I see you finally made it," said a cool, smooth voice. The human version of the macaw emerged from behind a screen of foliage and walked leisurely toward her. She looked exactly as she had on Earth: stunningly, effortlessly beautiful. *Effortless beauty must be a universal standard*, Anna thought with a touch of cynicism.

"Before I travel with people, I like to know a bit about them. I know as much about you as the last guy I fucked. What's your name? Are you a cosmic bum or what?" Anna began to approach her cautiously. She was intensely skeptical of this *puta*. Reflexively, she tried to shade her arms from the sun.

"My name is Ara. Relax, you won't burn here. You're a goddess," the mystery lady cooed.

"My other half and I are forces in the universe, greater than any deity. We cannot be summoned or worshiped. We simply *are*." Ara offered a gentle, knowing smile as she continued. "We feel most comfortable on Kala. I know it's *gauche* to have favorites, but this is ours. It's one of the most special of all our creations," she said, her eyes sparking with an inner light.

Anna, however, could not hide her skepticism. She was

too Russian, too conditioned by a life lived under authoritarian, atheistic rule.

Ara continued in her measured, cool voice. "My other half is Oragan. We balance each other, so to speak. Come with me now. You must visit your temple. Hopefully, it's not overgrown. Or worse."

Anna struggled to imagine anything truly terrible here. Everything felt so luminous, light, and fresh. The air was perfectly scented, the weather flawless. Yet, there was that persistent, faint whiff of despair, which she tried to push to the back of her mind.

A deep sense of calm washed over her as she stood on the shore. She felt a profound unwillingness to move. Anna wanted nothing more than to flop onto the beach, like a lazy tourist, and do absolutely nothing for an eternity.

"Do not let the scenery fool you," Ara said, a sudden, sharp frown creasing her face. "This side of Kala has not been consumed by the Shadow yet."

"Get out of my head," Anna snapped, scrunching her face in frustration. "What's the difference if I just stay here?" She paused, testing Ara.

"You weren't meant to come here for a vacation. I can send you back just as easily," Ara threatened, delivering the line in the most matter-of-fact voice possible.

Resigned, Anna followed Ara down a manicured path that sliced through the dense jungle. Unlike Cuba, there wasn't a single mosquito to be found. Various types of peacocks, parrots, and toucans lined the path as if they were expecting her, perched precariously on the edges of branches as though they defied gravity. They stared at her with unconcealed disbelief. She stared back with equal incredulity.

"Bless her heart, she looks just like Julia. The resemblance is uncanny. Rebirths have been known to screw with your looks, but she seems alright," squawked one particularly obnoxious toucan. Julia. That was the name of Anna's mother. Anna looked up at the toucan quizzically. It looked back at her, and they studied each other's faces. Anna determined that this was not merely an ordinary toucan.

"You knew my mama?" Anna had a strong gut feeling that this bird was entirely untrustworthy.

"Oh, sugar, you have a lot to learn! Everyone knows your 'mama,'" the toucan retorted with a sassy wink. The other birds immediately erupted in a chaotic, irritating cacophony that sounded exactly like snide laughter.

Ara responded with a sharp, commanding squawk of her own. Her reprimand silenced the peanut gallery. The entire jungle fell into a deafening quiet. There was no buzzing of insects, no chirping of birds. With that, the hundreds of birds lining the path simultaneously bowed, each placing their right wing formally in front of their breast.

"Apologies for the disrespect, Anna. We know that Kala is new to your current, eh hem, consciousness," quipped the toucan, rolling its eyes dramatically. "Now darlin', I know you are adjusting to this situation and all, but you should probably know something important. You too, Ara." *Of course Ara and this toucan knew each other*, Anna thought, utterly perplexed by the dynamic.

"Unfortunately for you, your gaudy temple thing is probably teeming with officers of the Shadow by now. Maybe if it hadn't been so hideous, it wouldn't have drawn something so insidious. A lot of the Kalans jumped ship and lost faith in you. Too afraid to worship there. They thought they would be conscripted, imprisoned, tortured, or killed. Can't blame 'em. Shit situation, really. Ah well, it's all about learnin' that lesson, right, Cousin?" The toucan preened itself as it spoke, drilling its gaze directly into Ara's eyes on that last word.

Indifference, Anna noted, seemed to be an inherent quality in talking birds. She could sense they were expertly masking fear. She had perfected that same tactic, and they were mirroring it back to her.

Ara looked troubled. Anna involuntarily bit the inside of her cheek. In the handful of times she had seen Ara, her face was always smug, cool, collected, and brimming with confidence. It was *never* troubled.

Anna was woefully confused. The very concept of worship fueling her powers befuddled her. How could she have done anything for this realm while merely residing on Earth? She didn't know the extent of her powers, much less that she was a deity in the first place.

"We have no time to waste," Ara declared, grabbing Anna's arm and pulling her into a brisk walk down the path.

Ara quickly glanced back at the toucan. "Thank you for your information, Callan. This is appreciated. It's much worse than I thought."

"Any time, cousin, but I don't know why you're surprised. You have much more faith in those mortal beings than I do. I don't mind helpin' em, but they can be weak-minded. And exhausting. We'll see y'all soon. Can't keep ya here chin-waggin' on my account. Best if you see the shit for yourselves," the toucan squawked.

"Cousin?" Anna gasped as they were now nearly running away from the birds. "You're that bird bitch's cousin?"

"Yes, it's an unfortunate cosmic twist," Ara sighed heavily. "There is no time to get into it now, as we need to get to Aranac." Anna looked confused. "Your temple. It and the surrounding grounds are called Aranac. You really lost most of your memory, didn't you? At some point, we need to take you to the lake near Lorsqanna." Anna's lips flattened, and she nodded.

Running through the jungle here was a stark contrast to Earth. Back in the oppressive Cuban heat, Anna had always despised running; it was her least favorite exercise. Trying to keep up with her brother Misha had left her feeling like her body would implode and her lungs would explode, a sensation, she now realized, that was similar to passing through a portal. But here on Kala, running was effortless. She felt weightless, like the famous dancer Nureyev suspended mid-leap. She felt she could maintain this pace indefinitely.

How fast were they running? she wondered to herself. It felt incredible. Her legs propelled her forward with divine energy.

"We're almost there," Ara whispered. The air abruptly changed. They detected the faint scent of decomposition, which started to grow oppressively humid and thick. Her skin twitched with unease. "Slow down and try to be quiet."

Ara slowed to a jog, and Anna followed suit. The familiar red feather began to creep out of the top of her bra, and she quickly shoved it back in.

"Clever as I thought you were, Anna. You have a part of me. Always keep that. No matter what. I know that Misha has a part as well. Curious how that will work for him. Probably wise of you both to keep those feathers. They should serve you well." Anna shook her head in exasperation. More riddles, more questions that would likely never be answered.

As they burst out of the jungle's edge, Anna and Ara

gasped, but for entirely different reasons. In the center of the sudden green clearing, framed by a jagged, lush mountain backdrop replete with plunging waterfalls, stood a stunning marble edifice. It was larger than the Presidential Palace back in Havana. It was surrounded by the most magnificent garden Anna had ever seen, overflowing with Birds of Paradise, Bromeliad, various types of orchids and lilies, and, of course, the requisite hibiscus and plumeria trees. Between the garden and the temple was a beautifully carved gray stone wall, which clearly depicted a long, intricate story.

Anna marveled at the temple grounds and the landscape. *Callan can fuck off, this isn't gaudy*, Anna thought, momentarily forgetting the danger. *Not the grounds at least.* Her admiration halted abruptly when she realized what had stopped Ara.

A gruesome sight lay before them. The temple's moat was not filled with water, but with dead/undead/formerly dead corpses. Anna gagged reflexively. A writhing, swirling horror of contorted, grotesquely animated bodies unlike anything she had ever encountered was packed into the channel. Above the temple and stretching as far as the eye could see, clouds the color of a hurricane sky swirled menacingly. Thunderless lightning shot across her temple. The air itself didn't move. It hung heavy, tinged with a hot, sickening stench of rotting food, excrement, and death. Anna gagged again. People in perfectly tailored gray and black quilted uniforms surrounded the moat. The temperature was at least thirty degrees Celsius, yet they marched unphased and unflustered.

"Those are officers of the Shadow, in the depressing couture. And the people in the moat, well, they were your followers." Ara stared directly into Anna's eyes, forcing her to confront the reality. Anna froze in horror. People died for her. Or they died *because* of her. Anna had blood on her hands.

She gagged again. No one should die for a deity.

Ara motioned to the top of the temple. Each immense marble spire floated unnervingly off the main structure. In Cuba, that would require a massive crane. Apparently, on Kala, it required unbridled, malicious power. Ara directed her attention to a man with an elegant mahogany staff in his hand. A red orb glowed intensely from its tip. Anna realized he was systematically dismantling the temple, piece by floating piece.

"Your temple is compromised," Ara stated dryly.

"You think?" Anna retorted sarcastically. "How is he doing that? Is he a deity?"

"No. Just a person."

Anna winced. *Just a person.*

"Just a person? As a former person," Anna said, motioning up and down her body, "I'm offended. People are deeply complex. That guy didn't just become evil overnight. People aren't like deities. Well, most of them aren't."

Ara's lip curled up to one side in a brief, dry acknowledgment.

"So you have learned something as a human. Contrary to the rumor mill, I'm not omnipotent. However, according to the Kalan rumor mill, one of Dalv's – Vlad's – priestesses tapped into the eternal power sources, including yours. They're making a mistake, though. Your temple is just a means to an end. It's not your source of power. Unlike Dalv, your power doesn't come from objects."

"Oh, let me guess, it comes from within," Anna trilled mockingly, her frustration boiling over.

Ara merely shrugged.

When Anna was a human, her repressed frustration manifested as heartburn and a headache. As a deity, however, a new, powerful sensation was churning deep within her sacrum, a tingling energy that ached to be released from her body.

"We need to find a house in Lorsqanna that worships you. They will restore you. Granted, their house won't be as nice as your temple," Ara said wistfully, eyeing the collapsing marble.

"Oh, so just a person might give power to a deity? Just a person in a normal house? I don't know, Ara, how could just a person have so much power?" With her hands firmly planted on her hips, she waited, demanding a real answer.

Ara opened and closed her beak multiple times before finally pursing it shut, electing not to answer immediately.

The temple was a magnificent object, but it wasn't home. Home was warm. Inviting. Safe. A retreat from the emotional and physical dangers of the world. A place of celebration and joy for family and friends. As the officers continued to dismantle each piece, Anna's fondness for the temple began to subside. Oddly, she felt a wash of relief. The temple was already a distant memory. Her temple was the cusp of a dream—vaguely something she knew, but ultimately forgettable. Sure, it was a bit gaudy and ostentatious from a distance, a thing to be admired like a museum piece. But as each segment was destroyed, Anna felt less and less attachment.

"Ara, did I have that built? What type of deity was I?" It was the second earnest, unironic question to come out of her mouth since arriving. She didn't want to imagine what type of thoughtless person would build something like that if people were suffering.

"There is a lot for you to learn, I think now -" Ara paused, her gaze distracted.

Anna wasn't listening. She was too busy staring wide-eyed at the moat when she interrupted Ara. "Ara, have you seen *Dawn of the Dead*?" Anna gulped, the horror movie image flashing vividly in her mind. She took Ara by the shoulders and forcefully turned her around. Ara's eyes widened in realization.

Her easy-breezy demeanor evaporated immediately, replaced by cold dread. "They know we're here. You're not strong enough to escape them yet."

The grotesque undead, now terrifyingly organized and in their matching, gray-and-black uniforms, began to march toward them in a unified wave.

Anna observed them with the detached fascination of an anthropologist. More energy gathered in her sacrum. It was a raw, primal energy, transforming her former human responses of flight, fight, freeze, and fawn into pure, harnessed power.

"Those 'things' were once your worshipers," Ara warned. She waved her hand dismissively, but the gesture only stunned the advancing creatures for a moment. Ara actually flinched.

Anna noticed the rare sign of weakness and firmly held Ara's shoulder.

"Inhuman. They have no souls. No free will. No spirit. And hey—calm down. You don't have your full power yet," Ara bristled, wiggling free from Anna's grasp.

A thousand years of concentrated rage engulfed Anna. A hundred atomic bombs worth of raw fury emanated from her *chocha*, stomach, and heart, surging outwards.

Ara smiled, genuine relief in her eyes. "Good, good, let the energy flow through you. For the injustice of the inhuman's fate. To enact revenge on Dalv. To bring order to chaos."

A human lifetime of repressed rage, societal injustice, revenge fantasies, and deep longing needed an exit.

Without conscious thought, Anna extended both arms out and slowly raised them upwards. The ground beneath the clearing shook violently. A solid stone wall emerged from the earth, surrounding and trapping the legions of officers within Anna's temple grounds.

"YOU WANT TO BRING MY TEMPLE DOWN? I WILL HELP!" Anna roared, her voice a cosmic thunderclap, as she raised immense stalagmites of rock from underneath her own temple. Crumbling marble made a deafening, final sound.

"Finally!" Ara exclaimed with genuine, unmasked relief, her breathing now slightly labored.

Instinctively, Anna grabbed Ara by the shoulder again. "Are you okay? Am I okay?" Anna quickly patted her body, confirming she was intact. Head. Heart. Stomach. *Chocha.*

"I'm fine," Ara muttered, clearly irritated by the show of concern. "Let's get to Lorsqanna now. No time for questions. Grab my talons as soon as I transform."

Anna ran in lock-step with Ara. When Ara suddenly transformed back into the immense, magnificent Macaw, Anna grabbed her talons as instructed.

She can carry me. She can carry me. She can carry me, Anna thought, clinging to the bizarre but necessary faith.

They soared over the jungle canopy, the surrounding cacophony of normal birds lifting them higher. Ara knew the way.

She can carry me. She can carry me. She can carry me, Anna repeated again and again, a new kind of mantra.

"Relax! You won't fall! And if you do, you'll be fine!" Ara

squawked, gleefully bobbing and weaving through the clouds.

Liberated air swimming, Anna thought. The energy continued to generate from her *chocha* as they flew. Was Anna still beholden to gravity? It was the number one unbreakable human rule. Death was number two. Ara looped sharply around the newly enclosed temple and flew directly toward the craggy rock formations and waterfalls behind it.

"Ara, I really don't want to be smashed into oblivion today!" Anna screamed, bracing for impact. At the last possible second, Ara swooped straight up, catching a powerful wind current that lifted them to the very top of the peak. Ara gently dropped Anna onto the pointy, green rocky outcrop.

"Thank you for not killing me," Anna said, catching her breath.

"I can't kill you, dear. You are nearly impossible to kill." Ara's large wings made a panoramic motion to the land as far as Anna could see. "Take a minute to take this in."

To the north of her temple, the clouds swirled with a deep, unsettling red hue that stretched thousands of miles. She focused her vision and realized she could see for vast distances. In the far-off distance, a snowcapped peak loomed. Looking at it caused her entire body to twitch.

"That's Dalv's temple," Ara explained.

The snake pit.

"I have dreamed of it," Anna whispered, the reality crashing down. Anna quickly composed herself. In the dream, Dalv had warned her that "they were coming." Still wondering who "they" were, Anna retreated to her default defense mechanism: snark.

"Of course. Honestly, could we be more opposite? He

likes the cold. I like the tropics. He likes being an asshole to people. I do not. I'm surprised that I didn't try to sleep with him in Havana." Anna said with a hint of sarcasm mixed with an uncomfortable truth.

Ara smirked. "Don't be so sure. Come on, we must keep going. They'll know that you're fully on Kala soon enough. We need to get to friendly territory."

Anna grabbed Ara's talons again as she dropped over the other side of the craggy outcrop, taking them outside the line of sight from her destroyed temple and the frosty, snowy mountains in the distance. The views were jaw-dropping as they flew through heavily forested canyons. As the land leveled off, about an hour later, Anna could see a warm, glowing light off in the distance.

"There it is," Ara announced.

Anna saw what appeared to be a small town. As they got closer, Ara descended and gently placed Anna on a sidewalk at the edge of a quiet neighborhood. Ara instantly transformed back into her human form.

They walked toward a small, bright orange house with a terracotta tile roof. Anna had never seen this house, yet it felt instantaneously like *home*. It was as if she was being embraced by her own mother. Anna's chest was pulled by an invisible thread toward the side of the house. Ara followed her with a knowing look on her face. Solidly set on the side of this bright orange house was a perfect replica of her temple, miniature, on a small platform, about a thousandth the size of her actual temple. She examined it closer, completely awestruck by the detail. It was a perfectly miniature replica, complete with miniature live orchids, bromeliads, and plumeria trees.

On the surrounding platform, Anna noticed fresh offerings: a cup of *cafe con leche*, fried plantains, a bottle of vodka, and fresh, beautiful mint and limes. Almost as if Ara could read her mind, she said, "People here pay homage to you by placing your favorite items in the temple. They believe it will keep them in your good graces. Does it?" Ara asked, though the answer was written plainly on Anna's face.

Anna was at a loss for words. She had never felt so utterly content and pleased in her entire life. Yet, she was merely staring at items that were regular occurrences in her life on Earth. She reached into the miniature temple to retrieve the *cafe con leche* and a plantain. As she sipped the dark liquid, she felt a beam of golden light ripple through her body.

"What was that?" Anna asked with utter surprise, nearly sputtering out the coffee.

"Take a guess," Ara said, tapping her foot with impatience. "Your power is further harnessed the closer you are to your worshipers and their offerings. This house is very faithful."

Anna had only learned the minimum about Earth's religions. The USSR was an atheist state. Her parents were not religious, though they were spiritually weird, one might say. Cuba had some not-so-hidden Catholics and those who worshiped ancestors and practiced *Santeria*. Some called them *brujas*. She wondered if the earthly deities were as pleased with their worshipers as she felt at that moment.

Anna had to protect this house. A brilliant gold light cascaded over the house and quickly disappeared.

"Clearly it works in currying favor with you. This house is protected." Ara said as she walked toward the front door.

It was a dumb question, but Anna asked anyway. "So, do we knock on the door?"

Ara nodded with big, encouraging eyes and pursed lips. Anna knocked. The door visibly shook. She made a mental note that her physical strength here was at Herculean levels. An older man opened the door and immediately dropped to his knees. He looked human, but had an iridescent shine to his skin. Anna stared intently, mesmerized and relieved, especially after seeing the gray, corpselike skin of the bodies at the temple. Finally, out of sheer embarrassment, Anna begged him to stand up.

"Anna! I have prayed for you to return order to Kala. I'm one of the few who stayed faithful. Our peaceful land is being engulfed by the Shadow. My two children went to your temple three days ago, in hopes that a pilgrimage would hasten your return to Kala. They are still away. I fear the worst as the birds have been talking," his voice trailed off, thick with fear and sorrow.

Ara whispered to Anna, "It was rare for deities to come to town and be seen."

"Fuck, I'm sorry," Anna spoke without thinking, the raw honesty escaping her. She panicked for a moment but was relieved when nothing terrible happened.

The man looked puzzled. "What do you mean? Are you not Anna?"

"No, it's a... nevermind." Anna gave Ara a look that pleaded for help. What was goddess etiquette? Could she help this man get his children back?

"Kind sir, we need to use your house for a while. Anna can protect your house from the Shadow if you can shelter us. Her temple has been compromised, and she needs a place to stay." Ara, visibly uncomfortable, was not accustomed to sincerely engaging with humanoids, unless she was flirting.

The man trembled, his eyes pleading and desperate. "Where are my children? Did you see my children?" Tears formed in his eyes.

Without thinking, Anna took his hand. He stopped trembling instantly. Serenity washed over him, radiating from her touch.

"We are going to conquer the Shadow. Anna needs to regain strength and power while she is here, as she was... fighting evil on Earth. Your children are out there," Ara said, not exactly lying, but bending the truth to the point of snapping.

He looked puzzled. Anna cocked her head to the side and stared intently at Ara. Bald-faced lie, unless serving up alcoholic beverages and dancing were somehow construed as fighting evil.

Ara rolled her eyes and stepped in between the two. "The Shadow kills the free will of the beings on Kala. It completely takes control and grows stronger with every human in its possession. Anna has not been in this realm for eons and needs to re-orient herself. How it resurfaced is a mystery, even to me." Ara was not omnipotent. Anna could tell that admission was nearly an impossible concept for Ara to accept.

"What the fuck can we do about this?" Anna tried to slow her breathing. The electric energy started building within her again, even though she wasn't in immediate danger. Her damn nervous system was out of whack, even as a goddess.

"Well, I can make you some food. No one else will make you a goddess-damned thing. They all lost faith, except for me. They felt that you abandoned them, but I knew better," their host said, walking toward the kitchen, immensely proud of his steadfastness.

Anna stifled a snort of laughter. This deity thing might be very serious, but surely she could have a little fun with it. "Why not? I'll have some black beans, rice, and plantains."

She genuinely didn't care what the others thought of her. But she never wanted to cause anyone's demise.

"I will make you food." With that, he walked to the kitchen and started a flurry of clanking and rattling.

When he was safely out of earshot, Anna loudly whispered between gritted teeth. "Ara, what is going on? What are we doing here, in this house? How can I remove the Shadow from Kala? Magical mojitos? Walls? Why is that man a shiny rainbow in the sun? How do I grow stronger? How do I use my powers without going crazy?"

Ara sighed with exasperation. "You're the worst version of you, you know that? Grow some *cojones*, as you say, or something. I'll start from the very beginning, a very good place to start. Clearly, you do not remember anything from the last time."

"Well, how the fuck do they know what I like to eat and what I do?" Anna wondered out loud, gesturing towards the direction of the kitchen.

"Anna, have you heard of the Bible? The Bhagavad Gita? Any religious books?" Ara spoke to Anna as if she were a difficult, slow-witted child.

"Of course. I know a bit about the religions of the world, but I know that there are always tomes that go with it. So, where's my book? The story of this mythology?" She asked, flinging her hands in the air.

Ara sucked in her breath, correcting her. "It's not mythology. It is very real. There is a book with your entire life written out, including your current iteration on Earth. It is the past, present, and future. It was written by a prophet approximately 100,000 years ago who received divine inspiration. There are tomes about each of the Earth-bound deities from Kala. Quite a few of you were exiled at the same time."

Anna repeated the words as she attempted to process the overwhelming information. "There are more 'Earth-bound deities' than me? Do they visit here? Are any of them from other countries?"

"Yes. Yes. Yes. Now remember, you are a deity. You can make almost any trivial item happen for this man, but keep in mind that you aren't a magic genie. You'll need to reserve your power for defeating the Shadow. It will take strategy, harnessing your power, and reserving your source of energy. Of course, you are free to do as you wish, but I suggest reserving the powers as much as possible."

Anna almost asked another question, but the man walked out with a plate of fried plantains and *crema*, beaming with pride. She was instantly embarrassed for him. It was all a façade. His children were likely dead or possessed. And here she was, eating his food while he believed that she held the key to all power. Anna didn't know where power came from. TBD. As far as she was concerned, at that moment, it came from food.

"Come sit by the lake," he summoned, and led them to his porch. They all walked out back to see a view of yet another stunning lake. He set the food on a four-top blue table with white chairs. He went inside and returned with bowls of black beans and rice.

"You have an incredible view. Before we go further, what is your name?" Anna inquired.

"Aranak." He served her a generous plate of food and then waited.

She realized that he would not eat until she did. She took a bite. Similarly to the coffee, it tasted like power. It felt intensely good, sending a wave of deep satisfaction and restorative energy through her entire body. She began to devour it. Aranak was beaming with pride. Ara kicked her sharply under the table, indicating that she should slow down. How could she slow down? With each bite, she felt stronger.

"May I speak to you, Anna?" Aranak asked with a slight bow.

"Yep," was all Anna could muster between rapid bites and slurps.

"The Shadow creeps slowly and runs quickly. It turns our people into Officers," he said, his eyes filled with weariness. "They lost faith in you. They lost hope. Dark promises kept their attention."

"Tell me more about this land. I have not visited..."

"...a few eons," Ara finished the sentence for her, her voice a low growl.

"Yes, a few eons. Tell me about Kala."

Aranak's weary eyes closed for a moment. He sighed and said, "Well, I suppose I should start with the beginning."

Ara rolled her eyes dramatically, knowing that this detailed history would take a near eternity, and they had minimal time.

"Kala is one of five habitable planets in our solar system," Aranak began.

Anna kept a perfectly straight face. Aliens were real. Deities were real. Multiverses. Life-sustaining planets outside of Earth. Mystical forces. All real. Surely if she were a mere human, she would have had a complete psychological breakdown with the confirmation of this knowledge.

"From what we have heard from other visitors, ours is the best. No, really, I promise." Aranak took a deep breath and continued, "All of our kingdoms were at peace. Each kingdom supported the other. Trade was prosperous. And we don't have these things that you call mosquitos. Deities from Earth hate those."

Anna was skeptical. But then she looked around, in an open-air, seemingly tropical place on a lake. Not one mosquito. She quickly wondered if they had cockroaches.

"Then how do you explain the Officers that we saw and this 'Shadow'?" Anna quipped. She finally felt satiated and vibrant enough to fully pay attention to Aranak.

"Well, we don't know. It first started to overwhelm the kingdom of Everbright. Reports came of a few Officers. It is rumored that their deity queens made a deal with the Shadow in hopes of securing more prosperity after a run-in with other deities. Then their people started moving to other kingdoms searching for refuge," his voice was filled with deep sorrow as he spoke.

"Would you call them... refugees?" Anna said in a sarcastic tone.

"Yes," he said, ignoring her tone, too focused on the tragedy.

Anna heard Ara mentally broadcasting: *Tone. It. Down. He is helping you.* Anna pursed her mouth into a straight line to keep steady.

"They fanned out across the kingdoms. Reports were spreading of their loved ones turning into Officers who would bend completely at the whim of the Shadow. Only ten of the fifty kingdoms remain intact as they have been. No one knows who controls the Shadow. Our leaders can't pinpoint who or when it started happening exactly. We don't even know why it is happening. We Kalans have been at a loss, not knowing what to do. I increased my prayers and offerings to you. My fellow citizens did as well, since our healers could not cure them. Our weapons can kill them, but they are not of sound mind."

Anna was stunned by the scale of the disaster.

"Of all the deities, it seems that you might be one of the

first to arrive. As you know, here in Lorsqanna, most of us worship you. Of course, you have some followers all over Kala, but you and your mother are the most worshiped goddesses in our region."

That was the second time that someone had referred to Anna's mother in the present tense. Anna decided that this was the wrong time to ask about her mother, even though every fiber of her being wanted to do so.

"What the fuck can I do?" Anna mumbled, focusing intently on chewing her cheek. Even as an alleged deity, her nervous tics prevailed. Internal and external pressure muddled around in her head. Yet again, she wasn't good enough. She couldn't save these people. She could barely save herself. And being raised as an atheist Soviet? The daily messaging of Soviet glory above all else remained embedded in a small, but vocal part, of her brain.

"You can have a fucking drink with me." He lifted up his glass, filled with a potent, clear concoction, to toast Anna's. Anna had to stifle a burst of laughter while Ara grew increasingly impatient.

"Aranak, I am going to take Anna to the lake. She needs the power of the water, not another drink. Clear head, clear heart, and all that. Please excuse us for a while." Ara spoke a commanding spell, not a polite request.

Aranak nodded, instantly obeying, and began to clear the table.

"Where is Oragan?" Anna inquired as they walked toward the lake. She only knew of Oragan and Ara within the same relational realm. It seemed odd that they existed separately now. Since they arrived on Kala, there had been no sign of him.

"He is working in Havana. He hastened these events. It's time that he is accountable and does something about it," she responded wryly. Something else was clearly at play there, Anna could feel it in her heart. In her state of profound overwhelm, though, she couldn't be bothered to ask about him.

"That is the least of what you need to know right now. Anna, you will need to listen to me and focus on me for the next infinite minute."

8

"Infinite minute? What's that?" Anna asked, her voice tight with suspicion. Anything with 'infinite' as an adjective sounded less like a gift and more like a carefully crafted form of prolonged suffering.

"An infinite minute is a process by which my other half or I transfer essence, power, knowledge... well, anything, to another being," Ara explained. She took a slow, deliberate sip of the shimmering lake water, her eyes never leaving Anna's. "Before we can continue here, you need to catch up. Clearly your banishment was extremely effective this time, and you learned a lesson or two," she added.

"Wait. My what? Listen, Ara, I can't take much more of your evasive, cryptic shit," Anna shot back, pushing off the bank and planting her hands on her hips. "Before today, I had *never* left Cuba! I had never been to my homeland. I only read about other countries and outer space. Now I am in another realm, one that feels completely impossible! It doesn't feel real. And, if I'm being honest, I feel like I'm doing this all to help you fix a monumental fuck up that you or your 'other half' made a thousand years ago..."

Anna's protest was cut short. Before she could finish her accusation, Ara moved with impossible speed, pressing her thumb firmly into the space between Anna's eyebrows. The touch was cold, electric, and instantly paralyzing. A blinding azure light flared, enveloping both of them. Their bodies levitated a meter off the water, held suspended above the placid lake. Anna was no longer in control; her consciousness became a spectator in a whirlwind of impossible memories.

Flash!

Anna was soaring over the entirety of Kala, a land of emerald mountains and rivers that stretched to the horizon. She felt utterly unburdened, the essence of joy and boundless power flowing through her. Her arms were outstretched, her laughter echoing as she playfully dove around the craggy peaks of the mountains and wove gracefully through the canopies of the jungle.

Flash!

Suddenly, she was home, standing within the walls of her temple. The moat was filled with clear water. Nymphs, their skin shimmering like mother-of-pearl, and pixie fairies, who looked like miniature versions of her Georgian father, flitted about, tending to her every need. "She is visiting soon, Anna!" one of the fairies chirped, its voice a musical chime. Anna's fuchsia hair, a vibrant cascade of power, was perfect and shiny. Her face, perpetually smiling in this memory, was glowing and radiant. Yet, a flicker of boredom crossed her features. With a languid flick of her hand, she commanded the creatures to leave her be. She was slightly bored and feeling a bit irritable, the fleeting nature of a goddess's contentment already showing its cracks.

Flash!

The scene shifted to the opulent, golden-draped throne room in Everbright. Anna stood before two deified Queens, powerful demigods who ruled the kingdom. They were pleading for her intervention. "Our powers aren't enough. We need your help, Anna. If Everbright falls, so does all of Kala. A Shadow creeps slowly through trickles of information, poisoning our people's minds;" said the mocha-skinned Queen with thick, flowing locs covered in beautiful, intricate shells, her voice heavy with desperation.

"Our powers can't contain the lies and dark magic," echoed the caramel-skinned Queen with the shiny, perfectly smooth head covered in tattoos of different constellations.

A sly, potent smile curved Anna's lips. This was the Anna who thrived on power and negotiation. "I can banish it for a price," she said as an eyebrow raised up.

Flash!

Her temple again, but the atmosphere was thick with the scent of sex and sweat. Anna was basking in the profound afterglow of a passionate fuck with Ivan, or Navi as the vision called to her, the immortal daemon of Kala. Their fiery chemistry left remnants of magic hanging in the air. The memory, impossibly vivid and tactile, made her entire body pulsate, a deep, warm throb beginning in her *chocha*.

Flash!

Anna was flying side-by-side with her mother, Julia, around Kala. Below them, clouds of yellow and vibrant green swirled in unnatural patterns. The violent creep of the Shadow they had been warned about was emanating like a plume of cosmic smoke from the kingdom of Merrat. They landed on a desolate plateau and walked, utterly unafraid, toward a menacing blood-red temple. The air here was electric, thrumming with the raw, untamed power of the Shadow. The temple belonged to Dalv, the deity worshiped by the Merratis. Dalv, always a fan of contemporary Earth weapons despite his ancient status, sat on his garishly gothic throne, sharpening a gleaming, razor-sharp katana. Huge serpents slithered and coiled themselves around the black ironwork of his seat like living ornaments.

Flash!

The tranquility shattered as Anna and Julia were battling Dalv high in the clouds. Diplomacy, as Anna had learned, was ineffective with him. Channeling an unknown, raw source of power, Anna made the motion of a parrot and an iguana with her hands, a gesture she had never attempted before. She succeeded in magically imprisoning Dalv within his temple, creating a cage of energy that was the most powerful force ever used in Kala. But in the immediate aftermath, a cold dread settled over her. Anna *knew* she was in trouble. Such a violation of cosmic law, even to save Kala, would have repercussions.

Flash!

The consequences arrived swiftly. Anna was sequestered in her temple, a gilded cage. The energy expenditure, the guilt, and the forced isolation caused her power to recede. She grew weak. Tired. Bored beyond measure. No visitors were allowed to breach the protective wards. She had everything she could need or want but she could no longer feel her people's adoration or worship, the very lifeblood of her divinity. Unable to serve her purpose, Anna began to waste away, her essence shrinking into a fragment of the goddess she once was.

Flash!

"Please! Take her to the Earth planet! She will wither to nothing if she continues without serving her purpose."

It was her mother, Julia, but she was pregnant and pleading desperately. She was talking to an Iguana and a

Macaw, whose eyes held ancient, knowing wisdom. The Macaw nodded, its feathers glowing, and the Iguana touched Anna's fading form with a claw.

Flash!

Anna was a young child again, her small hand reaching for a piece of *platanos fritos* in Elena's cafe in Havana. She sat between her mama, Julia, her papa, Anton, and her new baby brother, Misha. Elena, the cafe owner, rested her warm, strong hands on Anna's shoulders. Anna immediately felt an overwhelming sense of warmth and safety, as if a protective, powerful shield was placed around her fragile divinity.

Flash!

Anna was a little older, tucked into the twin bed next to her sleeping baby brother. But sleep was impossible. She could hear her mama speaking forcefully, her voice low and tense, to her papa in the other room. "Anton, you have no idea what this means."

"Julia, so what? Another Soviet Official from Moscow is here in Havana?" Papa sounded annoyed, dismissive.

"Anton, I can't fully explain, but you will not be safe here. We need to get you to Florida. Now."

Papa was genuinely taken aback. "I will never! Who are you even, to order me around?"

"Please, I am not an American sympathizer, but he will have a hard time finding you there," Julia pleaded, the fear in her voice a tangible thing.

"I am loyal to our country and the cause. And I love Cuba as if it were my own country. I am not leaving," Papa insisted, his tone proud and stubborn.

"Oh, please," her mama's tone suddenly turned from saccharine, mortal pleading to cold, inhuman malice in a millisecond. "This isn't your country. You have no home. None of us do."

Flash!

The nightmare of her Cuban life. On the outskirts of Havana, there sat a wrecked, mangled car. Her papa's lifeless body was gruesomely impaled into the windshield. Anna watched, a detached horror, as faint, bewildered spirits left his body and drifted lazily toward the city center. A single tear rolled down her mama's face. Before Julia could truly grieve, Vlad approached, his signature katana, a terrifying replica of Dalv's, unsheathed and gleaming.

In a split second, Julia fled, and Vlad followed her after placing a body next to Anna's father. Julia continued running. She made it to their garden by a combination of desperate grit and residual magic. She pulled a vibrant red feather out of her pocket with her right hand and, with her left, touched the intricate macaw design carved into the heavy iron gate. The gate opened just enough for her to slip through the gap. It slammed shut with a deafening *clank* in Vlad's face. A demonic roar emerged from his gut, shaking the very earth. Once safe in the garden, Anna's mother spoke to the stone fountain. She began to plead, an agonizing act that Julia had only done in her earthly life. The fountain, sensing the urgent, desperate power, acquiesced and, with a silent, rippling surge, pulled her in.

Anna's consciousness snapped back to the present with a violent lurch. Her feet landed hard on the soft earth by the lake's edge. In a state of overwhelming dizziness, she dropped to her hands and knees, fighting the urge to vomit.

The cool, healing water of the lake, and Ara's surprisingly gentle hands, supported her weary body like a parent teaching a child to float. The memories were a chaotic, fragmented collage. Parts of the story were glaringly missing, crucial connections severed. Ara was clearly hiding more than she was sharing.

"All things will come in due time, Anna. Thousands of years of power, consciousness, and painful experiences is a lot for a temporarily-mortal mind to take in," Ara said, her voice now back to its smooth non-emotive tone.

"Is everything okay? That was quite a light show!" Aranak yelled from his porch, his voice full of curiosity and perhaps a touch of concern.

Anna couldn't form a sound; her throat was dry, her mind too full. But Ara, as always, had an immediate, curated answer. "Everything is great, Aranak. This is Anna's rebirth and reconnection with her people and her realm. She is wonderful thanks to you," Ara spoke, skillfully weaving together half-truths and calculated omissions.

Anna maneuvered herself upright, pulling free of Ara's grip. Still unable to speak, she turned and dove into the lake. She needed the water, her favorite earthly mental health saver, the one constant in her fragmented human existence.

"Make it quick," Ara warned, her composure beginning to crack, an edge of impatience creeping into her tone. "You aren't human anymore. This kind of mortal coping mechanism isn't necessary. While your presence has *slowed* the Shadow's advance, it is still coming." Anna sensed Ara's growing, almost frantic concern, a stark contrast to the confident, alluring woman she had met in Cuba. Yet, Anna was sick of Ara's manipulation and decided to prioritize her own mental survival for once.

The lake was impossibly pristine. There were no submerged weeds, no muddy silt, and miraculously, no glass bottles. The water did what it always had done: it soothed her mind and body, washing away the psychic residue of the Infinite Minute. She effortlessly glided through the water, realizing that she didn't even need to breathe. *Dreams do come true!* She thought, a small, genuine smile touching her lips. She could easily be a mermaid here. Each powerful stroke propelled her forward like a dolphin. Tropical fish, impossibly vibrant in a lake, swam alongside her.

As she swam, Anna began the process of compartmentalizing the Infinite Minute into solid *certainty* and dangerous *speculation*. For all she knew, Ara could have implanted entirely fake, pre-earthly memories.

Before she could form her next coherent thought or stroke the water for another meter, she found herself standing dripping wet and shivering face to face with Ara on the bank.

"We need to return to Havana immediately and rescue my brother," Anna declared. The memories fueled her purpose. "Vlad killed my father and seems intent on killing my mother! I cannot let him kill Misha!"

Ara sighed, an exasperated, almost tired sound. "Your brother is fine, Anna, as long as Elena is near. Vlad has no idea who your Keeper is, or the true extent of the protective power around your brother. Besides, magical humans, especially one who can shield a fragment of a deity, have quite a bit of power on Earth. Unless... Nevermind," Ara stopped herself, catching a dangerous slip. "Listen to me, Anna. What you will discover will come to you in increments. It may paralyze you with shock or grief when you least expect it. But trust me when I say that your brother will be fine."

The problem, the deepest and most honest truth Anna currently possessed, was that she simply did not trust Ara. Not one bit.

9

Manny watched Misha lock up the brightly painted kiosk for the day. The oppressive, humid heat seemed to thicken the air. Off the coast, a greenish, murky cloud was spiraling, an unnatural phenomenon that Manny recognized with a familiar dread: it was not a tropical disturbance but a sign of other-wordly energies.

Misha, oblivious to the threat, unrolled and secured the metal hatch. He reached into his pocket and pulled out a single, crimson feather, turning it over in his hand to examine it.

"Do something," Misha whispered, a faint plea. The feather remained stubbornly inanimate. He swallowed, then made a conscious effort. "Caw caw." He attempted to activate the telepathic connection he shared with his sister, Anna, by imitating a local crow that he associated with her.

Manny barely contained his reaction, stifling a snicker so as not to shame his love. Misha's clumsy attempts at connecting with Anna's goddess-magic were, to the seasoned Keeper, endearingly innocent.

"Hello, can I please talk to Anna?" Misha tried again, as if the feather was a cosmic secretary. He approached quietly and tapped Misha's shoulder. Misha jumped out of his skin with a yelp.

"Hola, handsome," Manny murmured, his voice a low, a soothing counterpoint to Misha's panic. "Why are you talking to a feather?"

Misha's taut shoulders dropped, his expression softened into a radiant smile that melted Manny's composure. "Manny! You are a sight for my weary eyes," he breathed, clearly relieved. "Would you mind if we got dinner at Elena's? My sister has... gastritis, and I really do not want to be home with that right now."

Manny immediately caught the poorly constructed lie. He knew Anna wasn't suffering from a stomach ailment. She was in Kala, leaving Misha, a demigod, stranded and vulnerable on Earth. They were engaged in a subtle dance of mutual deception, a necessity that Manny, the Keeper, understood perfectly. Misha had his own silent narrative: *"Oh, by the way, my sister is a goddess from another planet, and I have magical powers. Also, there are weird talking animals. And you're hot!"* He added the last, personal bit to his internal monologue with a slight, private grin.

Manny shrugged with feigned nonchalance. "Sure, she is always happy to have either of you two around."

As they began walking, Manny felt an overwhelming, almost painful yearning to grab Misha's hand, to anchor himself to the man who represented so much light in his life. But he knew the consequences of such a public display would be dire. So, they walked side by side, their fingers occasionally grazing, a charge passing between them in the slight contact of pinky fingers. To give it extra-hetero flair, one of them would whistle or offer a flattering catcall to a passing woman. The women invariably went into a tizzy, especially around Misha. Manny was conventionally attractive, but Misha's fairy lineage gave him an almost irresistible, magnetizing effect that women could not control.

They navigated the chaotic evening streets, dodging bicycles and the stray dogs that often lounged in the middle of the sidewalk. As they approached Elena's café, which was usually a hub of boisterous activity and light at this hour, they saw that his *abuela* was unnervingly preparing to close.

Manny stopped abruptly, pulling Misha gently but firmly to face him. His eyes were grave. "Misha, whatever my abuela is about to do or say, please do not be alarmed or think we are crazy. You must also listen to her. It is only for your protection."

Misha stared back, his blue eyes searching Manny's. Manny, however, could feel the heat rising in his own body, a physical reaction to Misha's proximity and the charged moment. *Margaret Thatcher naked on a cold day. Ronald Reagan naked on a cold day.* Manny furiously chanted in his mind, utilizing the most reliable anti-arousal mantra in his mental handbook. The visceral distraction worked; all the blood instantly drained from his cock.

Misha nodded slowly, a deep, adorably knowing look in his eyes that suggested he understood much more than he let on.

Elena, her face etched with exhaustion, motioned them inside. There was no typical, warm, embracing smile. Manny knew instantly that this could be Elena's moment. Not every Keeper faces such danger, but exiled deities can be volatile.

The moment they were inside, Elena unrolled and locked the heavy metal storefront, sealing them in a small, secure box. No one could see inside; they could not see out.

Elena looked Misha dead in the eyes, her voice clear and strong. "Nice try. I am impressed, but my thoughts are my own."

Misha quickly looked away, a flush embarrassment rising on his cheeks at being caught attempting to spy on her mind.

Manny felt the complicated web of their secret knowledge: *Manny knows that Misha must know what they know, but Misha doesn't know that they know what he knows.* It was a magical, life-and-death game of "Who's on First." Manny thought, *If only Abbott and Costello could see them now.*

"Abuela, what is going on?" Manny asked earnestly, the urgency overriding his usual composure. There was no time for games.

Elena's voice became a firm command. "Manny, *his* powers are nearing their peak on Earth. You must leave Cuba for both of your safety. I have arranged for a boat at 2:00 AM. It will take you to Miami. The sea witch will protect you during the passage. It isn't safe for either of you if he knows where you are. You must go to New York City. Another Keeper, older and more powerful than me, is waiting for you there with her two charges. Only with them can order come," Elena commanded.

Manny felt Misha's mounting panic vibrating in the space between them. Misha's emotional suppression was futile. "I don't understand," Misha interjected, his voice trembling. "Whose powers? I am not getting on a boat. My sister is... ill. How will I be able to tell her where I am?"

Manny stepped closer, caressing Misha's cheek with his thumb, trying to offer a small island of calm.

Elena ignored Misha's deflection and reached for his hand, holding it firmly in hers. "Misha, listen to me. We know your story. We know more about you and your family than you do. Manny comes from a long lineage of Keepers, like me. I hoped we had a few more decades of mentorship before it came to this." Her eyes darted between Misha and Manny. Elena swallowed hard, keeping her tears firmly fixed in her ducts. Manny, however, smelled her grief - a mix of a doused campfire and saltwater.

Manny clenched his jaw, blinking back his own tears while simultaneously subduing the panic rising from his gut. He repeated a soothing mantra in his mind: *Hibiscus tea. Sea turtles hatching. Kind birds. Kids laughing.*

"Before it came to what? What is going on? I will not go to America!" Misha was desperate, the raw need for information overriding all else. Manny couldn't blame him. His sister was gone. His lover was a Keeper, and now, after a life in Cuba, he was being told to flee to Miami immediately.

Elena gently stroked the top of his hand, a tangible reassurance that instantly calmed Misha. She looked into his eyes and offered her usual, nurturing smile. Misha's jaw unclenched, and his shoulders visibly dropped.

"Misha, you will be fine if you are with Manny. But you must listen to him no matter what happens. Never leave his side, and you will survive," she warned. As the kind words left her lips, Manny noticed a slight, involuntary twitch in her eye, a sign of the profound stress she was under.

"Manny and I are ordered, by the universe, to protect you and your sister. We protect all exiled deities, demigods, and magical creatures."

Manny held his breath, waiting for the weight of that news to land. He contrasted the two siblings in his mind. Anna was the intelligent, deeply thoughtful, broody, and moody one. Misha was hot, joyful, and knew everything about pop culture.

"You will learn the full truth in time, but what is imminently important now is that Vlad is not from Earth—"

"That explains that mother fucker," Misha interrupted, his voice laced with venom.

"He is from the realm of your mother and your sister. Your mother and sister were self-serving deities, sometimes intentionally good, sometimes intentionally bad, but mostly chaotic neutral. Vlad was chaotic evil. There is no room for repentance or forgiveness in his world. He believes devotees should be afraid, and his devotees thrive in fear."

"That asshole is a deity?" Misha stared at her in disbelief, a harsh laugh escaping him. "Clearly there is no justice in the universe."

Elena merely shrugged. Manny inhaled deeply, knowing that a crash course in universal justice - or the lack thereof - was about to begin.

"What is justice, really? There is only the perception of order, chaos, justice, and injustice. Here, on Earth, similarly to your sister and mother, he had minimal power. His essence came with him, like your sister and mother. Unfortunately, an Earthling learned about the religions of Kala, even while remaining ignorant to its true existence. He started worshiping Vlad, giving him power. While I have an idea as to how the human learned of Vlad's identity, I cannot prove it. Regardless, the more Vlad is worshiped, the more danger awaits you."

Manny wished this inevitable, expository part of the process could move along a bit more quickly. *Inhale. Exhale. Listen and don't judge.* Buddhist mystics studied the patience of the Keepers, yet beneath his placid eyes, Manny found himself yearning for a cosmic void so he could scream into it. There were plenty of voids in the universe. Screaming into a void was his one, unfulfilled bucket-list item.

"Boris, that little doughy fucker. And here I thought he was the worst closet case at the embassy," Misha snarled, balling his fists as his nostrils flared. Manny, failing to stay present, found himself admiring the flexed muscles in Misha's arms.

"Right. Vlad has a thirst for revenge and death. Until now, he did not have the power to defeat me, much less come near me. That has changed. He is very dangerous. Vlad had a Keeper, like me, but Vlad turned on him," Elena said somberly, the weight of the memory heavy in her voice.

Now it was Manny's turn to blink back a tear, the gravity of her words finally hitting him. Misha, momentarily forgetting his panic, listened intently, paying no attention to Manny.

"You see, each deity sent to Earth is assigned to a Keeper. Keepers usually have two or three deities, but Vlad's Keeper only had him. They knew that he would need more attention than a typical deity."

"They? Who are they?" Misha asked, instantly curious.

Elena continued. "You know them as the Macaw and the Iguana. Anna called them the Mysterious Duo. I'm sure she has learned their true identities by now."

Misha tried, poorly, to hide his confusion behind a facade of comprehension.

"Querido, I can explain on the boat. Which you *are* getting on," Manny interrupted, an edge of urgency in his voice. The café's general aroma had shifted subtly. A faint whiff of pungent decay now mixed with Elena's L'Eeau de Grief. He knew, with a certainty that chilled him, that Vlad was arriving.

"I don't have much more time to explain. Vlad's Keeper was my son, Tonio, Manny's father. He died under 'mysterious' circumstances around the same time that your parents died, if you remember. It was a boating accident. But Tonio's peacock carried his final message for him: *'Vlad has a worshiper. I am sorry for the universe.'* Shortly after the finch shared that message, a part of my soul left the earthly realm, weakening me ever so slightly. It went with Tonio to the spirit realm for Keepers."

Misha had a torrent of questions. "How did he get here? Did he use the same garden as Mama and Anna?"

"No. I do not know where his portal is, but I think..."

Manny interrupted, his voice sharp. "Abuela, he is coming." The air, already heavy, quickly became stifling. The faint whiff had become an overwhelming stench of putrefying decay and excrement.

"Manny, quick! Take him to the docks. He doesn't know your identity." She pulled a tarnished silver necklace from around her neck and thrust it into Manny's hand. "This is yours now. Run out the back. Do not be seen by anyone. Take the darkest routes. I love you, queridos." She was saying good-bye forever, and he was completely unprepared for the emotional toll. His older sister had always been the strong one. Losing his sister and his second mother in one day was almost too much to bear. Misha stifled a sob beside him.

"My love, be strong. We can do this together!" Manny interjected, immediately grabbing Misha's hand and pulling him close.

Manny then quickly affixed the Keeper's pendant around his neck, tucking the small, stylized tree emblem under his shirt, where it rested against his heart.

Misha cocked his head to the side, his eyes examining Manny's face with a new, searching intensity.

Manny's psychic sense of smell registered a complex cocktail: vanilla, lavender, and a prominent hint of lime.

Regret and bitterness. Misha was questioning whether their love was real. The honey scent, however, turned quickly to new leather and metal: he was also profoundly aroused by Manny's sudden, assertive dominance and the danger they faced.

Manny kept his psychic olfactory information to himself.

The ground shook.

"Leave through the back window *now*." Elena's voice was a command, not a request. Manny leaned in and hugged Elena fiercely, a silent farewell, then grabbed Misha's hand and pulled him toward the kitchen. Manny balanced his foot on the sturdy propane tank, taking extreme care not to make a sound, and slithered through the small window into the back alley. He immediately reached back through the opening, feeling for Misha's arm. His physical magic hadn't fully integrated yet, making the simple task of hoisting a person difficult. He pulled Misha up just as they heard a loud, violent *crack* from the main café room.

As Misha stood, he almost fell, his eyes scrunched shut in pain. "I have to sit—" he whispered, breathless.

"We can't, my love," Manny said urgently, already trying to drag him through the dark alleyway.

"I can see what she sees," Misha whispered breathlessly, his connection to Elena's mind apparently forced open by the shock.

"Babe, you have to start walking, please. You must shut her out and open your physical eyes," Manny pleaded as Misha wobbled, fighting the psychic vision.

"He's hungry—" Misha whimpered, a sound of pure terror.

Manny knew that if he didn't act immediately, Misha would fall into psychic shock.

"He's sniffing up her neck, we have to help her!" Misha pleaded, trying to pull Manny back toward the window.

"We can't, Misha! This is her divine purpose: to protect you! It's mine as well! She is going to die. I cannot let you go along with her. I am sorry for what I'm about to do!"

With a surge of desperation, Manny flung Misha over his shoulder without much effort. Then, with a sharp snap of his fingers, Misha's wrists and ankles were bound together with an invisible, magical restraint.

When Manny ran along the beach with heavy sacks of sugar on his shoulders, his old training regimen, onlookers would never have known he was conditioning his body for this moment. *If only they could see him now.* They would all be mortified.

"Babe, please stop, please stop! It sounds like he is going to eat her! He said she smells delicious, like fine wine. Boris is there!" Misha's voice was muffled, panicked.

Ignoring the pleas of your new lover was physically agonizing; it felt like Manny's own heart was seizing. His beautiful, joyful lover was experiencing a horror movie unfolding inside his head. And it wouldn't stop until...

"He says 'You are a weird lot, you know. You're supposed to 'protect' us. But some of us do not need protection on this forsaken planet.' She's in pain! She can barely! Stand! If you're so powerful, MAKE THIS STOP!"

"He's trying to read her mind but can't understand your language... Manny Manny... we can save her please. She's your abuela," Misha went on, his voice cracking with tears.

"He just admitted to killing your dad." Manny froze mid-stride. The raw, gut-punching truth of Vlad's evil anchored him in the moment.

A Keeper's job is to protect their charge. A keeper's job is to protect their charge.

Manny repeated the mantra several times, the words a concrete wall against the rising grief and rage, before choosing his next action.

"Misha, I'm going to gag you if you don't shut up. I love you more than you can imagine. And I am doing this to save you!" Manny kept the *sack of Misha* firmly on his shoulders as he continued running, his pace relentless.

"She's dead! He sliced her throat with a katana! He is drinking her blood like a vampire. Oh my God, make it stop!"

And just like that, the psychic connection snapped, and the horrifying vision ended.

Misha struggled violently to release himself from Manny's grip and the magical bonds, but to no avail.

"Put me down, now. I don't know if I can trust you at this point. You let your own abuela get murdered. But I guess I don't have a fucking choice!" Misha's voice was raw with betrayal.

A void for screaming would have been profoundly cathartic for Manny right now, but he simply stopped and put Misha down. They stood on a darkened street corner near the old Occupiers compound, dangerously close to Anna's magical Garden.

Inhale. Exhale. Abuela died. His love hates him. Inhale. Exhale.

"My love, we must keep going, okay? You can do this. I promise when we're out of Vlad's crosshairs I will be here to hold you and listen. I am devastated, and I trained for this. Elena trained for this," Manny said, his voice flat with forced control.

Misha's eyes glazed over again, his breathing quickening as he focused on a new terror.

"Vlad smells you. He's foaming at the mouth like a rabid

dog. He's going to find us! We must leave. We must warn my sister! He doesn't want us! He wants to go back to Kala!"

"Change of plans then. Let's fucking go," Manny said, losing all composure. He grabbed Misha's hand and began to run again, the docks no longer the destination, but merely the first step on a new, desperate journey.

10

Manny and Misha ran desperately through the labyrinthine streets of old Havana.

A putrid stench violated their nostrils: Vlad was dangerously close. Their silence was critical. Instead, Misha strained his mind, searching the psychic ether for a glimpse into Vlad's intent.

"Vlad wants your blood," Misha finally whispered, the words catching in his throat, breathlessly thin. Manny seized his hand, his gaze plunging deep into Misha's soul. In any other moment, under the cover of darkness, this intimacy would have sparked a consuming passion. But the thought of an imminent, violent death at the hands of a maniacal deity caused Manny's body to be unresponsive.

Time. If only he possessed the rare ability of a Timekeeper. The sea witch's mission, however urgent, had to wait. Misha's assessment was chillingly correct: they had to warn Anna. They had to reach her in Kala.

"Misha, you have to trust me, okay? Completely. We need to get to your mother and sister's garden. Do you know the way from here?" Manny transmitted the plea telepathically. Misha, without breaking stride, simply nodded, his eyes fixed on the path ahead, and took the lead. Manny effortlessly bounded and weaved through the tight, twisting alleys, struggling only with the restraint of Misha's human-like pace.

"Oooh hoooo hoo! I smell you! Come out, come out!" Vlad's cackle was a jagged, high-pitched sound that scraped against the silence. Manny swiftly calculated the distance: two blocks behind them, and closing the gap with terrifying speed.

Misha glanced back at Manny, his face a mask of strain. He pointed a trembling finger toward a massive, rusty gate that blocked the dead end of the alley: the entrance to the secret garden. Misha swallowed a wave of vomit. His surge of adrenaline had vanished, leaving him depleted and terrified, so agonizingly close to safety. Manny's eyes pleaded with him, conveying the desperate need for one last push.

"You possess more power than you can possibly imagine, *amor*. Use it," Manny implored telepathically, sending a jolt of his own energy across their bond.

Manny stayed right beside him, matching his pace. They found themselves at the end of the alley. Previously, this section of buildings had been a monument to urban decay: paint peeled, faded, and chipped away by decades of sun and rain. Yet now, even in the deep shroud of the night, Manny could only perceive a brilliant, impossible splash of bright blue and vivid green. A clear, illuminated path had opened up just for them, guiding them to the garden.

They paused before the imposing gate, struck by a shared moment of awe. They admired the incredibly ornate metalwork, which Manny had known only as old and corroded before. *That chaotic duo really loved their dramatic magic,* he thought with a mental groan. The gate was a testament to their self-absorbed, gaudy, yet captivating flair for the dramatic: a ruby-encrusted macaw and an emerald-encrusted iguana formed a perfect, stylized yin-and-yang shape over the silhouette of a mahogany tree. *Typical. Always covering the Keepers,* Manny scoffed internally. Toucans were diagonally opposed in the top and bottom corners, while thick, coiled snakes occupied the other two.

"OH, TWO FOR THE PRICE OF ONE. A Keeper and a... Misha, what are you? Why I dare say, I had some idea that you would be related to this, but I would not have placed bets except that you two *maricons* are fucking." Vlad appeared as if by instantaneous combustion, seemingly manifesting out of the empty air. Boris finally caught up to Vlad, looking like the walking dead.

Manny spun around just as quickly as Vlad had materialized, tightening his grip on Misha's hand. He felt Misha's pulse skyrocketing to a dangerously high, frantic pace. The adrenaline was back, but this time, it was pure terror.

"And I am a gambling man! 'I know when to hold 'em, know when to fold 'em.' Kenny Rogers, no? You do like that American music, no?" Vlad, a master manipulator who instantly sensed Misha's surging fear, clearly relished toying with them.

Vlad brandished his katana whose blade glowed with a glacier blue light.

"Well, I originally wanted to find your sister, but you'll do," he purred, examining the razor-sharp edge of his blade with a connoisseur's appreciation.

"I should have known that a piece of shit like you was the reason Havana had been smelling like, well, shit lately," Misha spat out, but Manny's sharp elbow to his side cut him off instantly.

"It's the smell of power. The smell of a real man," Vlad

retorted, throwing his head back and letting loose a booming, guttural laugh.

Misha attempted to use his telepathy on Vlad, a power that had previously worked with startling ease. *Kill yourself.* Vlad, in response, unsheathed his katana and pointed the razor-sharp tip toward his own gut, mockingly. He then emitted a chilling giggle, and a blinding pressure exploded behind Misha's eyes, sending a painful throb through his head. Vlad then directed the katana toward Manny and Misha, wagging it back and forth like the condemning finger of an ancient *babushka*.

"Naive boy. Your powers are absolutely useless on me, especially now that I have had some Keeper fortification. Elena was delicious. Subtle, yet complex. I enjoyed her immensely." His tone was sickeningly light and airy, as if discussing fine wine. "It looks like you have nowhere left to go." He finished with a theatrical shrug. Boris slumped to the ground, covered in blood, whether it was his or Elana's, Manny couldn't tell.

A vital realization hit Manny: Vlad could not see the magnificent, vibrant gate to the garden.

"Misha, Vlad cannot see this gate. We need to get into the garden now. It is our only hope," Manny urgently messaged telepathically.

In the same split second that they turned to throw open the gate, Vlad raised his katana and made a single, effortless, blindingly fast slash. Misha was not quick enough. A thick spray of blood erupted from Misha's right calf. Blood oozed out, turning a startling, sickly black as it hit the night air. The wound immediately began to fester, a sign of its magical, toxic nature. Misha instantly looked woozy, staggering on his feet. Manny nimbly darted back, the tip of the malevolent katana missing his throat by a hair's breadth.

Misha dimly heard Vlad's enraged roar as the world began to fade in and out of focus. "Sister...Mama...Papa..." he whispered, his voice a ghost.

"Focus on me," Manny thought with a desperate, all-consuming energy. Elena had not made the ultimate, agonizing sacrifice for Vlad to simply kill them now. Misha's legs gave out, and he fell into Manny's arms.

"It's only a flesh wound, Misha. A typical earthling would be dead by now," Vlad observed with a detached, clinical curiosity, stating it as a simple fact.

In a millisecond of superhuman speed, Manny scooped up Misha, cradling him like a child. Misha's head rested heavily on Manny's shoulder, his left arm weakly clinging to Manny's neck. Manny straightened, defiantly facing Vlad, shield and protector.

"Where will you go, sad little Keeper?" Vlad laughed, a triumphant sound.

"Misha, stay with me," Manny whispered urgently, his mouth near Misha's ear. "Stay with me, please. I need you to hold the macaw feather with one hand and press the macaw figure on the gate with the other." Misha could not speak, but he managed a faint nod against Manny's neck.

Vlad, completely consumed by his self-important diatribe, was too absorbed to hear their quiet, urgent communication.

"Your father was delicious. But your *abuela's* blood gave me the most satisfaction. I feel, what is this, sadness? A little sadness knowing that this magnificent line of Keepers would finally die out." Vlad briefly frowned, a look of mock regret, and then shrugged it away.

"How can you be so sure, Vlad?" Manny was trying desperately to stall, to buy precious seconds. Vlad was so close now that Manny could see a tiny drop of fresh blood, a remnant of Elena, just above his lip. Sensing the presence of the warm blood, Vlad quickly licked it up.

"Obvious question, no?" he said calmly.

Vlad raised his katana across his body, the icy-blue blade out and ready, positioned for a deadly slash across Manny's exposed throat.

Misha, his mind battling the growing darkness, held the scarlet feather concealed in his pocket with his right hand while his left hand covertly pressed the sculpted macaw on the gate.

As Vlad finally unleashed his fatal slash, the ornate gate burst open. Misha and Manny fell backward, tumbling into the garden. Vlad let out a shriek of deafening frustration that pierced their ear drums. It morphed into a raw, powerful roar that sent a wave like a sonic boom across the humid night air. Boris clasped both ears with his hands.

"If you are thinking of entering a portal, you have cut my job in half. Misha will not be able to survive the trip after meeting the sword," Vlad chuckled, his voice laced with venomous certainty. "Sorry to break up the romance, boys, but that highway is only for true gods, demigods, and super magical beings. At best, this *maricon* has some leftover fairy dust from his father." Vlad let out a sinister, barking laugh at his own brutal joke and the thought of the Keeper's inevitable heartbreak and the death of Misha. Misha held onto consciousness for his life, determined not to give that repugnant human the satisfaction of witnessing his death.

The garden offered an immediate, profound respite, cutting off the stench and swirling heat surrounding Vlad. Manny knew that there was truth to Vlad's cruel words, but he clung desperately to the hope that Misha possessed enough of his latent magical properties to survive the journey to Kala. The only other option was to allow Misha to die in his arms, and that was simply not an option. He ran to a large, moss-covered fountain and sat heavily on its edge, gently cradling Misha in his lap.

"Love, this is going to hurt like absolute hell," Manny whispered, leaning down to place a feather-light kiss on Misha's clammy forehead.

Misha, unable to speak, simply nodded. His eyes fluttered shut. Manny wrapped his powerful arms around Misha, pulling him into a tight, protective embrace, and they fell backward, plunging into the water of the fountain.

Misha's eyes snapped open wide for an instant. Manny stared into his beautiful, suffering soul, their last moment of connection just before they violently broke the water's surface and the world dissolved around them.

11

Callan, whose very existence was a celebration of melodrama, watched the entire live-action telenovela unfold with undisguised delight. She lived up to her stereotype as a Collector. As a being who had been conceived at the dawn of time itself, nothing in the span of a few hundred millennia typically surprised her. But this particular storyline, featuring the desperate flight of the Keeper and his lover, truly captivated her. It was new. It was different. Callan was, as she always was, entirely here for the spectacle.

As Manny, Misha, and the brutish, lumbering Vlad and his potato sack sycophant tore through the streets of Havana, Callan flitted effortlessly, unseen, from rooftop to rooftop, keeping pace. The only thing missing from her perfect cosmic viewing experience was a bucket of popcorn.

God damn, this lot was dramatic, she mused as they approached the garden's boundary. *At least Manny and Misha are ridiculously hot.* She made a mental note: she would very much like to see them consummate their passion someday. It wasn't often that Callan found any type of human sex interesting, but she knew a hard-bodied, wild, steamy affair when she saw one.

She detested Vlad, though. Callan silently hoped he would finally get the karmic reckoning he deserved. He was, to her eyes, nothing more than a shit-filled sausage casing. Watching him fume in self-pity was, as the humans said, the chef's kiss.

Manny and Misha dove into the portal's watery vortex. *Misha is gonna be in a world of hurt,* she thought grimly, the vision of his blackened wound still fresh in her mind. *She hoped he would survive long enough for them to fuck.*

Vlad's toxic blend of entitlement and pure rage practically oozed out of his pores and into her divine nostrils. *Poor baby couldn't see the portal or make it through. Wop wop.* She played the world's smallest violin as he angrily sheathed his sword and stomped off in the direction of his apartment.

Vlad failed to notice Callan. He paid her no mind whatsoever as he walked through the familiar, twisting rabbit warren of old Havana toward his dwelling. Women crossed the street, their heads bowed low, going out of their way to avoid him. Callan studied them as they averted their eyes, while Vlad remained oblivious to the fear he inspired. He rubbed his temples,. Callan hoped this headache was only the beginning of his problems.

"Fuck, not this again," he muttered to no one but himself. Callan knew instantly: he was being summoned to Kala. His Fortuna siblings, the powerful Tridents, were beings not to be trifled with, yet she knew with absolute certainty that Vlad would try to bargain his way out and refuse to pay the price. They were, after all, Saturn-adjacent.

Callan loved the unforgiving universal checks and balances. Saturn and his tireless minions oversaw the scales of cosmic justice. Of all the deities, Saturn came the closest to true omnipotence. Most humans never witnessed the karmic correction in their fleeting lifetimes, but Saturn never missed a single step.

Callan watched as Vlad staggered and steadied himself against a crumbling wall for stability. His eyes sealed shut in distress. She squawked loudly, unafraid to add insult to injury. He shuddered violently as he used his blood-stained shirt to wipe the sweat from his brow.

Callan knew that dying on Earth was not a viable option for a deity of his stature. But perhaps he might perish right before her eyes. Vlad opened the gated door to his building and hauled himself up the creaking stairs.

She flew to his small balcony and perched on the railing. He entered the apartment. Callan had always wondered why Vlad had been afforded one of the larger apartments typically reserved for high-ranking Soviet officials. It was significantly larger than those of his comrades and even boasted an enormous refrigerator and a balcony. Senior officials in the Party, she guessed, were likely afraid of him. Some power indeed.

Vlad pulled a bottle of frigid vodka from the freezer, rubbed the icy glass over his face, and took a long, burning swig. His giant 'meat sack' of a body crashed heavily onto the couch. Callan saw the yelp of agony just before his mind ventured to the other realm. His body violently contorted to the right side for a few seconds before going completely comatose. To the unaware human eye, it would look like a tonic clonic seizure. Callan swooped silently into his flat and perched next to his head. *Dare she tap into his mind?* What a terrifying place, even for a goddess like her. *Ah well,* she decided, *curiosity was her eternal kryptonite.* She placed her sharp beak delicately on the crown of his head. Callan instantly saw a shimmering, vaporous image of Vlad, his astral self, hovering over a pathway in Kala.

Vapor Vlad looked toward a serene Japanese garden, much like the ones he had seen in his rare, treasured books. The three pagodas within the garden's perimeter were constructed of pure onyx, a material unlike any photo he had ever seen before. He hovered over a pathway paved with scarlet red rocks, lined meticulously with vibrant red camellias and striking red spider lilies.

"Dalv, come. Dalv, come," a crackling, ancient voice emerged from the first pagoda. Callan flinched involuntarily. Usually, she went completely undetected, but the Tridents, or Fortuna siblings, in Kala were different these days. They were angrier than usual, and they had tapped into a much deeper, more volatile source of power. Callan had no idea what she was dealing with.

He walked toward the first pagoda. In the center, suspended unnaturally in mid-air, was a single, perfect ruby the size and cut of a baseball. Callan swore she saw his vapor dick begin to get hard. Money and power were his absolute kinks. He reached for it, but his ghostly hands simply passed through the jewel.

A chilling cackle echoed throughout the pagoda.

A red-eyed, alabaster nude woman with a thick tangled black hair emerged silently from one of the massive onyx columns of the pagoda. In a blink, she was within an inch of his vapor face.

"Dalv, wealth has no meaning to you, you fool. You are the warrior god of Kala. This *fortuna*, the ruby, is your power source. I am Malv, protector of the Fortuna and one of your Tridents." She spoke without moving her mouth, a resonant sound in his mind.

Her dismissive, commanding tone enraged him. He

raised his hand to strike her, and she cackled again, louder this time.

"Ah ah ah. You did not learn your lessons on earth, did you? You do not deserve this power."

Now that makes sense, Callan thought, the puzzle pieces clicking into place. No wonder he couldn't see the portal gate. And yet, if they had to wait until this sack of shit learned a moral lesson, he would truly be stuck in Havana forever.

Malv swallowed the massive ruby in a single, impossible gulp, like a snake swallowing a rat whole. She vanished completely.

Callan was not disappointed in the least. This, she knew, was going to be epic. *Woo hoo.*

Vlad stood in his place, perplexed, humiliated, and seething with anger.

"Dalv, come come." He heard a crackly male voice from the middle pagoda. Vlad walked over to find the source of the voice: a seemingly bottomless pool filled with cerulean, glowing water in the center of the structure. He attempted to dip his foot into the cool water, only to have a pale, powerful hand grab it and forcefully shove him back. A pale male figure rose from the pool, and like Malv, he had long, matted black hair and round, blazing red eyes.

"I am Zalv. I'll make this simple for you as I am not so forgiving as my sister. I am the protector of your portal. If you can put aside your outsized human ego and find the true earthly portal, you'll emerge from here. But heed my warning... if you have not learned your earthly lessons, you will learn them here. Kala is not as kind to deities as earth is," Zalv stated, his voice a deep, hollow echo.

Vlad smirked dismissively.

Callan giggled to herself, a silent, mocking sound. Vlad

genuinely thought power and fortune meant an easy life. *Such a deeply human trait.*

"I wouldn't be so sure that you can outsmart me, a little... *maricon* as you say. My final *zibling* awaits," Zalv warned ominously, clearly reading the contempt and arrogance in Vlad's thoughts before submerging himself back into the pool.

A third voice called him from the last pagoda. Vlad's brow scrunched in confusion. His mouth fell slightly agape. *Cogs were finally turning,* Callan thought, amused.

"Dalv, come. Come to me, Dalv". He walked to the final pagoda. Hovering in the center was an iron key. The handle was perfectly shaped like a snake skull. A pale, androgynous being descended gracefully from the ceiling and snatched the key.

Callan knew that Yalv was the most powerful, the true peak of Vlad's three tridents. They were absolutely not to be trifled with, and yet, Callan knew Vlad would find a way to test them.

Yalv had both breasts and a penis. The sight reminded Callan of a prostitute that Vlad had accidentally solicited in Havana before violently beating the shit out of her. *Another moment for Saturn's scales to correct.*

Their eyes blazed with a terrifying, fiery red light. "You still have many lessons to learn, Dalv. My name is Yalv. I am the peak of your Trident. You have angered my sister and disrespected my brother. You are wise not to do so with me as I am the key to your return. The key to full restoration is to enter through my brother's portal, find my sister, and restore the Fortuna." Yalv instructed him with cold authority.

"What kind of cunt do you think you are?" Vapor Vlad hissed, his anger overriding his survival instinct.

Callan shook her beak in false disappointment. *He'll be stuck in Havana forever.*

Yalv reached down and grabbed his vapor balls and dick firmly. "I'm a cunt who knows they could destroy all of your power with the flick of my wrist," they said, squeezing with palpable force.

"Learn your lesson or languish on earth," they hissed through gritted teeth.

Vlad froze, immobilized by a primal fear of losing his manhood and, by extension, his power.

Yalv let go. Vlad exhaled a massive sigh of relief, his vapor body shuddering.

"Back to earth with you." Yalv snapped their fingers with an audible crack.

Vlad regained consciousness on his couch in Havana, his body jerking violently. Callan flitted silently to the top of the large refrigerator. He frantically patted his crotch as he bolted upright. Another sigh of profound relief. Vlad grabbed the still-frosty bottle of vodka and took two more massive chugs.

Callan couldn't believe that he still hadn't noticed her. He stared down at his knees, clearly reeling from the disorienting experience. She had seen it infinite times before. Everyone thinks they live in their own earthly version of a gaudy paradise. Some do. But the Vlads of the deity world live a different, much crueler reality.

"That pagoda, my god... go through the portal. Get the ruby. Appease Yalv. It seems easy enough," he mumbled to himself, already simplifying the complex divine command.

Damn, he really was out of it, Callan thought, shaking her head. She flitted out to the balcony.

Vlad stood up abruptly and stomped into his kitchen where he opened the freezer and grabbed a block of ice. All his pent-up rage was violently unleashed on that single, inanimate block. Callan saw ice shards fly everywhere, tiny white missiles of frustration. Vlad filled a glass with the crushed ice and emptied the bottle's remaining vodka into the glass. He sat heavily on his balcony chair, channeling his confusion and volcanic rage into formulating a plan.

"How the fuck did these sniveling little fuckers leave right in front of me?" he muttered to no one. "Surely Misha was dead, but that Keeper *maricon* was there," Vlad wondered aloud, his plan already a mix of arrogance and wishful thinking.

Clearly, this dipshit wasn't going to return to power by learning any moral lessons, instantly confirming Callan's long-held belief that he was, in fact, the worst of the worst. She had to step in. She was bored; she needed some excitement.

"How the fuck can I get back to Kala?" he hissed into the night air.

Callan squawked loudly, drawing his attention.

"Get the fuck out of here." He shooed Callan just as she transformed instantly into the guise of a dour, unimpressive old woman.

In one smooth, lightning-fast motion, he leapt from his chair and unsheathed his katana, ready to slice her in half without a second thought.

"Hey, whoah whoah, not so fast, dick-for-brains. Sheesh. Y'all all lose your decorum in this place." She made a sharp, flicking motion with her wrist in his direction. His arm jerked back violently, involuntarily pointing the sharp end of the sword directly towards the ground.

"I can help you get what you need, you know, that portal location, if you would just listen to me for a second before going all ape shit," Callan said, her voice dry and unimpressed.

Vlad stood there, his mouth agape, looking, as Callan judged, like a dumb ape. *Although apes were certainly smarter than Vlad,* she thought. Eons of experience had taught Callan that taking the form of an old lady was the safest approach for all parties involved, especially her.

"I'm listening," he grunted, taking another defiant swig of the cold vodka.

Callan pulled out a single, scarlet feather from her pocket and began to make a deal. She had places to go, after all. *Tick tock tick tock.*

12

The violent lurch of the interdimensional transfer spat them out onto the flat surface of the lake in Kala. As Manny's head broke the water, he was reminded why he never traveled via portals. Every muscle fiber screamed in protest, feeling as though it had been flayed, while his lungs burned for air. He gasped before the immediate reality of his situation set in.

He tightened his grip around an unconscious Misha, his sheer weight making it nearly impossible to swim.

I didn't go through hell to drown, Manny thought in a small pep talk to push him towards land. Manny kicked and pulled them toward the nearest bank. He dragged Misha out of the water and lowered him onto the white sand.

A hard lump formed in Manny's throat. Misha looked like death: his odds of survival were slim, but - Manny focused on the mathematical certainty - not zero. He pressed his ear to Misha's mouth, straining to detect the faintest sign of life. Respiration was almost non-existent. He felt for Misha's pulse. It was barely perceptible.

As a Keeper, he operated under the cruel, fundamental

law of the multiverse: that nothing was remotely the human equivalent of *fair*. Yet, his very soul, the core of his being, yearned for Misha to live. The raw wound of losing his *abuela* was too recent, too deep; he could not entertain the possibility of losing Misha, too.

Manny forced his focus outward, scanning his surroundings to assess the situation and plan his next move. The vibrant landscape would have captured his awe under any other circumstance, but he barely registered it.

Just then, as if appearing from thin air, a shockingly bright, cheeky-looking toucan landed with a light thud directly on Misha's head.

"Hey, Keeper," the toucan began, cocking its head, its black eyes glinting with unwarranted amusement. "You and he are looking real rough. I hope your stay in Kala proves to be better than the journey over," the bird finished, cackling as punctuation.

"That's not remotely helpful, bird. He needs immediate healing. Time is a luxury we don't have," he snapped, keeping his voice low despite the urgency. "Could you tell me if Ara and Anna are on this planet and, if so, where I may find them?" The toucan's distinct coloring and overly familiar manner pricked at a distant memory. He dreaded that this may be a Collector. They were notorious for their manipulation and the endless, petty trouble they caused.

"Yes and... *maybe*," the toucan replied as she raised a brow, hopping down from Misha's head to land squarely on his stomach. It gave Manny a distinctly coy look. "Who wants to know, and more importantly, *why*, Keeper?"

By now, an entire audience of parrots and fellow toucans had materialized, fluttering down from the canopy to gather in a chattering ring around them. It was, apparently, a rare spectacle. Nothing ever came through this particular portal, much less *twice* in one week. Manny treaded carefully, his instincts screaming caution. Birds, he knew, were the eyes and ears of this world. Birds knew *everything*. Birds gossiped. And, most dangerously, birds kept the best secrets. His mind, his body, and his very spirit were utterly wrecked by the harrowing events of the last few hours on Earth. But his role as a Keeper demanded a cool head and self-control. He had to play the game with precision and keep his focus locked on his objective: the safety of Ana and Misha.

"I do not have time for your games, bird. This man is gravely injured and may die if we do not get him to Anna's temple or an equivalent healer *now*," Manny stated, rationing the information he gave out to a strict, absolute need-to-know basis.

The Toucan threw its head back, leading the entire avian flock in a squawking cacophony that undeniably sounded like mocking laughter.

"Oh, honey, you certainly won't find them at Anna's temple. That derelict old place is completely unfit for goddess-level living at this point, bless her heart." The toucan ended its sentence by lightly pecking at Misha's well-defined abs. "My, this one is utterly beautiful. How did you manage to land a specimen like him? He looks... familiar. I can tell it's his first time traveling through a portal, lordy me," the toucan observed, its voice dripping with false sincerity.

Manny knew, with certainty, that she was lying about Misha's unfamiliarity. She knew who he was. The question was *how*? He had no choice but to play her games to extrapolate any valuable information she may be willing to give. Collectors were the worst.

"I am his Keeper. He was in considerable trouble on

Earth, but managed to activate the portal that led here," Manny disclosed, his voice carefully measured.

The toucan's black eyes narrowed, and a smile cracked the length of its beak.

"What a *terrible* Keeper you are, then. A deity-thing is nearly dead, and you're sitting here on the beach, having a leisurely chat with a toucan?" On cue, the entire feathered flock erupted again in a fresh torrent of laughter.

Manny's face felt hot, a flush of heat bubbled up his neck. Keepers were renowned, legendary even, for their unflappable, even temperament, but this creature was testing the very limits of his self-control. She *had* to be a Collector. There was simply no other explanation for the calculated, infuriating psychological torture. Keepers, as a universally upheld rule, absolutely loathed Collectors. But Manny knew the painful truth of their dynamic: she possessed something he urgently needed. That was their *modus operandi.*

Manny, by design and training, rarely used magic beyond subtly enhancing his physical strengths or the occasional, necessary bit of telepathy. Keepers were meant to maintain a low profile, to operate from the shadows. This was an extenuating circumstance. He flicked his finger. A silent wave of energy pulsed outward, and the toucan was instantly frozen, suspended mid-air. Every squawking bird shut up.

"You will tell me how to find Anna and Ara, the fastest, most direct route, or I will send you through the portal straight back to Earth," Manny warned, his voice now a low, dangerous growl that cut through the momentary silence.

"You know, I'm genuinely not sure if a toucan of your... *delicate* nature would survive such a trip. It might be worth trying, though, just for the data," he mused. The toucan struggled to speak, a desperate, silent croak emerging from her throat.

It remained immobile.

"As a matter of fact, I would be *very* interested to see if, upon your Earthly arrival, you would be able to communicate at all. Would you speak the native language of earthly toucans? Or would no one, ever again, be able to understand you? A life of silence, an irony for a bird who doesn't shut the fuck up." Manny made a slow, deliberate circular motion with his free fingers, and the Toucan's beak clamped shut with an audible *click*. Manny had never accessed such rage before and it felt liberating.

"Let's try this again. I'm going to allow you to talk, and you are going to tell me the fastest way to find Ara and Anna. No games, no tricks, just directions." Manny briefly wondered if he possessed the power to actually make good on all these threats.

The toucan, released from the spell, dramatically coughed and wheezed, rubbing its throat with its wings as if clearing a terrible blockage.

"Beg your pardon, Keeper," she said with a hint of respect detectable in her tone. "I... I did not realize how genuinely powerful you would be here in Kala. But you need to learn to take a joke. So damn *serious*, you lot are. Now, you were asking how to find Anna and Ara. My friends tell me that they are about a two day walk from this beach. They're heading over to the town of Lega, which is situated directly on the lake. It's a fine, fine walk. *Romantic*, even." The toucan gave a quick wink. Manny knew it then, knew for a fact: she had been watching them in Havana.

"Circle to the east, around this wide bay," the Toucan instructed, mimicking the path with a circular motion of its wing. "When you see a statue of Anna positioned right on the edge of the water, turn immediately inland and follow the narrow path through the dense jungle. After a full day of steady walking, you'll see a signpost for Lega. Just... best to avoid being on that path at night, though." The Toucan flapped its beak open and closed several times, as if loosening its jaw muscles.

"Thank you, bird. I appreciate your help," Manny replied, barely moving his lips as he spoke, his eyes still narrowed in suspicion. Normally, a Keeper would never, under any circumstances, trust a Collector. But unprecedented times, times of near-fatal injury and desperation, called for trusting an eternal enemy. Manny carefully gathered Misha into his arms and turned to follow the toucan's directions. He desperately hoped, as he disappeared into the exotic foliage, that he would never, for the rest of his existence, have to lay eyes on that particular toucan again.

13

Anna sat on Aranak's porch, unable to move. Her mind conjured an idealized past: a time when her parents were alive. She skipped the confusing, sorrowful period before her mother's death. No, she craved the simplicity of her early childhood, before the sudden, brutal blow of being orphaned. Misha, bless his rational heart, would always point out the technicality: she was an adult, not *technically* an orphan. But the cold, hard fact of having no living parents was dragging in her mind. It was this deep-seated need for security that had driven her to the monotonous safety of the kiosk job: a tiny bastion of order in a vast, chaotic world.

Yet, the universe was indifferent to Anna's grief. Time travel was impossible. It certainly did not pause for her yearning for a past that was, she realized with a lurch, mostly a fragile façade. *Is anything real?* The question consumed her. She sat there, lost in her own thoughts. A bitter chuckle escaped her, though her lips didn't move. *Even goddesses have severe anxiety,* she thought.

A new sensation broke through the fog. A primal alarm

screamed in her mind. Anna shot to her feet, muscles coiled and ready, adrenaline flooding her system. She scanned the porch, the empty yard, her eyes searching for a physical threat, but found nothing. Whatever "it" was, it wasn't a visible entity. It was an ethereal vibration that resonated through every cell in her body.

"Anna, would you like some food? Or perhaps hibiscus tea? Maybe a mojito with vodka?"

Anna jumped, the sudden, cheerful voice brought her to the present. It was Aranak, his gentle face beaming with concern. *What a fool he is to believe in me,* she thought. *What kind of goddess,* she silently wondered, *was so utterly broken, so prone to crippling panic attacks?*

"No thank you," she managed. Inside, a desperate voice screamed for salvation. She could easily slurp down five mojitos, the drink would be a welcome anesthetic. To fall blissfully into a drunked stupor felt like the only remedy for her profoundly fucked up mental state. She was an imposter, a fraud. This kind man, whose children were tragically lost, either dead or possessed, had given her unconditional sanctuary. And she, in her monumental self-loathing, felt she deserved nothing.

The universe, it seemed, was playing a joke at her expense. All Anna wanted was to disappear, to dissolve into non-existence. Yet, to save this entire realm, she was tasked with the precise opposite: she had to become fully visible, to embrace her whole, terrifying, god-self. The key to that transformation was right in front of her. She had to ask Aranak for help. Asking for help to become more visible, more exposed, felt worse than traveling through a terrifying inter-dimensional portal.

She inhaled deeply before finally uttering the request.

"Could you, um, help me, by telling your friends that I

returned? It might help me get more powerful and defeat the Shadow." As she made the request, Anna's stomach clenched and burned. She squeezed her eyes shut for a moment, waiting for the nauseating sensation to pass. It lingered before slowly abating.

"Of course, Goddess," Aranak said with a beaming smile, as if she had asked him for nothing more than the time. He turned and disappeared back inside the house. *Why?* Was it her ingrained, Soviet cynicism, or simply her own debilitating anxiety, that compelled her to question his motives, to search for the angle? Would his devotion, his profound worship, vanish the moment his children returned alive and whole? What would happen to her if she became obsolete on Kala? Wasn't that the very foundation of organized religion? A relentless, transactional system of quid pro quo? Anna's mind spun again.

"Anna," Ara's voice sliced through her thoughts, causing Anna to jump.

"There is something else that you should know. The book of your life, the one with the sacred text for dismantling the Shadow, the popular, widely circulated version, is not the original. Nobody, not even I, knows where the original version is located. It is imperative that we find it for the sake of Kala and your ties to other realms."

Other realms. Was she talking about Earth? The very thought was absurd. Earth had nothing to do with this cosmic battle. At least, none of the ordinary earthlings Anna knew. If Ara truly cared about Kala's survival, why was she still hoarding vital pieces of information? And if she was so omnipotent, why didn't she just fix everything herself? Anna had finally reached her breaking point with this evasive infuriating bitch.

"How," Anna spat, her voice laced with venom and a raw,

dangerous frustration, "is it that a truly immortal beyond-deity being doesn't know how to kill the Shadow? If you were truly powerful, you should know exactly how this all ends, or at least how we can destroy it. What the fuck is your endgame, Ara? These people are desperate, terrified!"

Ara opened her mouth, her gaze momentarily blank, then slowly closed it. She opened it again, as if to speak, and then, with an audible click, closed it once more. For the first time since Anna had met her, Ara's usual smug, self-satisfied expression was gone. In its place was a look Anna couldn't immediately identify. Guilt? Shame?

Ara gave a sudden, sharp shake, as if fluffing non-existent feathers, and then spoke, her voice lower, more dangerous. "My omnipotence can wax and wane depending on the circumstances. I can know what I have yet to learn and forget anything that I will ever know. Maybe you are not ready for this." Ara's eyes flashed, a brief, startling darkness. "You are not as strong as you should be. I overestimated your abilities. After all, your mother abandoned you and never taught you who you truly were," she finished, the deliberate cruelty of her words piercing Anna's heart.

Anna was simultaneously furious and grateful. This manipulative bitch had finally shown her true cards. Anna might be a goddess, but she was also fundamentally Russian, taught from childhood to mask her vulnerabilities. Her face, a mask of stone, rarely betrayed her emotions, especially when facing powerful authority figures. Elena's long-ago warning about Ara, a memory from what felt like eons ago, still echoed sharply in her mind. She would forever be cautious, calculating with Ara. A dark, exhilarating truth settled in Anna's core: she knew she could push Ara to the very brink of existence. And yet, it was impulse, a failure of self-control among other volatile traits, that had caused her exile to Cuba in the first place.

"Ok," she said, the single word devoid of any traceable emotion. "I will go on this quest with you. I can't stay at this house all day feeling sorry for myself. I need to help this nice man at the very least." The decision was made. A drink and some food would, in fact, be an excellent idea to fortify herself for the journey ahead.

"Aranak!" she yelled, her voice ringing out, her gaze locked squarely on Ara's eyes as she spoke, a small act of defiance.

"Aranak! Could you please make me a mojito and vodka for now and hibiscus tea, black beans and rice for the road? We have a journey ahead."

Aranak and a new person's head popped out of the back door, two sets of wide, surprised eyes. "Of course! And please, meet my neighbor Xebi. She'll help." By this point, Aranak was clearly a little drunk, pulling his neighbor into full view with a sloppy, uncoordinated gesture. Xebi's jaw dropped, her face a mixture of awe and terror. Anna felt Xebi's reverence and fear wash over her, an elixir that revived her tired body.

"Um, hi... Xebi. Am I saying that right? Not sure if Aranak told you, but I am reacquainting myself with Kala after a very long absence. Please do not be terrified of me. Thank you so much for making me food for my journey," Anna said, taking Xebi's hands in hers, a gesture of unexpected human warmth. Xebi's mouth slowly closed into a soft, stunned smile. The worried line between her brows melted away as she nodded, completely mesmerized.

"Yes Anna, we all know that you have been gone for quite some time. But your return was prophesied. I just did not expect it to be in my lifetime." Xebi stated as her lips waffled between a smile and an O shape. Anna, however, felt a sense of detachment, as if she were outside of her own body, watching a play unfold. None of this felt real.

When would she finally feel like a goddess instead of a freak? At least in Havana, she knew her place. Julia had always told her she was special. Anna had always assumed every parent blindly told their child that. But in her case it was true.

"Ara, what is the book called?" Every question she had to ask made Anna feel stupid, deficient.

"The Book of Kala. It's not very dense or informative, primarily because you walked among the people for so long. They didn't have a *reason* for a detailed explanation, unlike many of the dense religious texts on Earth. But it covers the basics," Ara said matter-of-factly.

Even the layperson's copy of The Book of Kala would help her.

"Aranak or Xebi, it would please me immensely if I could borrow your copy of The Book of Kala," she announced, puffing her chest out subtly, trying to project the kind of authority she imagined a goddess should possess.

Xebi visibly trembled beneath Anna's touch. Anna held her hand tighter, a silent reassurance. "Goddess, you may have my copy. It is from my maternal lineage, from the time when you walked Kala. It is very fragile, but I trust you will care for it, as it is irreplaceable. However, I should be so lucky to have *The Book of Kala created by you*."

No pressure with that one, Anna thought dryly. She had quit ballet when her parents died, but the lessons of poise, of holding a performance posture under intense scrutiny and pressure, seemed incredibly applicable at this very moment.

If Señora Maria, her tyrannical ballet teacher, had only told her: "I am yelling at you and smacking your legs with a ruler to help you become the goddess that you are meant to be," Anna might have endured it with more patience. She made a mental note that if she ever saw Señora Maria again, she might actually thank her for being such an absolute bitch.

"Xebi, please, no. It is too special. I know what it is like to have things given to you by your mother's side. Cherish them. I'll borrow Aranak's."

"Goddess, it pleases me greatly to let you borrow my copy. It has been in my family since you previously walked Kala as well." Aranak, ever eager to serve, pulled from a drawer a beautiful, leather-bound copy of *The Book of Kala*. The embossed lettering on the front looked strikingly similar to earthly, Celtic lettering and symbols, artfully framed by macaws and iguanas designed around the perimeter. *Those smug mother fuckers were on everything,* Anna thought.

"Fine," Anna conceded. "Is there anyone who can get me a regular, more common copy the book?"

"Anna, that book has not been printed since you left for Earth. The only copies that remain are older ones," Ara informed her, then shot a sharp look at the two Kalans. "Don't worry Xebi, your copy will be fine with Anna. Now please, if you both could hurry and bring us the food and the book so we can be on our ways." Ara then leaned in, her voice dropping to a conspiratorial whisper. "You need to put protection on the rest of this village. We do not know the state of things when we return to it."

For the first time in days, Anna felt a flicker of genuine purpose. She gulped down the mojito, hoping the potent concoction would get her slightly buzzed. She licked the sugar and mint from her lips, and then, without hesitation, waved her palms back and forth in the directions of the town sprawl. Gold and fuchsia flecks shot from her hands, drizzled over every building and then disappeared. She hoped that simple gesture would suffice.

"Anna, we need to go to Lega. Many of its inhabitants fled, but its library is vast and holds ancient tomes. Some say it's enchanted with Keeper magic. The original book may be residing there," Ara informed Anna.

Lega... Lega... *how did she know Lega?* Sweat beaded on Anna's forehead as a sudden, violent wave of nausea washed over her. The warning didn't come soon enough.

Flash! A circle of solemn, robed people were gathered, hidden deep in a catacomb beneath a lakeside town. They chanted, the sounds guttural and ancient Kalarian: "Sacred daemons of the realms, protect this tome from the malefic forces, weaken the miscreants, and protect the benefics who are worthy of your power." They chanted multiple times, the repetition creating a hypnotic resonance, before lifting the heavy, marble lid of a tomb. A bearded old man, his hands trembling, motioned for the book to be placed carefully inside the tomb. It was clear from their expressions and distance that no one wanted to touch it.

When Anna came to, the present snapping back into focus, she realized she had been unconscious, or at least in a trance, long enough only for a single, full blink of her eyes. Ara had perceived a slight disturbance, her gaze sharp with immediate suspicion.

"Are you ok?"

"I'm fine. Just thinking of the quest and how it reminds me of a book that is popular in Cuba - it's called *The Hobbit*. We're going on a quest like Bilbo." The image of the ancient magician in her vision, with his beard and solemn air, had strikingly resembled her imagined version of

Gandalf. Anna wondered giddily if Gandalf was a real person, perhaps a figure from another realm. Maybe J.R.R. Tolkien was another powerful being who had simply chosen to write about his home realm for the great joy of Earthlings.

Ara snapped her fingers. A rucksack instantly appeared, materializing out of thin air. Predictably, and perfectly on brand, it was elaborately embroidered with macaws and iguanas.

"For being so mysterious, you are so incredibly predictable," Anna said, the fatigue and nerves making her voice a little more forceful and less guarded than she had intended.

"Someday you will find out just how predictable I am," Ara retorted, her response predictably cryptic.

"Was that a threat or a promise?" Anna shot back, matching Ara's intensity.

"It all depends on the results of our quest, Anna." For a millisecond, a chilling perception struck Anna: she thought she saw Ara's face briefly contort into the sharp features of a vulture.

They said their farewells to Xebi and Aranak. Anna, though she had never been this way, clearly saw the entire route in her head, as if she were staring at a detailed map laid out before her.

"We need to walk to the other side of town. People should see me," Anna commanded, no question in her voice. Ara nodded in agreement.

The small town here was strangely similar to the small towns she knew in Cuba. They walked past a series of brightly colored, low-slung cottages. Each one had its own individual flair—some boasted beautiful, thriving gardens, while others had only brown, struggling plants and patchy grass. People went about their daily chores with a slow, relaxed pace. *It must be a weekend,* she thought.

As they continued walking, Anna realized there were no cars or motos, no internal combustion engines at all. The people either walked or rode something that resembled a bicycle, yet had no pedals or motors. *Was it powered by magic?* Anna wondered, filing the curiosity away.

Anna stared at the Kalans, and they stared back, their mouths mostly agape, their eyes wide with recognition and awe. Anna's skin crawled with the amount of intense attention she received. Being seen, being recognized as the goddess, was her new normal. It made her deeply sick. Being hidden, anonymous, had been safe. Being seen was inherently dangerous.

Every few houses they passed, she felt a powerful, almost painful surge of energy.

"Should I do something goddess-like right now? Like a protection thing or what? What the fuck am I supposed to do?" Anna whispered urgently, gritting her teeth against the pressure.

"That would be advisable, yes. Maybe start protecting some of these houses and shops?"

"You could have told me that from the start!" Anna whisper-yelled through clenched teeth, furious at Ara's continued failure to communicate basic instructions.

She flicked her hand as she walked, a dismissive gesture. In her mind, she felt a ridiculous, childish need for a wand. After quickly reassuring herself that she was absolutely *not* a witch, she decided her own hands were more than enough to protect the houses and businesses. A continuous, shimmering stream of gold and fuchsia mist shot from her palms towards the structures. The act of performing the magic was surprisingly meditative. As she focused on protecting the people and their homes, her anxiety, the constant background noise of her mind, gradually quieted. By the time they reached the other end of town, over an hour later, she had a following of over one hundred people behind her. They all looked stunned, their faces radiating a mixture of awe and hope. Anna realized that her former earthling body would have been utterly exhausted by the walk, but her new body - or rather, her *old* body - had sinuous muscles and seemingly limitless levels of energy for mundane tasks like walking for over an hour. Protecting the houses was another matter; it was a little more depleting, but it was nothing she couldn't handle.

"They are your people, Anna. Say something. Don't stand there like a fool," Ara hissed, her voice low and sharp.

Anna waited, praying for inspiration. Nothing came. Her face felt hot with embarrassment. She silently prayed to herself, begging for another memory flash, for a clue. What, exactly, does a goddess say to a throng of devoted, terrified followers?

"I am not the per—eh—goddess who left. I mean, I am. But I am different."

Fuck fuck fuck. The stammering words did nothing for the crowd. Anna shot a panicked look at Ara for help. Ara cleared her throat and gave a small, barely perceptible nod of encouragement.

Anna closed her eyes for a moment to center herself, to channel the powerful energy she now possessed.

"You deserve to live in peace. You deserve to be with your family and friends. Their love is the most important thing in the world. Their love and community creates magic and miracles, as my mama would say. Only the most putrid, defiled creatures would seek absolute power and the destruction of that love. I will do whatever I can to restore your way of life."

The crowd erupted into a powerful cheer, a wave of unfiltered love and belief washing over her. Anna felt a colossal surge of power flood into her core. It felt good. It was like the rush of good sex.

She wanted more.

Ara grabbed her arm with startling force, her talon-like nails nearly piercing Anna's skin. The sudden pain and shock brought Anna crashing back to the present.

"Before you make your next move, remember why you were sent to Cuba. It happened before. It can always happen again," Ara's voice was a low, chilling warning. Her claws released their grip, leaving a faint, painful mark on Anna's skin.

Anna understood the message perfectly. It was both a threat and a warning: never let Ara know the full extent of your power, or your ambition. Full stop.

As they walked away, Anna deliberately changed the subject, forcing a return to the practical.

"Is this protection a Band-Aid? Or will it hold?" Anna asked in earnest. She thought about all the wars she had seen on Earth's news feeds. Unless the root of the problem was solved, any protection was a temporary patch.

"It depends on the unfolding. I cannot know, as too many variables are in play." Ara's gaze narrowed slightly. Her slightly downturned lips told Anna all she needed to know without a single, definitive word.

Everyone is a fucking imposter. The thought settled into Anna's mind with weary resignation. *No one knows what they're doing.* Might as well go find a library with a magical book.

14

Manny's body screamed for a break. Every muscle ached. Carrying a grown man through a portal and then on seaside jungle trek was a little more than he had been trained for. As a Keeper, he had no choice. The Keeper's lineage mandated ultimate deity protection on Earth. However, he rarely heard tales of Keepers' ventures to other realms. Was it because they died? Surely not, Manny thought as he reassured himself.

Manny felt comfortable with the challenge, but he worried about Misha. He slowly pressed on. Adoration filled Manny as he stared at the man he carried. Manny did not intend to fall in love with him. Abuela told him that it happened with other Keepers, even though the consequences could be ruinous.

Through deductive reasoning, Manny concluded that Misha must be a demigod, or he would have perished from the katana slash and the trip through the portal. What was the extent of Misha's powers? If he was not born here, on Kala, how could he increase his powers? Manny yearned for more universal knowledge. The universe answered by giving him the ultimate experiential course. Grief bubbled up from his heart. He couldn't share his knowledge with neither Elena, his father, nor his mother. Keepers thrived on sharing knowledge.

Manny stopped. A faint crackle on the forest floor vibrated his eardrums. The unmistakable sound of feet on leaves came closer. He sensed a human presence, however the vibration was off. He took pride in maintaining a steady nervous system. In this moment though, his heart rate and breathing increased.

He wondered if this was fear. He tried to slow his breathing. The animal making the sound was still out of eyesight, but too close for Manny's comfort. Manny noted the sea as a possible exit on the left, but was unsure if Misha could handle that.

Eyes. Manny used only a fraction of his abilities on earth. Manny focused on sharpening his vision. He saw people, likely non-mythans. However it was neither dead nor alive. Eyes glazed and body shuffling, it appeared lost in every sense of the word. As the being turned the corner, her eyes met Manny's eyes. Manny heard countless footsteps on the jungle floor. Three more appeared behind Dead Eyes and paused. Outnumbered, Manny only had faith in his mandate to protect Misha, and not much else Misha remained unconscious, but alive.

"Hello Kalans. I mean you no harm and come in peace," he said, hoping diplomacy would work. They did not register his words.

Their commander, dressed in black quilted cuffed jacket over a black turtleneck, glistened with sweat as she held a peculiar staff with glowing scarlet orb, stood before Manny. He had seen that orb before but could not remember where.

Before Manny could remember its origin, the

commander roared and sprinted towards the Keeper and his unconscious lover. The others followed her in perfect unison.

With no time to think, Manny started running. Slick with sweat, he flung Misha over his left shoulder, hoping he wouldn't slide off, and firmly held him under his ass. He motioned right arm down and back, summoning the power of wind.

A gust with the force of a category four hurricane wooshed towards them. They stumbled and slowed but remained undeterred. Manny continued running while thinking of his next move.

The furious Glazed Eyes and followers roared in unison. Rage reverberated through the jungle. Manny didn't know their origins, but they were clearly foes and not friends.

The commander gained on him. How was that possible? Manny outran panthers on earth. Up ahead was a cluster of large shimmery mahogany trees. Alien mahogany. Well, alien to Manny. Technically Manny was an alien on Kala. The leaves called him in a new tongue.

"Manny, come to us," they whispered. When faced with the choice of the evil dead-eyed people or talking trees, Manny chose the trees. He approached the tree, with the commander on his heels. "Climb me now!"

Hand-sized knobs emerged from the bark, perfectly shaped for Manny's grip. As he went for the next knob, Misha slipped off Manny's slick shoulder.

"NO!" Manny yelled. Suddenly a branch appeared and in one motion, it caught Misha and passed him up the tree. Other branches gently pushed Manny to the top. As the commander grabbed the knob, she immediately screamed. Manny caught a glimpse of her hand. All flesh was gone.

Only tendons and bone remained as if she dipped her hand in fire.

The commander continued screaming as her followers gathered around. Manny knew the screams were both pain and fear. What was she afraid of? Surely nothing in this jungle.

A wooden platform appeared at the top of the tree, as if it heard Manny's weary thoughts. The tree placed Misha on the platform. Manny hoisted himself up and looked back at the Kalans.

"We know you are here, aliens. You cannot escape us. No one can arrive on Kala without them knowing. No one," one of the Kalans screamed towards Manny.

The leader writhed in pain and while her followers frothed at the mouth. Manny would kill them if he had to, but he intuitively resisted. Some form of humanity remained. He wondered if he could kill them. What would Elena do?

Elena's wisdom was always the key. BBQ Hand ceded the orb to Glazed Eyes. He cast red flares towards Manny and missed. Abuela would have immobilized them.

Summoning the energy of the earth, he wove a translucent sphere out of water, stardust, and sand. Manny sent the sphere towards the mass of beings. It sucked each one inside, like a vacuum. One by one, each Kalan was immobilized and suspended mid-air with their mouths agape and their eyes dark and wide open. Manny pushed the sphere to the center of the tree cluster.

He caught his breath. His abuela rarely spoke of her time in other realms. He wished that he asked her so many more questions while she was alive. Manny closed his eyes to remember.

"Always express gratitude when warranted". Elena may have been a Keeper, but she was also an abuela.

"Thank you for your safety. What type of tree are you?" Manny was profoundly grateful and curious..

The wind whispered through the trees. "We are just like you, Manny. We are Keepers." Manny looked down at the tree pendant on his necklace. The tree was an exact replica of the ones in this grove, iridescent blue as well. His abuela and mother told him that Keepers take different forms, but the tree formation was the rarest in all of the realms.

"Do you know what these are? Will they be on our path until Lega?" He queried as he motioned to the Kalans.

"These are Kalans who succumbed to the power and promise of the Shadow, as they call it. They are partially conscious of their actions. These ones are looking for their home, but they will never find it. It is their curse to serve a master without belonging. Every Kalan is in danger of succumbing to the Shadow."

Manny had so many questions, but as he was about to ask another, Misha sputtered blood.

"Misha does not have long. Get him to Lega. Be wary. Stay on the trail and keep moving," the tree warned him in a whisper.

Manny didn't want to hear this. Bone-crushing exhaustion consumed him. He wanted nothing more than to sleep on this platform while feeling the warm protection of these Keepers. A branch gently swung towards him presenting Manny with a cluster of berries. Manny popped a berry in his mouth. The perfectly taught berries exploded in his mouth in satisfying pops. Perfectly balanced sweet and sour berry juice coated his tongue. It was unlike anything he had ever tasted. He ate the whole cluster as each berry boosted his vitality more than the last. The weariness lingered, but he was ready to continue.

"Thank you, Keepers. May I leave the Officers here? It will be better for all, I think," Manny almost hesitated to ask so much of his fellow Keepers but he knew they would work in Misha's best interest.

"Yes, that is wise," the tree whispered.

Manny scooped up Misha and gently kissed him on his forehead. The tree's branches held the lovers as they descended towards the jungle floor, one branch after the other.

"I hope to meet again, forest Keepers. It has been an honor," Manny said with utmost sincerity.

"The honor has been ours, Manny. We shall meet again. Be wise. Be wary," the tree advised.

Manny restarted the journey. The setting sun's last light dappled the sky on his left. A bright full moon illuminated their path. Full moons usually ushered in a release, according to Keeper lore.

"I'm sure it's going to release more hell upon us," he mumbled to no one. Usually unflappable, Manny took this quiet opportunity to entertain his human emotions. His biceps and shoulders screamed under Misha's limp weight. His heart remained shattered. His mind continued to chastise his decisions.

A Keeper who fulfills their purpose never fails, Manny. Steadfast and one foot in front of the other. You were born with the wisdom and power to fulfill your destiny.

Manny's heart stopped for a moment. He swiveled around, expecting to see Elena. It was her voice, loud as it ever was. Elena was a part of every tree in the universe, just like every Keeper who died before her. Did she find him so quickly?

"Message received," he said, not wanting to unleash the torrential pity party about to burst in his mind.

He walked for about an hour, hoping the effects of the berries would continue. Misha's life was no guarantee. Manny remained amazed at Misha's survival. He enjoyed the peace and quiet as he walked on the trail, noticing the different varieties of flora and fauna compared to earth. Similar tropical vegetation, but everything had a slight iridescent hue. Many of the birds and beetles looked familiar, but were slightly different. Even though he carried a deadweight, the peaceful jungle walk revitalized him. Within a second of being lulled into a false sense of tranquility, the hair stood up on his arms. He felt a presence coming. Manny instinctively pressed his back against the closest tree.

A dour old woman, about 100 meters ahead on the path, shuffled towards him. She was alone. Manny knew that her looks were deceiving. Goosebumps engulfed his body. The Keeper warning system.

Misha's body chose that moment to cough up blood. Manny felt a twinge of panic, which was a new unwelcomed sensation for him.

The woman steadily walked closer until she was within a few meters. "Oh a Keeper! Twee hee hee hee! I haven't seen you in a minute. Welcome!" She said in a sing-song voice as she bowed deeply. The way that she bowed looked familiar. He found it odd. She was tall, seemingly frail looking, yet was carrying a giant sack on her back that was filled with items that were on the verge of spilling over the edge. Some were items that he recognized from Earth, like a pair of jeans, a wall clock and a snow globe that said "Disneyland" on it with a castle on the inside. Other items must have been from other realms or planets in the multiverse. He had no idea what they were. Manny hoped she wasn't a Collector, like that damn toucan.

Given his predicament, he turned on the charm, as he did so many times in Havana to protect an oblivious Anna and Misha. The stakes were much higher here.

His face softened and his mouth turned into a smile. "Are you a sight for sore eyes. You seem to know a bit about me, but I don't know anything about you. What are you doing on this path?" She looked very familiar. Almost a beaky nose. Her squawky voice had an air of familiarity as well.

"Oh darling, wouldn't you like to know. Who's your friend? Can't tell what he is. Looks and smells a little like an earth human." Almost on cue, Misha sputtered more blood.

"My friend is quite sick. We are walking towards a town that is past Lega and I'm hoping that Lega has some sort of healer," Manny said, afraid he had revealed too much to this stranger.

"Aren't you the luckiest son of a bitch in Kala! It so happens that I am a healer of sorts. I'm a Collector. My name is Callan. I can heal almost any being," she said, raising an eyebrow, "for a price."

Fuck. Manny knew it. They could do almost anything for a trade of something personal or valuable. Elena said that they were not to be trusted, were extremely deceptive, and very powerful. And immortal. Immortal beings were the most dangerous. They had nothing to lose. Manny maintained his cool face as he thought. He had two valuable things on his person, both of which he was unwilling to trade: Misha and his Keeper necklace.

"Don't strain too hard darlin'. It's easy. You trade me something that I value and I'll heal your friend."

Manny could give her sex. It was worth a shot. He gently set Misha next to the tree.

"You know, I'm feeling a bit amorous and would..." Manny regretted it as soon as the words left his mouth.

The Collector cackled, like a bird. When she regained composure, she said "Honey, you're beautiful but I don't want your dick and I know for sure that you don't want anything that I have to offer. No no no. I can tell that you have treasures more valuable to offer me. Now what is it that I want?" She said as she swirled her finger around his face.

Manny was trying to think of an out. Anything. His duty was to protect Misha. If she chose him, that would end terribly. For whom, Manny wasn't sure as Collectors and Keepers were never known to be at peace with each other, by their very nature. He wasn't sure what would happen if he traded the pendant. Elena made him promise to keep it safe. He could not break that. He trusted Elena more than anyone in the universe, even Misha.

"I can tell that you're new at this, darling. So let me help you choose what you'll give me in exchange for his life. You got him. But I don't want him. What can I do with a halfling earth human? Pretty useless."

Manny felt some relief.

"Your pendant is mighty lovely."

"I can't give you that. I can give you our ancient language though, with one spell."

She threw her head back and laughed.

"Eimim aptqasan lyngya ta katoch. I took that from the last Keeper I met. She was in a desperate situation on Yanos. Bless her heart. But now she can't speak the ancient language, which makes her job just a bit more difficult." Her lips curled up into a terrifying smile as her eyebrows each created perfect peaks.

"If you give me the necklace, then I promise I will never bother another Keeper for as long as I walk the multiverse."

Misha's breathing grew shallow. He began convulsing in Manny's arms. Manny crouched down and set Misha on the trail, laying him on his side so that he wouldn't choke on his own blood. Manny felt helpless and panicked. He knew the Collector could sense it.

As he lay Misha on his side, the parrot's red feather fell out of his pocket. The Collector's eyes lit up. Manny knew it was a risk, to offer the feather but what else could he do? If he let Misha die, he would fail his duty and lose his lover.

"Oh ho ho, that feather! That would do. Yes, that's what I want. I know someone who needs it a few hours ago. I don't need your pendant."

"A few hours ago?" Manny asked.

"Never you mind, I'm just a kooky old lady," she squawked.

If he gave Callan the feather, she may be able to access the portal. But clearly she has been to earth, so that's not the reason that she needed it. Why would she want the feather? As he was pondering it, Misha started foaming at the mouth. Bloody foam dribbled out of his mouth. His eyes rolled back into his head.

Manny knew he had to be specific in his request or else the Collector could take liberties.

"Fine, Collector! Heal my friend, no more than that, and I will give you the feather," he said exasperatedly.

Her wide, bright eyes sparkled with glee, as if she had just won the grand prize. "It's a deal!"

As soon as she uttered those words, Manny knew that he would eventually regret the decision.

She swirled her hands above her head and spoke a language he had never heard. It sounded grotesque, like listening to a record backwards. She nearly choked on every syllable. Green light radiated from her hands and cascaded around Misha to form a dome. His body contorted and writhed in agony.

"What are you doing? Our deal was to heal him!" Manny screamed.

"Calm your pants, Keeper. His injury was something from a deity. He didn't piss off a god or goddess, did he?" she said almost rhetorically, as if she knew the answer. Manny shook his head, knowing that the less she knew, the better. As she continued to heal him, Manny grew more impatient. Blue smoke fought to stay inside Misha, but Callan was winning. When there was nothing left to pull from Misha, she raised her hands into the air, holding the orb of blue smoke. Callan cawed at an earsplitting frequency and pushed her hands to its sides. The orb exploded.

Callan waved her finger at Misha's incision. Not even a scar remained. Manny was overcome with relief. With a snap of her fingers, the red feather appeared in her hand. A brief gust of wind swirled around her. Misha's face returned to its normal color and his breathing steadied.

The Collector shoved the feather into her backpack. "Thank you for my gift. It's exactly what I needed."

Manny couldn't return the pleasantries. "What are you going to do with that feather, Collector?" His distrust hung on that last word. She was so familiar... Manny wondered if she knew the toucan from earlier.

"Hee tee. I know someone who is desperate for it. But maybe oh maybe... shall I teach a lesson to the being to whom this belongs? Shall I use it for fun and games? Extract its power for my own? So many options! I can't dilly dally all day around here though, or else she'll come for me. Ciao bello!" She blew Manny a kiss and walked down the path in the opposite direction. Manny watched until she vanished, ignoring her nonsensical word salad.

Manny could no longer maintain decorum after everything that had experienced in the past two days. He burst into tears. Crying turned into sobbing. Sobs turned into heavy weeping. He looked at Misha's face and kissed it all over. His love was alive. He was still a Keeper, upholding his duty. While Manny knew that allowing the Collector to take the feather could have grave consequences, he upheld the duty of the Keepers and kept his lover alive.

Misha stirred. His eyes fluttered open. In a dry, crackly voice he managed to utter "What happened? Where am I?" With that Manny embraced him for what seemed to be an eternity. He pulled back and told Misha the entire story, not leaving out any details, thinking that honesty would protect Misha in this situation.

"You did what? That feather was the only way I could communicate with my sister!" Misha said in an angry, raised voice.

"I had no choice. You were dying in my arms." Manny defended his actions.

"Why didn't you do your magic or whatever you do? What is your problem? How am I supposed to talk to my sister?" Misha said frantically.

"Misha please, lower your voice. Remember what I said about this path? We need to get to Lega anyways. It was on the way to your sister and the parrot, who is called Ara." Manny tried to calm him.

"Do not tell me what to do!" Misha stood up and stomped his foot, like a child as he tried to steady himself. Manny caught him and tried to suppress an eye roll. He now fully understood why Keepers and their charges should not be lovers.

"I am going to look for my sister without you," Misha insisted.

Manny's eyes grew dark and serious. "You will not find your sister without me. We do not know the extent of your powers on Kala. You have been through a lot, but now it is time to continue the journey." Manny tried to understand Misha's motives. He endured more than anyone ever should by almost dying at the hands of an evil god and had a Collector use her magic on him, but he was acting like an ungrateful child. Perhaps a little bit of that Collector's essence rubbed off on him.

Misha let out a "Humpf" and started walking towards Lega. Manny walked next to him, not saying a word, unsure of what the future would bring in this strange land.

15

Ivan left the Soviet Embassy early that day. "Adios, Marlena" he said to the receptionist. "Ciao Ivan." She winked at him and made a O shape with her bright red lips. Whilst Marlena was the epitome of sexy, the only person he ever had a longing for was Anna. He fucked quite a few women in his time, but Anna was the only one who permeated his thoughts at all hours. Ivan's mind often wandered into fantasies of making love with Anna. The thoughts felt like memories, rather than a fantasy, or, at least, the feeling of sex with Anna felt like a memory. His dick remembered it.

In his favorite fantasy, he walked to her kiosk at closing time. It was Misha's day off and there were only passersby. As she rolled down the metal slat, he wrapped his arms around her waist and whispered "Amor" in her ear. She turned around and looked deeply into his eyes. During this part of the fantasy, a blue flame flickered in her pupils. "Ivan..." she said in a husky voice. She kissed him deeply and took control of the situation, grabbing his crotch to determine how erect he was. By this point, he was extremely hard, in his fantasy and in real life. She pulled him into the kiosk, released his cock and shoved it inside of her, dripping wet with arousal. Sex took various, adventurous turns that would always end in a fiery climax.

Ivan was on autopilot. When he came to, he realized that he was almost to the kiosk and had a huge erection. He faced a building and talked himself down. It wasn't too difficult as the air smelled like rotting garbage, shit and what he imagined a corpse would smell like. No one could locate the origin of the smell. It was all anyone could talk about. No doubt governments were paranoid that America had set off some chemical weapons.

When his dick went soft, he continued his walk. Something was amiss with the kiosk, even though it wasn't in sight. Ivan could feel it. As he got closer, he could vaguely see that it was shuttered.

"That's odd," he thought out loud. Either Anna or Misha worked. His gut told him not to approach the kiosk. He turned 180 degrees towards Anna and Misha's apartment to check on them. He knew that diarrhea wasn't keeping them from their job.

"Goddammit," he muttered to no one. Vlad and Boris were walking towards him. He was protected from them at work, but they were increasingly difficult to endure regardless of his connections. As they got closer, Ivan's skin tingled. It was more than goosebumps or a shiver. He breathed deeply to suppress it. It got worse as the foul duo got closer.

"Vlad. Boris. Buenas tardes," Ivan forced a flat smile, while attempting to obscure his physical discomfort. He observed Boris' doughy body. Sweaty and red as usual, but his eyes looked weary and sunken in their sockets. Ivan could sense that Boris was silently pleading for help. Help from Vlad? Help to recover from being a sycophant?

Vlad, on the other hand, appeared furious, radiant and powerful all at once. It was a terrifying new look. For as long as Ivan knew him, he looked purposefully intimidating, even though it was a facade. Now he was truly ferocious and chilling, no facade. This mother fucker achieved his dream.

"Buenas tardes, Ivan" Vlad said through gritted teeth. "Were you on your way to the kiosk?"

"I was." This would be a Soviet battle of brevity, Ivan thought.

"Why?" Vlad intently bored into Ivan's head. Or at least he tried.

"Thirsty for a drink." Ivan thought it odd that Vlad's face turned a darker shade of maroon with every word.

"Did you see Anna?" Vlad pressed.

Ivan felt a tiny ball bounce off of his head. As he mussed his hair, nothing was there. But the bouncing continued. This was the weirdest fucking day, he thought. Maybe the Americans poisoned the water supply.

"Nope," he said with confident resolve.

"Do you know where she is?" Vlad was growing increasingly enraged. Ivan knew that this must have something to do with deportation back to the USSR, but it felt much worse than that. Boris looked like he was going to faint.

"Nope." Deflecting, Ivan decided to play nice. "Hey muchacho - you don't look so well. Why don't we go to Elena's and get some food?" Surely Ivan could extract some information.

Boris shivered. "I am not hungry."

Vlad looked like his head was going to explode. He was focusing so hard with such futility. Ivan felt truly afraid but refused to let on.

Vlad let out an otherworldly roar. Ivan, Boris and all passers-by cupped their hands over their ears. Vlad flicked his hands around him and the pedestrians continued walking on their way as if nothing happened.

"What are you?" Vlad incredulously demanded Ivan.

"I am the fucking Cultural Attache. You know who the fuck I am. I am well connected and don't you forget it, *puta*," Ivan said trying to disguise how intimidated he was with some good old fashioned posturing.

Vlad placed himself inches from Ivan's face. "You sad fucking imbecile. Stop bullshitting me. I said what, not who. Your lineage means nothing to me. I am watching you, Ivan. I know you. I don't know how, but I know you. You better hope you find out before I do," Vlad warned him.

Ivan shrugged his shoulders. Vlad and Boris sped off down the sidewalk towards the empty, locked kiosk. Ivan hustled in the other direction. His mind raced as his face burned hot and sweat profusely. Feeling the urge to cool off, figuratively and literally, he walked towards his favorite nighttime spot. It was a small, impossible-to-find bar. If one didn't know where it was, they would miss it entirely. Aside from serving the best rum mojitos and playing the weirdest music, the bartender was rumored to practice Santeria. As a result, the crowd was always weird and served up great conversation, which Ivan thoroughly enjoyed. Weirdos were shunned in Cuba. Even though it was impossible to find, it was one of the few spots in Havana where one could find revelers from everywhere in the world. Ivan always left drunk, vibrating, and enlightened. He created his best art after a few drinks at Vongara's, Vong's for short.

After passing through an empty alley with discarded liquor bottles and the heavy scent of piss, he arrived at Vong's. The sign above the rusty metal door was almost illegible. White paint peeled and cracked on the wall around the door. There were no windows on the alley side of the bar. Cigarette and cigarillo smoke billowed out as he opened the door. The ethereal sounds of a Chinese duet unemotively singing a song that Ivan recognized as Starman, by David Bowie, filled the space. As Cultural Attache/Arts and Culture Officer/whatever Ivan wanted to call himself, he could listen to any music confiscated by the Party. All music electrified him, but certain songs felt as if they gave him power.

Everyone in the tiny bar, no wider than a 1955 Chevy Bel Air, and no longer than two of the same car nose-to-nose, froze mid-action and looked at him. Ivan looked at Catalina, the bartender. She motioned him over with her finger. The duet resumed their odd song and the handful of people in the bar continued talking.

Catalina's bar was full of weird shit, to put it bluntly. Aside from the best rum selection, it had odd religious icons from all over the world, ancient religious artifacts that were probably real, and some items that did not look from this planet. Everything was clustered on shelves, not by geographic region, but by some other classification that remained a mystery to Ivan. Every season, she reorganized them. Catalina insisted that it was required to keep everyone happy. "Everyone" meant her alleged spirit friends.

Catalina, or Cat to her patrons, was Afro-Cuban. The way that she dressed convinced the average Cuban male that she dressed for them, when in fact she dressed for the Cuban women. Bespoke tight, black, and short was her style. She always donned unpolished emerald stone earrings.

Ivan approached her with his usual easy breezy smile. "Ivan, what the fuck have you been doing? I got the sense that something real bad is going down in Havana right now and I am not talking spook shit. The chatter from the other side has been particularly annoying." She flicked her head to the side, rolled her eyes at an invisible something, and looked back at Ivan, wordlessly demanding an explanation.

"I, uh, well." She caught him off guard. "To be honest, I don't know what the hell is going on." He gave her a summary of his encounter with Vlad and Boris and the missing Anna and Misha.

She slammed a shot of rum between his hands and snapped her fingers at Paulo, one of the regulars. He immediately took her place behind the bar. "Come with me. We need to talk." Trepidation and panic filled Ivan and radiated outward. He gulped the shot of liquid amber and obeyed Cat.

In all the times he had been to Vong's, he had never gone beyond the toilets. Cat made a sign with her hands, pulled the curtain back and pulled Ivan through behind her. The room was not particularly inviting. It was a small, cramped space that was just big enough for the items in it and the two humans. It had a dark brown leather couch, an ornate looking altar embossed with human skeletal symbols on it, looking like the Mexican Day of the Dead skeletons. Hundreds of tapered candles were lit, at random, in the room. Many more remained unlit. He noticed the wax didn't melt and the wicks remained white.

"It's not meant for you, it's meant for me and my spirits," she informed him as he looked at her ass. Ivan smirked. Instantaneously, something smacked him on the back of his head. He turned around to see nothing.

"Watch what you say and think in here. This is my realm, and the spirits will disrespect you if you show any disrespect towards me or them. Usually they're here for me and themselves, not you. Until now. They are so intrigued by the shit that's going down. Nothing exciting beyond politics and political revolutions happen here." Ivan nodded. Nothing was out of the realm of possibility, he thought.

"BASTA! One at a time!" Cat's "friends" were quite chatty. It was difficult to have a coherent conversation with her at times.

"Do you know what you are?" Cat asked.

"Why does everyone keep asking me this today?" He said, not trying to hide his irritation.

"It's a great day for self-discovery, Ivan. Answer me. Do you know what you are?" She demanded.

"Ok ok, delving deep here. I am a Cuban-Russian. I am an artist. I am -"

"I'm gonna stop you right there. You obviously don't know what you are. Ivan, you are not from here." Cat's deadly serious face surprised Ivan. She was always dramatic, but never serious.

"Havana? Where am I from then?" He was slightly amused and a bit alarmed.

"ONE AT A TIME!" Cat pushed both hands down like she was silencing a room full of children. Ivan noticed that all the candles were lit at this point. "You brought an audience."

"You are from... what? Where is that? Ok..." Cat's face contorted a bit. "You are from Kala? Is that right? Ok. Ivan, does that mean anything to you?"

"Nope," he said as he shook his head forcefully. Cat was fully off her rocker. Ivan received an invisible thwack on the side of his head. "Ow!"

Cat continued to listen with her eyes closed while muttering the occasional, "No...Si... puta madre... dios mio..."

"Shit, that's intense. Ivan - you are what is known as a

daemon. Do you know what that is?" She finally spoke to him.

"Those things from Greek mythology? How can I be something from Greek mythology? I'm not even Greek," he said, feeling stupid as the words came from his mouth.

"I don't know. I'm just the messenger. You're from a place called Kala and you are a daemon. Oh gross, do I need to repeat this? Ick. Heteros." She cleared her throat. "You and that Russian chick Anna, the one who runs the shitty mojito kiosk on the seafront, were lovers. But not just average lovers. Apparently you are bound to be lovers in every lifetime.Why she would want you... anyone's guess. She should be with me."

Ivan gulped the rum in his glass. Sweat beaded on his forehead. "I, uh, well." Nothing made sense except that he was bound to be Anna's lover.

"Well, have you fucked her? Are you lovers?" Cat demanded.

"No, but circumstances have made it difficult. Right now, I have no idea where she is and it feels like it is going to kill me. I must find her, Cat. How do your friends know all this?" He said as his voice cracked. He knew better than to use air quotes this time.

"Think of them like the best spies in Havana. They haven't had much excitement recently beyond the typical political spying, so they float around looking for the latest telenovela. But it's not on the radio, it's in human life."

Oddly, Ivan understood that and nodded.

"Are you fucking kidding me?" She said over her shoulder. "Please sit down. I'm not sure you'll like this next part," she motioned him towards the tiny love seat.

Ivan sat. This was the weirdest fucking day ever. He

should have just gone home with Marlena. She gave good head at least, even if there was nothing else.

"Anna is, um, a goddess. Like an actual goddess. But only on this other planet of Kala. HA! I knew it! Misha, her brother, is fellow homosexual! OOOH! Gossip is juicier. I'll welcome him in here any time with his lover Manny, the guy that works in... oh." Cat paused and sat down. She took Ivan's glass and finished the rum for him.

"What? What the fuck, Cat? This is insane bullshit!" He stood up and unconsciously scrunched the hair on either side of his head.

"SHUT UP! Sit down! There is more. A lot more. Misha is a demigod. Manny is something that I have never heard of. A Keeper. His father was a Keeper and his grandmother was a Keeper. Oh no...That's horrific." Tears welled up in Cat's eyes.

"Elena was a Keeper, but she was killed by Vlad, who apparently has some insane power. Manny and Misha escaped into some secret garden. Wow, really? Man, I didn't know those existed. Cool." Cats eyes fluttered as she spoke.

"EH HEM." Ivan glared at her. He thought that she was absolutely deranged. But she was the only person who made sense. Maybe they were deranged together.

"Anna, Manny and Misha all went to Kala via a portal in a hidden garden. That is some crazy shit right there! Ivan, the spirits may embellish because I know these putas like their drama but the meat of what they say is true. They have no reason to lie," she emphatically stated.

Ivan processed all of this information. His eternal lover, her brother and their "keeper" are on another planet. Vlad is more insanely dangerous than usual. And Ivan is a daemon from another planet. Just an average fucking day in Havana, oh la la.

"Do your friends know what a Keeper is?" Ivan asked, trying to make sense of this.

"Interesting. It's a being that protects deities when they aren't on their home planet. Apparently, earth is full of them. And they are very difficult to kill, which makes Elena's death disturbing."

Ivan sat motionless. He had no idea what to do next. Except paint. After this, he would get absolutely shitfaced and paint.

"They feel sorry for you," Cat said with compassionate eyes.

"Why? I have cool powers and I'll get to fuck a goddess," he said with a weary smile.

Ivan felt like he was being hugged by multiple people. "Are they hugging me?"

Cat nodded. "They suggest that you go home and paint. Perhaps write poetry. Stay clear of Vlad. He is a maniacal hijo de puta and probably more. A human couldn't kill a Keeper. He did. He is inhuman."

That did not reassure Ivan. He grabbed a bottle of rum from the corner of the room.

"You and your fellow Kalans are always safe in this bar. Nothing can happen to you here," she promised.

Ivan nodded and hugged Cat hard.

He had nothing else to say. He wasn't sure if he could speak. Ivan walked out the curtain.

Cat sighed. "Well I hope he does too. He is one of my best friends," she said to the air.

16

Callan thought of her newly acquired feather as she flew above the path. She grinned as much as a bird could. She landed on the banks of the lake and morphed back into her human form, rucksack and all. It was only logical since she was going to earth. She hated everything about earth. The smell. The humans. The disregard for nature.

Callan turned to the jungle and squawked to an audience of tropical birds. "My friends, I apologize for what is to come. You will survive. You always do. Protect each other." The birds squawked back wildly.

"Quit your squawkin! It is my role in the universe. I am a Collector. I have no allegiance, only favorites. Consider yourselves lucky to be among them." Callan was accustomed to this type of name calling. She tightened her rucksack, waived her hand over it to protect its contents during the portal ride and swam towards the center of the bay. She loathed water. She was a creature of the air.

She swam until she was hovering over a glowing blue orb and called out to Zaris.

"Oh it's you, Collector. Again. And so soon. Trouble follows you like the slime trail of a slug," he said to her.

"You're just a bitter glorified security guard. My role in the universe is mine alone." Callan always sounded so confident when she replied to those barbs. But they still stung an eternity later.

Callan took a deep breath to prepare herself for the trip. Multiverse travel was painful for immortal beings. It never got easier. Callan has been roaming the universe for so many eons that she lost count. She was tired of Collecting. She was tired of traveling, but given who she was, she went on. It was her duty. To collect things for a trade in services. It was never personal for Callan. The most recent Keeper was so sincere and earnest that Callan almost felt guilty for taking the feather. Almost.

Right before diving to the portal she clearly said "Havana, Cuba, Earth, the right time," and wondered where exactly she would emerge. As a Collector, she needn't rely on the same portals as deities or other mythans. Portal travel was more accurate than trans-world apparition. If she aparated, she may have ended up in Aruba, instead of Cuba. Moments later, she emerged in a stinking, filthy alley. She shook as if she were ruffling her plumage. Her cousin loved earth. What a misguided twat. Ara loved "helping" deities that fell from grace. Boo-fucking-hoo, Callan thought. Ara and that damn lizard. If she knew anything, it was that their help fucked shit up more than it did any good.

Callan started walking towards an old Spanish colonial compound. "Oy abuela, do you need help with that?" "No, darlin', no need." Callan liked looking like a grandma when she was on earth. It kept her under the radar. If people ever said anything to her, it was in the form of offers to help. If she had to speak to them, they often listened to her. Most of the time, they ignored her, which was her preference. As she continued walking along the vile street full of humans, she thought of her upcoming rejuvenation in the Amazon. It was the only place on this rock where she could be herself and truly relax.

Earth could not take much more of these humans. Gaia left a few decades ago. Callan could see why. Why stay in a place where no one worships you and everyone disrespects your entire reason for existence?

Callan realized that she arrived at the Occupiers compound early. She waited for Dalv. He was one of her least favorite deities in the multi-verse. He never understood subtlety or elegance. Dalv was all brute force all the time. No charm. No wit. Straight shootin' as the Americans say. There were nuanced ways of achieving power. Although Callan understood that living on earth could do that to someone. It was soul crushing here. But still, it was no excuse for being an asshole.

"Dalv, darlin', it's been a minute. You're lookin' a bit... stronger than the other day." Callan could smell the power emanating from him. She wondered what he did to gain so much power so quickly. As far as she knew, that doughy spud next to him was his only worshiper on this planet.

"Callan. You're looking a bit like a hag, per the usual. Do you have your end of the deal?"

Callan smiled, taking it as a compliment, brought her rucksack forward and pulled out the feather. "Yep, one feather from Ara. A ticket back to Kala."

"Good." Vlad reached forward to grab the feather and it disappeared from Callan's hand.

"Not so fast, love. Whatcha got for me? You know the rules." Callan knew that these games would infuriate him. She took joy from that. But the rules were the rules. It was impossible for a Collector to give away anything without getting something in return.

Vlad's face grew increasingly more annoyed. "Yes of course. I can give you the language of the Keepers."

"What is this, Keeper's Language Day? I've already gained that from a Keeper a few decades back. Eimim aptqasan lyngya ta katoch. How did you acquire it? Nevermind, I don't think I'd like to know." She looked at the potato standing next to him. He looked almost green at the mention of the Keeper. Poor kid. Callan could tell he did not know what he got himself into when he started worshiping Dalv.

"You see, love, the thing is that I know how much this means to you and how much it will piss off my cousin. So if I am going to piss off my cousin, I need something good in return. And I know that you have something good to give. Better than what you want to give."

Callan couldn't believe that Dalv had a look of resignation. This must be good.

"I will give you the tail of the Iguana you so revile," Vlad mumbled.

Callan's eyes widened. She knew that there was a good story behind this offer. "Darlin' Dalv, you're gonna have to tell me how you got this. I must know."

"I don't have time for this!" he roared.

"Love, if you want the feather, you'll make time," Callan replied unamused at his bullshit.

"Quite a few years ago, when I first started remembering my true identity, the iguana visited. At first, he made me think that I was crazy, but then parts of my life began to make sense. He promised that he would help me return to Kala to become the deity that I am meant to be. He showed me the book of my worshipers on Kala. The Way. Of course it was my book! Everything was right and justice was swift. If my worshipers followed The Way, they were rewarded. It guided me to the power that I have today. I gained more power with each day. Boris helped me channel that power." Boris looked positively gruesome at this point.

"Then one day, Oragan told me that he made a terrible mistake. He would no longer help me in my quest to return to Kala. You see, Callan, my power here on earth is finite. But on Kala, my power grows infinitely as you know." Great, another malignant, narcissistic deity.

"When Oragan refused to help me, well, I got angry. I took my katana to him, but that little fucker moves so fast that I only got a portion of his tale."

Callan was riveted. Ara's other half was smote by a god! Oh ho ho, this was good. And Callan could add his tail to her collection.

"Well Dalv, my boy, you got yourself a deal." As soon as she said that, the tail was in her hand and the feather was in his hand. As soon as she held the tail, she realized that it did not belong to Oragan. She was duped.

Dalv roared and then started laughing maniacally. "You stupid old fool. Did you think I would give you anything of value?"

Callan squawked an ear piercing screech that caused Dalv to shudder and nearly-dead Boris to faint. Honestly, earthlings should not worship deities not meant for them, Callan thought.

"You are a fool. It is a curse to dupe a Collector, darlin'. I hope that I am around to see when it comes full circle, love." She blew him a kiss. Dalv reached for his katana, but before he could Callan had turned into a toucan. She heard Dalv's roar echo through the streets as she took off in flight. She was non-plussed by it. He would get his. If it was one thing the Buddhists got totally right, it was Karma. Applicable to all deities, and most magical creatures, in the multi-verse.

She circled over the city. It's been awhile since she graced the only human-owned establishment in Havana that she could stomach. There was a little bar off an alley in the old town. It was difficult to find, but she always took a moment there before going to the Amazon. Callan was sure that Cat would never allow Dalv to find her bar.

Callan landed on a gutter above the alley of the bar. When she was sure no human would see her, she swooped down and morphed back into a human. Just as she grabbed the handle, the door, Navi pulled it open..

"Well, darling, this is AWK-WARD, he he he. How are you?" Callan felt a twinge of guilt seeing Navi, although her face hid it.

He looked perplexed, like he didn't recognize her. Callan realized that she was in for a treat. "Oh sugar, I'm not sure where you think you are going with that bottle, but turn around. We're going back inside." She wrapped her arm around his back and turned him towards the bar's entrance.

This time, the band played the latest multi-verse hit, Thriller, by that daemon, Michael Jackson. Navi looked resigned.

"Sorry, but my name is Ivan," he insisted.

"Sure it is sugar, saddle up next to me," Callan said as she patted the bar stool next to her.

The back curtain floated open and Cat marched out like a soldier. "Callan, I don't want anything, nor do I have anything to give you." Callan relaxed a little.

"Callan, I don't want anything, nor do I have anything to give you" Navi repeated, trepidatiously.

"Wow, hun, you learn quickly. At least I can relax for a bit. Cat - can I have one of them mojitos?" Callan requested.

"Sure thing." Cat gave her the side eye as she made the mojito.

"Make it two," Navi said and turned to Callan. "Señora, this has been the weirdest day of my life. Who are you and why are you calling me Navi?"

"Lordy, earth sure does a number on your memories, doesn't it? Navi is your real name, if it wasn't obvious. Navi. Ivan. Seems so obvious. We know each other from Kala. Had a few exciting encounters, darlin'," she said, painting on her fakest smile.

"What are you?" he asked with true curiosity.

Callan sighed. "I'm a Collector. No doubt the next question out of your cute little lips is 'what's a Collector?' Cat, care to tell him?"

"A Collector is a puta who stores her excess shit in my bar." Cat glared at Callan.

"Testy testy! Don't be so harsh. I keep your friends entertained. Speaking of, eh hem," it was difficult for Callan to ask the next question in Navi's company, "may I store another little thing of the utmost importance here?" Callan could see wisps of the spirits nodding around Cat. Cat detected true sincerity in Callan's voice for the first time ever. Spirits swirled excitedly around them. Callan made intentional eye contact.

"Sure," she said hesitantly. Callan took her rucksack off of her back and set it on her lap. She reached in with her arm shoulder deep and felt around until she found it. Her hand emerged clasping a necklace with a fiery blue pendant. Navi shivered involuntarily and gripped the bar. She quickly gave it to Cat, who asked no questions as she left for her spirits' room. Navi stopped shivering once it was out of sight.

"What little miss meant to say before I rudely interrupted her was that I collect things in exchange for something. There is a lot that I can do for other people, but they need to give me something special in return. You and Cat let me off the hook when I walked in, so I can relax." Callan knocked back her mojito.

Navi's brow furrowed as he stared at her intently. This kid needs to lighten up. "Why so glum, chum? Were you just duped by Dalv as well?"

"Dalv?" He questioned her. Callan gave him a minute. "Oh you mean Vlad. Joder. I wasn't duped, but he is being more of an asshole than usual lately. And apparently I'm hot shit in another realm," Ivan said with a smug smirk and continued. "Cat's friends told me the tale of my alleged life on Karla."

"Kala sugar, and it's not alleged. It's real. Your backstory is delightful. If you want it, I can give it to you for - "

"No. I will figure it out. I know that I'm a daemon and that Anna and I were lovers in Kala," Navi interrupted her firmly.

"Suit yourself." Callan never gave pertinent information for free. It wasn't her style. However, she had an idea as to how to get him to Kala. It might thwart her Amazon plans, but Kala was better. And potentially ruining Dalv's day was even better.

"I know you must be reeling from all the weird shit that you learned about today. How would you like to see it?" She tempted him, knowing that Navi had a weakness for beauty and the potential for inspiration.

"CALLAN, no. He isn't ready and he has nothing to offer." Cat re-emerged from the back room, emphatic. Callan saw a flurry of furious wisps swirling around

"Quiet Cat and company. I've seen what he can do in Kala. He can give me a little somethin'. I don't even want a fraction of it. I can't keep it for myself of course, so it doesn't matter." Callan put on a slight frown and looked at her nails as if she were feigning boredom.

"While we're at this negotiating phase, Cat, could you get us a couple more mojitos. They sure are tasty." Cat glared at her and reluctantly made the drinks.

"I'm not going into this blindly, lady. Why do you want to take me to Kala? What's in it for you?" Callan knew his soul. She knew that he would be a hard sell.

"Well Navi, I was just duped. I don't have anything of major value to anyone, except the Keeper's language, but that seems to be going around like a common STD. What's a collector without something really valuable to give? Plus, I'd like to have a travel buddy." Callan left out the part about Dalv possibly returning to her favorite planet and turning it to a wasteland full of mindless followers all for the sake of his power.

Cat slammed the drinks in front of them. "Callan, what about these...relics that you store here?" she said as she motioned towards the otherworldly artifacts.

"Honey, I'm not quite sure I need those right now. But I need something of value, if you recall and those aren't currently in demand. I do love you storing it here for me, especially my favorite pendant," she said with a wink and smile.

"It seems too easy. What's the rub? Why do you really want my powers and or presence?" He said, not giving in.

Navi's questioning always irritated her. She should have appeared like a common hooker. Then he would do whatever she asked. Her eyes narrowed and her voice dropped an octave.

"It's better if I show, instead of tell. Your earthly brain won't comprehend it. Kala's beauty is unfathomable, especially the people. They serve as the inspiration for all the best artists on earth," Callan said knowing that the last one was a major stretch. It was a tiny bit true, not technically a lie, so her cousin wouldn't kill her for it.

"Ivan, do not enter into this lightly. You do not realize what this involves," Cat warned in a stern voice. Her hair swirled around her head as the whisps frantically chattered.

"Come with us," Navi said innocently, pleading with Cat.

"I can't. Humans don't survive multiverse travel," she said firmly.

"Now that is not entirely true, but yeah, it's mostly true. I've seen a couple of regular humans and humanoids survive. The end wasn't pretty though. Skin peeled off. Some bones were crushed. They were begging to be put out of their misery" Callan said nonchalantly.

"Ok enough! Cat, stay here and have your friends keep you safe from...well, whatever the hell is happening," Navi said.

Cat rolled her eyes. "Thanks for the clarification. I'm not sure what I would do if you didn't explain that."

"Callan, I'm coming with you. I need to take care of a few things first, like a good cover story." Navi looked like a dumb doe eyed boy at that moment. Bless his heart, Callan thought.

"Uh huh. That's a good idea. Tell them that you are following Che's Motorcycle Diaries. Believable. Buys a lot of time. Inspirational. Blah blah blah," Cat said, giving him the perfect cover.

"You're good, Cat. Sometimes I wish that you weren't human or else we could strike up something fun," she winked at Cat and turned to Navi. "Sweetie, meet me out front Vong's this time tomorrow. We'll need to get something to get you to Kala."

"Christ, not another deal. What more could you need or want? We haven't even agreed on our terms."

Callan threw her head back and laughed and started walking towards the door. "Oh ho no. It's to get you to Kala. I can't make a deal with this being. You'll need to get it. I'm gonna recharge just outside of the city. See you tomorrow."

Callan stepped into the alley and jumped into toucan form. She ached to get away from the humans. She flew, as the toucan flies - never as the crow flies, she didn't like them very much as they always worked for Morgana - to Pico Turquino to find a glorious tree with plenty of her brethren. Callan nestled into an abandoned branch. She thought about the upcoming excitement and let out a croak. It's been awhile since there was a threat of worldly destruction and she would be there to witness the drama. Grab the popcorn, as the Americans said. She drifted off to slumberland.

———————————

Ivan couldn't believe his parents bought the story. Not only did they believe it, but they were also genuinely excited for him. Before he retired to his room, he hugged them as if he never were going to see them again.

"Ivy, what's wrong? A mother always knows when something is wrong."

"Nothing, of course. A bit of nerves over traveling Che's route, otherwise it's no big deal." Ivan felt a breeze rustle his hair in the otherwise stagnant and hot room. Cat's friends were around.

"You'll be fine. You always are, son. I have a big day tomorrow. Vlad has a list of Russian artists whom he wants to deport and I need to provide rationale for them to stay," his mother said earnestly.

Ivan neglected to tell his parents that Vlad wasn't going to be at work tomorrow either.

He spent his last night painting. Ivan took the paint brush to the canvas. Inspiration took over. A trance-like state took over his body. When he came to, he looked upon the blue phoenix on the canvas. It was awe-inspiring. And a bit terrifying. Her talons held bones whilst its beak was as sharp as a sickle and the eyes conveyed a deep sorrow.

He intended to visit his studio tomorrow to bid farewell to his art work and collection. The allure of being a non-human powerful being on another planet was too much, even if it had the potential for being a bullshit scam. Surprisingly, Ivan had no hesitations about the trip itself, only about his travel companion. He knew Callan would be trouble.

17

Anna found the silence on the trail to Lega unnerving. Not a single traveler had crossed their path, making the journey feel strangely isolated. Ara, waffling between her human and bird form, offered nothing unless prompted, her presence a silent, winged enigma.

"So, how many people live on Kala?" Anna asked, breaking the oppressive silence with a question she didn't truly care about. Small talk, whether on Earth or this strange, new-old world, always felt like a necessary but painful formality.

"Very small compared to your Earth. Only 100 million people in total," Ara replied, her voice flat, the number delivered with the detached air of someone reciting a dry statistic.

"And how many countries are there?" Anna continued, trying to piece together a map of this planet she was meant to save.

"Expanses, not countries. There are 20. Not evenly

populated or resourced, just like on Earth." Ara's boredom was palpable, etched into the toneless delivery of the fact.

"Why are there no people on this path, then?" This question, at least, was genuine. The stillness was beginning to feel less like peaceful nature and more like an ominous vacuum.

"Everyone is afraid of the Shadow. No one wants to travel for fear of recruitment or worse," Ara explained. The 'worse' hung in the air, a dark, unspoken promise of true horror.

Anna sighed. "What jobs do people have here?"

"Similar to those on Earth," Ara repeated flatly, her patience wearing thin.

In a momentary pique of exasperation, Anna threw out a ridiculous question. "What's your favorite color, Ara?"

Ara's beak twitched, a gesture that might have been a wry smile. "You can't see it and certainly couldn't understand the word if I told you."

"Why are you doing any of this?" Anna finally asked the question that had been burning in her mind since their journey began. This was the true core of her curiosity.

Ara paused. She opened her mouth as if to unleash a torrent of cosmic truth, then closed it, the moment of potential revelation gone. She finally said, matter-of-factly, "Because I have to."

Anna's temper, already frayed by days of evasive conversation, snapped. "Of fucking course! Why are you so goddamn vague all the time?" Her face grew hot, the familiar internal combustion of her rage igniting. She chewed furiously on the inside of her cheek. A low, internal vibration emerged from her core, a seismic warning. For the first time, Ara looked genuinely anxious, her composure momentarily slipping.

"Now Anna, please. You are only privy to two planets in the multiverse. You cannot comprehend the reason," Ara stated with a renewed, if slightly strained, air of authority.

"Try me," Anna challenged her, leaning forward, daring the bird-being to expose the grand cosmic scheme.

"Maybe someday I will show you, but not now," Ara deflected, looking away towards the dense jungle canopy.

Anna fumed, the silent rage a heavy, humming presence between them as they continued walking. Two days in the company of Ara, felt like an unbearable eternity.

"Can you fly us there? Surely there is a faster way for the two of us."

"For reasons that I do not know, my powers are waning. You may eventually regain the power of flight," Ara said, looking down at her taloned feet, a hint of genuine shame in her posture. She quickly recovered her pragmatism. "But as I said, best not to attract attention."

They walked in silence for hours, the only sound the chirping and clicking of unseen jungle insects. The familiar, humid smell of the earthy jungle began to soothe Anna. Nature had always been her balm; she allowed herself a flicker of hope that she might know peace again. The slight smile returned to her face.

Of course, all good things must come to an end. Anna froze mid-step. Electrical pulses, faint but unmistakable, darted around her scalp and hands. The ground beneath her feet began to faintly vibrate.

"What is it, Anna?" Ara's voice lowered to nearly a whisper.

"Someone or something is coming," Anna whispered, the electricity a growing current in her blood.

A little girl appeared from around the bend. She couldn't have been more than six years old. Her eyes were wide with a terror that seemed too deep for her age, and she hugged herself tightly, walking towards them with cautious, uncertain steps.

"Hello. What's your name?" Anna asked, the suspicion in her voice making the question sharper, more curt than she intended.

The girl remained silent, her gaze darting between Anna and Ara. Anna realized that seeing a deity and a macaw might terrify a child. She tried a different approach.

"Do you know who I am?" She asked.

The girl nodded slowly.

Anna crouched down, forcing her gaze to meet the child's at eye level, and offered a soft, practiced smile. "Who am I?"

"You are Anna, worshipped by many on Kala." The answer struck Anna like a physical blow. Beside her, Ara adopted her usual smug expression.

Anna wasn't accustomed to dealing with children. She probed further: "Do you worship me?"

"No, my family worships another. One who stayed." The little girl's voice held a strange, almost adult attitude, a nascent bitterness. "She is in suspension. She tried to fight the Shadow and lost." The little girl barely held back tears, the reservoirs of grief nearly spilling over her lids.

For a split second, Anna's divine pride flared, thinking about leaving the girl for blaspheming her. But rationality, and her earth-trained sense of duty, took over. She knew her banishment was not her choice, and such matters were trivial to a child whose family was in danger. Blasphemy, after all, was merely a matter of perception.

Anna maintained composure. "What's your name, *diavushka*?" she asked, using the Russian term of endearment.

"Orlana," she replied.

"Well Orlana, we can help you," Anna said, offering the reassurance the child so desperately needed, even though she wasn't entirely sure it was true.

"I do not trust the one who brought the Shadow to Kala. You are the reason." Orlana's words, delivered with a child's brutal honesty, felt like a deep, unexpected wound. Anna felt the blood draining from her face. Her mind raced, processing the accusation. She chewed on her cheek. For all Anna knew, the rumor could be entirely false, a propaganda tool.

Her human instincts took over. She did what any other Russian would have done: lament life with her and offer her some food.

"Yes, Kala has gone to shit. Now then, Orlana, would you like something to eat?" Anna began to rifle through her rucksack for their meagre provisions.

The little girl's face brightened with a hunger that was quickly overshadowed by skepticism. "What are you feeding me? Will it turn me?"

"Turn you? Fuck no. It will feed you. Are you hungry or not?" Anna said, frustrated, thrusting the container of food toward the girl's face. Ara subtly dug a warning thumb into Anna's back.

The girl shrugged, took the container, and gingerly took one bite, only to promptly spit it out. "What is this gruel?"

Anna's cheeks burned with indignation. Small electrical currents began to dart from her core, fueled by her anger at the child's ingratitude in a time of desperation. She could never imagine refusing food.

Orlana, despite her complaint, took another, slightly larger bite. "I suppose it's okay." Then, as if a switch had flipped, she inhaled the rest of the food. Anna's anger and the electrical currents subsided. The girl was clearly starving. Orlana swallowed without chewing, nearly choking a few times in her haste.

“Slow down! You’ll make yourself sick,” Anna warned, alarmed by the speed at which her inner energy had built up. She breathed deeply, examining her hands, which were faintly electrified, the only way to calm the strange power. A few feet ahead, Ara, elegantly perched on a boulder, called them over.

“We can take a break. Come. Have a seat and rest while you eat,” Ara said, patting the smooth stone surface.

Orlana continued to eat and talk, a bit of color returning to her face. The poor child probably hadn't eaten in days.

“Do oo ave wa’er?” she slurred with a mouth full of food, bits of rice falling down her chin.

“Here, little one, have some hibiscus tea,” Ara said, handing over a canister, barely concealing her disgust at Orlana’s table manners.

“Are you sure we don’t want to give her the other drink? It might make her more enjoyable to be around,” Anna said, unsure if she was being serious or just deeply sarcastic. Ara simply shook her head, also unsure of Anna's intent.

Once Orlana was satiated, her mood lifted slightly.

“Orlana, are you from Idaz?” Ara asked, a question that was clearly rhetorical, as if Ara already knew everything. Anna had never seen Ara show such a gentle demeanor. Perhaps she had a soft spot for children. Anna decided to let Ara lead the conversation, as she was currently public enemy number one in the girl's eyes.

“I am. The best expanse in all of Kala,” she said, shooting a defiant glare at Anna. Children had an uncanny way of speaking uncomfortable truths to power. It had amused Anna when she was powerless, but now, with even a sliver of power, each truth felt like a personal attack.

Deep breathing again. Anna reminded herself of the vast power distance between herself and the small child.

Ara gently placed a hand on Orlana's shoulder. Orlana immediately relaxed further and managed a faint smile.

"Go on. Tell us a bit about yourself," Anna cleared her throat as she spoke, hoping to mask any residual ill-will towards the child.

"I am a dancer! I love to dance." Even that got a small, genuine smile out of Anna. She almost chimed in that she was a dancer too, but thought better of it.

"How wonderful! Would you like to show us a bit of it?" Ara looked truly joyful, a state Anna had not witnessed before.

Orlana hopped off the boulder, started to sway with an easy grace, and then stopped abruptly. "I don't want to show *HER* anything," she declared, shooting a look of intense disapproval at Anna.

Anna did not want to purposefully or accidentally smite a young girl. "Orlana, could you please tell me why you are so angry with me?"

Orlana clearly thought about it. Ara wrapped an arm around her small shoulders in comfort.

"Isn't it obvious? You brought the Shadow to Kala." Orlana spoke with absolute, angry conviction, her hands balled into tiny fists. She truly believed this profound lie.

"How is that possible? I've been on Earth for two decades," Anna said, truly perplexed. How could people believe such slanderous lies and rumors? It was completely false.

"My mama told me that you went missing when the other deities needed you. At the beginning. Before the planet fell into despair. You and your sister are the two most powerful ones on Kala who could be on our side. Our Idazi deities are peaceful, but do not have your destructive force. You failed to defend us." Orlana's eyes, fierce and accusatory, bored into Anna's soul.

She has some serious cojones, Anna thought, continuing the deep belly breathing to temper her internal power. She questioned the validity of the little girl's statement. *Destructive nature?* Ara looked at Anna with her usual, infuriating smug face.

"My mama said that you abandoned your followers as the first inkling of the Shadow crawled out," Orlana pressed.

"I was exiled, but go on," Anna huffed, her power dangerously close to bubbling over.

Before Orlana could utter another word, Ara clapped a quick hand over the girl's mouth. Anna heard it too: a low, resonant growl and the distinct crackle of sticks snapping on the forest floor. Tears started forming in Orlana's eyes, which were now wide with pure, instinctual fear. Her small body began to shake uncontrollably. Anna saw what she saw.

A tiger, the size of a pick-up truck, emerged from the forest's gloom. The moon, now visible through a break in the canopy, shone brightly on its magnificent and terrifying silhouette. It was unlike any tiger Anna had ever seen in books or zoos. Its fur was a mosaic of grey, white, and black stripes. Its eyes were horrifying: glowing orange where the whites should be, with pinpoint black dots for pupils. Blood coated its enormous mouth and paws.

Out of pure, primal instinct, Anna wrapped her arms tightly around both Ara and Orlana and pressed her back against a nearby blue-hued tree. In an instant, the three travelers were absorbed into the tree's trunk. Anna's eyes darted to her feet, which had morphed into wooden roots anchoring her to the ground. Her mind was hers, but her body had become the tree itself.

The tiger roared, a sound that shook the leaves. "I smell you," it taunted through a low growl. "I smell your fear, little girl. Do you smell the blood of your family on my paws?"

Anna held Orlana tightly against her bark-laden form. The child's tears dripped onto Anna's hands. Anna suspected, or perhaps knew, that only she could understand the tiger's language. Orlana simply heard a deafening, terrifying roar.

"Pity I couldn't have you as well," the tiger said, sounding bored now as it began to pace in a tight circle around the tree. Suddenly, the tiger sniffed the air frantically, its pupils widening. "Oooh, a familiar smell indeed. It would seem as though the prodigal daughter has returned! I know some people who would love to have this information." It let out a haughty, booming laugh that echoed through the woods.

"Welcome back, Anna. It's been a while." The tiger sat down, its massive body settling comfortably as it waited and licked its paws like a common house cat.

A bloodthirsty tiger spoke to Anna, and Anna was a tree. She was paralyzed, not knowing what to do. Ara was motionless beside her. Orlana was utterly terrified, shaking against her.

As Anna spoke, the sound emerged as rustling leaves, the tree speaking to its temporary occupants. "Anna, as much as I revile you, the other two are welcome in my tree. Gavin, the tiger, has a renewed blood lust for Kalans. You and Ara are safe, but Orlana is not." *Wonderful*, Anna thought. *A tree is disappointed in her as well.*

"Come off it, tree, I know you are speaking!" Gavin

roared, lunging slightly. The three passengers inside the trunk shook violently. "I am not afraid to take a bite out of your bark." Anna detected a thin layer of apprehension in his voice; perhaps even a magical tiger wasn't entirely keen on eating ancient, enchanted wood.

Gavin crouched into an attack position, bloody claws outstretched. Before Anna could react, he leapt onto the tree and dug his claws deep into the trunk. The tree screamed—a long, agonizing, rustling shriek—and instantly expelled the three travelers from its trunk. Gavin gave out a pained howl and dropped to the ground. His paws looked like raw meat, having been severely burned by the tree's magical bark.

Anna grabbed Ara and Orlana by the wrists. The tiger, recovering instantly, leapt toward them, emitting an ear-splitting roar. Without a conscious thought, Anna raised both of her palms, the electrical currents fully charged, and pushed them forward. Gavin rose into the air as if lifted by an invisible wave, slammed into a normal, non-magical tree trunk, and dropped to the ground, knocked out cold.

Orlana, traumatized, clung to Anna and would not let go. Anna felt an awkward but fierce surge of protectiveness, holding the child tightly against her chest.

"Anna, we need to move now. He won't stay asleep for long. Once he tells whomever he needs to tell, I'm sure our lives will get much more difficult," Ara warned, her voice strained.

Anna nodded, still slightly in shock but entirely aware of the urgency. "Uh, thank you, tree." The blue tree's branches blew gently, as if waving them off.

As they continued walking in silence, Orlana finally fell asleep in Anna's arms, her small, frightened face buried against Anna's shoulder. Anna looked down at the child and finally understood the source of her anger. She saw a reflection of her own youthful frustration and defiance in the girl and vowed, silently and fiercely, that she would protect her no matter the cost.

"Talking tigers. Right. Okey dokey," Anna muttered to the empty air, trying to process the latest bizarre reality.

"They only talk to deities and other magical creatures. Orlana had no idea what he was saying," Ara stated, her tone back to its usual flat matter-of-factness.

Anna was profoundly relieved. It would be a daunting burden for a child to know a creature was specifically hunting her to finish off her family.

She looked at Ara to see a face filled with renewed resolve, then looked ahead into the dark, foreboding jungle, and continued to trudge forward on the narrow path to Lega.

18

When Ivan first encountered Callan, the sight of the gold machete in her hand was jarring. It wasn't the sort of accessory one expected on an *abuela* wandering the streets of Havana.

"Hey Sugar! This is one of the most useful items in my collection," she chirped, her eyes bright with enthusiasm as she held the gilded blade. With a disconcerting lack of self-awareness, Callan began to engage in an elaborate, silent sword fight, her movements surprisingly agile for a woman of her apparent age.

Ivan instinctively bobbed and weaved out of the way, a flicker of genuine alarm crossing his face. "So why did you ask me to meet you at Anna's? Cut to the chase, please." He was tired and her bizarre theatrics were wearing on him.

"Here's the skinny. Dalv fucked me over. Royally. And you simply *do not* fuck over a Collector and expect to walk away unscathed. Ever. I know for a fact he plans to slip back into Kala. I want him to get what's coming to him, and what's more, I want a front-row seat to the reckoning." Callan's voice, which had been light, dropped to a hard, cold register, the smile vanishing as abruptly. She stopped mid-sentence, her focus shifting inward.

"And Anna's place... it's a portal?" Ivan guessed, trying to connect the disparate pieces of the puzzle she had thrown at him.

"Oh Sugar, you are cute, painfully so, but you really don't know shit about how this works. The purpose of this whole endeavor is twofold. Firstly, I can't personally use the items in my collection," she said, motioning dismissively to the gold machete. "They were made for others. Secondly, and more importantly, our friends on Kala can't effectively make Dalv's life the hell he deserves without *you* as the conduit." She leaned in conspiratorially, her eyes gleaming.

"Plus...nothing," she trailed off, her thought process seemingly interrupted by some private, inner dialogue.

"Querido, I know my attention span is criminally short when dealing with people like you," Ivan said, his tone thick with saccharine sweetness, a desperate attempt to rein in his mounting frustration, "but for the love of all that is holy, tell me exactly what the machete is for?"

"Why to chop off the Iguana's tail, of course," Callan declared with absolute, unblinking sincerity.

Of course, Ivan thought with a surge of deep skepticism. *Chopping off an iguana's tail.* He felt a familiar dread of worry that he had been dragged into some ridiculously elaborate hoax.

"You need his tail to access and stabilize where the portal is hidden, and I'm merely tagging along for the pure thrill of it all." She then reached deep into the pocket of her faded cotton skirt and pulled out a large, heavy silver ring, jangling with hundreds of antique, strangely shaped keys. After a moment of rapid consideration, she selected a small, brass one to unlock the building's heavy wooden door.

"Wait, the *tías* in these buildings are nosey as hell! They all know me. They're going to wonder why I'm breaking into Anna's apartment with a strange, elderly woman they've never seen before." He knew the Cuban neighborly code intimately: they looked out for each other, yes, but they also lived for exciting, new gossip to be shared at the next boisterous domino or card game.

Callan let out a booming laugh that seemed too loud for her frame. "Hun, I know more about these old biddies and their scandalous secrets than you will ever know. They can't hear us right now. Trust me on this." She punctuated her statement with a quick, conspiratorial wink.

Once safely inside the dim hallway, they made their way up the worn marble stairs to the third floor. Despite the danger and the bizarre company, a nervous energy buzzed through Ivan. He was finally going to see Anna's apartment, a place he had idolized from afar, though he had always fantasized the circumstances would be far less morbid. They slipped into the tiny, sparsely furnished one-bedroom flat. It was neat, surprisingly tidy, clearly kept by someone meticulous. One of them, Misha or Anna, definitely slept on the living room couch while the other took the actual bedroom.

"Are you ready to snoop around, Sugar? We must find a cassette tape player and a specific, coded tape. At least, that's what I've been told by my myriad of little birds around town," Callan whispered, motioning toward the closed bedroom door with her chin.

Given the almost minimalist, sparse nature of the flat's furnishings, Ivan didn't imagine the search would take them very long.

Fifteen frustrating minutes later, they had located an

old, but functioning, cassette tape player, but the vital tape remained elusive.

"Well, shoot-fire-dang-on-my-matches, darling. Where in the nine hells do you think this tape could possibly be hidden?" Callan asked, exasperation creeping into her tone.

Ivan pointed slowly toward the small, dusty bookcase nestled against the far wall. "It's worth a try," he muttered, more to himself than to her.

"It's an open, established secret that most people in both Cuba and the USSR who are involved in... sensitive matters... have hollowed-out books," Ivan informed Callan, his expertise momentarily overriding his caution, "for storing a whole variety of clandestine things."

He quickly scanned the worn spines. His fingers stopped on a thick, well-loved Russian copy of *Anna Karenina*. As he pulled it off the shelf, the perfect rectangle of a cassette tape slid out from the expertly cut hollow.

"You aren't quite as dumb as you sometimes act, Navi. Now, let's get this show on the road, sweet thing." Callan opened the window next to the small, rickety kitchen table, letting in the humid air. "We gotta be quick now. I don't know if Dalv is still loitering around here, or if he's already slipped back to Kala, but best to make haste either way." Callan handed the gold machete to Ivan. The moment his fingers wrapped around the leather-bound hilt, the metal quivered violently in his hand, immediately reacting to his touch. A raw, humming surge of unfamiliar power shot up his arm and flooded his entire body.

"Wow!" His eyes widened with a mixture of terror and delight at the intense, visceral reaction the object had to him.

"Don't get too sexy with that, now! You aren't trading me anything for it. It's mine, understood? Now, when Oragan, the Iguana, comes to the window, you need to hack off his tail. Swiftly. But don't go too far up the base. If you truly injure him, he'll get absolutely furious with you. And trust me, you do not want that." Her warning was sufficient for Ivan.

"Okay." Ivan said, the word barely a breath. He faked the confidence he definitely did not possess. He had never "hacked" anything before in his sheltered, privileged life as the son of powerful, well-connected government workers. He stood poised, ready, the powerful machete still humming slightly in his grasp, still unsure what the music she mentioned had to do with a talking iguana.

"Hold on. This part might make you feel momentarily ill." Callan quickly slotted the cassette into the player and slammed the 'play' button. A song immediately started, and on cue, a sudden, violent wave of nausea washed over Ivan. "Hide that!" she hissed at him, gesturing to the weapon. Ivan quickly obscured the glowing machete behind his back.

It was Michael Jackson's *Thriller*, of all things, playing at full volume. While the sound quality was jarringly clear, Ivan was on the verge of vomiting. To his utter shock and mounting disbelief, a massive, jade-green iguana with startlingly intelligent black eyes appeared perched on the window sill.

"Shit, Callan. To what exactly do I owe the honor of this visit, you bird-brained half-wit?" the Iguana rasped, his voice a dry and gravelly sound. Callan immediately stopped the music. Ivan cursed silently; he couldn't get a clear, clean strike on the creature's tail at this current angle. He simply marveled, momentarily frozen, at the sight of the articulate, oversized reptile sitting in front of him.

"Oragan. It's been a while, but honestly, it hasn't been nearly long enough," Callan retorted, a venomous edge in her voice that told Ivan she harbored a deep and enduring hatred for this iguana. "Why don't you give us the skinny on your buddy? You know, that evil asshole Dalv who's systematically ruining shit for everyone?" Callan said, carefully shifting her weight and moving subtly to the side of the window, meticulously hoping Oragan would adjust his position and bring his tail into clear striking distance.

"Now, now, Callan. How about a proper introduction first? This one looks distinctly familiar," Oragan said, his black eyes fixed on Ivan. Oragan knew exactly who he was speaking to.

"It's Navi, you shit-for-brains. You know that."

"Of course! You've grown up nicely, haven't you?" Oragan said, his gaze running Ivan up and down in a slow, appraising, and deeply creepy manner. Ivan scowled openly at the reptile, feeling thoroughly violated.

"Well, Callan, I won't lie. There is some truly serious shit going down on Kala. We have a solid idea as to who is behind it, but Ara and I thought it was prudent to bring all the other exiled deities back into the fold. Especially Anna, given that the few worshippers she had left were praying with such fervent desperation. We genuinely felt sorry for them. We knew the whole affair was going to be a bit tricky to pull off, but necessary." The iguana then performed a slow, unsettling lick of his own eyeball.

"Well, you condescending asshole, all my friends on Kala are in a complete twitter over this 'Shadow thing.' You and I both know that entire planets can go extinct, and Kala happens to be one of my sentimental favorites. I truly hope that your little intervention plan actually works." Just as she finished speaking, Callan leaned hard against the wall in a manner that subtly forced Oragan to perch perfectly parallel to the window sill. With a swift *swoosh*, Ivan brought the gold blade down hard on the Iguana's tail, striking a little higher up the base than he had originally intended.

"FUCK! God dammit! Ara loses a feather for this portal bullshit, and I have to lose a goddamn tail every single time!" Oragan yelped, grabbing the severed stump of his tail as Callan, with a minute flex of her hand, magically summoned the gold machete back to her before Ivan could attempt to hand it over.

"Awww, now you're suddenly a little more tolerable than you were a second ago. Why are you still here, you foul reptile? Why haven't you gone back with Ara to do your typical weird, mysterious deity thing?" As the two bickered, Ivan did his best to ignore the thick, twitching iguana tail now sitting, rapidly changing colors from jade to copper to blue, in his hand.

"I truly hate telling you this, of all infuriating creatures, but, I... uh, I can't get back. My powers are a bit on the fritz, shall we say, and I'm not entirely sure why. I'm sort of stuck here for the time being." He darted his eyes everywhere in the room except at Callan and Ivan. Ivan felt a pang of surprise; the all-powerful, immortal iguana actually looked profoundly embarrassed.

Callan threw her head back and laughed uproariously, a sound of genuine, unadulterated pleasure. "Well sugar, I'll be absolutely sure to tell Ara when I see her on Kala." She reached out and gave a quick, condescending pat on his scaly head. Callan then turned sharply toward the door and motioned emphatically for Ivan to follow her.

"Wait! I'm just as deeply invested in this whole mess as you two are," Oragan insisted, his voice regaining some of its old authority. He looked straight at Ivan. "I have a piece of crucial advice for you: Navi, take care of your mind, your heart, and, critically, your libido in Kala. That is the one and only way that you can be of true service to Anna. She will need you to be completely whole, and you must be there for her, grounded and stable, if you want the planet to survive this. Your reputation there is similar to here, except on an exponentially magical scale." It sounded less like advice and more like a dire warning, but Ivan, with his inherent arrogance, interpreted it as a grudging compliment.

"I think I can handle myself," Ivan smirked, puffing out his chest slightly. After all, he had a fantastic reputation in Cuba as a charming, creative and clever playboy.

Callan and Oragan both burst into simultaneous laughter. Callan laughed so hard and so long that genuine tears began to stream down her wrinkled cheeks.

"Oh, honey," Callan managed to gasp out, wiping her eyes. "You gallivant around Havana like you actually own the place! You have never, in your entitled life, truly known struggle or self-control! This whole trip should be a delightful treat to watch. Too bad you can't come for the show, Oragan. It's sure to be a doozy!" Oragan merely shook his massive, scaly head in evident disappointment.

Ivan, thoroughly humiliated, simply refused to believe the lies Callan was gleefully spewing.

"We're off to the garden now. See you sometime, unfortunately, in the future," she said to Oragan, giving him a slow, deliberate middle finger. Oragan simply rolled his little iguana eyes and began grooming his stump.

They left the apartment, walking with renewed urgency toward the Occupiers Compound.

Twenty minutes later, after navigating the maze of back alleys and forgotten streets, Callan and Ivan arrived at the wrought-iron garden gates. Ivan was gobsmacked. He had walked by the dilapidated walls of the old Occupiers Compound hundreds of times before and had never once seen this exquisitely maintained garden or the gate. *People only see what they want to see,* he thought, the realization hitting him like a physical blow.

"Welcome to Anna and Julia's special spot. To open the gate you need to hold the tail in one hand and press the iguana figure on the gate with the other--- SHHH."

Ivan saw nothing threatening, only Callan frantically rifling through the deep recesses of her large, frayed satchel. She shoved a small, faintly glowing crystal orb into his hand and mouthed the words, "SAY 'COVER OF NIGHT'". Ivan, recognizing the danger in her eyes, did it without hesitation, whispering the phrase. Just as the last syllable left his lips, Vlad and Boris, the duo from hell, lumbered around the corner. They marched toward the gate with a heavy, purposeful stride, completely ignoring Callan and Ivan's presence. The concealment spell, it seemed, was working perfectly.

"Boris, you will be adored on Kala. You will be a high priest of my people there," Ivan heard Vlad boom, clearly spewing one of his lies. The only thing Boris would ever be the high priest of was Russian potato salad and possibly bottom-shelf vodka. Ivan struggled valiantly to stifle a snort of derision. Callan's sharp elbow to his ribs ensured his silence.

They watched as Vlad dramatically produced a vibrant red feather and pressed it firmly against the parrot figure carved into the iron gate. With a low, grinding sound, the gate swung open, and they walked through. Callan motioned with a tense hand for Ivan to remain frozen, presumably waiting until the two had passed through the portal on the other side of the garden. Ivan wondered, his heart pounding in his chest, how they would know exactly when that crucial moment had arrived.

Suddenly, Boris screamed. It was the most horrific sound Ivan had ever heard. It was not a cry of pain, but a sound of unadulterated terror and agony. Callan instantly snatched the crystal orb from his hand and tossed it back into her backpack, the threat now gone, and gave the iguana's tail to Ivan.

"It's showtime, Sugar. Let's go."

They walked through the gate and straight into a nightmare. Vlad was nowhere to be seen, but a grotesquely inside-out version of Boris was twitching next to a small, ornate stone fountain. The sight was so horrific that Ivan vomited onto a nearby, beautiful plumeria tree. Boris had been skinned alive; his white, glistening fat, red sinew, and pale, shattered bones were on full, horrific display. Ivan clamped a hand over his mouth, gagging uncontrollably.

"Would you look at that?" Callan said, her voice filled with a detached, clinical curiosity. "It's been a while since I've seen the immediate aftermath of a human attempting to cross a portal."

Ivan finally managed to stop gagging, sputtering, "Can't you do something? Is there anything in your enormous bag of tricks for this? Please, put him out of his misery?" Thick, cold sweat beaded on Ivan's forehead. He staggered and had to steady himself desperately on the trunk of the plumeria tree.

"Afraid not, darlin'. Not many items in the universe can effectively reverse the aftermath of a regular human entering a portal. But really, would you truly want to waste that kind of cosmic power on this pathetic schlub?" Boris's low, guttural moans were barely audible over the gruesome sound of blood gurgling deep in his throat. His remaining skin seemed to be dissolving and melting off his body in sheets. Dark, viscous blood dripped steadily out of every orifice and onto the otherwise pristine white stone bench he was slumped against.

Ivan neared full-blown shock. His vision tunneled as he fought desperately to make any kind of sense of the immediate horror show in front of him. "We *have* to put him out of his misery! Now!"

Callan calmly reached into her bag and pulled out the gold machete, the very one that had just severed Oragan's tail. "You, Ivan, may have the honor," she said, a faint, cold smirk forming at the corner of her mouth.

"I have never killed anyone before!" Ivan's voice went up an octave, cracking as a result of his panic.

"Oh, sure you have, sugar. Loads of times. Think of the number of spiritual battles you fought for Anna. It's actually one of the primary reasons you're here, right now! You needed to cool off for a bit. Get a little bit of that non-magical creature compassion and reality check. You absolutely can do it, sweetie. Just don't think too much about the *him* part of it."

Ivan swallowed hard, looked at the strangely comforting weight of the gold machete, and walked slowly over to Boris. Boris's eyes, the only part of him that looked remotely human, were wide with blinding terror. Ivan had never witnessed such raw fear before.

"Just do it, Ivan," Callan commanded, her voice sounding suddenly bored, the moment of morbid curiosity passed.

Ivan raised the machete and, without conscious thought, decapitated him in one swift, clean stroke. Immediately, he vomited a second time, this time all over the now-still body.

"What do we do with—" Before Ivan could even finish

his stunned question, the body, the blood, and the head shimmered, dissolved, and disappeared, leaving the stone spotless.

"Universal weapons truly do come in handy, don't they?" Callan remarked, looking at the golden machete with something akin to respect. "Now, let's jump through this damn portal before you have any more time to think about any of this."

Without any hesitation, warning, or ceremony, Callan grabbed Ivan's arm and pulled him, the iguana tail still clutched in his other hand, into the churning, shimmering waters of the fountain. They were finally on their way to Kala.

19

Manny and Misha pressed on toward Lega, hypervigilant as ever. Manny's heart ached with the knowledge that the true Misha, the man he loved, was buried beneath the ungrateful facade wrought by the Collector. The 'faux Misha' was an irritating distraction during what was, otherwise, a stunning hike. The trail wound through a dense forest, thick with flowers and birds. In any other circumstance, this would have been a romantic adventure. Not today.

"Where in the hell is my sister? You swore we'd find her, you swore we'd help her! I'm absolutely sick of this; it's been two goddamn days of walking toward this stupid town!" Misha's petulant complaints sliced through the quiet every hour or so.

Manny felt his patience wear with every step. Whatever twisted magic the Collector had used, it had altered Misha's very being. "We are almost there, I promise. The village, Lega, will be a place for us to finally regroup and get some much-needed rest, *querido*."

Slowing his pace by the slightest amount, Manny subtly

raised his hand and cast a gentle, calming sensation toward Misha, hoping the magic would benefit them both. The effect was immediate; Misha, at least, fell silent.

Every subtle sound—the crackle of dry leaves, the snap of a twig—triggered a spike of adrenaline, a frozen pause, and a primal fear response. This time was no different.

Misha, his eyes wide and fixed, gestured abruptly toward a massive, gnarled tree. Manny's gaze followed, and he gave a quick, sharp nod of acknowledgment.

"No need to bother hiding. I wasn't looking for you anyway." A creature of impossible size, a tiger easily three times the dimensions of any earthly counterpart, stepped out from the shadowy depths of the woods, its massive head twitching as it sniffed the air. "Although... What a pity. You do smell *halfway decent*," the tiger remarked, its eyes narrowing on Misha. It moved with a slow, pained deliberation.

For an instant, a genuinely adorable expression crossed Misha's face. He gave Manny a look of bemused resignation. At this point, nothing truly surprised them, but a talking tiger was still awe-inducing.

"My name is Gavin." The tiger continued sniffing the air like a house cat. "You smell... familiar," he stated, his huge nose pointed at Misha. "You smell exactly like someone I just had a run-in with."

Misha's eyes lit up. "Did you meet my sister?"

Unfortunately, that was the wrong thing to say. Before Manny could even register the danger, let alone conjure a protective spell, Gavin lunged. The tiger's bulk slammed into Misha, knocking the wind from him and sending him sprawling to the ground. Gavin's massive, drooling muzzle was inches from Misha's face, hot spittle dripping from his whiskers onto Misha's neck.

Clearly, the answer is yes, Manny thought grimly, his hands instinctively crackling with the magic ready to immobilize the creature.

"Your *sister,*" Gavin spat, his voice a low, rumbling growl, "knocked me clean out! Because of her, I practically incinerated my paws on a goddamn tree!" He snorted a blast of hot, foul breath directly into Misha's face. Then, with a dramatic, weary sigh, Gavin seemed to deflate. He backed away in a theatrical show of resignation and flopped onto the earth. Misha slowly scrambled to his feet, trying to dust the bloody paw prints from his shoulders.

"If I had to make a guess, Gavin, you absolutely deserved whatever my sister did to you," Misha retorted, the petulance replaced by defiant anger. Manny jabbed him sharply in the ribs, a silent, urgent reminder that they were moments from being shredded by this monumental beast.

"Gavin, please accept my apologies for my travel companion's behavior. He is... unwell. Could you possibly tell us how much farther it is to the town of Lega?" Manny inquired.

"Why is it that *everyone* suddenly wants to go to Lega? It's a completely useless little town, nothing but a den of cowards who fled there the moment the first rumors of the Shadow's return started to circulate. Why, you ask? Who knows. All I know is that nowhere is truly safe anymore, not since *she* came back." Gavin frowned, casting a look of melancholy toward the sky.

"My sister is here to *help*! She has returned to protect the people of Kala, even the ones who are too ignorant to worship her!" Misha shouted. Manny elbowed him again, harder this time. Misha's new explosive temper was a constant source of stress. Manny desperately missed his old lover.

Gavin threw his head back and burst into a booming, rolling roar of laughter. "Your sister?!" He rolled completely onto his back, his legs splayed in the air, his laughter shaking his enormous frame. "Oh, you are truly adorable if you think I was referring to *your* sister! No, I'm talking about Julia. *She's* the important one now. Used to be just another deity of minor importance. Now, she is all anyone in this whole wretched land can talk about."

Misha's mouth dropped open, ready to unleash a torrent of words, but no sound escaped.

"What did you say?" Manny demanded, his voice tight with confusion and mounting dread. "Julia is dead. Vlad killed her." Manny's mind raced, scrambling for a rational explanation. The most obvious surfaced: Deities are inherently immortal. Of course, Vlad hadn't truly killed Julia.

"Honestly, both of you are starting to bore me. Why am I even wasting my time?" Gavin maintained his position on his back, his massive paws reaching into the air, kneading invisible biscuits. Then, his head snapped up, his expression shifting to one of sudden, shrewd calculation. "Say, you have some healing abilities, right? You're one of those Keepers. I can smell it on you." He sniffed aggressively in Manny's general direction.

"Yes, I am. What of it?" Manny said, instantly regretting that he hadn't lied. He absolutely did not want to make any more binding deals with magical, grumpy creatures.

"My paws are in a rather painful situation thanks entirely to this maroon's sister. Tell you what: I'll share everything I know about Julia, and you fix my paws." Misha's brows shot up, and he frowned, silently pleading with Manny to agree. Manny considered the offer. The tiger seemed to possess no extraordinary power, save for his ability to communicate with and track powerful deities and mythans, which, admittedly, wasn't *nothing*. But the sight of Misha's pleading eyes was enough to break Manny's resolve.

"I agree," Manny stated. "However, I will not heal your paws until you have told us everything you know about Julia."

"Fine. Good. At least we have one benevolent being around here." Gavin sighed again. "I'll give you the abridged version. Julia came back, went immediately to the country up north where most people worship the Great Dalv. Rumor has it that she wanted Anna to return as well, but Dalv was making that impossible for them on Earth. Julia may have subsequently disappeared into hiding again. His followers are really ruining everything here," Gavin punctuated his sentence with a sigh.

"He was always such a menace after my mother's... after my mother disappeared. He made everything unpleasant," Misha muttered, his tone shifting, a rare flicker of his old self momentarily returning.

"You know how vengeful deities can be, Keeper," Gavin continued with a dismissive wave of a paw. "She went to the expanse where they worship Dalv and, in a classic act of divine pettiness, decided to smite a high priestess who was intent on bringing Dalv back to Kala. She felt the priestess would only harm Kala." Gavin sighed, a massive gust of air that ruffled the wildflowers, clearly bored with his own tale. "Honestly, this is precisely why I am an agnostic. You lot," he motioned dramatically toward Misha, "are nothing but trouble with the way you casually play with people's lives. Now, where was I? Oh yes, so the smiting—or smoting? Smitten?—backfired. Julia disappeared again. Rumor is that Dalv, your Vlad, has returned. That's the end. Now, Keeper, fix my paws, please." Gavin stood upright on his hind legs, pointing his injured paws in Manny's general direction like a pet demanding a treat.

"One more question, Gavin. Where is Julia *now*?" Manny asked, his hands already beginning to glow with the soft, emerald light of a healing spell.

"You know how the deities are, all wanderlust and no commitment. Well, maybe you don't. So, she could be anywhere. But the latest rumor circulating around the jungle is that she fled for safety. So cliché. Now, for the love of the stars, fix my paws, please," Gavin pouted, his expression one of exaggerated suffering.

Manny made the motion of an upside-down question mark with both hands hovering over each massive paw. Gavin winced at the initial surge of energy and then breathed a huge, shuddering sigh of relief as the healing magic took effect. "Well, Keeper, I'll always lend you a hand, or a paw, when I can." He shot a final, disdainful look at Misha. "You, on the other hand, are completely useless to me."

"Where are you going now?" Manny called after the colossal tiger.

"Nowhere in particular. I used to have some lovely Kalans in the expanse of the Two Queens, that area known as Everbright, who would leave me generous helpings of food. I'd roam freely, chat with the other animals, and always return to their land for a good meal and a comfortable patch of ground to sleep on. But they were tricked into giving up their power. No one has seen them since. I've since had to hunt for food the old fashion way, like the common tigers in other expanses," Gavin said, his voice trailing off into a low, despondent mumble.

"Did you... did you eat people?" Manny asked,

wondering if he detected a flicker of shame in the tiger's eyes.

"Of course I did, but I'm hungry! I have to eat! I can't exactly subsist on birds, now can I? Squirrels are just a tiny little snack. I used to get a side of good beef every few days," he said wistfully, lamenting his lost, luxurious diet.

Manny and Misha exchanged a look and nodded in mutual understanding. They couldn't logically fault the tiger for his pragmatism.

"Promise me you won't kill any other people, alright? On Earth, tigers enjoy eating fish. Try some. You might actually like it," Manny suggested gently.

"I suppose I can attempt this 'fish.' They're just so... *fishy*. Alas. Good luck on your quest, Keeper. I'd dearly love my old life back, so I sincerely mean that," Gavin replied, his massive form turning to walk in the opposite direction from Manny and Misha, disappearing back into the dense, vibrant foliage.

20

"Anna, we're approaching Lega. Be prepared for anything." Ara's raspy voice matched her haggard appearance.

"Do you feel as bad as you look? You look terrible. And I mean that in the nicest way possible." Anna's concern was genuine, despite the blunt phrasing. The change in Ara was stark and unsettling. Her usually thick and lustrous hair was now thin, dull, and stringy. The familiar sparkle that always danced in her bloodshot eyes had been utterly extinguished, leaving them flat and weary.

"Anna, I don't know." Ara's hesitation worried Anna.

"Would you mind if I turned into my other self and sat on your shoulder? I feel weak in this form."

Anna nodded. She carried so many mental and spiritual burdens. What's the harm in a physical one?

Don't think about it. Walk. One foot in front of the other. Breathe. The mantra was a desperate, internal drumbeat.

Whilst Anna wasn't physically alone, she was engulfed by an overwhelming sense of loneliness and anxiety, a cocktail of emotions that caused her to chew incessantly on the inside of her cheek. Again. It was a nervous habit she couldn't break.

As they followed the footpath approaching the town, Anna observed a series of intricately laid cobblestone roads that branched out, weaving both into and away from the city. It was a stark contrast to the last settlement, which had been relatively modern. Lega reminded her of the older, forgotten parts of Havana, steeped in a history. The slight commotion of their arrival stirred Orlana awake.

"We're...we're in Lega." Orlana's voice was a tremulous whisper, laced with dread. "It isn't supposed to be consumed by the Shadow?"

"I am here Orlana. Don't worry, kid. I promise to keep you safe." Anna's voice was firm. Orlana's large, doe-like eyes fixed on Anna's, and for the first time since they had met, Anna felt the weight of the child's trust in her.

"I'm a bit rusty in this language. Help me out. What do these signs say?" Anna asked, gesturing toward some faded script on a nearby post.

"The town center is about a 20 minute walk on this road," Orlana translated, pointing a small, shaky finger toward the main, wide cobblestone street that led into the heart of the town.

They made their way down the street. The silence was unnerving and the city was eerily empty. It was unlike any city Anna had ever seen, even in the history books of Earth. Each building was a masterpiece, with intricate, ornate carvings etched above the door frames and windows. Each carving appeared to be telling a story.

"Ara," Anna whispered, her voice a mix of awe and disbelief, "what is this? It's...stunning and moving. The carvings are moving!" She actually squealed. The sight was awe-inspiring, and wildly trippy. She remembered Misha mentioning certain hallucinogenic mushrooms that could make pictures move. Anna questioned her sanity, yet again, and seriously wondered if she was on some Kala-specific psychotropic drugs.

"It's the story of all the deities of Kala. This block, specifically, was created as an homage to Orlana's religion." Orlana's lips curled into a faint, knowing smile as she gazed up at the pictograms, a small comfort in the overwhelming desolation. "Lega is a sacred place and a knowledge center for all of Kala," Ara murmured softly into Anna's ear from her perch on her shoulder.

They shouldn't keep all their knowledge in one location, Anna thought instantly. She had read enough about the history of wars and invasions to know that knowledge centers—libraries, archives, universities—were always the first targets to be destroyed during an invasion. Accounts of history were almost always omitted or dramatically rewritten by the victors.

Orlana's smile vanished. "Something moved in that window!" Tears immediately streamed down her face, the terrifying sight snapping her back to reality. Anna scooped up Orlana, holding her close to her chest. "We need to see what we are up against." They crossed the empty cobblestone street and peered cautiously into the darkened window. Anna's vision sharpened, honing in on the interior. She could make out four distinct forms huddled together inside. From what Anna could discern, they were hiding, terrified.

Anna crouched down to Orlana's level, her eyes earnest. "Orlana, listen to me. There are people from your expanse here. I think that you will be much safer with them than with me right now." Orlana immediately shook her head in a vehement motion of dismay. Ara, however, nodded her head in silent agreement with Anna's assessment.

"We don't know what we're up against, *querido*. I cannot allow you to get hurt again." Anna lightly knocked on the sturdy wooden door. She figured that most people realized that an evil goddess did not bother with the courtesy of knocking. The loud, metallic commotion of multiple bolts and locks unlatching echoed jarringly from behind the door.

"Stay away, demon woman!" The sound was a jarring, hissing whisper that belonged to a little old lady who seemed barely capable of standing without aid. Anna's infamous reputation needed no introduction on this planet. With a practiced, effortless flick of her hands, Anna immobilized the woman. She became a voiceless, wide-eyed statue, a momentary monument to prejudice. Anna knew this confrontation was yet another definitive nail in the coffin of her public image. Religious conversion, she realized with a sigh, would need to happen later.

"Yeah yeah, I know you hate me. But could you please help a fellow Kalan?" Anna presented Orlana, gently pushing her forward. "She has been orphaned by a giant tiger." Anna found it unbelievable that she was relaying the tale of a talking tiger with a straight face. She saw the intense desire in the woman's eyes to speak and, with a subtle wave of her hand, she allowed it.

"Gavin... Yes, he can be testy," the old woman acknowledged, her head tilting in a gesture of knowing agreement, her fear momentarily forgotten. She looked down at Orlana. "In times like these, we must rely on each other, especially when the deities refuse to intervene," the old lady said as she delivered it with an accusatory glance at Anna, who subtly rolled her eyes at the familiar slight. Orlana returned the smile with an nod, sensing the kindness. "I have a family myself. We've all been through hell.. No one is sure exactly when the Shadow will make its final move, but we're terrified."

"I will protect your home. I'm not sure how long the protection will hold," Anna began, searching for a way to complete the sentence without sounding overtly arrogant, but she couldn't avoid it, "since you don't worship me."

"We'll take our chances," the woman said firmly, as she started to gently usher Orlana into the safety of the house.

Anna gave the girl a quick, tight hug. "You'll be safe here." Orlana nodded, her eyes already looking toward the other hiding people inside.

They went inside, and the resounding clatter of every possible lock being secured echoed out into the empty street.

Anna raised her hands, palms up and spread out, facing the building. Instead of her usual, blazing gold energy, a cold, shimmering silver light encompassed the entire building, forming a protective barrier.

"That won't hold very long," Ara said without a trace of emotion, the assessment a flat, depressing statement of fact.

"Hopefully it will hold long enough for them to be rescued later."

After walking another five minutes, keeping prudently close to the buildings, which they noticed had evidence of people hiding, Ara ruffled her feathers in agitation. "Something is coming." Ara wiggled restlessly on Anna's shoulder, unable to settle into a comfortable or secure position. Anna instantly guarded herself mentally, preparing for confrontation. A surge of heat and light automatically surged through her body, settling as a warm, humming energy in her *chocha*.

"Stop," Ara whispered urgently in her ear. Faint,

rhythmic footsteps tip-tapped from the other side of the building they were passing. Ara was proving to be oddly out of sync with her heightened senses.

Callan and Ivan turned the corner and almost slammed directly into them. Anna stared in total disbelief, the sight of them a profound shock.

Ivan stood before her, and perched on his shoulder was a familiar, colorful toucan.

"Darlin', are you a cod fish? Why is your mouth hanging open like that?" squawked the toucan.

"Callan," Ara said calmly, a chilling restraint in her voice.

"Cousin! What a really great surprise, *truly*!" Callan retorted, giving a dramatic, theatrical eye roll with her large black eyes.

"Ivan, what are you doing here?" Anna whispered into his ear as she tightly hugged him, relief and shock consuming her.

"Dontcha mean Navi? Let's get the names straight. Why don't you tell her while I catch up with my cousin." Callan interjected, her beak tilting with impatience.

Anna and the man who was now Navi separated quickly but maintained an intense, steady eye contact, a silent conversation passing between them.

Navi regaled Anna with the tales of his harrowing homecoming, the revelation of his true identity, and the grotesque reality of a dead Boris. He finished with the fact that Dalv was likely somewhere on this planet. He could be in this very town, or he could be 10,000 miles away. No one knew his location or his plans.

"Would you look at their intensity, cousin. I don't have much to tell you since you know everything, but your little cosmic fuck buddy sends his regards." Callan said, disrupting the moment.

Anna saw Ara's eyes light up for a fleeting moment, a spark of genuine hope in the general exhaustion. "Oragan, how is he?"

"Well, sadly he is without a tail until it grows back. It was the only way that we could get here quickly," Callan said with a dramatic, feigned sadness that didn't fool anyone. Ara's sharp eyes, however, immediately spotted Oragan's missing, vibrant tail hanging half out of Navi's pocket. "Apparently, I'm part of the worst game of telephone. His powers are weakening and he doesn't know why. He can't change back to his human form. He's stuck as an iguana in Havana, it seems," Callan finished, totally nonplussed by the supposed tragedy.

"Don't you have something in your bag of tricks, cousin, that can help him?" Ara pleaded, even though a deep part of her knew the question was utterly futile.

"Now now cousin, you made the rules. You know that I can't do anything without a deal or a trade. Plus, Oragan's tail belongs to Navi now," Callan said with a dismissive shrug of her feathered shoulders. Navi held up the item—a disorienting iguana's tail that seemed to change color every few seconds, pulsating with weak magic.

Anna saw Ara ruffle her feathers violently in distress. Anna wondered if she could trust Callan. Ara clearly loathed her with an intensity that was rare for the usually calm creature.

Ara swiftly changed the subject. "Are you two ready to figure out how to restore the natural balance?"

"Not really. Maybe? I don't fucking know. We're in a city whose people are in hiding and everyone thinks that I'm an evil bitch." Anna said flatly, her eyes darting to the closed shop and house windows that were being shuttered as they spoke.

"Lordy, Anna, you're just as dense as your little boyfriend here. Where do you find information in Havana?" Anna could have sworn that Callan pursed her beak as she ended the sentence, judging her.

In Havana, you could find out most information from the local people, but you could definitely find historical and cultural information from the library. It even housed a few tattered bibles and other religious texts.

"The library. The cultural attaché knows." Navi said confidently as Anna mumbled "unearned" under her breath, referring to the knowledge he had just effortlessly accessed.

"Bingo, genius. Man, Ara, how have you been dealing with her ignorance for all these years? Don't you get tired of working these deities over and over again for the past few millennia? What's the rub? What's the pay off? You always got more time!" Callan said, sounding as profoundly exasperated as she looked.

Anna could tell that Ara's preferred, and perhaps only, way of dealing with Callan was to completely ignore her existence.

"Usually libraries are near the town center. We aren't very far from it, so I suppose we should continue on our way and will hopefully find it soon," Navi said, decisively taking the lead.

They made their way down the cobblestone path. Anna and Navi were both marveling at the brightly colored, impeccably well-maintained pastel buildings that lined the street. It looked like Old Havana, but a version where Old Havana was immaculately maintained and had beautiful, enchanted, ornate stories carved over every single door.

Anna noticed there were an unusually large number of birds in the carvings, a lot of representation of the *ziblings*, and the two queens that Orlana had mentioned. Curiously, there were no depictions of the main deities in the carvings, or so Anna thought initially.

Fifteen minutes later, and without incident, they found the town center. It was a spacious plaza with a beautiful, detailed map carved into a large marble slab in the middle of a plaza. The library was situated behind the municipal building that fronted the plaza. The sun rose from the east, but immediately following its ascent, an ominous red cloud engulfed it.

Anna and Ara exclaimed at the exact same time, their voices laced with terror, "It's here!" Anna violently yanked Navi by his hand and started running with all her strength toward the library. They heard a low, monstrous hum that sounded like a million flies rumbling toward them from the dark cloud. The wind shifted, blowing a fetid stench their way, which smelled remarkably like Havana did just before Anna had left: smoke, rot, and the metallic tang of decay filled their nostrils.

Anna and Navi ran as fast as they possibly could, with Callan flying effortlessly overhead, a watchful, manic presence. Sure enough, the colossal library was situated directly behind the municipal building. As they ran up, Anna fervently waved her hands all over the place, a desperate act of protection. Silver and gold streams of pure energy flew around the library, weaving a shimmering net of defensive magic. They ran up to the most beautifully set of ornate wooden doors, which appeared to be carved with yet more untold stories. Anna wished she had a moment, just a single moment, to admire and decipher the elaborate carvings, but there was not a second to spare.

She threw open the doors with a minimal effort and they all ran inside. She immediately spun around to seal the doors in the best way that her current power allowed. "Okay, hopefully that holds for a little while."

She looked at Navi's face, which held a look of surprise.

Anna, feeling a moment of confident satisfaction that he was admiring her raw strength, began to explain the mechanics of her powers when he abruptly interrupted her.

"No no, look over there," he said, pointing a shaking finger behind her. She turned her head, looking over her left shoulder, and her breath hitched. Standing there, impossibly, were Manny and Misha. Unable to process any more emotional surprises, any more shocks to her system, she collapsed in a sudden, sobbing heap at Misha's feet.

Misha hesitantly lifted her up, hugging her with a surprising tepidness. "Apparently goddesses look like a snotty mess when they cry as well." Anna didn't even register his typically judgy tone as she was overcome mentally, physically, and emotionally. New sights. New sounds. New smells. New cultural rules. And now, every single love of her life from Havana was suddenly alive and in one place with her, safe for the moment.

Manny immediately stepped in for a real, solid embrace, holding Anna tightly. She knew, with a certainty that settled her soul, that her Keeper would keep her safe. Manny was her anchor, keeping her grounded and at ease in the chaos. After a few moments, she lifted her head from his shoulder. Misha stared at them both, his hands placed firmly on his hips, which were cocked to one side.

"What's wrong with him?" Anna said, flinging her hand dismissively at her brother as she wiped her snotty nose with a clean handkerchief that Manny had instantly produced for her.

Manny quickly told them about their horrific time in Havana, including the details of Elena's death and how Misha had been brutally slashed by Dalv. He then went into detail about Callan, who saved Misha's life, but in doing so, left him a bitchy shell of his former self.

"Eh hem, YOU ARE WELCOME, hot stuff." Callan piped up from behind him, her voice dripping with mock offense. Manny frowned at the sound of her voice.

"Callan. I did not expect to see you, nor you, yet..." He motioned awkwardly to Navi, still unable to fully process the transformation.

Navi just shrugged, a look of tired acceptance on his face. He almost opened his mouth to reply, but at that exact moment, it sounded as if an entire freight train had just slammed into the exterior of the building. The Shadow energy, a clear sign of incoming officers, visibly swirled and pressed against the protective barrier around the library.

Suddenly, a group of four people emerged from behind a giant, solid wood reception desk that curved elegantly like a wave between the door and the stacks of books.

"You!" One of them hissed, his voice venomous as he pointed an accusing finger directly at Anna.

"You are why the Shadow is here! They will destroy our sacred library!" He hissed, his face contorted in a mixture of fear and rage.

"Look, I put some protections on this place. If you keep talking to me like this, I can remove them and let the Shadow have you all." Anna glared back at him, her own anger flaring. Manny's calming hand immediately settled on her shoulder, a gentle weight designed to cool her temper.

An old, weathered woman emerged and firmly pushed the upset man out of the way. She was adorned in an over-sized, flowing silk purple and gold kaftan, cinched with a large, elaborate belt made of dozens of peacock feathers. Jewelry made of a dull, blue iridescent metal dripped from her ears and wrists. "You need us just as much as we need you," she stated firmly, her voice authoritative, as she elbowed the man aside. "My name is Bianca. Come with me, but only you and that fellow." She pointed a bejeweled finger to Manny. "I think I know what you need to find. But only you two. The rest, well you're on your own for a bit."

"Will you all be fine without me?" Anna said earnestly, her gaze moving over the group, most concerned about her brother and Navi, who she'd just gotten back.

"Well beauty queen, we have all been fine up to this point without you. If I were you, I would worry about whether *you'll* be fine without us. But, to answer your question, I think we can handle it," Misha said with a smirk, blowing her a sarcastic kiss as Ara instantly jumped from Anna's shoulder to his.

"Ew, get off of me!" He flinched and flicked at her, and she flew immediately to Navi's shoulder, the thought of resting on her cousin, Callan, being unbearable.

"Someone replaced my brother with this asshole," she said just loud enough for Manny to hear, a weary joke. He nodded in silent agreement. The three other Kalans stood opposite of this strange, ragtag group of misfit beings, each sizing the other up with wary suspicion, except for Callan who looked exceptionally bored and was filing her long, sharp nails with a bedazzled nail file.

The old woman grabbed both of Anna and Manny's hands and led them briskly towards the back of the cacophonous building. Manny and Anna were looking from the polished floor to the towering tops of the stacks, marveling at the sheer scale of the library. The enormity of the glorious building was striking. The art painted on the ceiling was so intricate and detailed it was difficult to take in its full significance in a single glance. Anna guessed that it was a massive story, like everything else in this remarkable town. Manny looked up as well, his eyes scanning the architecture. Anna knew he would be subconsciously looking for some ancient lore or markings related to the Keepers.

"I am the head librarian here in Lega. Our library is the oldest library of record in Kala. We store almost every published book, map, document, text, really anything that has ever been published on this planet." She said it with an unmistakable sense of profound pride. Manny knew these types of universal libraries existed throughout the multiverse, but he had never seen one in person, only in vague visions. Anna, on the other hand, was nearly giddy with awe. She had never seen anything even remotely like this. The National Library in Havana seemed rather impressive to her then, especially when she compared it to the small provincial libraries. But she imagined that 15 or 20 national libraries could fit into this massive space.

Bianca was clearly mindful of the increasing, deafening roar swirling around outside the protective barrier. "Let's speed up. The Shadow waits for no one, and your barrier is only a delaying tactic." They followed her to the back, a good 10-minute walk from the front of the library where everyone was waiting for them.

They turned left down the second-to-last row in the stacks. They stopped abruptly in front of a shelf that housed every book ever invented on the subject of taxidermy.

"Bianca, out of all of the books in this entire library, you think that *I* need information on taxidermy?" Anna said incredulously. Bianca ignored her completely as she intensely studied the books. She pulled out a precise series of eight books and then immediately returned them to their exact spots. As soon as the last one was slid back into its rightful position, the entire shelf opened with a low grinding sound, revealing a stone staircase that went underneath the library.

Anna was genuinely impressed. Manny smiled as well, a rare moment of lightness. The library was full of surprises. How she longed to be able to explore it properly. They followed Bianca onto a small platform. Bianca snapped her fingers sharply, and the shelf immediately slammed shut behind them. The darkness that enveloped them was instant, the silence deafening. No sound nor evidence of the Shadow beyond the taxidermy stacks.

"Now you two must trust me implicitly. The steps are provided, but we must go down, okay? I don't advise that either of you use your powers down here—they may not react well in this environment." Bianca's voice trilled slightly as she spoke to them, a strange undercurrent of excitement in her tone.

Anna's arm hairs tingled, standing on end. Her body was experiencing a strange memory, an echo of either this specific place or of this particular woman.

"Why should we trust you?" Anna said, verbalizing the exact thought that was running through both her and Manny's minds.

"I don't think you have another choice right now." Bianca took the first steps further down the stone stairwell. Anna and Manny followed closely behind her. Both of them loathed the dark, but they decided to heed the librarian's advice and keep their powers dormant. Anna remained vigilant, her senses on high alert.

For ten agonizing minutes, they carefully walked down step after step in complete silence. Anna furiously chewed the inside of her cheek, her nervous system screaming, sending alarms to every part of her body. Pitch-black darkness deep under the earth was precisely the type of scenario that used to fill her worst nightmares in Havana.

"Bianca, how much further are we going?" Manny said uneasily, his voice barely a whisper. "If something happens to the others, I want to make sure that we're nearby."

"Don't worry about them. Not much further now." Bianca snapped her fingers again. Torches immediately lit up on both sides of the damp stone staircase, illuminating the endless path downward. It was a tunnel that never seemed to end. *Wonderful*, Anna thought sarcastically.

Manny and Anna looked at each other, sharing a look of mutual anxiety. They both turned their heads up toward the taxidermy stacks, unable to see the door by which they had entered, feeling truly trapped.

Anna had to speak. She had to choose her words carefully. "I am not moving a step further until you tell me what the hell is going on. Our friends and family are up there, and we are trapped down here." Manny stood beside her, his posture rigid in agreement.

"Silly goddess, they are fine. Or they are not. They are dead. Or they are alive. But honestly, do you really believe they are dead? Sure, harm may come to them, but they'll be fine. It is my duty to bring you to the truth, which can only be found in the catacombs of this library. You made a lot of people angry the last time you were here on Kala. Let's not repeat that, okay? This planet's survival is in my best interest. Not you, not your unstable powers. Although he is truly special," she said, nodding approvingly to Manny. "I have only met one other Keeper. You may know her. She goes by Elena on earth." Manny nodded slowly, but he was cautious not to reveal her fate to Bianca. Anna nodded as well, her heart aching.

"When I tell you it will only be a bit further, I mean it will only be a bit further." She humpfed, clearly annoyed by the delay. They continued walking. Always walking. They descended more steps, and Anna wondered if they would reach the very center of their planet before they found what they were looking for.

At long last, she saw a level stone path about 30 stair steps down.

"Now we truly are almost here. Let me tell you the truth about the library above versus the library down here. The library above has typical historical and current texts and maps. It has any reference information on anything that has ever happened in Kala. As a matter of fact, from what I can tell from speaking with one of the top librarians on earth, it is very similar to what earthlings find in their libraries."

"Excellent. Let me guess. Everything below the surface is where the really interesting information is stored. The information that I need to figure out how to stop the Shadow and how to save this planet," Anna said flatly, her voice dry with sarcasm and fatigue.

"Allegedly. There are some truly ancient texts down here, including the original Book of Reason, which won't give you too much *additional* information, but will confirm things." Anna remembered her vision of the tomb holding the book.

Panic once again sprung forth from the pit of Anna's stomach, a cold, sharp feeling. Manny sensed her alarm and squeezed her hand reassuringly.

"Why am I down here with you, then?" Anna asked in a higher pitch than she intended.

"I was instructed to keep you safe at all costs and this is, quite simply, the safest place on the entire planet," Bianca replied coyly, a faint smile playing on her lips.

On the verge of tears, realizing that the two people whom she loved the most in the world, Misha and Navi, could possibly be dead or captured, Anna yelped through her tears, the sound raw and desperate, “Who instructed you to do this?!”

“Your mother,” Bianca replied matter-of-factly, as if she were commenting on the weather.

21

The deafening sound grew louder from outside of the library. Navi, usually able to maintain his cool in any situation, grew concerned. It had been hours since Anna and Manny followed Bianca to the other end of the library. He looked at the librarians. They insisted that everyone wait with them. While they were respectable, indeed, he couldn't help but think that there wasn't a fighter among the bunch. He looked at his crew. They were a ragtag crew, he thought. A molting, sad macaw. A dour, sardonic toucan lady. And Doppelgänger Misha.

"I'm going to walk around the foyer for a bit." Navi was amazed at how much of his Earth-self still remained. Or how much his Kala-self went to Earth. In any case, he was in absolute awe of the architecture and carvings in the foyer. Electrical energy crackled through his body. He walked towards the doors to the library and noticed that the carvings told a story, much like he had seen in old cathedrals in Europe. Navi realized that the carvings were animated. The story was told from left to right, but quite a few of the pieces were missing.

Navi focused so intently on figuring out the story that he jumped when a librarian tapped him on the shoulder. He turned around to see the middle-aged man. He donned an outfit similar to the woman who whisked Manny and Anna away from them.

"I'm Maurn. No surprise that you're drawn to this. Rumor has it that you inspired the architect who designed this." Navi felt surprised and pleased.

"Don't get too excited. The architect went mad in the process. She ended up killing herself when they finished the door. She couldn't figure out the missing tiles. She spent months wandering Lega, mumbling to herself, as the story goes. When she couldn't take it anymore, she hung herself in the taxidermy section, way at the other end of the stacks."

Navi winced. That wasn't exactly how he expected it to end.

Suddenly he heard frantic knocking at the side door, labeled "Emergency Exit." He ran over and listened. "PLEASE! Help us! It's coming! HELP US!"

Maurn's face went pale. "I don't know if we have enough food and water to last us all, but we have to let them in." Before Navi could protest, Maurn opened the door. The hundreds of people pressed against the door flooded the library. They could see the Shadow Officers moving in rapidly from about 500 meters away. Navi jumped back as people poured into the library.

He looked back at the Rag-Tag Crew and saw the look of shock on Callan's face. "Close the damn door!" she mouthed. As much as he hated to admit, she was usually right.

Navi thought for a moment. These people were being sent to succumb to the Shadow. Maybe even death. But he knew that the greater good was at stake. Without thinking, he waved his hand at the people coming towards the door. They slowed, looking transfixed. It was just enough time for him to close and lock it. The sound of the screams from the other side was something that Navi was quite sure he would never forget.

"WHAT ARE YOU DOING? YOU'RE SENDING MY PEOPLE TO THEIR CERTAIN DEATH!" Maurn screamed as he shoved Navi out of the way. He was pulling at the door violently while screaming uncontrollably. Navi was stunned with himself. He felt like a monster, but knew this had to be done.

Navi grabbed Maurn by the shoulders and looked him directly in the eye. "Maurn, the people in this library are your only hope for saving all of Kala from the Shadow. Do you understand? However long this has been going on, no one has been able to stop it." Maurn sobbed into Navi's chest. Navi looked at Callan, pleading for help with his eyes. She laughed. Ara, however, made a hugging motion with her molting wings.

Navi, unaccustomed to showing affection to men, awkwardly embraced Maurn. Maurn immediately relaxed. His sobs slowed to silent crying and then nothing. He looked up at Navi. "This does not mean that I forgive you. I'm trying to understand." Navi gave a quick nod and walked over to Callan, Ara and Misha.

"Ara, how long will Anna's protection hold?" Navi had to nearly yell to make himself heard over the screams and Shadow Army outside.

"Hard to say. It could last a day. It could last a few months. I have no idea how much more power she gained since arriving in Kala." Ara's voice was barely audible. Navi wondered if she was dying.

"Well this is a fucking great situation that we've found ourselves in, isn't it?" Misha said as he sidled up to them.

"Oh sugar, you are just hilarious." Callan patted him on the back. "I like your spirit!"

"I learned it by watching you!" Misha said without missing a beat.

"We need to find Anna and Manny -"

"You won't. At least not for a while." Maurn interrupted Navi from behind him.

"What do you mean?" Navi wished that he stayed in Havana where nothing in his life was dire or an emergency.

"Bianca was under strict instructions to take them to the Tomb of Reason and Knowledge, which is only accessible by the head librarian of Lega." Navi's face fell. Maurn looked a little pleased at his dismay.

Before Navi realized what he was doing, he grabbed Maurn's shoulders and lifted him off the ground. "Maurn, don't fuck with me please. I know that I may have upset you, but don't fuck with me." Seeing the alarm in Maurn's eyes, Navi set him down.

"Keep your hands off of me daemon! I am not fucking with you. I never wanted you two to return. You are nothing but trouble. It's all you ever have been, self-serving ass hole. But she insisted that you could stop the Shadow. Excuse me, but I need to give my people some water." Maurn stepped away.

Callan looked bored. Misha was still put out. Then there was Ara, who Navi felt sorry for. "Between all of us, surely we have enough magic and intellect to figure this out."

"I wouldn't count on it sweet cheeks. You're a pretty boy with some skills and immortality, but you're no Keeper. The brainiac in the group is with Anna." Navi wished that Callan's mouth would disappear.

"And what about you and Ara? You're so high and mighty on yourself that surely you can think of a way out."

"Doll face, I think I know how this will unfold. I'm just here for the front row action." Navi knew that it was only partly true, but he wasn't sure which part.

He suddenly realized that if the architect hung herself in the taxidermy section of the stacks that maybe her ghost or spirit lurked about. He wondered if there was a santeria equivalent on Kala.

"There might be someone who can help us. Follow me - even you, Misha. Stop looking so put out. You're a demigod. Figure out what the hell that means." Misha scowled. Callan shrugged. Ara nodded. Off they started walking towards the back of the stacks while the librarians fed the refugees.

Ten minutes later, they arrived at a stack that said "Taxidermy". Navi and Misha, still growing accustomed to their new reality, were dumbfounded by the thousands of books on taxidermy alone. Navi stepped into the row. Immediately he found himself suspended 20 feet off the ground.

He opened his mouth to yell for help but nothing came out.

"Naaaaaaviiii...." a voice echoed around his head. "I've beeeeeen waiting for you." A large silver wisp swirled around him so quickly that he couldn't make out its original form. This must be the architect, Navi thought.

"Bravo, darling. Great idea," Callan whooped. He looked down to see that Callan had a slight frown. Misha was back to looking extremely annoyed.

The figure stopped moving directly in front of Navi's face. He recognized her, but it was as if they met in a dream. Her curly hair floated around her head while her studious and intense eyes bore into Navi's. If he had to guess, he would place her at the human age of 35. Impressive age to design something like this library and... suddenly his body writhed in pain.

"You tortured my mind for years. Now it's myyyyyyy tuuuuuuuuurn." She let out a cackle.

"Hey hun, I get that you're pissed at Navi. Really I do. But we have something that we have to figure out. You think you can help us?" The Architect looked at Callan and noticed Misha standing next to her.

She kept Navi suspended while she glided down to Misha. "Whoooo are you?" She swirled around Misha.

"Misha. I am A-" Callan jabbed him in his ribs "A long for the ride. Why do you ask?"

"You look like someone I could talk to forever." The Architect's face relaxed into a dreamy state. The hair on Misha's arms stood up. "I'll talk to him and only him."

"Well he isn't exactly known for his scintillating conversation. Sure you won't talk to me or the parrot here?" Callan muttered.

"SILENCE COLLECTOR. I want to talk to him."

"Suit yourself." Callan shrugged. Misha looked slightly smug.

Navi screamed voicelessly. Misha was one of the most charming people that Navi knew in Cuba. Misha was known for his charm and streets smarts but was never accused of being a genius.

"I'm happy to chat with you. As a matter of fact, I'd love to get to know you better." The Architect skeptically raised her eyebrow. "I mean, not in that way. Sorry, I don't like women in THAT way, but I really love this library. It's stunning. Did you design it?"

She smiled. "I did. I was the youngest Architect ever awarded a project of this size."

"Incredible. What a feat. How long did it take?" He asked, sounding genuinely intrigued.

"Not long, only a year," beamed the Architect.

"Wow!" Misha was impressed. "How were you able to design it so quickly?"

Wrong question. She roared and screamed "Because of HIM!" The Architect tortured Navi again.

"Oh yeah, tell me about it. He irritates the fuck out of me too." Misha was clearly speaking from the heart. The Architect floated back down and rested near him. Through the searing physical pain, Navi felt a sting of emotional pain from Misha's comment.

"He continued to push me with creations and ideas. All day. All night. I couldn't sleep. I could barely eat. The only thing that I could think of was the story. The story. The story. The Reason of Kala. It was like he possessed me. I couldn't stop thinking of Anna and the Reason of Kala. It drove me mad. I had to channel it all into designing this." She gestured at the entirety of the library.

"What's the Reason of Kala?" Misha asked innocently.

"Oh you really must get by on your looks and charm," the Architect said.

Callan nodded, as if to say "I told you so."

"The Reason of Kala is the book for the Annasts. The people who worship Anna and Julia." Misha tried not to react. Frustration built inside Navi. His face was hot. His contained body begged to be released. He remained voiceless. He must interrogate the Architect.

"I never worshiped them, but Anna's lover... he was a man about Kala. He was inspiring and cunning. Really a horny asshole that couldn't keep his creativity and his manipulations to himself." She looked up at Navi who, on cue, writhed, in pain.

"I thought he left forever. But I just saw Anna and her Keeper walk by and hoped that he wouldn't be far behind. And here he is." She smiled widely. "What's that they say on Earth? Payback is a bitch?" She sent another shock through his body. "I've learned a lot about the planet of banished deities. Earth is odd, isn't it?" she said to Callan. Callan nodded.

"You saw my - friend Anna? Where was she?" Misha probed.

"Bianca took her to the Tomb of Reason and Knowledge - which happens to be right here." She pointed to the end of the row. "You'll never get in there though. And she's never coming out of that entrance. Bianca was under strict orders to ensure that Anna and her Keeper did not return through the library. I swear to goddess, the things that these head librarians are put through. Almost as bad as what this one put me through."

"The library is so beautiful. Where is the story?" Misha inquired earnestly.

At the same time, Callan and The Architect replied "The Library is the story!"

Misha realized, later than everyone else, that Navi must know the story as well.

"Excuse me dear, but are you interested in makin' a trade? As you guessed, I'm a Collector, which means that I have quite a few items that could be of service to you."

"I've read about your type. I'm curious to hear your deal. Do tell." The Architect swooped down to Callan. Navi wiggled in protest. He knew the deal would be something unpleasant at best and completely agonizing and torturous at worst. It was Callan, after all.

Navi couldn't hear anything from their whispers. He saw the Architect nodding. Callan pulled out the same locket that he gave to Cat in Havana. Navi cried, tears dripped from his frozen face. He tried to yell but couldn't. He was confused and overwhelmed, trying to fathom what could happen to him.

"That sounds like a deal worth considering." The Architect looked up to see tears dripping from Navi's face. "Done."

Callan reached out her hand and they shook on it. Navi dropped to the ground in a crumpled heap.

"We needed to figure out our next move, but if you haven't noticed, we're a bit short on time. The Architect just gave me the Cliffs Notes version of what we need to know."

"What did you promise her in return Callan?" Navi sputtered through grit teeth.

"Oh you know I can't tell you that, sugar pie. A deal between a Collector and another is secret." She winked. "Think of it as a sacrifice that you're making for the greater good." She smiled like a Cheshire cat. Navi shivered. "Don't ask me again, hun, if you want to ever be reunited with Anna.." It was a warning.

"Hey pretty boy, gather round." She waved Misha over. "We must make our way north. Rumor has it that there is a High Priestess in a snowy hellscape called Merrat. The gossip queen told me that she controls the Shadow for Dalv in anticipation of his return. It's said to be colder than a witch's tit in a brass bra. Gotta promise me that y'all won't wuss out along the way."

"How can I trust you when I don't even know what you promised of me?" Navi spat.

"I got ya down didn't I? What are you gonna do? Hang out here with your protege and that lot?" she said, motioning to the refugees. "She sure as hell won't tell you how to get into the tunnel. Now be a dear and do something useful. We need some warm clothes for this journey. This bright guy is a demigod - he can make shit happen with the right inspiration."

Navi scowled. Misha smiled. With Ara's meek guidance, they started with the first task at hand. Navi put his hand on Misha's shoulder. Misha felt electric. A force surged through his hands as he thought of the winter wear that he had seen in Soviet photography books. Three human sized ushankas appeared along with a miniature one for Ara.

"No no no, I am not wearing a hat. Callan, you know how humiliating this is," Ara lamented.

"Sure do cuz, but you don't really have a choice now do ya with you molting and all." Next up, full length fur coats and fur boots appeared, including three backpacks with provisions.

"I can't do any more," Misha said in a raspy voice as he plopped down to the ground.

"Misha, that was impressive." Navi encouraged him. Misha reminded him of Anna. Navi felt a bit aroused.

"Whoah tiger. Now we need to get a map. Navi, you built this place. Figure out the map situation. Get," Callan ordered.

Thirty minutes later, Navi returned with multiple maps. "I know fuck all about navigation and map reading." He threw four maps on the ground. Callan knew they would all be relevant at some point.

"Nice job, bud. Now, it's time for the first challenge. We gotta get outta this joint."

Ara whispered "I know how to get past the Shadow, but we'll need to wait for Misha to regain some strength." She told them her plan. "Let's rest until morning."

"I couldn't agree more," Navi said as he made a little nest with his coat.

"Ooh, I'll be little spoon!" Callan laid in front of Navi as he frowned. "He's not her. Watch it," as if she could read Navi's mind. Within a few minutes they slept soundly for the last time.

22

"Do you mean to tell me we're going underground the whole way?" Anna couldn't believe it. The tunnel system was nonsensical to her, nor could she grasp the true objective of their journey. So far, she's trusted strangers, all of whom have guided her through hell. She continued her relentless speed walking through the passage, her footsteps echoing on the uneven stone floor. The tunnel was a maddening construct: rock walls lit by self-igniting, self-extinguishing torches that flared to life precisely as they approached and extinguished barely three meters behind them.

"Anna, honestly, act like the deity that you are," Bianca snapped. "Yes, we need to navigate the tunnels for much of the journey. The surface is...complicated now." Anna's heart weighed heavy with the constant admonition to 'act like a goddess'. The only person who might truly understand the overwhelming burden was her mother, Julia. Yet her mother's presence felt everywhere but seen nowhere.

"What about..." Manny began, the name he wanted to

say catching in his throat. He feared that mentioning the creature would draw it to them.

"Shhhh... don't mention them," Bianca warned, her eyes darting nervously back at the recently extinguished torches as she held Manny's hand. Knowing the Keepers' power of telepathy, she wordlessly squeezed Manny's in a silent warning. He frowned. Anna, walking far ahead, didn't notice.

"Anna, *querido*, please. Slow down," Manny called out. He was the only one who could settle her nerves. "Take this opportunity, as Bianca said, to re-educate yourself about Kala and your past. Pay attention to the walls. There are carvings, you know. They might spark a memory, offer some insight." Anna finally stopped, her shoulders slumping in reluctant acceptance.

"Okay, fine. Then tell me this, since you're all so informed: Why was I banished to Earth? Why does all of Kala seem to hate me?" she demanded, turning to face them, her eyes blazing.

Bianca's detached, authoritative posture appeared to be a defense mechanism. "Your hubris got the best of you. You were reckless with the prayers that you answered and the deals that you made on behalf of your worshipers. Not every prayer is meant to be answered, Anna. You disrupted the natural flow. You really messed up with the two queens. Chaos spun out of control, and now, Control, in the form of the Keepers and the Shadow, is filling the void. You need to restore some balance to the realm."

"I just love how a librarian is telling a deity how to do her job," Anna retorted, a bitter laugh escaping her.

"You asked, I answered," Bianca spat back. "My business is retaining history for scholars and deities to study, to ensure that the worst parts of the past aren't repeated. Clearly, one of us failed to study properly."

Something about Bianca gave Anna pause. Beneath the librarian's starched indignation, Anna sensed a guarded secret but she refused to engage further. They continued their trek in silence for what felt like hours. Anna reluctantly studied the carvings along the tunnel walls, intricate murals that combined pictograms with the alphabet. Most were generic, depicting ancient Kalan myths, agricultural cycles, and various constellations, appearing useless to her mission. However, she began to take specific note of the ones that distinctly resembled her, her mother Julia, and Dalv. She noticed, with a jolt of recognition, an intricate symbol of an embellished, thorny flower deeply carved onto Dalv's wrist in all of the pictograms. She had taken money from Vlad hundreds of times, seen his hands close up, and never a marking or bracelet on his wrists.

"Bianca, what is this?" Anna said, pointing to the flower symbol etched onto Dalv's wrist in the stone.

Bianca approached and traced the carving with a long, slender finger. "It's a bracelet, or so the legends claim, that was sealed to his wrist during his last, most tyrannical stint as the deity for the people of Merrat. No one knows of its origins, but prior to him receiving it, he was on a level playing field with you and your mother. Afterward, he became more powerful. He was able to do anything he wanted, including mind control. When he was finally banished, the bracelet disappeared. Or so everyone was led to believe."

"And..." Manny prompted. No one on this journey was particularly forthcoming. Perhaps it was cultural.

Bianca hesitated, a deep furrow in her brow. "I hate rumors. I am the head librarian of Lega. We value truth above all. What can be verified, or clearly classified as fiction if it is of the imagination. Rumors and gossip are explicitly forbidden to leave our mouths." Bianca's look was serious.

"Spit it out. We don't care how you classify it," Anna said, her own patience worn thin.

"Manny, come here. I am truly forbidden from speaking anything that I cannot verify personally," Bianca insisted. Manny, understanding the silent plea, reached out and grabbed her hand, linking their minds. His eyes widened immediately, a shock of revelation passing through them.

"She says that it's rumored," Manny relayed, his voice low, "that the high priestess who is controlling the Shadow is doing so by wearing his bracelet. And she's calling Dalv back to Kala, right now, to give him the bracelet and restore him to his full power." He pulled his hand back, a clear look of distress on his face, holding something back.

Anna couldn't understand the reason for the pained, horrified looks on her companions' faces. "This seems obvious, no? It would explain almost everything. The Shadow, the priestess, the fear of Dalv's return."

Manny approached Anna, his expression grave. "There is more to the story, Anna." They continued walking. Bianca followed closely, glancing over her shoulder repeatedly.

"Stop." Anna whispered, holding up a hand. The air was suddenly filled with the dust of disturbed rock. "Something is coming." With a *crack*, pieces of the tunnel ceiling began to fall from above, narrowly missing them.

"The only thing to do is run!" Bianca screamed, her librarian dignity instantly forgotten. They all took off at a desperate, frantic sprint. Anna assumed the Shadow itself was hot on their heels. She looked back, ready to instinctively throw a protective, desperate burst of divine energy toward Bianca, but she was too late.

A creature of Anna's most visceral, recurrent nightmares

on Earth had breached the tunnel and was already upon them, a monstrosity disemboweling the Head Librarian of Lega. It had the segmented body of a centipede, ending in the serpentine neck and hissing head of a venomous snake. Anna stopped running and violently threw up onto the stone floor.

Through thick, gurgling sounds of blood in her throat, Bianca managed a final scream. Anna was paralyzed by panic. The gore and reality of the monster that regularly haunted her human sleep, was too much. The creature, sensing the cessation of movement, realized that Bianca was not the only prey in the tunnel. It locked its cold eyes first onto Manny, then onto Anna. Its mouth curled up on both sides of its serpentine head in a horrifying smile. Anna froze in place, rooted by terror.

"*Naganta*," Manny whispered, his voice a choked breath, his own fear only barely less than hers. "Anna, get it together or we'll be next!" Manny, seeing the monster charge, lost his composure entirely. Anna instinctively raised her arms. A weak, uncoordinated spark of yellow-white energy flew out and struck the massive snake, deterring it for a split-second. It immediately resumed its charge. She tried again, faster, focusing harder, forcing the divine energy, but nothing happened.

"Anna, please hurry!" Manny screeched, his voice cracking with desperation. The Naganta was mere meters away, its fangs dripping venom onto the floor. Anna felt a gentle, feather-light brush against her cheek, and a familiar, comforting voice whispered directly into her mind, *"I'm always with you."* She reached into her pocket, pulled out the macaw feather, and concentrated all her focus, her panic, and her will into the object. A sudden, blinding force of shimmering black light, a force of Chaos, shot from her hands towards the snake. For a few terrifying seconds, the colossal creature fought the energy, writhing and coiling in the tunnel. Then, with a deafening *thoom*, the Naganta exploded into a million pieces of viscera.

Manny and Anna found themselves completely covered, head to toe, in hot Naganta guts, sticky gooey innards, and black, extra slime. Both Anna and Manny were stifling gags..

"That was the creature from my nightmares on Earth. What was that?" she asked, furiously trying to wipe the thick, nauseating slime from her face and body.

"That was a Naganta," Manny replied, wiping his own eyes with a sleeve slicked with gore. "I had never actually seen one before. They aren't usually a threat to surface dwellers, but they are the primary reason Kalans never mined anything from their planet, unlike earthlings. Any type of extractive, deep work was far too dangerous because these things inhabit the soil. Some of the Naganta are really small, like the size of a common snake, but no less deadly."

She looked back at the mangled, bloody remains of Bianca and immediately sank to the floor, her energy completely drained. "Why did you not warn me? Why did Bianca agree to this, knowing those things were down here? She was a smug bitch, but she was more valuable than I am! She had all of the recorded knowledge of Kala!" she cried, looking up at Manny, her brow furrowed with grief and rage. This time, her cheek chewing was so forceful that it drew blood.

He crouched down immediately, wrapping a comforting, if gooey, arm around her shoulder. "Anna, she knew that this was probably going to be her fate the moment we started the journey. But she also knew that you were the last hope for her people. She believed in the Book of Reason, and in her interpretation, this was written to happen." Anna stifled a tear.

"How did you know to grab the feather?" Manny inquired, staring at the miraculously clean piece of plumage she still clutched.

"I heard Ara's voice," Anna murmured, looking at the feather with sudden focus. "We need to go back to the Library now, especially since we have no one to stop us from taking all the answers we need."

Manny frowned. "Unfortunately, we can't. The door was sealed behind us to ensure that nothing from below could ever enter the library. Bianca was the only person who possessed the key and the knowledge to get in and out of that specific door."

"I just caused a giant carnivorous earthworm to explode. I think that I can open a goddamn door," she said, her voice dripping with angry defiance.

"Anna, trust me when I say no. Not this door. Not this time. We need to keep going. Give me a moment." He closed his eyes and went into the Keeper's slumber, a meditative state that allowed him to locate his charges across vast distances. The mental picture was fuzzy, unlike on Earth, where he could always locate them clearly, like a crisp TV screen. His mind was clear, but the picture of Misha was indistinct, like a bad television reception. He focused intently on Misha's distinct scent and bright, comforting smile to force a clear view.

"Found them," Manny said, his eyes fluttering rapidly under his lids. "Callan, Misha, Ara, and Navi are walking along a road... It's... snowy. They are all wearing heavy winter clothing, except for Ara. She is still in her macaw form and is perched on Misha's shoulder. She doesn't look well but is wrapped up tightly in a scarf."

Anna stood up, her jaw set with renewed determination, wiping the last of the Naganta slime from her hands. “They are going to Merrat. I know Navi and Misha. Those idiots want to help me, and they will run headlong into Dalv’s stronghold. Let’s go.” Anna was ready to abandon the planned tunnel route. “How do we get out of this tunnel and to the surface?” Manny startled from the meditation.

“Anna, we don’t want to attract too much attention as we approach Dalv’s stronghold. A surface route is unwise,” he argued. “I do not think this is wise.”

“Sorry, Manny, but I don’t give a shit what’s wise, to put it bluntly,” she snapped, her eyes hard. “We’re going. I need to start acting like a goddamn goddess, right?”

Resigned, Manny knew that Anna wouldn’t take no for an answer. Anna couldn’t bear the thought of anyone else’s death weighing on her shoulders.

23

Navi was in a castle, fucking a woman whom he had never seen before. In the next second, he was in the forest, caressing the face of another woman whom he had never seen before. She leaned into his face for a kiss and swoosh! This went on for eons. In the final second of the dream, he made love to Anna. Right before the climax, he woke up in a panicked sweat. Callan stood over him with Ara on her shoulder. Misha looked down on him with a scowl. He had a pained look on his face, not that of unrequited arousal, but of confusion.

"Get up, lover boy. We don't got time for your memories, in case you couldn't tell." Callan looked in her bag and pulled out a cafetière and some espresso. Navi and Misha's eyes lit up.

"Well Callan, I can't say that I've been more happy about anything that you've pulled out of that bag than the espresso maker," Navi said with a feeling of relief.

"Who said this was for you?" She said, "Just kidding!" She howled. "You should see your faces! Hon - make a little heat, will ya? Go on," she motioned to Misha.

Misha looked skeptical.

"Come on Misha... just try. Please. Put yourself in Elena's cafe. Her warmth and smile. The screech of the metal chairs on the tile floor as you would sit down for a cafe con leche with Manny. Feel the energy of that moment. The laughter coming from the regular tables. The laughter from your table between you and Manny. The electricity that you felt the first time his knee touched yours under the table," Navi said almost breathlessly. Ara's eyes were wide. Navi saw a glint of hope.

Misha's gaze softened with that memory. He made a sweeping motion with his palm and then faced it up. A small blue flame sat above the palm of his hand. He smiled with shock. Callan, having already prepped the cafetière with the water from the bathroom, was ready. She placed it over his palm where it levitated until the exquisitely satisfying pop happened, signifying that the espresso was ready.

Callan pulled out three brown coffee cups and shrugged. "That's all I have for this. I made a deal with a Keeper in New York City. She gave me these diner mugs for some safety charms. Ooh wee, those charms are keeping those ladies safe alright."

Navi couldn't hear her ramblings as he was so intently focused on the cup of coffee. A moment of normalcy. Misha sat next to him.

"How did you do that?" Misha asked him.

"Do what?" Navi wondered.

"You know, make me start that flame." Misha said, irritated.

"I don't know. Maybe you needed something to remind you why coffee is so good," Navi laughed uncomfortably. Misha gave him the side eye.

"It's coming back," Ara said with a knowing look, or at

least as knowing as a bird can get. "And in good time. We need to leave here now. Are you ready?"

Misha and Navi shook their heads at the same time, even though they both knew that staying wasn't an option.

"Ok Tweedle Dee and Tweedle Dum, store up some courage." Callan snapped and the coffee accoutrement disappeared.

Navi reluctantly spread the maps out on a nearby table.

"Sugar, we can do that later. Right now we need to get out of here fast and make sure that neither of you are left for dead and we have to do that before this place opens for business."

"I refuse to leave until I know where I am going." Navi studied the map. It appeared that there was a network of footpaths all over this hemisphere with accompanying shelters. He couldn't tell how far Merrat was though. The scale was so bizarre, it didn't make sense to him.

"Ara, could you help me?" Navi asked.

Ara flew off Callan's shoulder and landed softly on Navi's. A mild jolt went through his body. Something was awakened from within. Ara gave him a nuzzle in his ear, silently communicating that it was okay.

"Kala is at a different scale than earth. It's twice the size with less than a third of earth's population. Hover your palm over the map and draw it up."

As Navi did that, a holographic image of the topography of Kala appeared.

"The scale appears off because the maps are at true scale, unlike those of earth. Here you can travel through. Through mountains. Through water." Ara continued. "Unfortunately for us, I don't recommend those types of transportation. Dalv and the Priestess will know. She has spies everywhere. We'll need to go up, over, around and across until the very end. Merrat is only accessible by a high speed train network through the mountains."

"Shush!" One of the librarians said through an echo cone. They stopped talking. They could hear the deafening roar of thunder. The sky darkened. Children began crying from within the crowd.

"I told ya so. But nope. You don't listen to women, Navi. You never did," Callan whispered through her clenched teeth. "Git your shit together."

They hastily gathered their maps and clothing while dropping them in the satchel. The ground rumbled a bit.

"Naganta," Ara whispered, her eyes looking mildly concerned.

"What's a-" Misha and Navi said at the same time.

Callan, in human form, interrupted. "Follow me, boys." She could run quickly for an older lady. Navi and Misha took off after her with Ara resting on Misha's shoulder now.

They ran for at least five minutes through the library before they got to a nondescript steel door with a copper latch and handle. Everything else in Lega was so ornate and thoughtful. Each piece of every building was part of a story of the history of Kala.

"I don't think we should go through that door," Navi whispered urgently.

Hun, I hear you. And your memory must be coming back, but we don't have a choice." Callan ushered them to the door. "Open it Misha."

Misha opened the door to a black void and Callan pushed them through.

———————

They fell for at least 10 minutes. Navi could only see a black void. Eventually he looked down and saw a crack of blue. Then green. They rushed towards the ground. Navi braced for impact when his body came to a halt two feet above the forest floor. After a moment, he dropped.

"Oof! What the hell was that, Callan?" He demanded.

"That, my dear, is one of the perks of being hot shit on Kala. That Jesus fellah gets to walk on water. The Buddha is connected to all the consciousness of the universe. Those Hindu deities get way more perks than that. And you get the equivalent of a Kalan bus pass. Been awhile since y'all have upgraded it. Like hundreds of years. Maybe it can be a priority once you restore it." Callan said matter-of-factly.

Misha flicked dirt off his arm. "Where are we? This is trying my patience," he said.

Navi looked around. He's been here before. He could see it in his mind's eye and on the map. "I have good news and bad news," he said as he smiled. "The good news is that we're headed in the right direction. The bad news is that we're, if I am correctly estimating, one hundred kilometers from the closest rest area."

"Fuck that. I'm out," Misha exclaimed as he threw his hands in the air. Ara pecked the side of his head as he swatted at her.

Callan got in his face and hooked his chin with her finger. "And where do you think you will go exactly, limp dick? What will you do? You can't just shake your ass here and expect results. Get it together. You had coffee. Enjoy this part of the journey. It'll be the most, uh, peaceful."

Navi nodded. "Misha, listen to Callan. Let's go." He began the walk north, hoping they wouldn't see anyone or anything on their journey.

24

Filth covered Anna and Manny as they emerged from the earth, blinking against the bright sunlight. Anna's mind was a blank slate where the concept of time had been, a casualty of their trek through the goddamn tunnels. Her eyes burned as she struggled to blink away the grit.

"How many days was that, Manny?" she finally managed, her voice hoarse.

Manny dusted off his clothes. "Only three. Though, you must remember, time is slower here than on Earth, Anna. You'll continue to adjust."

They had emerged right adjacent to a worn footpath at the fringe of a town nestled in the foothills. The rising topography gave her a strong indication: they were getting closer to Merrat.

They exchanged a look, a shared acknowledgment of their present, unglamorous state. "You look like absolute shit," Anna quipped, offering a playful wink.

"You don't look much better yourself, Goddess," he retorted, and a genuine, shared laugh broke the tension.

Anna closed her eyes, concentrating deeply, trying to focus her divine will on a vision of clean, dirt-free versions of themselves. The dirt and grime vanished from their bodies.

"Ah, that's much better." Buoyed by the small success, she tried to visualize new clothing, the way she had easily conjured garments when she first arrived in Kala. Nothing. She tried again, pouring more focus into the visualization. Nada.

"You don't have my worshipers here, Anna," Manny stated, his tone flat and matter-of-fact, anticipating her frustration.

Anna frowned deeply with the familiar look of frustration and self-pity.

Noting the visible change in her demeanor, Manny continued, "I don't think this is cause for alarm. Most people in this region worship other goddesses. From my recollection, two queens have benevolently ruled this realm for ages. It's a great theocracy. And there is a lesser deity as well, though a locally important one. He is the very epitome of chaotic neutral."

"Oh. OH. Oh no," Anna breathed out, a chilling memory resurfacing in her mind.

Manny sighed, his impatience showing. "What is it now?"

"Well, we need to keep a low profile," Anna said, wincing and sucking in a sharp breath. Once again, she realized she had left a path of destruction and bad feelings in this specific corner of the world. She could not bring herself to share it until she had a chance to somehow make amends with the queens.

"If we are to make it to Merrat safely, you need to tell me

what you know," Manny pressed, his eyes narrowing, demanding the truth.

Just then, a couple of locals zoomed by on sleek hover bikes. They craned their necks, almost breaking them as they did a sharp double-take at the sight of Anna, their attention clearly drawn by something about her appearance or aura.

Once the hover bikes were out of sight, Anna let the forced, slightly manic smile drop from her face. "This region is where my exile was set in motion." She winced inwardly, knowing she should admit that she had likely set the events in motion herself, through her own arrogance and poor judgment.

"Right, so low profile," Manny repeated, his eyes critically assessing their current attire: shorts and t-shirts. Their clothes screamed 'Lega,' a land far too hot and casual for this cooler climate, and certainly not conducive to blending in.

"The first order of business is to find a shop and acquire the proper clothing," he declared, and Anna immediately nodded in agreement.

They walked toward the outskirts of the city. The boundary wall was unusual—similar to the low ramparts Anna had seen in historical books about ancient European cities, barely a meter high. She could easily see over it. From their vantage point on the west, looking east, the city seemed well-organized, with multiple entrance points: a wide lane for hover buses, a designated track for hover trains, and a narrow entrance for foot traffic.

"Do you want to tell me about your last *experience* here?" Manny pushed again, his Keeper persistence surfacing. *Damn Keepers*, Anna thought. Good, protective intentions were behind their every move, but a deep, debilitating shame prevented her from divulging the full truth.

"I will, but first, let's get clothes," Anna stalled, deflecting the question.

Manny stopped, gripping Anna's shoulders firmly. He looked into her eye. "Trust me when I say that you are different now. You changed, for the better." Anna swallowed back a wave of tears and guilt, nodding her acknowledgment.

"Come on. Let's get into something cleaner and warmer." Manny, ever practical, had the foresight to check Bianca's pockets for money and any other useful objects after her death. *It wasn't stealing if she was dead and no one could retrieve the body,* he rationalized to himself. He pulled out a handful of the global currency and a few odd, unidentifiable items.

They veered off the forest trail and moved towards the city, attempting to maintain a low profile while searching for a clothing kiosk. The two obvious foreigners continued walking closer to the edge of town, and passersby looked at them, only to immediately avert their eyes in a way that felt deliberate, almost practiced.

"Something isn't right," Manny murmured. Without warning, he grabbed Anna tightly by the wrist and darted into the woods, keeping parallel with the footpath, but fully concealed by the trees.

"We need to stay off the paths from here on," he instructed, the hair on his arms standing on end.

"What is the point in being a goddess if I can't wield my powers to protect us, huh?" she demanded.

Manny shrugged, maintaining his vigilance. "That's not how this works, Anna. You are a deity, not a wizard casting spells on command."

"Are there wizards in this world?" she asked, following the question with a loud, exasperated "humpf" as her exclamation point.

Manny merely shrugged again, a gesture of helplessness.

"Great. You seem to know just as much as I do about this place," she griped.

"Look, regarding the deity thing," he began, shaking his head in frustration and shrugging one more time. "Your power is complex, Anna. It's not a switch you flip. It's not infinite, yet it's not truly finite either. I simply can't explain it."

"Wonderful," she drawled, rolling her eyes in sarcasm.

Ten minutes later, they stood at the true edge of the town. It presented as an odd, deceptively simple-looking place. No building rose higher than a couple of stories, and every single structure was built with whitewashed brick, giving the town a uniform feel.

"We wouldn't be on this detour if I could just activate my powers," she muttered, a buzzing starting behind her eyes. Anna closed them for a fleeting second, and a clear, internal vision burst forth: a shop selling warmer clothes, just two streets over. The city was a maze of curved, ancient-looking stone walkways. Clearly, no hovercrafts of any type were permitted within the city center.

"I know where we need to go," she announced, grabbing Manny by the hand. They turned right, emerging directly into a square dominated by an enormous statue of the Two Queens. Anna froze in her tracks. Her eyes rolled back into her head, and she crumpled towards the ground. Manny reacted instantly, catching her and holding her upright.

A few seconds later, she came to, looking utterly dazed.

"How long was I gone that time?" she whispered wearily.

"Just a few seconds," Manny confirmed.

She shook her head. "This really is not a friendly place for me. This area was under the rule of two queens..." She hesitated, her shame making the next words difficult.

"Thank you, dear, I believe we already covered that part in the exam prep," Manny interjected with a wry, supportive smile.

"Well...I might have tricked them out of their power. A full-on power grab of their powers, if you will," she confessed sheepishly. "And of their other local god, Moaz. I tried to strip it all away by promising their people more wealth and knowledge if they worshipped me instead of the queens and Moaz. Only one person got more power from that deal, and it certainly wasn't them."

"Noted," Manny said, his voice grim. "That would certainly explain why your powers have diminished here. It is highly possible that Moaz is actively protecting the area from any external deity influence. That's good news, though. It means that Dalv and his ilk have no power here either. Let's truly try to keep a low profile, shall we? And no more fainting," he finished deadpan. The pair looked nothing like anyone in their surroundings, an issue they had to rectify immediately.

"I'm not worried about Moaz; I'm much more worried about the queens," Anna replied, wincing. They reached a shadowy alley, which curved around the corner from a row of shops.

"You go in, Manny. I'll stand guard out here. You just look like a generic foreigner. I, unfortunately, look like, well, me," she said matter-of-factly, acknowledging her own unavoidable divine aura.

He hesitated, still worried about leaving her alone.

"Go. The sooner you buy us normal clothes, the sooner

we can blend in. Besides, I promise I won't move from this spot. I won't get into trouble."

Manny knew, with certainty, that this entire trip was marked for trouble, and she could easily get into it without moving an inch. But the risk of them both being discovered inside the shop was greater.

"Fine," he conceded, pulling out the bag of currency. "But scream if you need me." As soon as the words left his mouth, he regretted the instruction.

Anna doubled over in immediate, loud laughter. Manny sighed heavily and turned the corner to enter the shop.

The local fashion in this part of Kala was profoundly strange. There were clearly people from Merrat, dressed in stark black and gray, looking severe yet stylish, and people from Lega, in their bright, primary colors, though here they were long-sleeved, long-panted, and paired with warm, equally brightly colored outerwear.

The true locals, however, were decked out in their seasonal autumnal wear. Everything they wore was voluminous and billowy, colored in the exact shades of changing leaves—russets, golds, deep reds. The entire vibe was overdone and lavish. Manny, who could usually appreciate almost any type of fashion, judged this look to be borderline hideous.

He walked into the shop after observing the passersby, hoping he could find something far more conspicuous for the rest of their journey, rather than the plume-like clothing he saw here.

"Ulloo. How ez ya?" the shopkeeper greeted him without even looking up from a large log book he was meticulously scribbling in. Manny felt a pulse in his dick. The man who stood before him was unmistakably hot. The shopkeeper had the build of a runner, skin color of mahogany and perfect locs down to his shoulders.

Their local dialect was almost as difficult to parse as their clothing choices.

"Feen," Manny replied, profoundly grateful that his role as a Keeper allowed him to speak and understand thousands of universal languages.

The shopkeeper, immediately detecting an accent, looked up. His large hazel eyes narrowed in suspicion, then softened as he smiled, looking Manny up and down with an unmistakable gaze. Manny was, for the first time since they arrived in Kala, feeling in desperate need of a good fuck.

Clearly, the body language of attraction was universally understood. Manny smiled back, feeling a brief, fleeting sense of liberation. It was freeing to be on a planet without sexual hang-ups or cultural baggage on desire.

"Yee not from eround here. Leet me hulp ya." The shopkeeper walked towards him with seductive confidence.

Manny knew he could not be distracted, although his mind wandered for a second, imagining retreating to the changing room... *No. Focus.*

"I need some more muted clothing for myself and a friend," Manny requested. The shopkeeper sighed audibly, the romance momentarily draining from his face.

"Reeght theees wuy." Manny could tell that visitors often had disdain for the local fashion sense.

Manny quickly found two pairs of lined, heavy wool-blend gray pants and two black sweaters. Not exactly fun or fashionable, but considered boring everywhere in the universe. Perfect.

He also bought hats, gloves, and scarves, anticipating the colder temperatures of Merrat.

"May I change into these now?" he asked.

The shopkeeper's eyes lit up again. "Yes."

Manny walked towards the changing room, the shopkeeper following closely behind.

Apparently, a blowjob was a blowjob no matter where you were in the universe. Manny desperately needed the release. He was not a monastic; he was a man with needs, and the brief, intense encounter made him feel at ease for the first time since their arrival on Kala. He returned the favor, ensuring the experience was mutually enjoyable. Even a Keeper had desires.

After the escapade, Manny emerged from the dressing room fully dressed in his new gray and black layers, the shopkeeper winked. Manny guessed this was his standard operating procedure.

"Thank you for everything," he said, zipping up his black coat as he walked out of the store, clothes for Anna in tow. He turned the corner to see Anna waiting impatiently, the bag of clothes held tightly in his hand.

"Took you long enough," she snapped, scowling at the delay.

"It was an intense shopping experience," he replied, a hint of mischief in his tone. "Let's change and get back on the road." Before they could open the bag and change, a voice startled them.

"You know, next time you really should be careful about whose dick you suck, Manny," Moaz said, standing directly in front of them, his presence an immediate, unsettling shock.

Manny's face remained flat, a mask of composure. Anna, however, looked at him incredulously, her eyes wide with surprise and a touch of amusement.

"But seriously, these are my faithful," Moaz continued,

gesturing vaguely to the town. "The Officers asked us to keep an eye out for you all. What did you expect? Please don't tell me that you are still that naive after being here for a few weeks." Moaz's face contorted into a fake, mocking pout.

"Moaz, it's been awhile," Anna said coolly, stepping forward. "We have no business here, so please just let us on our way."

"Oh, but I have business with you, if you recall," Moaz countered, his voice losing its playful edge. "I know that once a deity is exiled, we're *supposed* to forgive you. Time served and all that. But I'm having a hard time welcoming the prodigal daughter back from purgatory." Moaz wasted no words, cutting straight to his resentment.

"Calm down. I do not want to influence your faithful or cause trouble. I have other, more urgent concerns right now," Anna said, her voice as tranquil as she could muster, trying to de-escalate the confrontation.

"You nearly took it all from me and the Queens! This is a neutral, peaceful zone, and you tried to ruin it! We are hanging on by a thread here with the threat from Merrat looming. You have no idea what you're truly up against, Anna." Moaz began to levitate as he spoke, vibrating visibly with barely contained anger.

"I know Dalv. I know how powerful he is. But I have powerful friends as well. We can and will defeat him and his priestess," Anna declared with forced confidence.

"You don't get it, do you? It's more powerful than Dalv. Nearly everyone here worships me, prays to me, offers sacrifices—"

Anna and Manny both winced at the word 'sacrifices.'

"Well, I happen to like certain animal meat and skins. What can I say?" Moaz dismissed their judgment with a wave of his hand. "The point is, I am more powerful than I have ever been, and it's only out of the fear of my faithful, not for any other reason. I have a few million active worshippers, and still I am no match for—" He stopped suddenly, his eyes widening.

"They're here. You need to leave now," Moaz urged, his anger instantly replaced by fear. He raised his arms and pushed his hands outwards in a powerful, desperate gesture aimed at Anna and Manny.

Manny and Anna were sucked through a terrifying, disorienting vortex. In the next instant, they were spat out into a silent, frozen forest. A light dusting of snow covered the ground and the low-hanging evergreen branches. They were both severely disoriented.

Flurries blew gently in the breeze around their heads.

You're getting close to Merrat...

They both snapped their heads up, looking wildly at each other.

"Who said that?" Anna asked, her voice panicked, spinning around to search for the source.

"One of the trees," Manny replied. It was exactly like their earlier, strange tree encounters, only the voice was clearer, more urgent.

Anna opened her mouth to protest, but Manny quickly shushed her. A stronger breeze blew through the trees again.

Your friends are much further than you. They are nearly there.

"Let's go!" Anna started running immediately, her panic fueling her speed. A tree branch blew down in the breeze, waving them over as if beckoning them to slow down.

"Let's take a moment to change our clothes and maybe plan a bit, okay?" Manny said, motioning to a thick evergreen about ten meters off the main path. Anna reluctantly took the large paper bag full of clothing out of his hand.

"These are so drab. You couldn't find anything with a splash of color?" Anna complained, pulling on a black woolen turtleneck sweater and thick gray wool leggings. She slipped on a pair of flat, black boots. She felt significantly cozier than before, which was at least one small victory.

"Not unless you wanted to look like a turkey, Anna. Besides, Merrat isn't exactly known for bold and bright fashion," Manny countered. After he changed, he felt hideous but undeniably cozy. He hated being cold.

"Moaz actually did us a significant favor by expelling us like that," Manny admitted, his concern focused on any potential passersby on the footpath, even though they were safely hidden by the dense trees.

"How are we going to do this? How are we going to find them with my ridiculously shit power levels?" Anna's voice was filled with a fresh wave of anxiety. "And how in the hell does Dalv have so much power if it comes from the number of worshippers? My realm is bigger than Merrat's! I know I don't have his numbers, but Dalv and I have been here for the same amount of time!"

Another breeze whispered through the trees.

Keep walking towards Merrat and stay off the trail and out of sight as long as you can.

A tree had whispered directly to Manny.

"Okay, now we go. Come on, Anna."

"Hang on, you're listening to a tree?" Anna said, exasperated by the absurdity of the situation.

"The trees on Kala are directly connected to Keepers like me. They have served me well so far, and I trust them implicitly," Manny said firmly, brooking no argument.

Frustrated, Anna let out a small growl as she started

jogging through the thick forest. Manny immediately ran at max speed to keep up with her powerful stride. She stopped abruptly after about thirty minutes of hard running.

Her eyes rolled back into her head. Another vision, more intense than the last.

She trudged through the muddy river in the darkness of night so as not to be seen by anyone. When she emerged on the other side, she meticulously checked her impermeable bag to ensure that the six fortunas *were intact. She was mildly shocked at how easily she had obtained all of them. Nothing in Kala had strong supernatural protections anymore. Kalans used their primitive weapons and good will to guard items that they deemed valuable, but they were so blind to the immense power available to them in the absence of fierce deities.*

The deities that remained on Kala were impotent. Too benevolent. They responded to what the people thought they needed instead of what they truly needed, failing to recognize what they desperately required for survival. She would ensure that Kala was brought back to its rightful, powerful state.

The fortunas shined back at her: six iridescent gemstones, each one harnessing the power of the deities. They were capable of strengthening or weakening any deity, like a cosmic voodoo doll. Two of the fortunas *were easily found at abandoned temples. She used a series of cunning tricks to get the other four. If her calculations were correct—and so far they had been 100% correct—the seventh and final* fortuna *would be the most difficult to obtain, but not impossible. It was the only way that she could create a new, undetectable portal. The other portals were too heavily guarded.*

The platinum dagger rested between her teeth as she scaled up the side of the rocky mountain face, attempting to avoid detection by using the perilous bridge to get to Dalv's temple. The dagger was the only way to defend herself without alerting the local authorities. Dalv was known as the most wrathful of the deities of Kala, but he also rewarded his loyal followers with great, terrible gifts. Even though he was currently gone, she expected his most devoted worshipers to be present, making fervent offerings and praying for his immediate return.

The wind rushed violently up the side of the mountain as she finally made it to the stone bridge. Covered in mud and exhausted, she ducked into an abandoned offerings center.

"Ha. His followers aren't as loyal as he thought," she chuckled to herself, the sound dry and humorless. She began to bath herself in the holy water trickling out of the ancient fountain. It felt instantly reviving and energizing, and the mud came off easily.

"YOU. It predicted you would come. I have been expecting you." The old man cackled, pointing a knobby, accusatory finger at her from the shadows.

Without hesitation, she turned around and threw the dagger at the high priest of Dalv, piercing his thick breastplate and hitting him directly in the heart.

She walked over and immediately noticed the final fortuna, a glowing red iridescent stone, set in a broach that attached his ceremonial scarf. He coughed and sputtered up a thick rush of blood. His eyes were wide with pure contempt. She reached down and pulled the broach off, tearing his bloodstained scarf. "It is written," he coughed up more blood, his final words.

"Thank you. It's unfortunate that you won't live to see the new paradigm unfold." She threw her head back with a triumphant, maniacal laugh.

The priestess turned her back, making her way up the granite steps to the discovery pool, missing the fact that the priest, in his last, conscious breath, pulled a red feather and a lizard tail out of his pocket and dropped them into a hidden slot.

She carefully placed the seven fortunas *around the pool in a perfect heptagon. The water immediately formed a gentle, swirling whirlpool. She began chanting, "Ad ihim mallimara ed mureod" as she placed the very last fortuna. The whirlpool became violently agitated and turned into a powerful water spout. She held her ground, raising her arms high during the process. The water spat out an intricately carved bracelet with seven miniscule* fortunas *set into it, which landed directly at her feet.*

At last. It was hers. It was all hers.

Anna snapped back to consciousness. Disoriented and woozy, she wobbled until Manny squatted down next to her, helping her find her balance. Anna forced her breathing to slow, trying to reconcile the vision with reality.

"How long was it that time?" she whispered, still shaken.

"Only a few seconds again," Manny replied gently.

She shook her head in disbelief. "It wasn't my history, or a vision of my past life. I could only see the back of the woman and it was dark, but it had to have been the priestess. She had a bag of incredibly powerful hourglass-looking items. And she just... killed a temple guardian. She and Dalv together..." She couldn't finish the sentence, unwilling to voice the terrifying implication of what their combined power could accomplish.

"But that's... impossible," Manny breathed, knowing instantly that she was talking about the *fortunas*. "How could a priestess touch the *fortunas*? They are protected from all but true deities."

"Of course you know the *fortunas*," Anna sighed. "Anyways, the best way to answer that question is to ask in person. Let's go find her," Anna said, her voice now filled with a true, unwavering determination.

With that, they continued their difficult journey into the silent, snowy forest.

25

They all laid in a pile after their rough landing.

"I reckon we gotta stick to the woods, probably off the trail. Unless you lot want some excitement." Callan lectured to the group.

"Not particularly. Are you sure that a trek is the only way? Can't we take a taxi or a train?" Navi said with the resignation of already knowing the answer. On earth, his life was so certain and easy. He had power and influence within the Communist Party, which was akin to being a deity of a micro-kingdom.

"Here we go again, genius. Have you seen a taxi anywhere?" Callan motioned outward to the land. Navi shook his head.

"Cuz they don't have 'em. Trains, yes. But again, lots of quick moving communications on this planet, not like earth. If we're seen on a train, then our lives will get exciting." She smiled gleefully.

"Fine." Navi resigned himself to being out of control. Unaccustomed to being constantly berated and accused of being responsible for heinous acts, he could only stare at the ground as he walked. Unable to remember his past whilst being blamed for it made him feel like a pariah.

The damp chill of mist permeated Navi's skin. The low hanging clouds looked like cotton candy being drug across the tops of the craggy, leafless trees. The rocky, rooted trail was lined with gnarled, knobby trees and varieties of moss that looked unreal with their chartreuse and fuchsia colors. He could only see about 10 meters ahead due to the low cloud cover and mist.

Misha nodded in agreement with Callan. "I, for one, agree with her. We're strong enough to fend off whatever comes our way. Besides, I'm feeling a bit energized now," he said with that Soviet stoicism that was all too familiar to Navi. Navi had to suppress the urge to touch Misha. A hunger enveloped his body. He felt an insatiable desire to fuck him. Was it Misha's power his aphrodisiac? Was everyone's power Navi's aphrodisiac? That seems to be the pattern of his relationships on this planet.

He shook off the thought. He knew that Misha still had his Soviet mindset, regardless of being a lifetime from home. Soviet stoicism and secret-keeping was prized above all. Navi himself was frightened by his own sensations and feelings. He couldn't shake the simultaneous sense of power and foreboding. As he has learned, his powers in Kala seemed to have bizarre or dangerous consequences.

They walked in silence with their rucksacks. He was grateful that Callan could shut the hell up for awhile at least.

Misha started making small talk. Navi joined, even though he didn't enjoy conversation with this new petulant Misha. He complained about the pedestrian life that he had in Cuba, showing slight emotional wavering when Manny came up in the conversation. Navi nodded. Laughed when appropriate. Inserted a few key words to indicate that he was listening all whilst staring at his feet. Tuned out. Thought of Anna. Noticed the earthy funk of the fertile forest floor with the seemingly winter-ready trees on each side. His senses were further activated by the flora.

Peculiarly, the trees knobs and gnarls appeared in a pattern that looked almost like a language. Navi spoke in earnest when Misha stopped talking.

"Do you all see this?" He walked up to two trees that emerged from the same root system that formed a U shape coming from the ground. There was a clear message in the bark from the top left of the U to the top right, but he couldn't decipher it.

"Oh honey, I want whatever you're on because you are seeing some shit." Misha said tartly.

"Welcome back sugar, Kala has missed you," Callan said without inflection. Misha swiveled his head towards her in disbelief.

"Can any of you see it?" Navi said, in a bit of a frantic tone, hoping he wasn't going crazy.

"Nope, that's your gift. You and nature have a special relationship," Ara said, looking as pleased and relieved as a bird could.

Navi had to know what it said but he couldn't figure it out.

"You'll be literate again. Incorporation takes time," Ara said coolly.

"I'm sick of all the fucking time that this is taking," Navi snapped.

Misha shrugged, oblivious to the Navi's feelings.

Navi gave up as they continued walking. Confusion washed over him as he absorbed the feelings of the fog, the earth, the woodland creatures and the trees. He was lost in the world of sensation for hours. Every natural element of this world spoke to him simultaneously. His mind swirled like a hurricane. Lost in perception, his physical body walked with the crew whilst his mind was oblivious to their reality.

They walked for three days. They slept in tents off the trail and survived on Callan's favorite American junk food that she pulled out of her bag of tricks. Navi's favorite was something called a Hostess Cupcake. Misha devoured hundreds of a version of an eclair called a Twinkie. The lack of excitement lulled them all into a false sense of security.

On the fourth day, they meandered along the trail as they had every day before, the topography was ever changing and morphing into a more rocky and frosty environment. Suddenly, there was a loud crack in the mist just ahead. It morphed into the sound of multiple smaller pops.

They all froze. Four days on the trail and they managed not to see any other sign of life. Instinctively, Navi grabbed Misha's hand. A shadow of a human form emerged from the woods. It was neither good nor evil.

Navi was perplexed. He looked at Callan who, for the first time, seemed genuinely puzzled. She shrugged her shoulders.

A voice came from the figure. It sounded like a poorly tuned radio.

KSSHHHHHHKKKKKSHHH "- he is a pawn -" KSSSSHKKKKSHHH "-do not advance" - KSSSHHHH "-the cause" KSHHHH.

Navi could swear that voice was from Anna.

"Anna?"

KSSSHHHHH "the fortunas" - KSHHHH.

By that point, they were all wincing at this message from beyond.

The figure disappeared and so did the sound.

"What the hell was that, Ara?" Callan asked. "I've seen a lot of shit, but that beats all I ever saw."

Ara looked perplexed. "I think that perhaps, it's a message from another time and place. Perhaps Oragan?"

"It sounded like Anna. How is that possible?" Navi demanded. The air brought no warnings, nor did the energy signal remain in this realm.

Ara shrugged, matter-of-factly.

Another crack rippled through the air. This was the unmistakable sound of a tree branch breaking. Before any of them could react, a branch swooped them into the multi-colored mossy embankment just below its trunk. They were all flat-backed against the trunk with branches around their mouths, arms and legs. Navi felt his legs absorb into the root system. Relief and calm washed over him for the first time since they arrived.

A group of five Officers paused about three meters away.

"I just saw these assholes, I swear!" said a figure dressed in all black with utility boots. She and the other five officers looked like they were not to be trifled with.

They looked around. *The tree must be camouflaging us,* Navi thought.

Another one, apparently the leader, paused in front of their tree. He sniffed around them. Navi saw his beady little eyes and red puffy skin up close. Whilst other Kalans had a lovely iridescent hue to them, his skin reflected light making it painful to look at.

"You tree," he said while knocking the tree with his orb, "tell me what you've seen."

I do not see.

The tree said in a sighed whisper that sounded like the wind.

The man knocked what he thought was a tree, but hit Navi in the head. Navi used all of his willpower not to yowl. Aside from the blunt force, it burned his head.

"I'm not interested in semantics, tree. Tell me." He then pressed his orb into Navi's shoulder. Tears welled in Navi's eyes. A burning sensation permeated his shoulder and radiated down his right arm.

Of the experience you wish for me to discuss, I did not have. Be on your path, the tree whispered sternly, *the forest is not your domain.*

"Come on. These cunts are powerful," a woman warned.

He flipped his staff so the orbs faced the path. In unison, they levitated off the ground and took off in the southern direction.

Five minutes later, the trees dropped their charges.

Navi's face, stained from the pain of the burns, winced as he emerged.

"What in the fuck was that?" He said as he rubbed his left shoulder.

Misha rolled up Navi's sleeve to see the damage and frowned as he inhaled sharply.

"Ew, Navi. That looks disgusting." Misha stared at a perfectly red half sphere branded on Navi's shoulder.

Navi bit his lip to keep from screaming. The pain intensified.

"It fucking hurts!" He screeched as he looked at his shoulder with his brow knitted together.

The tree raised its moss-covered roots toward Navi's wound and pressed it on Navi's shoulder and used the fuchsia moss from another root on his head. Navi drew blood as he bit his lip. The pain intensified for a minute and then sweet relief washed over him. The tree lifted its branch. Navi looked to see that his shoulder was completely healed.

"I - Thank you. Why - " Navi stammered. The hurricane returned to his brain, rendering him unable to speak.

Time is not here. Go north to subvert their search. Go now. The tree said.

For the first time in days, Ara took flight up to the tree top, through its branches and dove down. Callan remained shockingly silent. She landed on Callan's shoulders and fluffed her feathers. All of them picked up the pace and continued north on the trail in stunned silence until Misha opened his mouth.

"What was that? What was that? What was ALL of that?" Misha said as he swooped his arm.

"Don't ask me. I just visit here. Cousin?" Callan looked at Ara, who was on her shoulder.

Ara sighed. "It's involved."

"Try me," Navi said sternly.

Ara opened her beak to say "Your type, the daemon, share a kinship with the elements. It's complex and intense, but similarly to the elements, you inspire. For whatever reason, regardless of what you do to the people and other beings here, the elements will mostly be favorable to you."

"Mostly?"

"There's always some unsavory elements," Ara winked.

Callan groaned. "Cousin, keep the jokes to me."

"Y'all, those Officers are like the Cuban Policia for the ruler of Merrat. Best if we keep out of their way, capiche? Merrat, even without an evil priestess, isn't known for its laissez faire approach to life." Callan informed them. "Let's get going. The refuge is only a few more hours."

"Wonderful. Will there at least be a shower?" Misha said flatly.

Callan and Ara shrugged.

They walked in silence for over an hour. Ideas in Navi's

head flitted from disconcerting thoughts to disconnected memories. Within seconds, he clearly created an entire city and infrastructure in his mind. But there was nowhere to put it. No one to inspire. It spun around like a centrifuge. Perfect plans for piping water into the refuge were clearly visible in his mind. Stuck. In the middle, with nowhere to go. Memories of Kala flashed and disappeared as quickly as they came.

He closed his eyes and shook his head.

Misha noticed. "Navi, *apareces como mierda*." Navi knew that he looked like shit. He surely felt like it.

Ara landed on his shoulder. "Incorporation is painful. It's the simultaneous merger of atonement, magical restoration and memories from the past, present and sometimes future." She said quite matter-of-factly, without any sympathy.

"Can I go back? Go back to Cuba?" He whispered as his brow broke into a bead of sweat. He felt crazy. Like those poor old schizophrenics on the streets.

"You won't want to." Her voice echoed in his head.

The weather turned colder as they walked further north. Navi sweat profusely as he battled a searing headache. Bile crept up his throat. He froze. Electric tremors jolted through his body. He put both hands on a tree and dry heaved. Each piece of bark beneath his fingertips sent a message to his core. At that moment he felt connected to the tree. The nausea and headache subsided.

"You ok?" Misha said.

"Why the hell did you let me do that?" Navi yelled at Ara. "Why didn't you tell me to touch the fucking tree?"

"It changes every time. Contrary to belief, I don't control the universe and I'm not psychic." Ara said and shrugged her wings.

Navi deeply inhaled and exhaled. The sweat and tremors were gone. His stomach was settled.

"I'm fine." Physically he was fine. Emotionally, he was not. Every moment felt like an excruciating decade of emotional torture. Pieces of information and images flashed in his mind. If Ivan from Cuba saw Navi from Kala, Ivan would have Navi committed to a mental institution.

As men did in Cuba, however, he kept silent and trudged forward as he always had before.

26

Callan's own demons kept her from flying away. She never incorporated, but she sure as shit felt like she atoned. It was lonely on the side. She was never at the top. Always on the side. For eternity.

They approached the refuge.

"HUSH." She shut up Misha and Navi real quick while waving them to the side of the trail. Callan could smell people in the refuge.

"I think it's just hikers. Lemme check." She transformed into the toucan to get a closer look, for herself of course. It wasn't like she was trying to develop a soft-spot for Misha or Navi. Those fuckers could take care of themselves, she was sure. But in case they couldn't...

Callan knew that the limits of her human body resided in her mind. But God damn, every time she returned to her natural state it felt like a layer of rock had been chiseled off of her skin. She took an extra few seconds to soar up, just to the top of the trees, before diving towards the refuge. Every fiber of herself desired to take a short detour around Kala. Forlorn, she settled for a quick graze of the canopy's top before returning to her mission. Her sleek black wings expanded as she swooped down and perched on the windowsill of the octagonal shaped refuge.

Ooh eeee, this is a good one, she thought. It sat protected by ancient cedar trees, like those redwoods on earth. She quite liked it there, but those damn golden eagles were territorial mother fuckers. Her thoughts drifted to one of her encounters with a particular white-tailed kite. "Get the hell out of here! Collectors aren't welcome by birds nor humans in these parts." All she wanted was to fly through those majestic trees along the coast while inhaling the smell of the redwoods. At least this part of Kala was similar.

This is some Navi shit, right here, she thought. The trees formed in a perfectly symmetrical octagon to protect the refuge. Cerulean water trickled in a glacier creek behind the structure. Moss carpeted the forest floor and smoke rose from the chimney. The exterior was constructed of a stained wood overlaid with a stretched waterproof cloth top, like the yurts that she had seen in her earthly travels. It was impermeable to the elements, and hopefully angry deities.

She peered in to spy two weary females who looked like they were from Lega. They were cooking a stew. From her esteemed judgement, and her judgement was very esteemed, they were the refuge managers.

She swooped back towards the rag tag team of misfits to inform them of the good fortune, for once.

"Good news y'all, the refuge managers are from Lega. Y'all calm your extra. We don't want to scare them off and have them alert the buzzkills," Callan stated.

Misha and Navi nodded skeptically. Those damn boys. Misha was a lost cause. At least he was cute. Navi slowly got it, but damn. No wonder he was exiled.

She then opened her bag. "Hop on in, cousin, I'll make it nice and cozy just for you."

Ara begrudgingly hopped into her bag.

They walked up to the refuge and knocked. A Black woman with short cropped, shockingly blue hair answered the door and smiled.

"Don't look so relieved, these guys stink!" Callan squawked and then laughed at her own joke.

"Eh hem, we're weary travelers looking to stay in this refuge. Would you be so kind?" Navi said.

"Of course. Please come in. We were worried that you... it's just that these times are uncertain." She ushered them in.

The refuge had four sets of bunk beds with cozy blankets along four of the eight walls. The kitchen set-up was on the fifth wall, with a chimney that vented the smoke outside. There was a giant pot of stew simmering in a cauldron within the hearth of the fireplace carved out of a single giant slab of stone.

Navi and Misha's faces relaxed when the smell of the stew hit their noses. It smelled like a pot of rice and beans with all their favorite spices.

"You'll have to pardon my travel companions. They have no home training. I'm Karina," Callan said, hoping Navi would take her lead.

"I'm... Natto," Navi said. Callan was impressed with his fake name.

"I'm Misha," the idiot said proudly. Callan knew that fool would fuck it up.

"Misha, that's an odd name. I'm Benya," said the woman who answered the door.

"It sure is. His parents were really odd," Callan said.

"This is my partner, Joiya," Benya said. Joiya smiled and

waved from the far wall as she stirred the pot and added more spices.

"We manage this refuge and were hoping for some nice company as things have been a little tense in these parts for a while. Given everything that's happening, we thought this would provide a peaceful respite from the world," Benya said wearily.

"How's that workin' out for ya?" Callan asked.

"It's ok. We could do without the regular visits from those Merrati goons." Benya shrugged.

"What's that like? We don't see many of them where we're from," Navi said.

"Where are you from?" Benya asked, raising an eyebrow in curiosity.

Callan knew that these shits would ruin it all.

"A little bit all over Kala. Family reunion trek. Thought it would make us bond. Turns out we're just making each other nuts with each passing day!" Callan laughed. Benya and Joiya both chuckled.

"We've heard that before!" Joiya hollered from the other side of the room.

"You're lucky then. We don't know much about those Officers since they're new. They visit here every few days asking for our resident logs with detailed descriptions. They clearly have an orb up their ass about it. We oblige to keep the peace. We're just glad that we're Legalans and don't have to deal with them regularly." Benya sighed. The group didn't dare break the news of Lega being overrun. "Our friends from a few refuges up inside Merrati said that they have strict reporting laws. If anyone is looking for, let's say, a more off-the-path experience, they shouldn't stay up there." Benya said as her eyes narrowed on Callan.

"Good to know, sugar." Callan nodded knowingly. These women were allies.

"Dinner's ready," Joiya said. Callan watched Navi take in the table. Mesmerizing as it was informative, the table was clearly another piece of art inspired by Navi. From what she could tell under the place settings and food, the intricate carvings told the story of the Birds. If Callan were capable of sincerely emoting, she may have shed a tear at the beauty of the table.

"Beautiful table ya got here. What's it of?" Callan said slyly.

"It's an antique from our area of Kala. Isn't it stunning? If you get the chance, you should visit the library in Lega. I'm not a historian, but I think this was created during the same period as our library." Joiya said proudly. "Apparently there are hundreds of these tables around Kala," she added. A prickly sensation overtook Callan. What was that? Genuine curiosity? Sincerity? It's been a millennia at least.

As they sat down to their meal, Callan noticed that Navi's fingers delicately traced around the table as he ate. Maybe he could tell her a little somethin' about it later. The boys inhaled their food and kept the conversation to small talk with the managers.

Callan felt a little peck through her sack. Shit, Ara. She wished Ara could see this. It told something of their origins, to them it was only whispers of their ancestors, who have existed for an eternity as well. Callan and Ara lived through space and time for so long that they forgot where they came from. Callan surreptitiously fed her cousin in the sack.

Ara nipped her finger in frustration. Callan pulled it closed in retaliation. If Ara wanted to be a little bitch, fine. But she didn't have to take it out on Callan. It wasn't Callan's fault that Ara's life mate was on earth. Callan fed her anyway. Obligations or some such bullshit.

"Alrighty y'all, it's time to get a good night's sleep. We gotta be up at the butt crack of dawn tomorrow morning," Callan hollered. "Natto, clear the table with me, would ya? Be a doll to these hosts," She added.

Joiya laughed. "You are so interesting. I can't say I'm familiar with your accent or your diction. Where are you from again?"

"Not here." Callan said flatly.

The couple's lips pursed and their eyes widened as they nodded. Callan's tone made it clear that they shouldn't ask any more questions.

Navi got the hint and walked over to help her clear the table. "Would ya look at this Natto? Gorgeous, right?" Callan studied the table. The famed corvids of Kala and the mountains of Terram were intricately carved into the table. Various corvids were carved throughout the entire piece. She hated corvids. They were smug assholes. They thought that they were so smart.

Navi's eyes widened as he brushed the table with his fingers, clearing the plates. Callan was dying to know the origins of that story. She also wanted to know if there was any dirt on those damn birds.

A single giant cedar had been carved to create the table and, by Callan's estimate, it was 5,000 years old before it died. The magic and power still emanated from it. Evergreens, carved in exquisite detail, adorned the legs. Crows, magpies and jays were dispersed throughout its branches, detailed down to the barbs of each singular feather. Choucas floated playfully around the carving of a mountain range. The sun set above the crows as they looked east towards a tree on the other side of the table. The evergreen on the other side had two owls looking west towards the corvids. They guarded a nest filled with gems and objects that looked like hourglasses.

A flurry of activity filled the space in between. Mindless, idiotic songbirds flitted about.

Callan's thoughts. She realized exactly what events needed to transpire to restore balance to Kala. Anna's presence alone wasn't going to restore the balance, but Anna was the only one who could bring them back. Fuck a duck (although not literally - ducks were terrible lovers). She knew this was going to be epic but holy hell. She kept her face flat to hide her shock.

"Best we get some sleep before we continue this lovely time for family bonding, eh?" Callan said. She knew these poor kooks would need their feeble sleep to get through the next part of the journey.

They climbed into their beds and slept soundly, except for Callan.She didn't need sleep. But if she did, she would've laid there with her eyes wide open. In all her history, Callan never anticipated she would experience anything like this: growing fond of humanoid magical creatures and deities. If only she could be more like that asshole collector in New York City.

As everyone else slept, Callan thought of the contents in her possession and how each trade would play out, as if she were playing a cosmic game of life-or-death chess. It kept her mind busy until the sun crept over the horizon.

27

Before the day broke, Callan woke them up one by one. Navi could have slept for another decade.

"You stink Natto! Please wash that stench off before we go."

Navi groggily made his way towards the bathroom for another shower.

"Misha, get up. You're next, bucko," she belted to Misha.

The hot water hit Navi's body. Like the sleep, he could have showered for an eternity. He emerged from the bathroom to the smell of Joiya and Benya warming up last night's stew.

Navi felt so fresh and so clean after his shower.

"Do you have coffee?" He asked, still half asleep.

"What's that?" Joiya asked curiously.

"It's a drink from our neck of the woods. You know, it gets ya going in the morning."

"Oh yes! Here we call it challa. Sure, I'll make some." Joiya pulled a collection of dried herbs from a sack, boiled and steeped them. Callan balked. Navi inhaled the funky smell. It didn't smell like coffee or tea.

"Welp, thanks but we gotta run!" Callan chirped.

"But I just made this. I insist," as Joiya handed a cup to Navi and Misha.

Navi held his breath as Misha, the wild card, took a sip. His face puckered slightly but he pulled it together.

"Energizing," he said with a fake smile.

"Natto, ya wanna have some before we go?" Callan said.

"Uh, sure." He took a sip. It felt like home. Misha gave a full mug back whilst Navi gave them his empty one. Indeed, it was a refuge in every sense of the word.

"Ok we'll be off!" Callan said as she walked towards the door.

"One last thing," Benya said, "You'll need to register," she said, tapping a clipboard on the table. The act of overlord compliance threw off Navi. What was Benya playing at with this?

Name. Expanse of residence. National ID.

"We're regularly observed," Benya said as she cleared her throat, her eyes looking more nervous than her voice sounded. Joiya came up from behind and placed her hand on Benya's lower back.

"No doubt they will be by later to check," she said with a forced smile

Navi was going to sweet talk their way out of it when Misha stepped in.

He registered everyone.

"Thank you! Be safe and take care. And stay on the trail. I've heard some crazy stories about what's going on out there." Benya said with a deadly serious tone. It was clear that these allies had an idea as to who they were.

As they stepped out into the chilly air, Navi felt a little optimistic.

"Misha, I hate to say this but you done good in there kid.

How did you know what to do for the ID information?" Misha beamed at Callan's rare praise.

"Please, Callan. I was the queen of forgeries in Cuba. A lot of homos made their way to the U.S. because of me. I paid attention to everything official that we've seen thus far. I'm not some 'shit for brains' princess, as you would say," he smiled proudly.

"Touche," Callan retorted.

Ara popped out of Callan's bag.

"That was miserable. Remind me never to do that again," Ara said in a huff.

"Lookin' a bit naked their sis, you ok?" Callan said. Navi felt sorry for Ara. He knew what macaws should look like. And then there was Ara: scraggly with thin, greasy feathers.

"I'll be fine. I've been without Oragan for much longer than this," Ara said, not fooling Navi nor anyone else.

Onward they marched for 12 hours without stopping. Ara perched on Callan's shoulder, looking wearier. Callan wrapped Ara in a thick piece of green velvet from her sack.

The climate grew increasingly colder and more biting. Navi and Misha kept warm in their winter clothes to ward off the chill. Misha had never worn so many layers in his life. He looked miserable. A good night of sleep, hearty food, and a hot shower gave Navi hope for the rest of their journey. Maybe the worst was behind them, he thought optimistically.

"Oooh weee. It is colder than a witch's tit in a brass bra up here." Callan exclaimed. "I don't like these northern climes. The birds are often smug shits as well."

"How is that any different than you?" Misha said pointedly while looking at Callan.

"I really like you. You got spunk." She winked at him. For the first time since they had been on Kala, Mish cracked a wry smile. They managed to sneak past the Shadow Army and out of the Library, trek through the forest, find refuge, and make their final journey to Merrat.

They sat around a smokeless and woodless campfire just inside the border of Merrat. Misha managed to conjure it up with some inspiration from Navi. Navi felt a shift in the power dynamic of the land compared to that of Lega. He had a feeling that this may be their last moment of peace for a while.

The librarians gave them the lay of the land and insight about what to expect as they got further north. Merrat wasn't known for its hospitality regardless of being controlled by an evil priestess. The hover buses were fine for transport between cities. They had privacy pods, allowing people to travel discreetly. Inside the city, walking or a hovercraft was often the only way to travel without being recognized.

Throughout their journey toward Merrat, they argued over the best way to overcome the Shadow. Their only unifying hope was that Anna and Manny would meet them there. Navi brooded over the deal Callan made with the apparition in the library. What would be his fate? There are so many fates worse than death. Given how callous she is, Navi knew it had to the potential to be excruciating. He distracted himself by mentally devising a plan for when they arrived at the temple. One that would involve escaping from Callan by any means necessary.

"Ara, do you still have a connection to Anna?" She nodded. She mentioned that she felt a surge of power at one point, which was likely Anna using her feather. "Good. I think we can use that to pinpoint Anna, Manny and the Librarian's location."

Ara squawked.

"Callan!" she proclaimed.

"Yes cousin?"

"Have you seen it? It's following us," Ara spat.

"Oh yeah, darlin. I can smell a magpie from a mile away. We haven't done anything to it. I'm hopin' that this shifty S.O.B. will respect us, but I doubt it. You never know with them. They are as selfish as they come." Callan scowled as she said "magpie". It amused Navi. They were in a huff over a magpie?

Callan cleared her throat and cawed in that guttural, toucan way. Three choucas flew from nowhere and twittered in her face. For the first time ever, Navi saw Callan's face transformed from smug to ruffled to sinister. She screeched at them. They zipped away.

"Well? How about some translations for the rest of us?" Misha said.

"Those smug little shits are minions of Marge the Magpie." Navi and Misha snorted at the name. Not exactly as foreboding as Ara and Callan were making her out to be.

"You think it's funny now, but she is one of the most powerful birds on Kala. If we make her happy, she will be of high service to us, serving as a guide. If we piss her off, which you never know what will get her goat, she'll fuck us over six ways from Sunday. She is watching us. We are in her territory now and she won't let us forget it," Callan said pointing at Navi.

Ara nervously flitted to Navi's shoulder. "Ara, what are you doing?"

"You never know with Marge and Callan they hate each other, but sometimes they can play nice." Again, Ara's tone was serious. Navi felt the air change. Electrical currents shot through his arm hairs, warning him.

Misha, mostly oblivious to the undercurrent of tension,

stated the obvious. "Well, shouldn't we keep walking? According to the map - it's that lit city on the side of that mountain. Probably only a day of walking left. I know Anna is on her way up to Merrat's capital as well."

"I agree with Misha. Enough wasting time anticipating a bird who may never show up. Let's keep moving," Navi said authoritatively. The others looked at him, surprised that he spoke with such command.

"Well, well, well, look who got their big boy britches!" Callan said with a wry smile. Navi rolled his eyes and led the charge through the forest.

As they continued further north, the looming pine-type trees became increasingly frost covered in what looked like perfectly formed red iridescent ice crystals. Navi marveled at how stunning it was, for being in enemy territory and all. Frost crystals crunched underfoot, bringing him slight satisfaction with each step.

"Callan, where is Marge? Until we talk to her, I don't trust that she isn't spying for the priestess," Ara said, her voice wavering and fading.

On cue, a bitter gust of wind bit their faces. A large magpie and a flock of choucas raced towards them.

It was as if Ara called Marge by speaking her name.

"Hullo Callan. Ara. Navi. Misha." Navi was a bit disconcerted by the fact that this stranger knew his and Misha's name. The look Callan shot to him validated his feelings. The crew halted.

"Yer in mah zone. What eez tha perpose?"

"Dear Goddess, your accent..." Navi dug his heel into Callan's toe before she could finish "... is just lovely. Hello Marge. Surely you must know why we're here."

"Rehmors are flying. They appear to be tre-u." At that moment, the choucas flapped incessantly around her. "Yer trying teh stop her." Callan noticed a brief flash of desperation in Marge's eyes before the look went back to smug. "Yeh can't. Eets fuhtile." The choucas laughed as they flit about."

Callan opened her mouth but Navi spoke first. Electricity flickered through his body. Microscopic drops of magic were slowly activated from deep within his core. Navi knew that he could get them out of this situation.

"Marge, you know who I am. No need for introductions." Marge's face softened as she hovered at his eye level. "Your knowledge and power in this land could prove useful for us. We are a mostly humble -" he shot a side-eye look to Callan "- group of people who only want to restore Kala to its previous state where animals and people lived without fear of the Shadow. If you help us, you'll get your old life back." Navi smiled confidently.

"Navi, ye are coming unto yer powuh. Someting so alluring aboot that, right?" The Magpie's eyes were intoxicating. Navie couldn't look away from her gaze. Brief scenes flashed through her eyes. Navi tried to decipher what he was watching.

Marge screeched hurriedly to the choucas. Callan's face dropped. Marge turned back to Navi "Ye arroghent preck. Yeh don't remember do yeh? I thought mehbe earth made ye remerseful. I gess not." Navi's smile faded. He wished hat he hadn't been such an asshole in his last iteration on Kala. "Let me show you a bet about yerself."

Before anyone could intervene, Marge pressed both of her wings to the sides of his head. Suddenly, Navi was in this same forest, but closer to the capitol. "Marge, Marge, Marge. I have a job to do on behalf of my goddess," Navi said as he sauntered up to her. You know that I love you though. I'll try to make sure that this doesn't hurt too much. You're my favorite in this northern area, after all."

The words dripped out of his mouth, delivering a false promise.

Navi cringed at the entire scene (including his wardrobe: tie dyed billowy pants, no shirt, a gold goatee and a bun on the top of his head), however he knew himself. Past Navi was scared of something. Current Navi was deep in thought, trying to remember the origin of fear. He continued watching the movie unfold.

Before Marge could fly away, Navi raised both hands and singed almost all of her wing feathers beyond recognition. Marge screeched and fell to the forest floor. She writhed in pain as the choucas swirled around her.

"Navi!" Marge was sputtering and gasping between words. "Thes will not be eer last encounter. Ye well wish eet to... be. Tek meh to him! Now!" The choucas zipped her away. Navi shrugged and leapt up to the sky, taking flight somewhere.

Marge transferred the pain from the past to Navi in the present. His body grotesquely contorted. He saw Callan and Misha wince, but they were helpless in the moment.

Marge let go of his throbbing head. The scene replayed repeatedly. What did he get from her? What did that accomplish? With pleading eyes, Navi apologized. "I am so sorry, but look - you have your wings now. Fully restored. All's well that ends well? It looks like whatever I took merely resulted in a flesh wound." Navi had no idea why he did that to her, but surely there was a reason.

"Oh you are a fool, sugar. Just stop talkin' right now. Honestly, I can't wait to see my trade through. It will be better for everyone," Callan warned.

"Lesten tah Callan! Teh only rason that I have wings is because I had ta make a deal with the Shadowmancers. Before they were successful. All yeh deities and daemons are the same, but teh get mah wings back. I had to be loyal to the Shadow for eternity." Her eyes blazed red.

Before Navi could react, Marge pecked each of his eyes out and swallowed them whole. Navi emitted an unholy terrified scream. Ara leapt onto Misha's shoulder as he came to Navi's aid, unsure what to do. "Ye'll get tese back when you can finally see the error of yer ways," she squawked as Navi's eyeballs rested on her tongue.

"Kem on boys" she yelled to her choucas. They flew away before anyone could say another word.

Everyone froze in stunned silence.

"Well, that was the worst possible outcome," Callan said. Navi heard her rifling through her sack. "Put this scarf around your eye sockets, darlin. No one wants to see that. I am letting you borrow this. Ya can't keep it though. It's my own." She placed it in Navi's hand.

Navi violently hyperventilated as he struggled to wrap the blindfold. Misha placed a trembling hand on Navi's shoulder and took the blindfold from Navi's hands. Misha wrapped it around his eye sockets whilst making gagging sounds. Navi could only imagine how grotesque he looked.

"Callan, surely you have some eyeballs in that Mary Poppins bag of yours?" Misha pleaded, if not for Navi then surely so the others did not have to look at his grotesque face.

"You know the deal Misha, you gotta give me something to get something valuable. I got about all that I can take from you lot," she said with a hint of remorse in her voice.

Navi whimpered "what did I take from Marge?"

"Oh, probably one of her gifts. She looks like she fell out of the ugly tree and hit every branch on the way down, but that bitch has some serious gifts that only she can give."

Navi, barely able to form a thought, wondered who wanted him to take a gift from Marge.

Callan was useful for inviting trouble. Ara was useless. Navi, from his own perspective at least, went from gorgeous and confident to a grotesque sad sack.

"Navi, get up. It's only a matter of time before Dalv and the priestess find us. Stop being a fucking asshole. Get up and let's go. We must get through the tunnel. We must find Anna." Navi was shocked at Misha's sudden resolve.

Electricity sparkled through Navi's body, making him a conduit to Misha's growing power. At least he was good for something, Navi thought about himself. He sensed Misha's emotions as his power became more fully formed.

Misha picked up Navi by his coat collar and wiped the spittle and blood from Navi's face. Navi collapsed in Misha's arms under the relief of being held by a dear friend.

"I just want to go back to Havana," he whimpered to Misha.

"Not an option. We're stuck here. Now suck it up, buttercup because as Nancy Sinatra said these boots were made for walking." Knowing new Misha, Navi was quite sure that he just cocked his hip to the side and flipped his hair back. "We have a job to do. And I, for one, rather like being a gay demi-god than a gay in Cuba. I don't want to go back to Havana."

Navi stood motionless while the rest of the crew debated the best way into the city. There were a series of footpaths leading into Merrat. They were warned that the Merrati police kept watch on the perimeter of the city, footpaths included.

"Can't I just fly and meet y'all over there?" Callan whined.

"No!" they all said in unison.

"Look, they probably assume that we'll enter the city via the forest. Why don't we use the train? It's a large city right? We can blend in. Plus it's the fastest way into the city," Misha proudly proclaimed.

"This is a SHIT idea, you know that? We'll be discovered by the snitchy spies. I'm sure they're all over the trains," Callan said in a pouty voice as Misha charged forward with Ara on one shoulder and holding Navi's hand on the other side. Navi heard Callan keeping in step with them, no doubt reluctantly.

"Callan, he's right. They can't walk. We need to take the train. The station is about a kilometer that way," Ara said. "Once we're there, you'll have to hide me. We cannot be discovered on the train."

"But what about me? How can I travel like this?" Navi stifled a sob.

"You'll have to trust me, Navi," Misha said as he held Navi's hand tightly.

28

The discussion subsided as they trudged towards the Merrati Tunnel Terminal. It was the famous dual purpose tunnel that was about 15 earth kilometers long and passable by hover train or hover vehicle. The bottom level was for the hover train while the top level was meant for the vehicles.

"Navi, don't talk to anyone. You seem to have fucked over many people on this planet," Misha said as they approached the tunnel.

"Wow. I wish you could see this tunnel though," Misha said to him.

It was quite the site, especially for Misha who had only ever known a flat tropical island. Navi could feel him marvel at the incredible engineering feat. The tunnel went into the base of a giant mountain peak. Allegedly Merrat was just on the other side.

Navi remained silent.

"Come now, Misha, you think he had something to do with this? This ain't no art project. This is one of the best feats of engineering in the universe." Callan said it without an ounce of her usual sarcasm.

They stopped for a moment to admire the tunnel. It was still about 300 meters away, but clearly visible as it stood on a trail off of the main road. A perfect cylinder that was about 50 meters tall and 50 meters wide, it was unlike anything Misha would have seen in Cuba. Hover trains zoomed in and out of the bottom level while hover vehicles zoomed in and out of the top level. Misha looked on with his mouth agape. It was like something he imagined from a science fiction novel. He knew there were tunnels burrowed deep into mountains on earth, with quite a few of them being in the U.S.S.R. However, none of them resembled anything close to this in modernity and scale. The Art Deco designed rock carvings on the tunnel looked like the art deco designs in central Havana, but on a significantly larger scale.

"She's a beaut. Now let's get," Callan commanded.

"I don't think this is a good idea. I'm sure there are Officers patrolling the train station," Navi said nervously.

They were standing in front of a fork in the trail: to the left was the footpath into Merrat, including a trudge through snow and ice; to the right were stairs down to the station, which they couldn't quite see.

Misha, feeling more in control and in command than ever. He commanded Callan to do a reconnaissance mission. She smirked, hating that a humanoid was telling her what to do, but he had a point.

"I gotta dress like the locals," she said.

Pop!

"I didn't know you could be a chouca," Misha muttered.

Once she was out of ear shot, Navi thought it was safe to speak. "Misha, please don't trust her. She does nothing but get us in trouble."

Misha couldn't help but laugh. "Typical. Poor little rich boy. Never wanted to take responsibility for your actions. While my sister and I were grieving over the loss of our parents, you ignored us in favor of that fuck boy life. Turns out it is who you are! You did the same thing here. This is on you, not Callan." Misha's words pierced Navi's heart.

Navi opened his mouth to respond but couldn't. Misha was not lying.

Callan returned and morphed back in her human form.

"Aight y'all, miraculously, Misha was right. It's crowded. People everywhere. I'd say it would be easy to blend in, but we need to clean up a bit. We look a bit rough." She motioned towards the snow.

Misha pulled Navi towards the snow. "Come on, let's wash our faces." Navi removed the bloody scarf. They both sucked in their breath as the snow wash felt like tiny needles in their skin. There wasn't much to be done with their tattered hair. Callan tried to tame Navi's hair, but it was mission impossible.

"Well y'all, at least Misha's hair looks mildly manageable. Navi, good thing you don't have a mirror. Here - take these." She handed Navi a pair of aviator sunglasses and said "You may actually look cool for once."

"I thought you couldn't give us anything without something in return?" Navi said sardonically, hesitating to grab the sunglasses.

"Hey now, these are mine! All the rage in the U.S. I'm letting you borrow them. They are regular old sunglasses. But you gotta give em back. I keep losing 'em. Maybe next time I'll buy a cheap pair. Anyways, we can't walk around with a blindfolded guy. Now that would attract attention."

Navi stood there, refusing to take them.

"Look, I can't give you anything from my sack that has

been traded or has any universal value. It's the rules," Callan said with no hint of emotion.

Begrudgingly, Navi took the glasses.

"Thank fuck, that's so much better," Misha exclaimed with relief. Misha took Navi's scarf off and wiped any remnants of blood and dirt off of his face. At least someone was taking care of him, regardless of Misha's motive for doing so, Navi thought.

"You look presentable, sugar. Now cousin, what are we going to do with you? You want to get in my sack? You'd fit." Callan said to Ara. Navi could feel Ara's humiliation in that moment. It caused him to shiver. Deep, unbridled humiliation. She wasn't meant to be a molten bird in a sack. Sitting with Ara's humiliation was almost too much for Navi.

"Ara, it won't be like this forever. I promise," Navi said. Remarkably, that tempered the intensity of her feelings. He may not have eyes, but he sensed Ara's feelings.

Callan stuffed Ara in her sack and then produced three tickets that she bought during reconnaissance.

"Keep these on ya. Don't look anyone in the eye, ya hear? The identification technology here is about 60 years ahead of earth."Misha nodded. "Well, Navi doesn't have too much to worry about. A lot of it is eyeball based." She snorted.

Navi lunged for her, forgetting for a moment that he was blind. He fell flat. Misha grumbled at Callan as he helped Navi up. Navi would never understand her. Was she there to help or hurt? Or maybe, just like Navi himself, a little bit of both.

"Listen Callan, taunting him and being a bitch isn't going to keep a low profile, ok?" Misha calmly, but firmly, said. Callan shrugged.

As they approached the platform, Navi felt Misha's awe over the fashion and was woefully embarrassed by his clothes. Navi was shocked by how two of the most powerful people whom he has ever met feel shame. They hide it so well. What else are they hiding? Navi wondered.

"Everyone is elegantly draped in black, red and gray silk and wool. Their outfits are perfectly tailored. Some are quilted. Some are flat. It's stunning!" Misha explained to Navi.

"Sounds like a shitty dress code," Navi murmured while he felt Misha ease up. Navi didn't take Misha as someone who liked such formal wear, but maybe this is part of his evolution. Amidst all the chaos of the recent weeks, these perfect people on this perfect platform provided him with some calm. But Misha surprised Navi with how at ease he felt about the origin of their current tragedy.

A loud bong echoed from the speakers. A cool voice informed them that the train would arrive in two minutes. They stood there awkwardly alert, unsure of what to expect yet trying to evade attention.

"I don't much care for these northern snobs. They all look the same and dress the same. Boring and smug if you ask me." Callan said, as if she could read Navi's mind. "At least they get a lot of visitors and immigrants from other countries to make it interesting."

The three kept their faces down as they boarded the train, with Navi following in tandem with Misha.

"Hold on to your britches. You've never traveled so fast," Callan said.

Misha shot Callan a look, reminding her of the portal travel.

"Let me rephrase - you have never traveled so fast on something that won't kill you." Misha nodded.

The train lurched forward. After a loud woosh, they were inside the mountain. It was Misha's first time on a train. Navi felt him observing and analyzing every detail. Navi had only been on the rickety coal powered trains in the U.S.S.R. This train was crammed, which was better for them.

The trio, plus Ara, stood by a door.

"Apparently we're not the only ones keeping our eyes down," Callan whispered in the mostly silent car. Navi heard a few whispers, but decided not to eavesdrop. .

After 15 minutes, the train stopped.

"Holy shit," Misha gasped audibly in awe. "I've never seen a landscape like this. Navi, the city was surrounded on all sides by mountains with craggy, rocky, snow-covered peaks. It looks nothing like anywhere we've been here or in Cuba. Could parts of the USSR look like this?" Navi enjoyed this feeling of wonder exuding from Misha.

A flash of a vision came to Navi. He clearly saw the peaks, the rocks, the ice, the snow and the engineering marvels of the modern funiculars and gondolas that effortlessly transported people around the mountain range.

"I think I know this place," Navi muttered out loud.

"Of course you know this place, sugar. You helped design half of it," as Callan spoke, Navi felt a hum beneath his feet and the familiar electrical surge throughout his body. He frowned at Callan's words though. Everything he touched seemed to have turned against him.

BONG. "Next stop Matzi station."

"That's us. Come on." They followed Callan off the train and towards the city.

29

"Why don't we have a drink and warm up first? I need some assistance to cope with these northerners. Brrrrr." Callan started walking towards the city on the hill. Misha took Navi's hand and pulled him along. Navi found it strangely comforting to hold Misha's hand. In Cuba, he would have rather died than be seen holding hands with another man.

"Come on. This way you go." She led the lot. The route from the station ended on a city sidewalk. Misha, who had never left Cuba, felt giddy with admiration for the city. While Lega and the surrounding area vaguely reminded him of Cuba and a certain tropical aesthetic, this architecture evoked awe, power and a bit of fear in its severity. The buildings were made of granite blocks with intricate art deco embellishments and carvings around the door frames and windows. The buttresses were especially modern and severe. The perimeter of the city consisted of a series of six to eight story buildings that went on for a few kilometers. Between each building was an alleyway that undoubtedly led to a rabbit warren. Misha shuttered at the thought of entering the maze. In paying attention to the architecture, he wasn't looking forward and ran into a streetlight which glowed red like a garnet.

Callan cackled.

Navi jumped. He was basking in Misha's pleasure, not paying attention to much else. "What happened? Callan? What did you do?"

"Navi, it's not always me. Halfling here bumped into a light pole," Callan said defensively.

People milled around, going about their day.

"No one's smiling. Everyone's staring at these gorgeous slate tile sidewalks!" Misha exclaimed.

"Now I'm 'bout ta get serious, are we ready?" Callan said as Ara flew out of her bag to rest on Navi's shoulder.

"Once we go in this city, we're in Dalv's and the Shadow's crosshairs. This here city is a maze. A meticulously planned maze inspired by none other than someone we know, do we have any guesses?"

"Me, of fucking course. It's always me," Navi replied.

"Correct, Navi! But you weren't all bad with this one. The good thing is that even though you designed it like a maze, you probably know your way to the other side when push comes to shove. Capiche?"

The two guys nodded.

They entered the first alley. The alley was no larger than 10 feet at its widest point and probably 5 feet at its most narrow. The granite exterior walls were tall and dark, creating a feeling of mild claustrophobia in Misha.

Moss perfectly outlined each cobblestone on the street. "I'm guessing this street doesn't get much sunlight?" Misha observed out loud.

"Correct you are, Captain Obvious." Callan rolled her eyes.

Five minutes into the alley, they came across a bar so innocuous that one might miss it if they didn't know it was there.

Navi stopped. "Here. This is the place." The ground hummed beneath his feet as they approached the bar.

"Navi, um, sweetie..." Misha said hesitantly as they stopped in front of a wooden door, not much larger than his six foot frame. Misha peaked inside the window on the door to see, in fact, a bar.

"I don't know about this Callan. It's empty." Misha said hesitantly.

Callan peeked inside. "Oh this is perfect hun, unless you have any other ideas Einstein."

"I know this place. I can feel it." Navi said, feeling Misha's skepticism and Callan's glee.

"Sugar, that's good to hear. You aren't useless after all. Now let's go in and get warm. Ara - get in my bag. You'll draw more attention to us as a macaw in this frosty hellscape."

They opened the thick, wooden door and trudged inside the dark bar towards a red leather covered booth in the back, past the watchful, narrow eyes of the bartender and a couple of patrons in hushed conversations. Misha, noting the culture of the area, did not smile at her. He knew his usual charm, that worked so well on earth, would not work here. Misha paused at the bar to get them drinks while the others made their way to the booth.

Misha focused on his desire to speak the local language. He took a deep breath and in Merrati said "Hello, I would like three glasses of cat piss." The bartender looked at him, completely offended, and said "You aren't from around here, are you? Your accent is funny." He could see Callan laughing hysterically and Ara, peeking out of Callan's bag shaking her head in dismay. She slammed the three glasses of something that resembled beer on the bar. Misha pursed his lips tightly and brought the glasses to the table.

"You just asked her for cat piss. Oh mercy me." Callan took five minutes to compose herself. Misha rolled his eyes as he tried to make himself comfortable in the hard wooden booth.

"What is this?" Misha wondered. "Tastes like apples."

"Oh this is cider. I've had this at the Embassy. One of the ambassador's babushka would make it at her datcha. So he has it imported for parties." Navi smiled, pleased that he could identify it.

Misha scowled in jealousy for a moment, then quickly dropped the scowl. Navi's smug face had no eyeballs. Not much power to flaunt anymore. At that thought, he almost smiled, but refrained. Navi sighed as he felt Misha's jealousy. He much more enjoyed inspiring (maybe coercing as well) people rather than feeling their feelings.

They started discussing possible locations for Anna. Ara was sure that she would go directly to the priestess' hold out at the base of Dalv's temple. Misha, knowing Manny, knew that Manny would advise a more cautious plan. Navi found that being without vision to be disorienting but noticed that his hearing quickly sharpened.

"Could you please lower your voices? The sound is unbearably loud." He could hear a mouse scurry across the back room. "Plus, we don't know friend from foe."

"Speaking of, the bartender keeps looking at you Navi. Another woman whom you pissed off?" Callan sassed, unable to conceal her annoyance with him.

"What does she look like? What is she doing?"

Misha began "Well, she has long black curly hair, black eyes and that red iridescent skin. She has quite angular features, sort of like a model in one of those American magazines, not that I would know anything about that." Misha's response was out of habit.

Navi felt a tingling sensation hovering above the crown of his head. He saw a clear vision in his mind's eye: a scenario with him speaking to the bartender in a previous time. The bar was bustling with average people of Merrat. People weren't exactly jovial, but it didn't have the current ominous atmosphere. He was friends with the bartender. It was a true friendship, similar to Cat at Vong's in Havanna. Stavina. That was her name, Navi remembered.

"I know her. She was a friend from my previous time here. I didn't fuck her or fuck her over. Her name is Stavina." Navi said cautiously.

"Well Casanova, why don't you meander on up there and get some information. We don't have all day. I may have something for her if she has something for us." Callan pulled Ara out of the bag as she rifled through it for something moderately useful for a boring old humanoid.

Navi cleared his throat and pointed to his sunglasses. Misha sighed and led Navi to the bar. Stavina kept her unflinching eyes on them. "If looks could kill, we'd be dead, Navi," Misha whispered.

"Hey pretty boy, are you going to try to tell me that I served cat piss again?" Stavina spat.

"Stavina. It's me." Navi didn't want to give too much away, in case she was an Officer.

For a split second, Misha could have sworn that her eyes softened and her lips curled up slightly, but then it was gone. Her eyes got more serious than before. "Navi! I thought that was you," she said in an urgent whisper then pulled him by his collar to within inches from her face.

"What happened to your eyes? Nevermind. You need to

leave this bar. Now. I don't want any trouble here. You can go out the back and walk through the alleys. They will take you where you need to go," she said in an urgent whisper. Navi could tell that she was scared. Her fear radiated through his body, causing him to feel queasy.

"Why? Please tell me. What do you know about me here? Help us!" He said in an equally urgent whisper. He was feeling a bit desperate.

Stavina motioned for them to follow her to the backside of the bar area so they couldn't be seen. "Navi, anyone who is important here knows you. Now those people know you have returned thanks to Marge. You must go." She pleaded. "All of you need to leave now."

"Please. Anything." Navi pleaded.

"Rumors are swirling about Anna's return. Julia is waiting for her. Now get out of here!" She hissed.

Navi sucked in a sharp inhale. He felt Misha's confusion, surprise and longing. Julia. Mama. She was here. Misha wanted to find her. She will fix all of this. Misha suppressed tears at the thought of seeing his mama. It was time to get to Julia. Navi had a feeling that the reunion wouldn't be as joyous as Misha anticipated.

"We're going. Now - Navi come on." Misha led him back to the booth.

"We gotta go right now -" Misha implored to Callan.

"It's too late." She tilted her head towards the door. Two people in fur lined uniforms walked into the bar, carrying batons with red glowing orbs on the top. Misha motioned for Callan to duck her head and follow him while yanking Navi along.

"Stavina," they said in monotonous voices "we're here to search your place." Just as Misha heard that, he heard the sound of the batons slam in unison on the floor. The door to the alley closed behind him as they began to jog away.

A red glowing light came from under the door.

The rabbit warren of alleyways in Merrat reminded Misha of old medieval cities he had seen photos of in the National Library in Havana, except not nearly as warm and welcoming. Navi could tell that Misha had no idea where he was going. Callan kept pace behind them, while Ara rode in her sack.

"The Collector, the Halfling, the Daemon. You cannot hide." Misha glanced behind him to see the two Shadow officers holding steady with their pace and their glowing orbs. They were running too fast, it was as if they were levitating. Why didn't he say Ara? Is Ara undetected? Navi wondered. Very curious.

"Well shit, I really hate carrying people, but I gotta do it. Navi - make yourself useful and hold my sack." She placed her rucksack on Navi's back. "I'm gonna start running, keep close behind. When I say 'Now' grab my talons, ok?" They both nodded.

Callan took off running, with Misha and Navi barely able to keep up. "NOW!" She transfigured into an alpine vulture. Misha and Navi grabbed onto her talons for dear life. They hurtled higher above the city and towards a cluster of lights at the base of an incredibly intimidating mountain. No doubt Dalv's temple was on that mountain.

"What the---?" Misha wondered aloud.

"Well you can't expect a toucan to survive up here? It's too cold."

The flight was jerky, but it seemed to get the job done. They were on the precipice of escaping the officers. Navi remained silent, trying to focus on the vision he had earlier.

Suddenly Misha screamed "CALLAN! They can fly!

They are right behind us!" The edge of their red orb lights got closer. Misha figured that nothing good came from those lights.

"Well I guess there are some benefits to following Dalv's bullshit. Here we go!" She swooped down so close to the ground the Misha's toes grazed the cobblestone streets. She then pulled up immediately before they almost slammed into a granite wall along the edge of the city, just before the ascent to the temple and town on the hill.

"We lost them!" Misha shouted with glee as Callan lifted them over the wall.

In the next moment, they were motionless in mid-air, wrapped in glowing red light, unable to move.

"We told you that you cannot hide," they said in unison.

30

The odd feeling of being suspended comforted Navi. He lost his identity. He was blinded by a vindictive bird. Nothing was as he believed. His life on earth was an illusion. His former life on Kala was an illusion. The only thing that brought him comfort was the thought of reunification with Anna.

Another vision came to him. He and Anna made passionate love in a temple. Was it something to come or something that happened? He couldn't be sure. The only certainty was that it was real, whether it was in the future or past. A smile crept over his face for the first time in days.

He thought that he was stuck with his thoughts, alone, when he suddenly heard "Stop thinking about my sister like that," Misha's voice intruded in his head.

Navi was jarred into reality, unsure of what happened. "We were caught by the officers in the Army, suspended in midair. I'm sure I look ridiculous."

"The fact that you are thinking about how you look at this moment, this insane moment, shows that you definitely

ARE ridiculous," Navi thought towards him, hoping that he would get the message.

"At least I have my eyes. Listen. We are in some type of orb, floating above them. Even Callan. From what I can see, they are taking us to the high temple. I'm thinking of it as a free ride," Misha thought optimistically.

"Right. Only good things come from being captured by army officers." If Navi had eyes, he would have rolled them.

"What if Anna isn't there and we end up imprisoned?" Navi thought.

"What if? Hopefully Callan and Ara have some extra-magical universal power play. For now, stay close to me." Misha sounded almost excited at the thought. Navi wasn't so confident. He felt faint vibrations that increased in frequency as they got closer to the temple.

What are Callan and Ara's thoughts on the situation? Do they have a plan?

"Did they have a plan this whole time? Probably not. What the hell good are these so-called immortals of the universe without a plan? Is this fun for them?" Misha thought.

"Try," Navi firmly stated.

"FINE."

Navi rested in this moment of relaxation. For the first time in a few days, he didn't feel panic. He eased into being captive quite quickly. His thoughts went to his previous life. He longed to be back in Havana, when his life was easy. He had power. Respect. A loving family. And his eyes. He could see. As he thought that, his eye sockets started to sting.

"Callan just said that if I read her mind, my tiny human brain would explode. We're approaching a large wooden door, with intricate carvings and a glass overlay that looks like a Scottish kilt,."

"Mix-medium tartan, probably red, white and black tartan. Door handles resemble icicles," Navi thought.

"How did you know?"

"I think that I, eh, inspired its design. I believe that I drove another artist mad in the process. She was revered by the deities though," Navi winced as he thought about his past.

"Your track record is worse than those putas on the Malecon," Misha observed matter of factly.

Navi didn't want to think except "get out of my brain NOW." And like that, Misha was out. It felt like there was a wall around his thoughts. It was satisfying.

Suddenly they dropped to the marble floors in a pained crumpled heap. At least the floors were warm. Upon touching the marble with his cheek, visions flooded Navi. The temple was telling him its story, reminding him of his past, leaving him speechless.

In a split second, the temple told Navi of a time when he worked with all of the deities as their muse and confidant, but he was Anna's true love. Navi's only other insatiable desire was to create. Each time he inspired an artist or created something himself, he wanted to do more. It was an addiction. He cherished the accolades and praise from the politicians and the deities. He designed this particular temple using the forest and mountains as the inspiration. The temple told him that the seven spires, the height of an Olympic pool on earth, were carved in the shape of the local area pine trees, ensconced in a special glass to make it look like icicles. Granite was used to create the dome of the temple. Mount Zem served as the inspiration. Each of its neeld-like, rocky points were distinctly visible as a mirror representation at the top of the dome. Mount Zem towered over Merrat from the north. Floating star lights in the shape of the various constellations adorned the interior of the dome. Navi took inspiration from constellations that are only visible in winter, when Dalv was most powerful and gave the most abundance to his worshippers.

Navi was shocked that some of the constellations were also visible from earth - like Orion's belt, Aries and Capricorn.

"Stand up. We're taking you to your prisons. You'll be comfortable." The flat voices said together. He felt an odd sensation around his wrists - like handcuffs, but made of no material that he was familiar with, at least to the touch.

Navi decided that blissful ignorance was the best approach for now. He didn't care about Callan, Misha or Ara. His eye sockets started stinging again as he thought about them. Navi forced the resent back down.

"Make sure my room has heated floors and a heated toilet seat." Misha piped up. Navi could tell that he was serious.

"Misha, I knew you had some diva tendencies in ya. Make mine the same! Ooh and can I get a tree in my room? How about some local whiskey?" Callan sarcastically chirped.

Navi wished that the two of them would shut up. He welcomed the idea of being imprisoned if only to get a break from them. The officers remained silent and drug the prisoners to their cells.

Navi paid attention to how far they walked from the front door. Suddenly he had the entire blueprint for the temple in his head. Every resplendent detail clarified in his mind. If his sense of direction was correct, they were going to the Hostia wing. People and animals were kept in this wing as sacrifices. Non-human beings were kept imprisoned there for eons. Dalv was one of two or three Kalan gods whose favor could be curried via human and animal sacrifice.

He felt a surge of nausea and thought LET MISHA IN.

"Misha, listen to me. We're on our way to the wing where they keep people and animals before sacrifice. No matter how nice your room is, they intend to kill us all, or at least me and you. I don't know about Callan and Ara."

Misha didn't respond.

"Can you hear me?" Navi thought intently.

"Yes, it doesn't matter which wing we're in. Callan and I are coming up with a plan. You and Ara need to play along no matter what. Ara will stay with Callan just in case things go tits up. She cannot be allowed into the hands of Dalv and that rumored high priestess," Misha thought.

"I know this. I designed this place. I can help." In his telepathic communication, he tried to keep thoughts of Julia out of his head for fear of disturbing Misha.

"You've had enough help," Misha thought emphatically.

The one-time Navi could be of service, no one would listen to him.

They deposited Callan, with Ara in her sack, first. From what he could tell, it was the first room on the left of the corridor. That room was impenetrable by anyone other than Dalv himself. Once someone entered, they rarely emerged unless Dalv commanded it. Upon Dalv's banishment, they released the last prisoner from that room. Navi had no recollection as to whom it was, but it must have been something very powerful.

"Not the nicest accommodations. I'm puttin' a complaint into management. Please send my breakfast at -" before she could finish her remark, the doors slammed shut.

They continued their journey to the unknown, passing four doors on the left before arriving at an open door.

"Navi, your room is here," they stated. It was the Olleper Cell. Nothing could be created or conjured in this room. Navi had other daemons in mind when he helped create it. Karma rained down on him at every turn. He was certain that in his previous iteration, he thought of himself as immune from Karma, a concept he had only read about. Navi reaped the karma that he had sown, unable to reconcile his past self with his current state of being.

The temple guided him to his bed through vibrations on the floor. Navi walked to the bathroom knowing that a natural hot spring tub awaited him, after all Dalv did not want dirty sacrifices. If anything, he could relax for an eternity.

The warm marble floors hummed beneath his bare feet as it guided him to the tub. He stuck his hand into the warm mountain spring water as it continuously flowed through the bath. The mineral rich water soothed his dry, weather-ravaged hands.

He peeled each dirty layer off clothing of his body, starting with the top fur layer, followed by the tech fabric and finally his preferred clothes. "Burn 'em," he thought. The smell of his own clothes made him wretch a bit.

Once in the tub, his entire body relaxed. He took off Callan's aviators. There was no one to see his hideous, weeping eye sockets.

Little ripples formed in the water at the edge of the tub, sensing his presence. The building spoke to him. He clearly saw, in his mind's eye, Misha, being escorted out of the Hostia wing. Misha looked slightly frightened and extremely confused. Navi's nervous system heightened with fear that Misha could be immediately executed. It would be out of Dalv's typical protocol. Perhaps Dalv was not the mastermind.

Nope. They continued walking past the funeral pyre and up another set of marble stairs at the end of the hall.

They were taking him to Dalv's living quarters. Navi was frightened for Misha, unsure as to what Dalv would do to him. Misha presented a stoic face, but his tightly pursed downturn lips said otherwise. The severe decor, meant to intimidate anyone approaching Dalv's quarters, didn't help.

Navi saw that Misha's mouth dropped open. His mind's eye swiveled to see what Misha saw. At the other end of the living quarters, in clear command of everyone in the room, was she. His fear was confirmed. The one in control of everything. The Reason. Julia. Misha's mother.

31

Anna and Manny were caked in grit and grime by the time they reached Merrat. Anna found the extreme cold of Merrat merely an inconvenience. But Manny's misery was etched on his face in a subtle frown. Even bundled in thick, woolens, his body was clearly accustomed to tropical life. She knew he was missing the humid embrace of Havana, but he suppressed it with the discipline of a Keeper.

She reached out and clasped his hands, their fingers laced together in a brief moment of shared warmth.

"Manny, please, you can leave now. I give you permission." Her voice was barely a whisper, a plea bordering on desperation. With every footstep closer to Merrat, a chilling sense of dread swelled within her. The thought of endangering her best friend was a burden she couldn't bear.

"I can't leave. Even if I wanted to, I couldn't sever the bond," Manny replied, his voice flat with resignation. "Keepers are bound by a magic that is universally pure and absolute. We cannot leave your side until the moment we die. We will always be with you, watching, guiding. Once we pass on, the bond is transferred, and you'll receive another Keeper, and the cycle continues." He looked exhausted.

Anna swallowed a sudden rush of tears and pulled him into a fierce, tight hug, burying her face for a second in his coat.

The respite was brief. They continued their trek, the air growing colder, the destination looming. As they finally emerged from the dense, pine-choked forest, Manny and Anna stood at the edge of a massive, industrial train station, a structure unlike any Anna had ever imagined. The sleek, silver lines and humming platforms were an extraordinary sight. After eons of walking, even a goddess grew weary, and the allure of rest was a powerful temptation.

"No, absolutely not. As much as I want to hop on that thing, we can't," Manny said, shaking his head. He pointed a weary finger toward the colossal, snow-capped mountain range that stood directly in their path, dwarfing the station. "We have to take the long way, over the peaks. The train station is undoubtedly monitored. We'll alert them the second we step onto the platform."

"If that's the case, then you have to hop on." Anna turned her back to him, pointing pointedly over her shoulder. "Otherwise, with all due respect, it will take us for fucking ever to cross those mountains." He couldn't argue. Her incredible, almost boundless speed and strength were the only advantages they possessed. He hopped onto her back, his arms snaking around her neck. Manny recently recalled a clandestine viewing of an American movie where a wise, green goblin named Yoda rode the back of his charge, offering guidance along the way. Manny was now entirely convinced that film had been written by a disillusioned Keeper.

It felt less like running and more like flying. Anna

launched herself across sheer crevasses that stretched fifty meters wide, scaling mountainsides and leaping down icy slopes with an effortless grace that defied physics. Manny struggled to maintain his grip, careful not to inadvertently choke her. He shut his eyes tight and buried his face in the warm spot just below the nape of her neck, trying to block out the elements.

After what felt like the longest hour of his life, she stopped, abruptly and completely. He lifted his head, opened his eyes, and the edge of a severe, yet undeniably stunning, city swam into focus: Merrat.

A wave of tension bled out of his body as he unfolded his limbs, untangling himself from his human backpack form. It took a moment to regain his footing, then he jumped down, shaking himself vigorously like a wet dog.

"Fucking hell, you must be freezing. This place is the antithesis of warm. Let's find a place to thaw out." She tried for a confident tone, but neither of them was truly convinced. Anna's powers were fading rapidly, a consequence of venturing so far from Lega. Coupled with the fact that their faces were now plastered across every available surface in this entire hemisphere of Kala, hope was a scarce commodity. Giant, glaring 'WANTED' posters adorned the walls of every hover bus depot, every public square, every dingy alley entrance.

"Follow me." Anna moved forward, driven by a powerful, almost magnetic instinct, even though the actual route was a blank slate in her mind. They examined the city's immediate outskirts: a towering wall of ancient, stone buildings that loomed over them. The city was a warren of narrow streets and tight passageways, clearly designed to baffle and thwart any invading force. One such narrow passage, little more than a crack between two monolithic structures, was the only viable entrance. It reminded Anna of the images of old, fortified European towns she had seen in her history books at the National Library, but it felt deeply and unsettlingly familiar.

The streets were so narrow that they could barely walk side-by-side. They walked quickly past tiny, shuttered shops, keeping their heads down, their eyes darting nervously. Few people were out on the streets this late in the evening.

Anna followed her intuition, which ultimately led them to a nondescript, dimly lit bar.

"We need to stop here," she announced, pulling up short.

"Seriously? Now is truly not the time for a fucking drink, Anna," Manny chided, irritation creeping into his voice.

"Are you actually questioning me? No. We're going in," she snapped back. She pulled the heavy, cold metal handle of the door, and as she did, a rush of energy flooded her, a powerful, familiar vibration that screamed of Navi, Misha, Callan, and Ara.

Inside, the bar lit only by the flickering light of hurricane lamps at each table. The most striking feature was an incredible back wall constructed of a hundred amorphous tree stumps stacked one upon the other, creating an organic quilt. Only a handful of patrons were scattered inside, all hunched over, keeping to themselves, none of them lifting their eyes. The atmosphere was somber. The bartender, a woman dressed entirely in stark black, was instantly familiar. The moment her eyes locked on Anna, they widened, not with recognition, but with a mix of shock and... was it lust that Anna detected?

Anna and Manny had been made. Before the bartender could even blink, Anna lunged, swooping in front of the bar and grabbing the woman's shoulders in a tight grip.

"I am on your side, Anna, believe me," the bartender whispered breathlessly. "Your friends were here, yes, but the Officers came. They ran, but they weren't fast enough. Navi and his friends were captured. I am certain of it. You need to leave. Right now. I cannot afford trouble."

"How do I know you're telling the truth, Stavina?" Anna challenged, testing the name on her tongue, hoping it would unlock another piece of the terrifying puzzle. In Havana, she was great with names. She hoped that Stavina was this woman's name.

Stavina offered a slow, knowing smirk. "We go back a ways, darling," she said with a seductive wink. "Or at least, it's a way for me. Probably just a millisecond for you. Navi and I, though? We go back even further."

Anna's face grew hot, a strange mix of emotions churning in her gut. Was it jealousy? Arousal? Whoever this woman was, Anna felt an undeniable, deep-seated connection to her.

"OH, not like *that*," Stavina laughed, shaking her head, understanding the flicker in Anna's eyes. "You're much more my type than he is, sweetie." She winked at Anna again. Anna felt the first hint of arousal she'd experienced in what felt like an eternity. Her rigid expression softened.

"Follow me. Maybe you'll remember," Stavina murmured as she led Anna to the back room. Before Anna could move, Stavina closed the distance and kissed her, deeply and passionately, her hands sliding down to rest intimately on the small of Anna's back.

In that instant, Anna's mind exploded with a flash of lost information. The memory returned, vibrant and unmistakable. "Stavina," Anna gasped, breathless, her face breaking into a wide, genuine smile. Stavina's expression was one of deep satisfaction. Her finger trailed lazily across Anna's hand. Anna pulled her into a tight, grateful embrace. The memories of their past sexual escapades, their fun, carefree days, flooded Anna's mind.

"So you remember how much fun we used to have?" Stavina whispered, her eyes dancing with mischief.

Anna simply nodded. "Come on. We can't leave Manny out there on his own," she said, pulling away, reality crashing back in.

They returned to the bar area, where a few more silent patrons had shuffled in.

Manny looked profoundly irritated, arms crossed tight over his chest. "What? You have needs. I have needs," Anna said, shrugging. It was a gesture that made Manny's eyes narrow with genuine fury.

"Do you have any idea how reckless that was?" he hissed, his voice a strained, low whisper, perhaps the most angry tone she had ever heard from him.

"This is neither the time nor the place for you to indulge in a casual fling, Anna," Manny continued, leaning in close, his intensity suffocating. "We are standing in the belly of the beast. This is precisely the kind of impulsive, self-serving shit that got you exiled the first time!" Anna was momentarily stunned into silence. Manny had never spoken to her with such unvarnished rage.

Suddenly, the bartender's demeanor changed entirely. "You both need to leave. *Now*. Officers are on their way. Do not come back here, or I will be seen as a sympathizer." She glanced slyly over Anna's shoulder. Two more Merratis, grim and silent, had just walked into the bar.

The air around Anna crackled with sudden, raw energy. She grabbed Manny's hand in a death grip. The next moment, before he could even register what was happening, they were outside in the narrow alley.

"There was something off about the people who just came in. A low hum, like the sound of a live wire, was radiating from them. I could sense it," Anna said, her senses screaming danger.

"They could be under some sort of trance or compulsion, perhaps from Dalv himself," Manny mused, thinking aloud for a moment.

"I think—" Anna began, but Manny cut her off.

"We can outrun them, Anna. Out the back. Into the deeper alleys. They are absolutely no match for your speed." He started to pull her hand, trying to lead her toward the alley's darkest recess. But Anna planted her feet, standing firm.

"No. We need to turn ourselves in," she declared, her voice resolute.

"My brother and Navi are imprisoned in the temple. We need to get in there anyway, so why not do it the easiest way possible?" She knew, with chilling certainty, that this was their only logical path.

"And then what? Let's try to think through this strategy first," Manny countered, unable to fathom any good outcome from her plan.

"Ok fine I - " And just as she said the words, two heavily armed Officers burst into the alleyway.

Without a moment of hesitation or thought, Anna flicked her fingers, sending a directed wave of energy that slammed the Officers against the solid steel door of the bar. They crumpled into two motionless heaps. Anna's eyes went wide with surprise. *Did I just acquire some worshippers in Merrat?* she thought. *How could that have happened?*

Manny's eyes were also wide as he smiled. "Wow, that was necessary and a little too easy. You know how this works. You are not a witch. You can't just conjure spells out of thin air. That spontaneous burst of strength is no match for Dalv's entrenched power in this region. I believe the objective must be to get in, locate and rescue our friends, and then return to your stronghold, to Lega. You do not possess limitless power. At least, well, nevermind."

A look regret washed over Manny's face, and he clamped his mouth shut.

"Limitless power? What did you almost say?" Anna pressed him, her voice suddenly intense.

"Nothing. Absolutely nothing. Either way, you don't have it now."

"Please, Manny, try to be more vague. It's so soothing," she deadpanned, her voice dripping with sarcasm.

She grabbed Manny's hand and ran toward the end of the alley. Without any warning, her body seemed to fold in on itself, a shimmer of light, and then instantly unfurl. They were no longer in the alley. They stood at the base of the mountain, staring up at what appeared to be an enormous temple complex carved in its side. Anna and Manny looked at each other in stunned, speechless silence.

"How is this level of raw, spontaneous power surge even possible within Dalv's stronghold?" Anna posed the question to the indifferent night air, to no one in particular.

"I... I genuinely don't know," he admitted, shaking his head. In all his decades of studying deities, their behavior, and their lives in various realms, he had never once encountered an example of a deity gaining a sudden, dramatic surge of strength and power while standing inside another deity's place of worship. While Anna was clearly delighted by this development, Manny was deeply unnerved.

"Be incredibly wary of this power surge, Anna. Whatever you have tapped into, he possesses exponentially more," Manny warned, his voice low and urgent.

"After this entire thing is over, do you think you can take a vacation and calm the fuck down?" she blurted out, the words escaping before she could filter them. The moment the words were out, Anna remembered that the stoic Manny had feelings too. She immediately regretted her thoughtless statement.

"I fulfill the duty of the Keeper, a purpose I was born into, a purpose that runs through a long line of ancient Keepers. My role is to protect you, to keep you safe, to re-educate you, and to guide you. I do this because of my bond, and in part, out of love for your brother. I know nothing else. I cannot desire to be anything else. Unlike you, Anna, I am fundamentally bound to this life until the moment I die."

What did he mean, that unlike me, he was bound to his Keeper life? Anna filed that disturbing thought away for later.

"Boo-fucking-hoo," she blurted out again, her self-control dissolving in the stress. And yet again, she instantly wondered why she couldn't keep her mouth shut.

"Do you not think that I would rather be with Misha in Havana, dancing and laughing? Do you not think that I would do absolutely anything to bring Elena and my father back into the picture?" His voice was rising now, filled with genuine pain. "That is not our fucking reality, Anna! The reality is right now. Right here. We are standing at the foot of this icy, art deco hellscape, to put it mildly, and our only duty is to rescue our friends." She followed his gaze to the temple complex. He was right. It did, in fact, look like a massive, icy art deco hellscape. The wall surrounding the temple grounds seemed to stretch boundlessly. Spire after spire rose behind the wall. Behind all that impenetrable stone and ice, where were their friends hidden?

Anna shivered at the thought of not finding them in

time, though she wasn't sure what "on time" even meant. Death? Prolonged torture? Eternal purgatory? Manny swished his hand back and forth in a dramatic, exaggerated wave, casting a veil over them, shielding them from their enemies' sight.

"What did you just do?" she asked, a touch of awe in her voice.

"Something nice, in spite of having an ungrateful charge," he retorted, his tone still sharp. "We are now invisible to our enemies, but we will remain visible to our allies, should we encounter any."

"Look, I am grateful. Truly. I'm just... I'm ready for this to finally be over. Can you tell me when that will happen?" She asked the question rhetorically, more for her own sanity than for any actual answer. She knew this struggle might never truly be over for her. Even though the warmth of his magic elicited a moderate feeling of relaxation, Anna still deeply longed for the simplicity of her old life.

She stood silently for a moment, letting the cold air clear her head. Suddenly, she noticed a faint, electric tingle, a familiar echo of Navi's unique vibrational signature.

"Manny, I've been here before. I know this place. Fuck. Fuck. Fuck." Anna closed her eyes and concentrated with all her will. Memories and fragmented images flashed before her, but they vanished just as quickly, leaving her mind frustratingly blank.

"Anything useful from your little special voodoo vault?" she asked Manny, her voice strained.

He shook his head, a muscle twitching in his jaw. "It's not voodoo, and no. While the general structure of a temple complex is often similar across various realms, I don't know the specific intricacies of this one. But there appears to be a large map... inside the main gate." He pointed toward the heavily guarded entrance beyond the immense, icy gate.

The guarded entrance. Flanked by Shadow Officers. Each one carried a long staff, its tip crowned with a pulsing red orb. *Fuckers*, she thought bitterly.

Anna knew they needed to be captured, but she needed to know the layout of the place first, just in case everything went tits up.

She bolted toward the entrance, moving with the speed of a projectile, knowing Manny would have no choice but to chase after her.

"Why did you do that?" he whisper-yelled, his voice tight and strained through gritted teeth.

"It worked, didn't it? You're always at your best when you're surprised," she whispered back, a hint of triumph in her tone. "I still don't know exactly how much power I have right now, and I refuse to waste it on a long-winded argument." Even though no one could see it, she smiled wide. She had finally, utterly outsmarted her Keeper, and the feeling was immensely satisfying.

"It won't always work, Anna. I am here to help, remember that. Please, for the love of the gods, keep the surprises to an absolute minimum," Manny whispered again, resignation heavy in his voice.

They walked silently, invisibly, past the guards flanking the massive gate. As Anna and Manny slipped by, the red glow of the orbs on the guards' staves intensified momentarily. The guards exchanged puzzled, uneasy looks, sensing a ripple in the air but seeing nothing.

They quietly approached the map, both immediately beginning to study it in minute detail. Neither of them had ever seen anything quite like it—or at least, nothing Anna could consciously remember.

A giant, polished slab of smooth white and black marble propped up the map itself. The map was enormous, about two meters tall and a staggering four meters wide. Its exquisite, complex detail was intricately carved into the stone. Anna reached out instinctively to touch it. Manny's hand shot out like a viper, grabbing her wrist just centimeters from the map's surface.

"Bad idea. A very bad idea. Chances are, Dalv already knows we're inside the perimeter," Manny whispered, his eyes scanning their surroundings nervously. "Once you enter a deity's temple, they can pick up the energy you emit. And if you touch something that belongs to them, something of theirs... that signal makes you an easy target," he warned.

She let her hand drop but continued to study the map intensely. The animated stone, reminiscent of the walls in Lega and the enchanted Library, was one of Navi's distinct design genres. She sucked in a sharp breath and immediately recognized the influence. The glacier waterfalls depicted on the map flowed with tiny, glistening water. The fire pits on the map were ablaze with miniature flames. Most importantly, it clearly showed the main path leading to the receiving room. Surely someone as overtly flamboyant and pathologically power-hungry as Dalv received offerings, sacrifices, and worshippers night and day. Yet, Anna looked around the colossal hall and saw no one entering or leaving. It struck her as profoundly odd.

The main path wound steeply upward, leading to two identical ice gardens, one immediately to the left and one to the right. They appeared, on the map, to be filled with glistening winter flowers, small, stunted pines, and bubbling water fountains. In this high-altitude winter hellscape, Anna had to admit the gardens looked rather beautiful and peaceful, at least in the carving. It was peculiar, though: the garden on the right led directly to the overly designed (sorry, Navi) receiving areas, nymph zones, and various guest quarters designated for pilgrims, powerful beings, priests, and priestesses; however, the garden on the left abruptly stopped. The map led one to believe there was nothing beyond that garden wall, a sheer face of rock. That couldn't be right. Navi was obsessed with perfect symmetry. It calmed him.

"I don't think that we have much time. They—" she began to whisper urgently to Manny.

"That's absolutely right." A sultry, low female voice spoke from directly behind them. "You don't have any time at all."

32

Before Anna and Manny could fully spin around, they were encased in a shimmering, tightly sealed orb of force, instantly unable to move a muscle or utter a single sound.

At least we got caught, Anna thought with a grim sense of success, trying to force a smile to herself.

The orb rotated slowly, allowing them to face their captor. Anna saw a pale, white-skinned woman with a faint hint of red iridescence to her complexion. She wore a severe black tunic and black leggings. Her long, curly black hair lay in perfect, cascading waves down her back. A beautiful silver and red tartan sash was draped diagonally across her body, secured at the shoulder by a bright red orb that served as a clasp. *This is the priestess,* Anna concluded instantly. *She is the one responsible for all of this.*

Anna's blood boiled. She wanted to lunge at the woman. She willed a bright blue light to surge through the containment orb, a desperate, raw burst of power, but nothing happened. Manny, next to her, merely blinked rapidly, processing the data.

"Now, you'll have plenty of time to show off your parlor tricks," the priestess laughed, a rich, dark sound. She then began to sing, humming a melody that seemed to pierce the air.

It's close to midnight...

Anna's ears rang with the familiarity. She knew that song. It was the song that had supposedly heralded the arrival of Ara and Oragan. *How did they know?* How could this priestess know *this* particular, American song?

The priestess continued humming the tune as she walked toward the ice gardens, Anna and Manny floating helplessly behind her, encased in their sphere. Anna felt sick to her stomach. She had trusted Ara and Oragan, foolishly, blindly, and now she was certain. They must have been working with the priestess all along.

Powerless and immobilized in that moment, Anna's oldest, most unwelcome friend, paralyzing anxiety, began to creep back in. Manny, on the other hand, was operating purely on instinct, taking note of every detail in their surroundings. As they floated through the complex, he noticed the intricate way the beautiful frost crystals built up around the plant leaves of the ice plants. White, star-like flowers hung heavily from the immense stone walls of the complex. The pines bore cones that were a shocking, vibrant red. He attempted to tap into the aura of the pines, but they were shielded, blocked by a counter-magic. Steam curled off the surface of the bubbling water fountains. It must be water from a hidden hot spring, Manny thought. As they drifted past one of the fountains, he could have sworn he saw the faint reflection of hibiscus and plumeria blossoms in the water. He missed Havana with an ache in his chest. Perched next to this hibiscus fountain was a pure albino peacock. As far as birds went, it looked profoundly despondent, especially compared to the other majestic creatures he had encountered on Kala. The peacock slowly lifted its head, looking Manny directly in the eyes. Manny saw a tiny, shimmering laser tether, a thin line of light, connecting the bird to the base of the hibiscus fountain.

"Manny... *querido.*" The voice was a soft, familiar Spanish whisper, and it caused Manny's stomach to drop out from under him.

A flash flood of childhood memories overwhelmed his mind. Most of them were with his father, Antonio. The father who had loved and patiently nurtured him. The father who had taught him the rigorous, sacred ways of the Keeper. The Keeper who had been tasked with keeping both Dalv in line. The father who had allegedly been ruthlessly murdered by Dalv himself.

He screamed for the priestess to stop walking, for her to let them go, but the orb muffled the sound entirely; no sound came out. He realized, with sudden, terrifying clarity, that Anna's plan was fatally flawed. He, a humble Keeper, would face sudden, agonizing death if he was brought directly before Dalv. They needed their friends. Manny knew this was life-or-death and summoned what he could from the elements. In that instant, the orb surrounding him and Anna shattered, exploding into a million glittering pieces, and they tumbled violently to the frosted ground. Anna was on her feet without hesitation, a raw energy coursing through her veins. She shot a searing wave of brilliant green light toward the priestess, who was hit full force and slammed into the ground like a sack of rocks.

"Shit, did I kill her?" Anna leaned over the motionless body and poked it gingerly with the toe of her boot. She didn't move. She tapped her head in frustration. The priestess's tongue lolled grotesquely out of her mouth.

"Probably. That was a hefty amount of raw power. Now, *get back here*!" Manny hissed in an urgent whisper, pulling her by the arm.

"But I only wanted to knock her out! I didn't mean to kill her. Well, maybe I did," Anna confessed, shrugging dismissively and stepping over the body.

"You just completely fucked up my plan!" she whisper-yelled back at Manny.

"Well, to use your own language, *your* plan was already fucked! Now be quiet and follow me." Manny had a grip on her wrist and pulled her forcefully back toward the hibiscus fountain with the albino peacock. Manny could see a desperate, pleading intelligence in the peacock's eyes. Manny walked slowly toward it. The bird nudged its silky head into Manny's outstretched hand and then pressed its body against his chest, the exact way Manny would nuzzle his father when he was a small boy. "Father..." Manny whispered, the realization hitting him like a physical blow.

"What? What the actual—" Anna whispered, utterly bewildered. Yet, she recognized Tonio, her former Keeper's spirit, in the bird's form, in the knowing sorrow of its eyes. She mentally added "dead dad turned into a bird" to the growing list of bizarre items in her new reality.

"More mysteries unfolded with my death, my son. But I don't have much time to explain or mourn. You are in a life-threatening situation and you must hurry if you want to save your friends," Tonio implored, his voice coming through Manny's mind.

"Where are they, Father?" Manny asked, his voice shaking.

"They are imprisoned. In the area that is deliberately missing from the map." Both Manny and Anna knew exactly where that area was supposed to be—off the left garden—

but they weren't sure how to penetrate the sheer, solid granite mountainside that formed the temple's back wall.

"You must rescue them and immediately return here. This is a portal, the only way out of this hell," Tonio explained. "But there is a catch, a powerful curse. Even if you make it back here, you must either fight me to gain entrance to the portal, or you must sever my tether, which is a nearly impossible task. *She* cursed me to guard it no matter what." Tonio frowned, the magnificent crest feathers drooping.

"But she's dead. I just killed the priestess," Anna said, truly confused.

"Not her—" Tonio stopped mid-sentence, his focus suddenly snapping away. They heard the distinct, loud crunching of heavy steps on the frost-covered garden path. All three, froze instantly, well camouflaged by the thick, swirling steam from the hot spring fountains. Two more Officers walked briskly onto the scene, stopping dead next to the priestess's body. One of them immediately let out a loud, wrenching sob.

Manny couldn't believe the words he was about to say. "Carry me. On your back. Again. We need to get to the other garden on the map. The one that actually goes somewhere."

Anna wordlessly bent over, motioning for him to jump on. She knew that as soon as she started running, the sound would be too loud for them to maintain their obscured presence. They had no choice. She bolted back the way they had come, but instead of heading down the main trail leading back to Merrat, she went right, toward the sheer, forbidding rock face into which the entire temple was built.

"I hear them now. They're coming!" Anna hissed. She had just killed their priestess, and now their presence was fully known. *This is going to be a party,* Anna thought with a sick, adrenaline-fueled excitement.

"I don't know what to do! We're at a dead end!" Anna whisper shrieked, her hands frantically feeling around the smooth rock wall, desperately searching for a seam or a hidden door.

"The feather! Use the feather!" Manny pointed to her pocket.

She fumbled through the woolen fabric, retrieved the damn macaw feather, and without a second thought, touched it to the most logical place a gate or door might exist in the sheer stone.

A massive piece of the rock wall shimmered, then cracked with a grinding sound, and opened just wide enough for a body to walk through sideways. Manny and Anna ran inside. The moment they were through, the rock slammed shut behind them with a deafening, final thud.

The walls inside lit up with soft, tiny glowing lights that illuminated a long, narrow path. Icicles had formed dramatically around the lights, hanging like chandeliers. Anna thought it might actually feel magical if only she weren't running from a psychopathic, revenge-driven deity on the other end of the tunnel.

"What. Was. That? How is your dead father a peacock?" Anna demanded, her voice echoing strangely in the confined space.

Manny shrugged, the motion jostling her slightly. "Something to ask him later, assuming we both survive this. Right now, we need to find our friends and get back to Havana. It won't solve our larger problem, but at least it will give us time to plan something in a power-free zone. Plus, Dalv won't dare come back for us there. He has no power in that realm."

"But what about the other woman your father mentioned? The one who cursed him?"

"She—" Manny paused, thinking hard. *No, it couldn't be Julia.* It had to be a different woman, he falsely hoped, but deep down he knew the truth.

"Don't worry about her for now. I'm not sure who she is, but our goal is singular: get our friends out of here and back to Havana in one piece. Let's go."

Their feet slid violently from underneath them as they stepped onto a path that had turned into ice. They instinctively grabbed each other's hands to keep their balance.

"Keep holding my hand. I think I've got this." Anna focused with every ounce of willpower she possessed, envisioning a stable force steadily pushing them forward. Within seconds, they were effortlessly gliding through the tunnel, their feet floating just above the ice, a bizarre, improvised ice-skating experience. Ten minutes into their first unintended foray into winter sports, icicles began dripping from the ceiling, a clear signal they were nearing the exit. They arrived at the end of the tunnel to find another heavy door, carved from the same solid stone.

"I hope no one is waiting on the other side of this one," Anna muttered nervously.

You and me both, Manny silently agreed, bracing himself.

They held their breath, pooling all of their combined powers, and tried to push the door open. The door groaned, scraped, and finally opened just enough for each of them to pass through sideways. After the frosty journey, they both stopped for a moment to marvel at the empty, echoing, cacophonous hallway before them, carved perfectly and flawlessly out of smooth stone. *This is Navi's work*, Anna knew instantly. The building whispered it directly into her mind.

He's here. Second door on the right... But be warned. This isn't your temple. We aren't loyal to you.

Anna nodded slightly, as if the massive structure could understand her. They were completely exposed in the middle of the hallway. If anyone entered, there would be nowhere for either of them to run or hide.

33

"Navi is in the second door on the right," she whispered to Manny. She felt his presence not just beside her, but deep in her bones. They crept forward, their footsteps muffled and soft against the cold stone floor. "I have zero hope for success," Anna confessed, the raw truth a bitter taste in her mouth. "I am persona non-grata here. I am the enemy."

The door to Navi's chamber was an intricately carved slab of ancient, dark wood that dominated the wall. It was not just a door; it was a museum of the macabre, detailed with gruesome sacrifice scenes that turned Anna's stomach. A wave of nausea washed over her as she imagined the brilliant, gentle Navi confined behind this monument to savagery. *Dalv was such a gross motherfucker,* she thought, the simple insult feeling profoundly inadequate for the architect of this horror.

Each animated panel detailed a relentless cycle of death. Animals and humans were depicted being beheaded, disemboweled, or burnt alive in an eternal, wooden tableau.

Small, articulated wooden figurines moved stiffly, reliving their final, agonizing moments over and over.

"Did you see that?" she whispered, clutching Manny's arm, her eyes wide with shock and morbid fascination.

"See what?" He murmured back, his voice a low vibration near her ear, his focus on the space ahead.

"I swear," she insisted, her breath catching, "the one getting decapitated over and over again just pleaded to me with his eyes. He looked right at me." The idea was insane, but here, in the heart of Dalv's temple, reality was a fluid, terrifying thing.

"Anything is possible here, Anna. Knock on the door already," Manny commanded, his impatience laced with a desperate urgency.

She raised her hand and knocked. The wooden door didn't just rattle; it vibrated with a deep, resonant *thrum. That can't be good,* she thought, a knot tightening in her gut. She heard heavy, quick steps on the other side.

"What?" Navi's curt voice came through loud and clear, but it was stripped of its usual warmth.

"Navi! Navi it's me and Manny. We're here to help!."

"Anna! You must leave now! Get out of here! He knows you're here!" Navi pleaded, his voice muffled but desperate.

"I'm not leaving without you and my brother," Anna stated, her resolve hardening. Ara and Callan could fuck themselves, as far as she was concerned, but the only people that mattered now were in this prison.

"It's too late for your brother, he—"

"NO!" Anna shrieked, the denial tearing from her lungs with an almost physical force. She refused to accept Misha was gone. As she screamed, the entire building seemed to respond, vibrating violently, shaking the very foundations of the temple. Within moments, the silence was shattered by the pounding of boots as a squad of Officers barreled towards them from the end of the hallway. Instinct took over. Without thinking, Anna raised her arms, throwing out an invisible wave of power. All the intricately carved doors lining the corridor, including Navi's, burst open simultaneously with a resounding crack of stressed wood and stone.

"Anna!" Manny yelled, his voice struggling to penetrate the cacophony, trying to re-center her, pull her back from the brink of a dangerous emotional breakdown.

Navi stumbled out from the suddenly-opened doorway, blinking against the corridor's dim light. Anna gasped. Where his gorgeous, amber eyes should have been, there were only empty, smooth sockets.

"What did they do? What did they do to you?" she whispered, the tears finally starting to fall as she cupped Navi's ruined face in her hands.

"They didn't—" Before he could finish his sentence, a blinding flash of light erupted in the corridor. Suddenly, they were all suspended, trapped inside glowing, impenetrable orbs of energy. Immobilized. Callan and Ara emerged from their own opened room down the hall. Ara looked like a bird who was clearly not long for any world, her vibrant feathers sparse and dull. Callan looked, well, like Callan always looked: annoyingly composed, a picture of insouciant self-interest.

And yet again, after all their efforts, they were all completely immobilized.

Anna's frantic mind could only think about Misha. She desperately hoped that her mother, her *real* mother, would miraculously appear and save them from this nightmare. A fantasy.

"No point in struggling. It's impenetrable. The High Priestess will decide what to do with you now," the Officers droned, their voices unsettlingly flat and in unison.

Creepy fucks, Anna thought, the small rebellion her only comfort.

The Officers marched with the captured crew floating helplessly above them like macabre balloons. As she was carried along, Anna marveled, caught between awe and horror, at the sheer artistry of the intricate stone and wooden carvings that covered every surface. They all appeared to be gruesome, cautionary tales—a tapestry of backstabbing, revenge, loyalty, and brutal sacrifice. Occasionally, Anna swore that one of the carved faces, mid-scream or mid-death throe, made deep, significant eye contact with her, drawing her into their silent suffering.

They passed through another massive door into a circular stone room. It was lit with a flickering orange glow from torches mounted on every wall, the air thick with the smell of smoke and dried blood. The room's grim focal point was a central pyre. A perfectly symmetrical path, chillingly lined with human bones, led directly to it. Surrounding the pyre were ornate designs made up entirely of human and animal bones, twisted into dark, complex symbols. The designs were simultaneously ghastly and undeniably beautiful, a masterpiece of dark devotion.

They floated through yet another door. It was a cathedral-like structure, almost as large as the grand library in Lega, but nearly empty by comparison. It was impossibly taller than any building Anna could ever imagine. It was Dalv in building form: a monumental, egotistical display of power. A surge of disgust for Navi mixed with pity; she felt disgusted that he had helped Dalv build this monument to cruelty. But then she reminded herself that Navi had also built *her* temple, her true home. She truly wished she had gotten the chance to visit her fucking temple in its full, majestic splendor before this.

"Once we get to the rejuvenation point, we will release you," the officers intoned in their synchronized, soulless voices. "We don't advise that you try to escape. You are no match for the power resident here."

They floated through the long nave. Anna, despite her predicament, used the time to scan for exit points. There were doors everywhere. She closed her eyes and, focusing past the pain and fear, thought of the temple map she had glimpsed at the grand entrance. In her mind's eye, the layout coalesced, and she clearly saw the distinct way to the frost garden and Manny's father.

Suddenly, the orbs holding them flickered and vanished, and they all fell with a jarring, painful *thud* onto the stone floor.

"Mercy me you turds, you could at least set us down gently. I may be immortal, but these ole bones don't like being dropped from twenty feet up." Callan grumbled, instantly back to her usual, irritating self. *Callan's back and at it,* Anna thought, a grim amusement touching her.

Suddenly, all twenty Officers collectively shouted, "Stand before the rightful deities of Kala!" and thumped their heavy wooden staffs on the marble floors three times in a deafening, unified beat.

Anna and Manny braced themselves, expecting the inevitable, arrogant emergence of Dalv from the wings. Instead, the figure who stepped into the main chamber and stood before an imposing, empty throne was Julia. She was instantly, unequivocally, in command of the entire room, radiating an unquestionable authority. Anna gasped, unable to process the betrayal, the sheer impossibility of it. Her mother stood before her as a goddess. All the subtle clues, the warnings, the small coincidences that her mother had preceded them here, were suddenly irrefutable facts. Anna was strong, fiercely strong, but denial was proving to be a much, much stronger force.

34

"MAMA!" Anna screamed, her carefully constructed composure disintegrating in an instant. Julia entered the colossal main hall of the temple and took her place standing to the right of an empty, majestic throne. Manny, trailed Anna, trying to focus on the situation and not the temple. He had never been in the residence of a true deity before. He quickly noted the five giant stone and metal fireplaces, each a mixture of polished black granite and elaborate wrought iron. Overstuffed floor pillows, covered in a black and silver tartan print surrounded each hearth, creating a cozy, yet macabre, aesthetic. He noted that two of the fireplaces weren't lit, a prudent precaution perhaps. The heated marble floors, however, were a silent, comfort to his weary, battered body. The five massive chandeliers, mounted at least twenty feet above, looked like menacing clusters of dripping icicles. Navi's handiwork, no doubt, and impeccably executed.

"Mama mama!" Anna sobbed, the sound childlike and broken, as she mindlessly ran towards Julia, arms outstretched.

"Anna stop!" Manny yelled, recognizing the danger, but he followed suit immediately, ready to intervene.

She ignored Manny completely and slammed into her mother, embracing her tightly. Julia returned the hug with a strange, cool efficiency, and then firmly grabbed Anna by the shoulders, pushing her back just enough to look into her eyes.

Anna saw, in that moment of forced distance, that this was goddess Julia, not her simple, loving mama-in-Havana Julia. This Julia had skin of alabaster with a faint, iridescent red hue, and her shock of hair was a fierce, deep red. Her eyes were an impossible ice blue. The was the blue eyed devil. Anna always thought Cubans were joking, but no. Julia was the Blue Eyed Devil. She was adorned with glass jewelry consisting of delicate, crystallized structures that dripped down her neck and ears, catching the torchlight.

A million fragmented moments and memories—snapshots of her life with her 'mother'—flashed through Anna's mind within a split second, a dizzying, painful montage. Manny, sensing Anna was on the absolute verge of losing control and ruining their entire mission, put his hand firmly on the small of her back, a silent, vital reminder to stay focused. She understood the implicit command from Manny and immediately maintained the charade of her enthusiastic, tearful reunion.

"Oh Mama! I thought you were dead until we arrived in Kala. I don't even know where to begin," Anna played along, forcing a smile.

Julia's lips curled upward in a movement that did not reveal her teeth. It was a smile, in the technical sense of the word, but it was devoid of warmth, of love. "My dear, I have so much to tell you," she said. "Maybe it's better if I simply show you."

Manny subtly flicked his finger at the small of Anna's back, a sharp, unmistakable warning shot.

Julia then walked towards the throne. The backing was made of what looked like solid, crystalline glass, molded to resemble a massive, jagged glacier. The seat cushions were upholstered in the same black and silver tartan pattern that dressed the floor pillows.

She took her place on the throne, every movement a calculated display of power. Anna followed her, moving against every instinct.

Anna stood before Julia, grabbing her hands without thinking, a reflex of the lost daughter. Julia twitched ever so slightly, a fleeting moment of discomfort. "I knew you would overcome Dalv. Please, Mama, see that you can let us return. Let's free Kala from the forces of the Officers for good," Anna pleaded, playing the role of the dumb, naive hero in order to desperately stall for more time, to think of a way out.

It was then that Dalv floated casually out from the side of the chamber, a triumphant, sickening smirk plastered on his face. *That rapist fuck,* Anna fumed.

His power emanated from him like a toxic fog, nearly bringing Anna to her knees with its oppressive weight. This was the worst possible timeline. Her mother, now her worst enemy, and Dalv, the most repugnant rapist, were united. In the classic flight, freeze, or fight scenario, she felt an overwhelming urge to make like the birds and fly far, far away. But her focus snapped back: *Where was her brother?*

"Fancy seeing you here, Anna. Want to make me a mojito con vodka?" he laughed at his own stupid, worn-out joke. He stepped closer to Julia, leaning in conspiratorially. "Oh yeah, I've been fucking your precious mama. What do you think of that?" he said, his eyes glittering with malice as he made an exaggerated air-humping motion with his hips.

"Bloody hell, Dalv, why do you always have to go to the vulgar place?" Julia said, but her voice held a tone of playful exasperation, and she lightly slapped him on the shoulder.

Anna maintained a flat, emotionless smile, the kind she had always used with Dalv. He was a creature that thrived on reaction; she would not give him the satisfaction of her disgust or anger.

"So the secret is out," Julia announced, waving a hand dismissively. "I'm sleeping with Dalv. Also, spoiler alert! I am not your mama. Nor was I your real mama on earth. I re-birthed you on earth, *sister*, when we were forced to take a sabbatical from Kala." Julia finished with a fake, theatrical pouty face. "Likely a sicker twist of fate for me than it was for you, having to play mother."

"Great, I always wanted a sister to fight with," Anna replied, her voice remaining as flat and unreadable as her smile.

"Come now, Anna. Don't be jealous now that *I'm* the one with the most power in the entire pantheon," Julia taunted, basking in her revelation.

"And look, I'm one of those feminists. I'm letting her have the power," Dalv chimed in with a smug smirk on his face. His smirk instantly vanished, however, as soon as his eyes connected with Julia's. Anna noticed that, for a brief second, he looked genuinely terrified, a flash of pure fear in his eyes. That almost made all of this worth it for Anna.

"Oh, I see how it is," Anna stated, completely non-plussed, as the grand, horrible plan clicked into place in her mind. "You're killing off all the deities in Kala and forcing conversion to gain absolute power. An obvious tale as old as time, at least on earth. How transparent and unimaginative," she stated, her lack of surprise stinging more than any angry accusation.

"My dear," Julia purred, rising from the throne, her ice-blue eyes blazing. "It's not only Kala that I want. BRING THEM TO ME!" She bellowed the command, and the sound echoed throughout the vast temple. Officers instantly scattered at her powerful command.

"And you, Manny, aren't you just so cute," she said, turning her attention to him with a condescending sweetness. "You've proven to be a better Keeper than your father and grandmother. You haven't died yet." Manny felt the blood rush to his cheeks, a mixture of shame and fury.

Anna immediately reached out and touched his shoulder, a silent reassurance and anchor.

"Ah, here they come," Julia said with an evil, satisfied grin, turning back to the approaching door.

Callan, Ara, and Navi were ushered through a large door to the left of the glacier-like throne. Navi's energy was a terrible thing to witness; it waffled desperately between profound despair and numb apathy. His shoulders slumped over in resignation as his lips remained in a frown.

"Ah yes, your precious boyfriend," Julia said, her voice dripping with venomous pleasure. "Not sure if you remember, but he literally and figuratively fucked over a lot of people during his previous time on Kala. Karma is a bitch, as they say on earth. He is paying the price now, aren't you, Navi?" Navi didn't move a muscle.

"WHAT DID YOU DO TO THEM, JULIA?" Anna shrieked, finally unable to control her temper. She took a step forward, unable to run towards them, stunned by an invisible forcefield. She was on the precipice of losing everyone she loved, and this sight was the final push.

"She didn't do anything to Navi," Callan chimed in

matter-of-factly, adjusting his collar. "He pissed off Marge, so she ate his eyeballs. Just a simple dinner." Callan paused, then glanced at Ara with a theatrical frown. "Now Ara here, well maybe Julia can explain that one because I don't even know what's going on with that bird."

Ara looked like a desolate shell of her former, magnificent bird-self. There were no resplendent feathers left. As a matter of fact, very few feathers remained at all; her skin was patchy and visible.

"Blah blah blah," Julia interrupted Callan with a bored wave of her hand. "I'm simply harnessing Ara's powers through the Avirapto stone." She pulled a glowing, dark gem out of her pocket, holding it aloft. Callan shrugged with feigned indifference. Ara let out a weary sigh. Anna, however, was completely lost, having no idea what she was seeing.

"What is that?" Anna demanded, pointing a rigid finger at the stone.

"Callan gave it to me. She should know," Julia replied, laughing a cruel, high-pitched laugh.

"You know you can't go blamin' me for this, sugar," Callan protested, stepping forward, her eyes suddenly serious. "But yep, that little beauty there pulls energy and power from the fortunas, the universe, hell, everywhere, not just the planet where the deity is worshiped. It's sort of a yin-yang thing. The power must come from somewhere, and clearly, it's coming from Ara." Callan sincerely frowned for the first time since Anna had ever met her.

"Monster," Navi said, obviously directing it towards Callan.

35

"Why all of this, dear sister?" Anna questioned Julia, her voice a low, strained whisper.

Julia's smile was a terrifying curve of triumph, devoid of warmth or sanity. "Because you told me I couldn't. That I shouldn't. That I wasn't powerful enough. You always looked down on me, didn't you, Anna? Always the power-hungry goddess whose faux-carefree exterior tricked everyone: your followers, Navi, and, the best trick I must admit, the two Queens. I had to prove you wrong. After all, I got a little bored. It was time to spice things up and play," Julie said, the last word landing with a sting.

Anna's jaw tightened, every ounce of her patience gone. "No wonder you lost worshippers. I'd leave you for another deity as well. This is the shittiest party that I've ever attended," Anna snapped, knowing the insult was a match to the fuel of Julia's boundless anger, but no longer caring about the consequences. All facades were gone. Their immortal sisterhood was a smoldering ruin. "Where is my brother? Where is Misha?"

Julia threw her head back and let out a dramatic laugh

that echoed off stone walls. "Oh now dear, sweet sister. You'll love this. He is truly my son. So that would make him your nephew? You see, I really did marry and fuck the brains out of that fairy from the U.S.S.R. A regular human wouldn't suffice. He was delicious. In bed and when I drained his blood. I'll give him that."

Everyone winced, their divine or mortal sensibilities revolting against her casual horror.

"Misha! Love! Come out!" Julia called, her voice suddenly shifting, infusing the raw command with a sickeningly sweet hint of maternal softness.

The massive, carved stone doors behind the dais ground open, and Misha emerged. He was clad in a perfectly tailored all black ensemble, the cut so sharp it looked dangerous, accented by a black and silver tartan sash slung across his chest and affixed at the top with a pendant that looked like a sickle in a nod to his Soviet ancestry. His stern and impassable expression made him difficult to read. He moved with a stiff, almost puppet-like grace, his focus fixed entirely on his mother.

Manny, ever observant, thought he saw a brief, desperate moment of hope flicker in Misha's face: his dark brows relaxed slightly, an almost imperceptible micro-expression of relief, when their eyes met.

Anna didn't hesitate. Hope surged through her. She ran towards him. "Misha! Misha!" She threw her arms around him, desperate to connect with her lost brother. He did not return the hug. His body was rigid and unresponsive. Anna felt the emotional recoil. She stepped back.

"The universe's worst family reunion, I see," Anna stated.

"I've seen worse, sugar, you've never been to Zarlogue. Hell of a place and the families... well..." Callan, ever eager to divert a scene with a bizarre tale, prepared to launch into a full-blown anecdote.

"Callan, shut up," Manny said, his voice unusually sharp and low, a rare demonstration of his temper that cut off the story immediately.

Julia, oblivious to the undercurrent of tension, beamed. "Well, this is all going accordingly. I have my temple. My son. What more could I ask for?" She wrapped her arm possessively around Misha's shoulder, giving him a tight squeeze. Anna studied Misha's face, searching for a clue, a sign of resistance, but his expression was unreadable. Did he enjoy this new power? Had his mother truly warped him? Did he hate it?

"Excuse me," Dalv said incredulously as he stepped forward. He was clearly taking offense at being forgotten.

"Oh yes, how could I forget." With a fluid, dramatic movement, Julia stood up, sauntered towards Dalv, and planted a long, passionate, open-mouthed kiss on him. Dalv's eyes fluttered shut in surprised delight. Anna stifled a gag, the sheer vulgarity of the power dynamic making her sick. Callan looked profoundly bored, already checking her nails. And Manny saw the ritual for what it was. He figured it out a second before the first sign of agony.

"STEP BACK!" Manny commanded, his voice booming.

Suddenly, Dalv's eyes did not open to pleasure; they rolled back in his head in white-hot agony. A guttural, tearing sound escaped from his mouth. His feeble attempt to push Julia away only seemed to feed her, making her stronger. A blinding, violent flash of crimson light shot out of Dalv's chest and was instantly sucked into Julia. Dalv dropped to the ground into a sack of bone and muscle.

Without hesitation, Julia turned her attention from the corpse to her son. She leaned over to Misha and placed her open mouth firmly over his. It wasn't a kiss of passion, but a deliberate, horrifying transference.

"So that's how they do it in their family," Anna heard Callan mutter under her breath, her boredom momentarily replaced by horrified fascination.

Initially, all eyes, including Misha's, were filled with disgust and shock at the perverse act. Then, Misha's eyes rolled back entirely, showing only the whites of his head as a powerful, energy surged into him. Julia had transferred Dalv's power, his very essence as a deity, to Misha.

Julia straightened, wiping a stray drop of blood-tinged saliva from her lip. "Guards, please take poor Dalv here into Navi's old room." Navi knew that wasn't a good sign for Dalv.

"Julia, what have you done?" Manny's usually steady voice quivered for the first time in millennia.

"Oh come on, is anyone really sad to see Dalv as a powerless sack of shit?" Julia gestured dismissively at the small, pathetic heap on the floor as two armored guards approached to float the unconscious form to his new, temporary quarters.

"I mean, I'm not too upset by this development," Callan said with a careless shrug.

"Yeah, I'm actually going to side with Callan on this one," Anna chimed in, still reeling and not entirely comprehending the monumental violation of universal law that had just occurred. She just saw Dalv get what she felt he deserved.

Manny brought his hands to his head, gripping his curly black hair, as pure, unrestrained panic set in. He understood the cosmic ledger.

"He knows what's up," Julia said, her golden eyes twinkling with wicked delight as she looked at the distraught Keeper.

"But you don't! You have signed Misha's death warrant! You have signed your own!" Manny yelled, his voice cracking with the strain of revelation. Everyone else, even Anna, was woefully confused by the apocalyptic pronouncement. Everyone except Julia.

"That's where you are wrong. Misha, my dear, is a new god. Powerful beyond anything he could imagine," she proudly stated, staring at her latest, most terrifying achievement as if he were a particularly splendid piece of stolen art.

Misha looked utterly dazed, his pupils dilated, his body radiating raw, unstable power. The new divinity hadn't settled yet.

For the first time in his existence, Manny did not know what to do. He had nothing to advise, no ancient scroll to quote. The universe was going out of balance and spinning violently into chaos. Chaos was meant to balance the universe. Now Julia had enough power, both her own and Dalv's, to wield it arbitrarily on two planets. Transferring the power of one deity directly to a demigod violated the most fundamental laws of creation. He had only heard tales of what happened post-transfer. It involved the explosive, agonizing death of the recipient and the destabilization of entire star systems almost 99% of the time.

"Manny, please stall them." Ara's voice, a crystal bell of ancient authority, spoke directly into his mind. *"I have a plan. It's the only thing that will keep us alive."*

"Julia, you are a monster," Manny started talking, trying to buy time, forcing his mind to focus on the triviality of an argument. Julia rolled her eyes, already bored with the Keeper's righteous indignation, and casually looked at her perfectly manicured nails.

"I know what you're doing and your quest for universal control will never succeed. And you've ostensibly killed your only son. You never learned anything from the Greek gods of earth, did you? Hubris will kill YOU if Dalv's followers don't do it first," Manny railed, clinging to the only weapon he had left: ancient history. Julia just laughed, a sound entirely lacking in sanity.

"Manny, love, you're jealous. You're just a sad little Keeper. Look at you with your sad little dirty outfit. You disgust me," Misha spat in Manny's direction, the words laced with cutting malice that wasn't Misha. His eyes were now wild with power, a sickly green light behind the pupils that elicited an unnerving evil.

Manny allowed a single, perfect tear to fall down his face. The sudden hatred from the boy he adored nearly shattered his composure, but he forced himself to breathe and hold it together. "This is Dalv talking. I know how *YOU*, the true Misha, feel about me. You can never take that from me." Manny tried to breathe through his words as his heart physically ached.

"Do you want to place a bet on that? I never took you for a gambler, but here we are," Misha retorted, the cruel edge to his voice cutting Manny even further.

Julia's eyes widened with glee. "This is going even better than I expected."

The stall was over. Ara flew from Callan's shoulder to Anna's shoulder in a blur of iridescent blue and scarlet feathers. Her razor-sharp claws gripped Anna's shoulder and pierced the flesh, sinking her talons through the skin, into the muscle. Blood streamed down Anna's back. Anna yelped in shock and then started shaking uncontrollably. Her body levitated several feet off the ground and convulsed violently as the macaw integrated into Anna.

"I did not expect this!" Julia clapped her hands together manically and laughed, believing the sudden outburst of pain and power was simply a dramatic reaction to her triumph. She was so absorbed in Misha and Manny's drama that she failed to see Anna absorb Ara.

Callan, however, took advantage of the distraction to fulfill her end of the bargain with the Architect at the library. In a flash, she pulled out the Xeratu stone necklace, a blue stone pendant of anti-power, and yelled, "Enterominu Navi!"

Navi disappeared with a faint, silvery pop. Callan placed the necklace around her own neck. "Welp, I've had enough of this. Time for me to bid you all adieu. Bye y'all!" She then instantly transformed into a massive, magnificent bearded vulture, her immense wings beating the air once. She flew out one of the unlit fireplaces of the temple before anyone could stop her.

Anna was unharmed and transformed. A surge of power and strength coursed through her veins, a feeling more potent than her own divinity. She looked over her left shoulder to see an incredibly detailed, perfect tattoo of a resplendent macaw, Ara, in her truest form, etched permanently onto her skin.

"NOO. NOOOOOOO." Julia's laughter morphed into a high-pitched scream. She finally understood. Ara had merged herself into Anna, potentially making Anna her true equal, a combined force of two deities. A power she had not planned for.

Julia screeched as she raised her hands high in the air. Misha was equally enraged. He ran towards Manny, a blur of dark fury. Large chunks of the stone ceiling crumbled and rained down around them as Misha unleashed a fraction of his new, unstable strength. Without another thought, Anna grabbed Manny's arm. The two figures disappeared out the side door and re-appeared instantaneously in the frost garden outside the temple.

Pieces of the temple continued falling into the main chamber, threatening to bury Misha and Julia.

"STOP!" Misha yelled, his voice echoing with a command. Julia turned to him, seeing the panic in his eyes, and instantly stopped her own destructive fury. She flicked her hands, and with a grinding sound, all the fractured stones went back into place, sealing the massive hole in the ceiling.

"What now?" he asked. Her lip curled up on one side.

36

"Father! Help!" Manny said, his voice a frantic plea as he sprinted toward the towering fountain where the white peacock, Tonio, perched. Julia, in the maelstrom of the power transfers, must have severed the protective tether. No laser-red leash existed.

Tonio extended one of his feathers toward Manny. "Manny, take my feather now—you need to find the other Kalan Keeper. They will be of service to you." Manny wondered if Tonio had been reborn as some type of Collector, or, as Manny hoped, something else.

"What about Anna?" Manny questioned, trying to keep his voice level.

"Yeah, what about me? I can't do this alone! I am all alone! Please," Anna pleaded, her voice cracking with raw emotion as she turned to Tonio. "You come with me!" Tears streamed down her face as the violent events of the last hour finally caught up with her.

"Anna, you must go to Havana. I am best placed here as eyes and ears. Both of you need to get to earth! *Pronto!*" Peacock Antonio screeched the command.

"Manny, where are you going?" Anna asked, wiping her eyes but turning back to her Keeper. Before he could formulate a coherent answer, a stream of armed Officers rushed towards them. He yelled as he leaped into the churning waters of the portal fountain, "Newyoooooork!" His voice was swallowed by the vortex.

"Anna, you must go to Havana NOW!" Tonio's warning escalated into a squawk.

Anna pulled the red feather from the pocket of her coat and plunged headlong into the portal.

The sensation of inter-realm travel hadn't improved, Anna mused, as she tumbled through the dizzying kaleidoscope of time and space. The violent wrenching felt like she was being turned inside out and then stitched back together with reckless speed. It wasn't a journey designed for comfort; it was a means to an end, and she knew it was never meant to feel great.

A wave of relief washed over Anna the instant she emerged, gasping, in the familiar, humid air of the secret garden in Havana. A new sensation pulsed through her: a strange, almost painful power surge. Energy, sharp and electric, coursed through her veins. *It must be Ara's influence,* she thought. As a deity, she had no power here. She wondered, with a flicker of apprehension, what was the power and how long it would last.

Pushing herself up from the fountain, she shivered despite the heat. She looked down at her Merrat-styled clothes: all black woolen clothes would never work in Cuba. She envisioned herself in her old Havana uniform: jean shorts and a red t-shirt. As she tilted her head to wring out her hair, her gaze fell upon a disturbing sight: dead flowers clustered at her feet. In all her years of visiting this garden with her fake-mother, Julia, nothing here had ever died. Looking around, the anomaly became a crisis: exactly half of the carefully tended garden was withered and brown, while the other half remained as lush and vibrant as ever. She sank onto the weathered bench near the portal fountain,alone, save for the molted Ara merged within her.

She forced herself to take inventory of the events. Manny was somewhere in New York City, USA. Ara was inside her shoulder. Callan, the puta, had flown off with Navi, disappearing into the wider multi-verse. *Fucking puta,* she thought, the vulgarity a small release for her mountainous frustration.

She couldn't cry. She couldn't scream. She could only sit, immobilized in a state of mild, stunned disbelief. Deep down, at the core of her being, she had always harbored the cynical suspicion that this journey would not deliver the promised utopia for that arrogant bird and the perpetually smug iguana. The Iguana. *Where in the hell was that fucker in all of this?*

Observing the peculiar, split garden, Anna began to gather her resolve, ready to step out into the city she had once loved. That was when she felt it: the unmistakable sensation of being watched. She snapped her head toward the top of the garden wall and saw him, Oragan, staring back with his beady, ancient eyes.

"Mother fucker, get down here," she commanded, pointing a rigid finger at the ground.

The iguana, clearly sensing the shift in her power and her mood, reluctantly crawled down the sun-baked wall and toward her feet, maintaining a safe, respectful distance.

"Eh hem. I think I can help you," Oragan began, his voice a cautious croak. "But you must help me." The implication was clear: at this juncture, Anna was indisputably the more powerful of the two.

Anna's first instinct was to lift her foot and crush his head, telling him to finally die. But then, for the very first time, Ara's voice spoke, resonating from a deep place within her. *Help him and do what he says. If for no other reason, he is wise.* A sharp, burning pain ignited on Anna's shoulder. *Ara will leave a scar,* she thought, a grim acceptance settling over her.

"Fine," she ground out, "what the fuck do you need?"

"First things first, can I hitch a ride? It's easier for me to be an iguana with things this way," he said ominously, flicking his tongue out.

"What way?" Anna pressed, her patience already threadbare.

"You'll see. Now, can I get a ride?"

"Listen, lizard, we've been through some shit, alright? I've lost almost everyone and everything I care about. I don't know if I should trust you." Anna said, her bitterness palpable.

"I understand. Nothing is normal, anywhere. Everything is desperately out of balance. Things aren't how you left them in Cuba either. But please, I am not safe out there in this iguana form, and I can't really transform. Everything is off," Oragan pleaded, his words laced with a terrifying crypticism Anna utterly loathed.

She rolled her eyes, the thought of having one animal deity inside her and another perched on her shoulder making her feel like a bizarre, traveling menagerie. She also noticed, with a flash of vanity, that her skin was starting to turn a noticeable shade of pink sun. She darted under the nearest palm tree, an instant reminder that she was more human than goddess on earth.

"Okay, fine, hop up," she conceded. "BUT, there are rules. One: you must help me, no matter what. Two: if you don't help me, I will not hesitate to maim you," she threatened, finding pleasure in the declaration.

"Yes, yes, fine," Oragan replied nervously, scrambling up her shoulder and settling near her neck.

"First, there is something that I should warn you of before we leave the garden. Cuba is not the same as when you left it. A lot has happened on earth since you've been gone."

Anna's stomach dropped like a stone. *Nuclear holocaust.* That was the only thing that could drastically change Cuba in the few short months she *thought* she had been gone. Images of fiery, horrific destruction flashed in her mind. "How much could happen in a few months? Did the Americans finally bomb us?"

Oragan let out a surprising, dry chuckle. Anna's face darkened instantly. He cleared his throat and straightened up on her shoulder.

"No, nothing like that. But, well, time is different on different planets, at different times. You've been gone for almost six years of earth time. It's 1991."

She nodded slowly, as if a profound, terrible understanding was finally dawning, all while trying to shake off the unbelievable fact that she had traveled not just through space, but through time as well.

"We are in a 'Special Period' in Cuba. The Soviet Union is no more. The U.S. is more greedy and power hungry than ever. And Cuba is, well, desperate," he stated matter-of-factly, his voice devoid of emotion.

Oragan had compressed an entire, devastating historical epoch into a single sentence that was difficult to process. Her entire identity and all her cultural associations on earth were now obsolete. Navi is supposed to be her touchstone, and for all she knew, he was who-knows-where with Callan.

"You seem to know everything," she said, her breath slightly short, her teeth gnawing on the inside of her cheek. *Stop that. You're still a deity. You don't have bad habits,* Ara whispered in her head. She ignored Ara. "Where is Navi? He disappeared. Call that puta Callan."

"Well, that's the tricky part. He might be in Havana. Or he might not," the iguana said, shrugging his shoulders with an infuriating lack of concern.

"Helpful. Thanks for that," Anna retorted, pushing herself to her feet.

She stepped out of the garden and sighed. The alleyway looked structurally the same, but a pungent, sickening smell, like raw sewage mixed with decay, filled the air. As they walked out onto one of the main streets, Anna's steps faltered. She could not believe what she was seeing. The buildings were visibly decaying. People were listless, almost sickly, looking unnervingly skinny. Very un-Cuban. Many of the classic American cars were rusting hunks of metal on the side of the road.

Sweat beaded instantly on her forehead. Her blonde hair frizzed out wildly. She began to laugh maniacally, unable to stop until she was breathless. Then, with a sudden clarity, she stood up, as if she weren't emotionally falling apart inside, and commanded, "*Vamanos.*" They began to walk, heading toward the one place where she might yet find some answers.

ACKNOWLEDGMENTS

How can one properly acknowledge the thousands of people, places, and experiences that feed one's subconscious to eventually create a work of fiction? It's a herculean task, but I'll try.

My heartfelt thanks to Bonnie Braudway, Jennifer Legge, Dan Cook, Mona Fetouh, Sally Walkerman, Thodleen Dessources and Meghan Corneal, all of whom are and were my emotional support animals during the most difficult years of my life.

Big thanks Debra Moffitt for hosting a retreat that unleashed this beast of a trilogy; John Wilson, the beta reader extraordinaire; and everyone who donated money to me at a time when I needed it most. There are too many to list but the biggest donors were Bill Brown, Jeremy Cannada, Cathy and Vivek Ayer, Siobhan Healy, and many more!

Thanks to Chloe (Naomi) Swickard, my former partner of 16 years and co-parent. She encouraged me to attend the writer's retreat that unlocked this epic adventure. Even though our lowest lows, she believed in and encouraged me to keep going with my book.

And finally to the women we've lost whose energy left an imprint on the characters in Precipice: Nana, Erica, Esther and Mom/Gigi.

www.ingramcontent.com/pod-product-compliance
Lightning Source LLC
LaVergne TN
LVHW100507110826
845146LV00002B/548

* 9 7 9 8 9 9 4 7 1 7 2 1 9 *